THE FLAME GAME

A Magical Romantic Comedy (with a body count)

R.J. BLAIN

THE FLAME GAME
A MAGICAL ROMANTIC COMEDY (WITH A BODY COUNT)
R.J. BLAIN

Bailey and Quinn are back for one last action-filled adventure!

A corrupt police chief is on the loose, and it falls to Bailey and Quinn to put an end to him before he finds some way to weaponize the spreading rabies virus, create yet another batch of potent gorgon dust, and otherwise wreck Bailey's happily ever after.

With a pair of orphaned gorgon whelps to care for, more animals she can shake a stick at, and her husband's determination to make the world a perfect place for her, Bailey has her hands full. To protect everyone she loves, she must embrace her dubious role as the Calamity Queen and rain hell down on those who stand in her way.

The Flame Game is on.

Warning: this novel contains two fire-breathing unicorns on a napalm bender, action, adventure, chaos, mayhem, humor, and bodies. Proceed with caution.

Contents

ONE

Crazy man.

THE FATHER I hadn't met until this morning walked me down the aisle, but Quinn's hands holding mine kept me from running in terror at so many people witnessing *me* marrying someone like *him*. I questioned everything about my odd life. *Me*, the Calamity Queen, marry *him*? It took a few moments to remember I'd already married him once. I'd asked that same question then, too. He'd laughed, and then he'd goaded me until I'd done what he wanted, which involved me marrying him.

Crazy man.

There'd been a bunch of witnesses to that courthouse madness, too, and I'd survived through it mostly unscathed. Most of the witnesses to our first wedding had been too busy brawling with each other to pay any attention to me signing the papers that gave Samuel Leviticus Quinn certain rights to me, but that didn't matter.

Reminding myself his signature on the same papers meant I got rights to him did a good job of steadying my rattled nerves.

No matter how many times I failed to tell him properly, I loved him.

To endure so many people staring at me, all I needed to do was remember a few key things. After the vows came the food, after the food came a show of gorgons petrifying each other during a brawl, and after the brawling came the pampering in our suite, which would be devoid of children for at least twenty-four hours, courtesy of an assortment of parents and grandparents.

I needed a lot longer than twenty-four hours to come to terms with having two pairs of parents.

One set hated me.

The other, who I'd learned about just yesterday, loved me.

I needed a lot longer than twenty-four hours to adjust to my life's new circumstances.

First, I needed to survive through my second wedding. Tomorrow, I would resume my quest to be the best mother possible for our pair of orphaned gorgon children, who would spend the rest of the day and most of tomorrow socializing with the other gorgons in attendance, most of whom were related to my husband in one way or another.

Staring at Quinn and refusing to acknowledge anyone else in the Venetian's canals would help with that, at least until we made it to the food portion of our wedding day. Once the food came around, I didn't care who watched me devour steak, steak, and even more steak.

The fire-breathing, meat-eating unicorn in me loved steak almost as much as I loved the man who'd turned my life upside down on me.

My husband made no effort to hide his amusement, and he squeezed my hands while we both ignored the minister, who did a pretty damned good job of impersonating Elvis while reading the scripted sermon. He went on and on about the responsibilities of married couples, husbands, wives, mothers, and fathers, along with the death-do-we-part stuff I doubted applied to us at all thanks to our mishmash of crazy relatives, most of whom were in attendance.

A few too many gods and goddesses for my comfort joined almost every damned cop in our precinct to witness us confess our love to each other. Or, at a minimum, blurt 'I do' in some horrifically embarrassing fashion.

I had trouble with the basics, and nothing had changed since I'd married my gorgon-incubus doohickey the first time.

"You can look somewhere other than me if you want," Quinn whispered, leaning closer to me.

I debated stealing a kiss before the official kissing portion of the ceremony, although the dumb veil kept getting in my way. Quinn had already shunted the damned thing back, but it kept falling wherever it wanted, to the point I wanted to light it on fire.

Nobody had warned me how much of a pain in the ass wedding dresses could be. And the heels? The heels might do me in. What had I done to deserve the damned heels, especially with the asshole pair of parents uninvited from the ceremony? While inserting my heels into their asses would have made my day, having a pair of parents who actually wanted me trumped my petty desire for revenge.

Huh. Somehow, I'd grown up since meeting Quinn, although only a little.

I forced my attention back on my husband. "If I look anywhere other than at you, I will see them staring at me. You're prettier than they are, and I absolutely refuse to be ashamed of this."

A few months ago, I would have gone and cried in the bathroom had I said that where anyone might hear me.

The Elvis impersonator grinned. "He really is prettier than everyone else here. You're a very lucky woman."

Oops. I shrugged, but I also smiled. "It's true. I can't help it. He's in a suit. He can't wear dress uniforms at home. I get ideas. I am enjoying this while it lasts. Someone is going to take a picture of him in his suit, and I will end up being bribed for copies of the pictures. I'll have to ration the pictures out. I make him late for work if he wears anything other than his normal uniform. He has to change at work."

Well, maybe I couldn't keep my blabbering mouth under control, but I could make people laugh. The entire audience had a field day with my runaway commentary, but beyond blushing over my nervous tendencies, I resisted the urge to dash for the door. If I bolted, Quinn would catch me, drag me back, and laugh about it for the rest of eternity.

It amazed me how much could change in such a short period of time. Six months ago, I'd been bitter, alone, tired, and hungry more often than not. I no longer worried about what I'd eat; if I skipped a meal, Quinn chased me down and hovered until I did what he wanted, which involved eating whatever offering he had brought for me.

Greasy fries and burgers showed up almost as often as healthier fare. He even tolerated me trying to shove fries down his throat, as he deserved to enjoy greasy goodness, too.

I had issues.

I had a lot fewer issues than six months ago.

I deserved a gold star and an entire bucket of napalm for how much progress I'd made.

Quinn chuckled, which captured my attention, and he stole a gentle kiss. "Don't worry. I'm going to have as much trouble as you when I get you into a dress uniform."

I loved my gorgon-incubus doohickey. "Serves you right, you freak." Aw, damn it. There I went, calling my husband a freak on our second wedding day. "I'm blaming the absurd number of cops in this building for my inability to behave like a normal adult."

The cops snickered, which helped mitigate most of my urge to run away and hide from my ability to thoroughly embarrass myself. Then again, if I did run away and hide, Quinn would cheat and use his body to lure me to our room. Running so he'd chase me tempted me, but I stood my ground for a rare change.

Sometime within a few hours, he would lure me to our room, and I would be rewarded for handling our second wedding with a little more grace than our first. Mostly. Maybe with less grace but properly dressed. I could work with properly dressed for our second wedding.

Then again, if we got through the vows without Quinn's relatives brawling with each other, we would be way ahead compared to our courthouse wedding.

The Elvis impersonator grinned, waited for the laughter to subside, and resumed his lecture. To my relief, he wound the whole sermon thing down, beginning the important exchanging of vows part. Thanks to my general inability to handle life normally, I'd made a single request: short, sweet, and to the point.

Wedding number three could be more elaborate after Quinn had a year to help me get over some of my more problematic issues. Blurting random shit out in the middle of my own wedding counted as one of those issues.

After some deliberation and some whining from the Devil, we'd settled on Catholic vows with some alterations offered by Quinn's various relatives.

My husband smiled at me and said, "I, Samuel Leviticus Quinn, take you, Bailey Ember Gardener, for my lawful wife, to have and to hold from this day forward, for better, for worse, for richer, for poorer, in sickness and health, until death do us part."

While I had issues, memorizing my lines, such as they were, wasn't one of them. "I, Bailey Ember Gardener, take you, Samuel Leviticus Quinn, for my lawful husband, to have and to hold from this day forward, for better, for worse, for richer, for poorer, in sickness and health, until death do us part."

Considering who my parents were—the pair I actually liked—the death do us part thing might cause us some trouble. Could the daughter of two divines and two horrid humans complete with a shapeshifting problem actually die? Did fire-breathing unicorns with a fetish for magically enhanced gasoline with some delicious additives age? What about gorgon-incubus doohickeys?

I had questions. I doubted I'd get answers, as we were related to a bunch of immortal assholes who enjoyed toying with us because they could. Three such assholes lurked in the front row, and I couldn't tell how many of them were fucking assholes or just standard ones. Sariel, formerly known as Sylvester but forced to change his name due to our adoption of Sylvester, the gorgon whelp, lifted his hand enough so I could spot him holding three fingers up.

Damn it. The last thing I needed was three fucking assholes, also known as archangels, making a mess of the wedding. Angels, the standard assholes, were bad enough. But to have three archangels *and* the Devil in attendance?

I would make enough of a mess of the wedding without help, and I had a lot of help available.

The Elvis impersonator made it through the rest of the predetermined speech and informed Quinn he could kiss the bride. My husband did an excellent job of redirecting my attention to him and only him.

Somebody needed to give his tongue a hazard rating, and as he wasn't above cheating, he enhanced his claim over my lips with a touch of his incubus influence, warning me what I'd have in store for me after the eating, the brawling, and whatever else needed to happen before we could head to our suite.

Once he finished with me, all I could manage was a whispered, "You're pure evil."

He grinned at me. "And now you get to

stew until I get you back to our room tonight. I will be the luckiest of men."

"Are we going to fight over which one of us is the luckiest?"

"Absolutely. But only once we're in bed."

Whee. "I forgot what I'm supposed to do now. You distracted me with your mouth."

"It's an art I've been cultivating with daily practice, making sure you're incapable of even thinking once I've had my way with your mouth." Quinn linked my arm with his. "Now we walk through the gauntlet of people eagerly waiting to throw things at us, as this is somehow romantic."

"Are they flinging money at us? That would be romantic."

Despite having mostly whispered my question, everybody laughed.

"Alas, you're getting rose petals rather than dollar bills. You're my bride, not a stripper."

As I'd probably die from mortification if I even thought about stripping for anyone other than him in the privacy of our bedroom, I couldn't blame anybody for chortling over his reply.

They knew me well, especially the feathered menace giggling a storm in the front row, who could read my mind at his whim.

I still wondered how a headless being could giggle.

"I'd be a terrible stripper," I conceded. "I'd

be trying to add layers rather than remove them."

"You really would." Quinn shook his head, chuckled, and had to drag me the first few steps to get me to move through the gauntlet of cops and family. As warned, we were pelted with rose petals, and because some cops had a twisted sense of humor, a few bills fluttered our way. Quinn's grip on my arm kept me from chasing them down, but he caught one and handed it to me. "I'm sure you can figure out what to do with that later."

Whee. If someone wanted to get my dollar, they would have to pry it from my cold, dead hands—and get through my gorgon-incubus doohickey first. As I was in no hurry to escape his clutches, I'd enjoy his hovering. When I did finally tire of his overprotective ways, I'd transform into a fire-breathing unicorn and nip him until he behaved. Or he joined me as the world's best cindercorn stallion.

Janet and Tiffany, both of whom had been recruited as bridesmaids so I could pretend I had a somewhat normal wedding, waited until we reached the end of the gauntlet before they both offered me twenty dollar bills.

I looked my husband in the eyes while depositing the cash in my bra.

"Thank you, ladies," Quinn said, grinning at our friends. "I very much appreciate your donation to my post-wedding activities. I'd say evening, but I suspect it'll be closer to morning before we escape."

Janet snickered. "The Devil told me I had to make sure you both showed up for dinner. It seems everyone went present shopping today, and you're to accept all your gifts at the restaurant. Apparently, this will be done in an orderly fashion and in pairs so Bailey doesn't try to bolt for the door from embarrassment. Also, you owe me, woman."

"I do?" I asked.

"I convinced your father to let you brawl a little with that gorgon you keep wanting to pick a fight with. You can thank the angels in the front row. They suggested it would be good for your little ones to be exposed to all forms of your magic early, including shapeshifting."

"Does everybody know?" I whispered.

"Yes." Janet pointed at the front row, where the Devil sat with his brothers, chatting while waiting for us to get out of the way so everyone could follow us to dinner. "It's his fault."

Technically, being pregnant with twins was the Devil's fault, along with some help from his winged menaces of brothers. While Quinn took steps to prevent our family from growing unexpectedly, his incubus powers didn't stand a chance against his divine relatives. "That is true. Quinn, we should get revenge on him. Perhaps as unicorns, after we have some napalm."

Janet grinned. "And this is where Tiffany gets to give you a present!"

I gave Perkette my undivided attention. "I deserve a present, especially as you made me leave my precious puppies and kitten upstairs rather than being part of the wedding party."

In reality, we'd left them upstairs in the care of an angel, as the sheer number of people present would scare them. While Blizzard handled crowds well, the husky puppy became excessively energetic, and while Avalanche was remarkably chill for an ocelot, they'd be happier playing with their toys in our suite. Sunny had been invited, as she had more than a touch of the divine influencing her, but it hadn't seemed fair to include her but exclude the other two beasts.

I already missed my furry babies.

Perkette giggled, and she spun around, showing off the dress the Devil's wife had acquired for her. The woman, a snow leopard shapeshifter of some sort, sat with her husband and seemed like the adult of that relationship. "You get to have a cup of napalm a week while a unicorn, and once a month, you get an entire bucket for your enjoyment. I have the documentation for it. We put it together earlier today with some help from the Devil, his wife, and his brothers."

I freed myself from Quinn's grip and doubled back to the front row, and as the Devil and his brothers were all conveniently located together, I flung myself at the quartet and indulged in a group hug. The Devil's wife dodged my affection, although she caught my veil before it could be ripped off my head or otherwise cause me trouble. Behind me, my husband laughed.

"You fucking assholes are the best!"

Quinn's angelic grandfather chuckled. "While I am most pleased to take some of the credit, my brother is the one who has done the research. He will also, with some help from your father, teach you how to better control your shapeshifting abilities. Your little ones need exposure to all of your magic, so outside of a ban from alcohol and too much sugar, you will find the next few months of your life disturbingly enjoyable when your offspring are not doing their best to kick you in the ribs. Cindercorns have an easier time with pregnancy than human women."

Uh oh. I saved myself from exposing the surprise by not looking at Perkette, who would be dealing with quadruplets after having been barren her entire life. "You're about to tell me I'm not human, aren't you?"

"You are sufficiently human for your new job's needs," the archangel assured me.

I grabbed Sariel's hand, kissed the back of, and repeated the process with the other archangels before planting a kiss on the Devil's cheek. The Devil's wife laughed and warded me off before shooing me away. I bounced back to my husband. "I get napalm, Quinn!"

He caught me in a hug and kissed my forehead. "Heaven forbid you are forced to suffer without any napalm. There's going to be a catch. There's always a catch when it comes to you and your favorite fiery treat. You should find out what the catch is now to limit your disappointment later."

As Perkette would do something like dangle a treat in front of me and then make me pay for it in some horrendous fashion, I asked, "What's the catch?"

"You have to exercise," the mad scientist replied. "You'll probably survive, and the exercise will be good for the babies."

I would remember that when she was waddling around, thanks to her four incoming children. "I'll try to limit my whining somewhat. That is a catch I can live with."

Perkette feigned fainting against Janet, and she flung her hand against her forehead. "It's a miracle. Your napalm supply will be rationed, however. There will be no unapproved napalm benders."

Heaving a sigh, my husband turned me around, planted his hands on my shoulders, and pushed me down the aisle in the direction of the steakhouse deeper within the canal's shopping district. "And I would prefer if there are no approved napalm benders."

I couldn't blame my husband for his opinion. Bad things tended to happen when the

CDC authorized me to use napalm, and it usually involved mass destruction and a requirement for construction crews to remove the rubble once I finished. Add in how I tended to scare a few years off my husband's life, and it amazed me anyone let me near napalm at all. And the hangovers. I could live without the napalm bender hangovers. "That doesn't mean there might not be an approved one. Come on, Quinn. We're the *best* at playing with fire."

"I'm sorry, Bailey, but you're still outclassed by phoenixes," my husband said.

"Just because phoenixes can fly doesn't mean they're better than cindercorns. We have hooves, we breathe fire, meat is delicious, and so is napalm."

Laughing, he shook his head and continued to push me along. "It is my solemn duty as your husband to feed you as much steak as you can stomach. If we stand here chatting, the hungry horde of police officers might toss us in the canal for delaying their dinner. It's bad enough more cops than I anticipated showed up, so we've taken over every damned restaurant in the hotel, and I think we took over some of the restaurants across the street, too. Including a buffet. The only good news is we're not paying for it, although there's a battle royale going on over who will foot the bill in progress. I want nothing to do with that battle, by the way."

"My father?" I guessed, as I couldn't imagine Ra liking to lose to anybody.

"Among others, including my grandfathers, my uncle, and most of my relatives. While you were getting dressed, I got to listen to some of the dispute. It's going to be entertaining. I did suggest your father handle processing all of the payments to keep things orderly and to fight over it after the wedding. That earned me some father-in-law favor, which I'm happy to take at this point."

If our families wanted to bicker over the wedding bills, I wouldn't get in their way. "I get to fight your grandfather, Quinn! That is the only battle I care about."

"It will be a light skirmish, and you two will not beat each other to a near-death state. We can discuss strategy over dinner."

"There's a strategy for fighting gorgons? You mean I can't just pet his snakes after I catch him in a headlock? I figured I'd get him in a headlock and cuddle with his snakes. They like me. Amanda has been teaching me the many ways I can put people in headlocks. I suck at everything else, but I am good at headlocks!"

I bet the instant we got home, Quinn would be doubling the number of self-defense courses I took. With luck, he'd join me.

Few things beat sanctioned brawling.

My husband laughed. "You know what? Forget I said anything. If you catch my grandfather in a headlock so you can pet his snakes, I will reward you appropriately."

"I've been extra good today, so I deserve an even better reward." Six months ago, I wouldn't have dreamed of asking anyone to spoil me, especially not my personal heaven and hell rolled together in one smoking hot package. "Maybe I deserve two extra special rewards for saying that out loud without running away."

"I am very impressed you didn't imitate a lobster or attempt to flee to the nearest bathroom. I figure you still have some time tonight to do so, although I'll enjoy catching you and returning you to where you belong." Quinn made sure I'd keep walking before releasing my shoulders, stepping to my side, and wrapping an arm around me. "I have you where I want you, and I intend to keep you here for the rest of the evening."

"Who has the kids? Are they going to be having dinner with us?"

"They're socializing with the gorgons. My cousin brought his whelps to start socializing them, so they'll probably play all night."

I wrinkled my nose at the memory of having beaten Quinn's cousin, who lacked common sense when under the influence of alcohol and an incubus. "Oh, he's useful for something other than annoying me?"

With a low, wicked chuckle, my husband led me to the steakhouse for my next conquest. "Shockingly, yes. It's their first time with other gorgons their age, so we'll let them socialize and have a good time. As Darrel never wants to experience you trying to shove your foot down his throat again, he promises the children will be tended properly and kept out of trouble. Not only that, when we get them back in a day or two, they'll be exhausted."

"Exhausted is good, because they're going to be exhausting us soon, won't they?" I couldn't wait to get the children and our new animals home so we could settle and get started with the rest of our lives.

"You would be right. Enjoy the quiet while it lasts." The smoldering look my husband shot me promised there'd be nothing quiet about the rest of our evening, once we got finished with the eating and the brawling. "But for now, you must enjoy your steak. You need plenty of fuel for your fight."

Once inside the steakhouse, the hostess took us to a booth for four in the heart of the restaurant, which was set up with candles and place settings for two. Two nearby booths had been commandeered for presents, which made me laugh.

I sat, rubbing my hands together. "Nobody told me I got prizes for marrying you in front of a bunch of people. And here I thought you were the prize."

"I am the prize. You're just getting consolation gifts for having to put up with me daily. Consider the gifts to be payments for getting too little sleep lately."

With my change of job, I looked forward to sharing the same shift with Quinn, being able to go home with him, and being able to spend time with him without sacrificing as much sleep. "Six hours a night, Quinn."

"I'll aim for letting you get eight unless I'm feeling particularly needy, in which case I'll just carry you to the car and let you sleep on the way to work—unless we sleep in, in which case, I will make use of a quicker form of transportation after calling it in so you're not chased all the way to Manhattan."

"You can transform and run with me. We could race!" Would New York survive two fire-breathing unicorns galloping from Queens to Manhattan to get to work on time? We'd find out, and I'd love every minute of it. "I won't even teleport so you have a chance of beating me."

"I'm game to try it." He chuckled, sat next to me in the booth, and held me close. "I like this part. I get to be a king for a day, and everybody has to shower my queen with gifts. And I've learned there's little more my queen loves than presents. I thought you would have been tired of presents after this morning, but it seems I underestimated you yet again."

"They have two tables for presents, Quinn. Isn't that crazy?"

"At last count, five hundred cops and their families came from our building, and that's only the folks who could make last-minute arrangements to come out. I was expecting fewer, but it seems you have a strong following. I bet it has something to do with your evil coffee-making ways."

I grinned, as I made a point of going to the station and taking over my husband's floor at least once or twice a month to make coffee for people.

It'd taken me a few months, but I'd discovered I missed being a barista sometimes, and I enjoyed making coffee for a bunch of starry-eyed cops who tended to follow me around like lost puppies whenever I paid them a visit. "That's going to be awkward once I'm working there."

"Not particularly. We'll just give you twenty or thirty minutes a day working the machine and set a rotation so everyone gets a chance to have your coffee. That'll give you an outlet for your wicked coffee-making ways, and it'll make everyone happy."

I liked that idea. "We need to look at increasing our training, too. Once we're—"

Quinn rested his fingers over my mouth. "We're not working until January. You can turn the station upside down on me our first day back, but you have to wait until then."

I stared at him with wide eyes and kissed his fingers.

As always, his smile narrowed my world to him and only him.

Once he seemed satisfied he'd quelled my

need to work, he lowered his fingers. "Play now, work later, and if you *really* need to get some work out of your system, you can express yourself in our suite. Be warned, however. I will do my best to thoroughly distract you from any inclination to work."

"Yes, please."

TWO

To my amazement, Ra indulged
me.

SOMEONE NEEDED to talk to the cops and our family about excess. Presents, which we weren't supposed to unwrap until after everything was ferried to our suite, towered on the tables, piled on the floor, and otherwise transformed the restaurant into a maze of red, green, silver, and white boxes and bags. At a complete loss of what to do or how to respond, I hid under the table and abandoned Quinn to his fate.

He peeked under the tablecloth. "Would you like your dinner?"

Hiding with steak seemed a lot better than hiding without steak, so I held up my hands in an acceptance of his offer.

The bastard cheated, and he gave me his plate, which had a lot more steak on it than on mine.

"Pregnant cindercorns need to eat more." He grinned. "I'll make them bring out another one for you."

"Rare, please." With the issue of too many nice people around me solved, I went to work making his steak disappear while my husband resumed chatting with his cops, who insisted on loitering for as long as possible.

"Don't mind her," he said with laughter in his voice. "She has reached her limit for people for one day, especially people she's embarrassed herself in front of already today."

I chewed on my steak, considered his words, and swallowed. Unable to smother my need to giggle, I said, "It's true."

Someone lifted the tablecloth, and my father bent over to peer at me. "Enjoying yourself?"

After a moment of consideration, if I sat on my husband's feet, there was sufficient room for my father under the table. I scooted over and waved for him to join me.

To my amazement, Ra indulged me.

Despite the tablecloth falling to the floor, I could see surprisingly well in the dark. I showed off my plate. "I am. I'm tasking you with making sure Quinn actually eats enough, because he gave me his steak."

"He will get plenty to eat, never fear. Making certain he is fit for your enjoyment later is in the forefront of his thoughts, and he plans on getting a steak for himself while ordering you another. I spotted you crawling under the table and wanted to make sure everything is all right."

"I'm fine. This steak is not long for this world, and I have never seen so many presents in my life. What am I supposed to do with so many presents?"

"Enjoy them. You will find there are many you will like, and as word has spread you shall have twins, many gifts come with something for your little ones as well. You will enjoy your time opening them later with your husband. As he does not expect me to discuss serious matters with you today, I thought it would be prudent to do just that."

I giggled and had another bite of steak. "Now we're talking. He's in vacation mode. I can't blame him for that, because he doesn't get to go on vacation, but I'm in a different mode. It involves me having a salary for the first time in my life, so I want to do a good job."

"You get your vigilance from me and your ethics from your mother, which means as long as there are problems you are aware of, you are not happy until it is dealt with. I will help you learn to control those tendencies."

I considered my father, eating more of my husband's steak. "You say that like I have an actual desire to change those tendencies."

I'd only met him earlier that morning, but Ra's sigh implied I tested his patience. "That comes from your mother's side of the family. It is part of your mother's charm, but it can be quite the source of frustration from time to time."

I could think of a few things I might do to annoy Ra, and one possibility rose over the others. "She tells you no, doesn't she?"

"As a matter of fact, yes."

I twisted around and tugged on Quinn's leg, and when he leaned over and lifted the tablecloth, I said, "Do you like when I tell you no?"

"When it's important and you're right, yes. When you're trying to convince me that you're not the perfect woman for me, no. What sort of no are we discussing here?"

"The first category," my father answered.

It was well enough he'd answered for me, as I would have found some way to insert my foot into my mouth. "What he said."

"Yes, I do. I told you at our first wedding, an asshole like me needs a bitch like you, Bailey. I want you to be you. If I wanted someone who wasn't you, I wouldn't have married you twice. I love you. Please enjoy my steak, and another one will be here somewhat soon. Apparently, when the groom asks for more steak, we get to jump the line of hungry people. I could get used to this." Quinn grinned at me and dropped the cloth, leaving me to chew on his words.

"He's weird," I informed my father.

"He would have to be to enjoy how hard of a time you give him."

Oh, wow. I would feel that burn for at least an hour, maybe for an entire day. "You're even worse than the fucking assholes.

Did you teach them their tricks? I bet you did. That was a good one. I'm going to use it on Quinn at the first opportunity. He should get to marvel at the majesty of that one."

My father chuckled. "I do enjoy when I get to toy with the Judaic pantheon, especially the archangels. They are delightfully prudish while also having an interesting sense of humor. I find myself quite amused over how conflicted your husband is, as he is heavily influenced by several pantheons. Even the influences within one of those pantheons creates chaos for him. The devilish side of his ancestry, in particular, clashes with his angelic side. Anubis's influences help temper that so he is able to tolerate his conflicted nature. The Sphinx? She holds a great deal of responsibility for his protective nature. As you are also the product of multiple pantheons, he will require a high tolerance for the absurd. And trust me when I say your mother's side of the family is rather absurd."

"And yours?" I asked.

"My side of our family is perfection, of course."

Of course. "Right. How could it not be perfection? What did you want to discuss?"

"I have spoken with some of your husband's relatives about the current situation, and while there are rules I must abide by, there are ways I can involve myself. Mostly, it involves information and giving you a general direction to apply your natural tendencies. There are three issues that need to be addressed, and I would rather you be ready for them than flail around. I have been warned you often indulge in aimless flailing."

I both hated and loved my father's honesty.

After a few minutes of thought, which I spent devouring my second steak of the evening, I could think of two possibilities that might warrant Ra's attention. "The rabies outbreak and that asshole chief?" I guessed. "That's only two, though. I'm not that math inept, I just can't think of anything else that important."

"Yes, those are two things you should be addressing. You should also be investigating how your husband's former companion became involved with gorgon dust manufacturing. That is the third issue. The third issue is, in some ways, a larger issue than the other two, but as my child has a tendency to rescue rabid animals from dumpsters, the rabies situation is my current top priority."

As I couldn't argue about my animal-rescuing ways, I focused on the one damned woman who kept haunting me. Even dead, my husband's ex-wife insisted on creating trouble. "Audrey again." I wrinkled my nose at the memory of her having deliberately used gorgon dust and becoming a gorgon with a general plan of using me as a surrogate to gain access to my immunities. "You have no idea how relieved I am that my gorgon-incubus doohickey does not require three-somes to successfully procreate."

My father chuckled. "He is likewise grateful, as he is entirely incompatible with gorgon society despite his position as a future king. I spoke with his father this morning while you were getting dressed. He is a most interesting man. He is human, but when he is exposed to mild transformatives, his serpents make an appearance. Asps. I was given a demonstration. It seems your husband's family does that trick to make certain they are aware that the line is intact despite the current king being mostly human. Gorgon politics are quite intriguing. Your husband's cobras are superior, and few can compare. While his father appears mostly human, your husband is rather prized. I will get to see his true shape soon enough. That will make things interesting for you, as he will be in high demand among gorgon females."

"I will light them all on fire if they even think about it."

"That is something you have gotten from me. I am quite jealous when anyone looks at your mother."

"I've been known to show up as a cinder-corn to defend my territory," I admitted.

"You get that from me."

I pointed at my husband's legs. "He likes it."

"He does like being the center of your universe. So, back to serious matters. I recommend you begin researching how Audrey McGee became involved with gorgons, as she was unaware of your husband's heritage. They were not close. Love had nothing to do with their union, although it is one of his regrets in a way. The regret fades day by day and will soon be gone, as he comes to terms with the role that union played in his union with you. He would not have had the patience or the fortitude to handle you without having coped with someone like that woman. He learned much about patience and tolerance from that relationship."

"I'm very good at testing his patience."

"Most would not be proud of that."

"I've been doing better. I only make him sigh a few times a day now, and I have to work at it now. Either he's become even more patient, or I'm doing better at being a reasonable adult. Do you think caring for two gorgon children will help when the helpless human babies come along?"

"You will be fine. Yes, caring for them will help you handle your offspring, although I would not assign them as humans. They will be adept shapeshifters and will need to learn early on how to control their powers. The first time they witness you or your husband shift, they will do their best to mimic you, as that is what young things do. They will not have your struggles with shapeshifting."

"But will they be legally human?"

Legally human mattered; while we had

weird abilities, Quinn and I still classified as humans. Barely. When it came to the law, classifying as human made a huge difference.

"In the eyes of the law, they will classify as humans. All of your children will have a majority of human genetics, but they will be shapeshifters. You'll find you'll throw many fillies, and your first son will take after his father more than you. The fillies will be proper little cindercorns, although you may find the existence of wings to be vexing, especially as they grow older."

"Winged cindercorns could take over the world. I've seen what I can do to a skyscraper. Give me enough napalm, and it's *gone*."

"Yes, I have been educated on your skills at destruction. That is definitely from my side of the family."

It amused me that my father seemed so determined to categorize all of my behaviors by who had contributed to my general inclinations. "We don't talk about the skyscraper incident, however. It makes Quinn twitchy."

"Yes. He is reminded he feared losing you, although he is very appreciative of the aftermath. He has come to terms with that, for the most part."

"You're nosy, aren't you?"

"I am," my father replied with zero evidence of shame. "I have a great deal of spying to do to catch up for lost time. As compensation for my ways, you will find you will often have easy access to a babysitter should you need one during the daylight hours, and your mother will likely show up to introduce herself soon. She can be shy, and she may try to stealthily make herself known. Your charming awkwardness comes from her. Just look for a woman who trips over her own feet when the moon is visible in the sky. That is likely her. She tends to manifest in a form that will not draw attention to herself, as she is somewhat shy and reclusive."

"You are anything but shy and reclusive."

"She does tend to enjoy hiding behind me for some reason, much like you do with your husband."

"Well, I know where *that* tendency came from now."

My father chuckled. "When you begin researching Audrey McGee, start with your husband's career in the police force. The scheming began early, even before his union with Audrey McGee. His awareness of her first corruptions will be a better guide for the investigation than anything else."

"And they were still together for a while before he filed for divorce."

"Yes. He's not the quitting kind, although she ultimately forced his hand. He could not enter his own home without being sickened by her crimes against him. You have done a great deal towards healing those old wounds, but a larger house for your new pets would not go amiss, so he can fully bury the reminders. With your twins and the two young gorgons in your care, plus Sunny, your charming kitten, and your new puppy, you will find yourself challenged in terms of space. If you would like, your mother and I can begin searching for a new home for you, one that will handle your familial needs without requiring you to move in a few years."

"Let me guess: I will be incapable of stopping after the twins, because I look at him and get ideas, and then I'll want to fight for every orphaned gorgon whelp to cross my path. Then I'll end up with even more little gorgons under foot."

"You have guessed correctly."

"There are worse ways to go. Hey, do you like babysitting?"

"You will find yourself having a difficult time getting rid of me now, and your mother will do what I cannot."

"Try not to cause a multi-pantheon war arguing over whose turn it is to babysit, please. I like Quinn's family even though they're crazy."

"Your tolerance for the weird and weirder will serve you well in the future."

"Are you game to come to Easter dinner? We invited Quinn's uncle. It should be hugely entertaining."

"I have not participated in that particular religious ceremony before, but we shall be there, although your mother will have to wait for the moon to rise to make her appearance."

"I'm sure we can figure something out if the moon isn't up during the day. If she can't manifest, she can somewhat be present, correct?"

"It is tiring for her, but yes. I have more restrictions than she does."

"Because the moon reflects the sun's light?"

"Yes."

"Will you two be wed? Or do divines not do that?"

"Would such a ceremony please you? If such a thing does, she is a most sentimental creature and would likely enjoy bringing me low as often as possible."

"As it seems like she'd enjoy it, absolutely."

My father's soft laughter reminded me I'd never heard such sounds from my human asshole of a father. I announced, "Then you absolutely should, but only because she would like it. Then you'd make those pesky archangels bring you presents, because it'd be rude for them not to. You are family. And you're not like the other part of the family. They'd just get smited."

"I believe you mean smote," my father corrected. "I was asked about your sensitivity to angelic song and their halos. Your mother's ability to reflect my light is the primary source of those woes. I do not know if you will be able to overcome that, but you will find the angelic host will be cautious around you in the future. There are some benefits to their powers."

"Like their ability to reboot my immune system when it fails?"

"That is one of those benefits, yes. One day, you may even learn how to do that yourself. It is within your grasp, although it will be more of a learned trait than a natural inclination."

"I'm a badass."

"You are, although those powers do come at a price."

"Like being smited."

"Smote."

"Smited!"

Quinn peeked under the tablecloth. "Are you really arguing with your father over that? It's smote."

"Smited," I replied, and I dared to lean forward and steal a kiss. "I win."

"Smote is still the correct word, but if it means I get kissed when I argue with you over it, I see no problems with this. Are you ready for your next steak? It just arrived."

I checked Quinn's plate, which I'd picked clean of meat while talking to my father, and I handed it to him. "I left you some potatoes and green things."

He took the plate, and he replaced it with one with a new piece of steak, which took up the entire plate and lacked any of the potatoes or green things Quinn often tried to feed me. "That is good, because I stole your potatoes and green things, and I will sit here and enjoy eating it all. I refuse to share, so you'll just have to eat that big steak all by yourself."

I claimed my prize, set it down, and rubbed my hands. "You are guarding our presents?"

"I am making sure your presents are safe and sound, and I'm even telling them you're spending some time with your dad—and not the asshole one. I have to specify, because a lot of the cops hate your human parents."

"Well, they are assholes, and *someone* told them about the courthouse incident."

"I may have asked the cops in Queens to keep an eye on our neighborhood in case they decided to pay you a visit," my husband confessed.

I sighed, rolled my eyes, and wondered how I'd gotten lucky enough to win someone like him. "I can transform into a unicorn, and I breathe fire. I can handle a pair of stupid vanilla humans."

"They might have a gun," he replied.

Being shot sucked. "I do not like being shot, and this is a very valid point. I do not wish to be shot."

"Again, my walking bomb squad." According to my husband's expression, he'd be getting payback in some form or another. As his version of payback involved the bedroom, I'd enjoy every minute of his scolding.

"You can punish me for that stunt when

we go back to our room and need a break from opening presents."

He laughed. "Is it a punishment if you like it?"

"It is now."

He lowered the tablecloth to resume his conversation with whomever had come to pay him a visit. I went to work cutting up my steak. "Do you want some? I've totally made you hide under a table without offering to feed you."

"After you return to keeping your husband company, I will dine with Anubis and the Sphinx, as we have much to discuss. In your excitement, try not to forget the investigating you should be doing."

"I won't," I swore. "Morrison is the kind of asshole who'd try to get revenge solely because I still exist. Add in the charges? He'll be back. I know this, and Quinn probably does, too. I'll do my best to keep from worrying about it for a day or two, but I don't want him to get too much of a head start. Since the gorgons were targeted and many of them killed, I'll get the Quinn family to help. I'm pretty sure the gorgons have a network."

"Your husband fears the possibility of retaliation, but he is uncertain about the probability of it happening. His grandfather is aware of the certainty of such things, as he saw your memories on the matter."

"Sariel told you about that?"

"He deemed it to be a wise decision, as I

will not be a benevolent being should he hurt you. We are limited in what we can do, but there is nothing in the rules stating I cannot prepare you for what I feel will be an inevitable conclusion."

"Because he's an asshole, and that's what assholes do."

"Yes."

I took a bite of my steak, debating how best to handle the situation. "Well, this will be fun." The instant Quinn perceived a threat to me, he'd freak out. Given ten minutes and an excuse, he'd involve the entirety of his crazy family. If his crazy family joined in, I'd be watching the kids and caring for the pets while they created havoc, which would give me an excellent opportunity to take the kids and deal with the problem myself.

"Your logic concerns me," my father admitted.

"It concerns overprotective over there, too." I pointed at my husband's legs just to make sure my father understood which overprotective individual I discussed. "Worse, can you think of any part of that logic that was wrong?"

"Alarmingly, I do believe your logic is founded on reality, which is as concerning as your general thought process."

"I feel I should warn you that I'm going to be a pretty terrible daughter, but in good news, the human ones survived me, so that's something."

My husband poked me with his shoe, and a moment later, he peered under the table-cloth. "I heard that, and I'm enrolling you in therapy to address your self-esteem problems."

"What part of that wasn't true?"

"The part about you being a terrible daughter. The Gardeners are the terrible ones, and I'll be implementing corrective training immediately."

I scowled. "Corrective training?"

My father snickered. "I will, with some help from her mother, make certain she realizes she is not the terrible party. I wish you the best of luck with your efforts to correct the self-esteem damage, but given time, I am certain she will begin to see for herself how we view her."

I pointed at my father with my fork. "You are an unreasonably biased party."

"You will get used to it, I'm sure. Being the perfect child of divine perfection is challenging to come to terms with. I'm sure your husband will have no difficulties helping you on your quest to accept your perfection."

With that, my father disappeared in a flash of fiery orange light.

"Huh. They normally poof off in silver or gold."

"That they do. Are you ready to come out from under the table now?"

I considered it, nodded, and handed over my plate before rejoining him at the table to deal with the endless line of those wanting to wish us well.

AS I DIDN'T WANT to destroy my wedding dress picking a fight with a gorgon, I changed into a pair of jeans and a black top. Black tended to hide the stains better, especially when covered with pet fur. Anyone who thought I'd resist the furry charms of Sunny, Blizzard, and Avalanche counted as crazy, and I only wanted specific crazy people in my life. As the rescued ocelot kitten needed the most care and attention to questionably count as domesticated, she got the lion's share of my attention, although the puppies didn't seem to mind.

Their new toys helped with that.

To make sure I wasn't late for my date with Quinn's grandfather and have enough of a fight to please the unicorn in me, Quinn grabbed me by my waist and dragged me out of the suite while the angel watching over our pets gently took my ocelot from me.

"Cruel," I whined, and as my husband enjoyed when I put up a fight, I grabbed hold of the door frame and made him show off his muscles.

He chuckled, pulled until I lost my hold, and hauled me towards the elevator. "I'm the cruelest of men, taking you from your puppies and kitten so you can pick a fight with my grandfather. You'll just have to punish me later."

"Think the hotel will let me do any demonstrations as a fire-breathing badass? Cindercorns are so much better than gorgons." As my husband was wise, he kept me out of range of anything I might use to put up a fight. I giggled, tried to dig in my heels, and enjoyed making him work for his victory.

"I'm going to let you have that, as I've experienced what it's like to be you—almost. I'll admit, playing with fire is quite enjoyable, although I'm somewhat saddened napalm doesn't function like pixie dust for me."

"Those hangovers are the *worst*."

"They're easily resolved. I just have to make sure you drink enough water afterwards. Your napalm rations will come with plenty of liquids afterwards. You'll be okay." Quinn pressed the down button, maintaining his vice-like grip while pinning me to his side. "I am thinking I'll condition you to accept you're also Police Chief Quinn through the careful rationing of napalm. I already refused to allow them to call you Police Chief Gardener. You're *mine*."

I loved when my husband became possessive, although I missed when he growled Gardener at me. As it was our second wedding day and nobody lurked nearby to catch me, I asked, "But will you call me Gardener when I've been really bad?"

"Call? Or do you mean growl or snarl it at you? There are other options, including purr."

Yes, my husband could purr, and I loved it. He also hissed nicely, especially when he shifted to his gorgon-incubus doohickey form. "Growl, snarl, purr, and hiss are all good options. Call is so tame compared to those."

"In private, I'll do whatever you want me to."

He really would. "Talk, talk, talk," I complained, sighing when the elevator door opened. To my amazement, no one was inside. "That might be a first."

"Well, we're on the upper floor and there's entertainment to be had in the canals. I'm betting the hotel is about to make good money off you and my grandfather, and I can't even blame them for monetizing your little scuffle." He dragged me inside and hit the button for the first floor. "Your goal is to headlock him and braid his snakes *without* getting bruised in the process."

"He'll probably just stand there while I crawl all over him attempting to knock him down and put him in a headlock. I've learned how gorgons operate. Unless I'm a cindercorn, I probably won't be able to budge him. But I'll just climb him, put him in a headlock that way, and braid his snakes together while he explains why it's a bad idea to do what I'm doing. Then he'll probably bite me a few times. *Somebody* mentioned testing my immunities while pregnant was good for the babies. As such, I'll probably get bit by every damned gorgon on the planet. Just to make sure I've had exposure to all types of snake venom. Then you're going to get all annoyed and insist you get to bite me more often than any other gorgon."

"You do realize that's more because my bites are like an aphrodisiac for you, right?"

"I may have noticed something along those lines, because gorgon-incubus doohickeys are the *best* doohickeys, and I have a full claim on the only one. Mine, mine, mine." I rubbed my hands together. "You act like I don't con your little serpents into biting me. Although it was sweet they tried to make the hangover better, but really, Quinn? A heart?" I pointed at my chest, where his serpents had indulged in body art. I blamed one of the angels or archangels loitering around the hotel for the scarring, as snake bites didn't usually do anything other than annoy me for a day or two. "And now it's permanent body art! I bet one of the fucking assholes is responsible for that travesty."

"I like it," my husband replied, grinning at me. "I like it almost as much as I like our bracelets."

"Like is not a strong enough word for what I feel about my man repellent. I will become very upset if it somehow becomes gorgon-incubus doohickey repellent, however." Considering an archangel had marked us with the magical equivalent of a ball and chain, which bound us together until death did we part, I wasn't particularly worried about that happening.

Chuckling, Quinn shook his head. "I thought about bringing my Lakers jersey just to screw with you," he confessed. "But I decided you were getting the suit model for Christmas rather than annoying you. When you least expect it, I'll show up in my Lakers jersey, though."

Evil, evil man. "Do I still get a picture of you shirtless to carry around in my purse along with a picture of the suit model? I'll take the dress uniform model, too." As my husband hadn't grimaced at the reminder I'd spent a disturbingly long time in the hospital thanks to my immune system shutting itself off, I added, "I am definitely pursuing the naked model later."

The elevator made a few too many stops on the way down to the lobby, and I sighed, forced to almost stand on Quinn's feet when we got shunted into the back corner. While I appreciated being close to him, I contemplated murder by the time we reached the ground floor with the lobby, the canal shoppes, and the location I'd finally get to pick a fight with Quinn's gorgon grandfather.

I escaped without killing anyone, but I wanted to scream at the crowd barring us from reaching my destination, a nice mat the hotel had brought out so we'd be able to fight without damaging their pretty floors.

"We can go around the back way," Quinn said, taking hold of my hand and dragging me towards one of the hallways that circled the canal shoppes. While there were still people loitering around, we entered the shoppes from the other side of the steakhouse and worked our way back to where I'd have my chance to be pummeled by a gorgon.

The jerk would probably stand still and sigh while I climbed all over him.

Quinn's parents spotted us, and his mother waved, and when my husband didn't immediately acknowledge her, she waved faster and bounced up and down.

"She really won't stop until you tell her you love her," I whispered to my husband.

"I know." According to his grin, he liked it that way.

Crazy man.

Quinn's father had more restraint, although he joined in waving at us, which drew a lot of attention, most of it unwanted.

"Dad, did you feed Mom sugar again?"

"She got into some pixie dust earlier."

I heaved a sigh at the unfairness of it all. "Just once, I want to know what it's like to get high on pixie dust. Just once."

"I'm sorry, Bailey. But you get high as a kite on napalm. I just get a little frisky and like fire."

"That's so sad."

"Not really. I get to watch you get high as a kite on napalm, and that makes everything all right with me. Last time, you wormed through it while on your back with your hooves in the air. Tiffany got a good laugh out of it, too."

"Where is that devil woman, anyway?" I needed to tell her a thing or two about laughing at unicorns who could breathe fire. After she finished laughing at me for attempting to tell her off, she'd probably get me in trouble.

"I'm pretty sure she and Arthur went to bed."

"Which type of bed are we discussing here?"

"The kind where they pass out into an unconscious and exhausted stupor. They both got a fairly heavy dose of influences from succubi and incubi in the past week, and they need to sleep it off."

Oops. "You didn't, did you, Quinn?"

"It wasn't me. The Devil's wife did some, my grandfather showed up to play for a while, and I'm fairly sure the Devil amused himself throughout the hotel. He can't behave all the time, and Darlene took her eyes off him for ten whole minutes."

It took me a moment to remember the Devil's wife was Darlene. "That poor woman."

"Don't worry about Darlene. She loves all the trouble he creates. If she hadn't wanted him creating chaos in the hotel, she would have stopped him. Probably. Then again, she *is* a succubus, and the Perkins weren't the only people wanting Christmas miracles this year. They're just getting the lion's share of miracles."

Well, yeah. Perkette being barren until the Devil and an archangel had gotten a hold of her counted as quite the miracle. "If she finds out I'm technically part of the reason she's having quadruplets, she'll kill me. Protect me."

"And who is the reason we're having twins?" my husband asked.

While I could have blamed his grandfather, I shrugged and pointed at myself. "For every one we add to the chaos, we have to adopt one. It's a new rule I just made up. I expect the adoptees will be gorgons, though. For some reason."

"Life will be interesting if our children don't inherit your immunities. We're really going to need a new house if that's how we're going to approach expanding our family. Also, I'll be adding to our evening ritual to ask if you'd like to add any new members to the family along with how many new members you'd like." Still laughing, Quinn dragged me over to his parents, letting me go long enough to hug and kiss them both. "Are you going to be roped into a demonstration, Dad?"

"Not today, much to my disappointment. Your grandfathers and uncle feel it's best to let Bailey show off. No demonstrations for you, either."

"He better give me a demonstration when we're back in our suite," I muttered.

"I'm sure you can handle any negotiations with my son as you see fit, Bailey. Are you having a good night so far? I was worried when you went under the table." Quinn's father chuckled. "But then your father joined you under the table, and at that point, I decided against checking in on you myself."

"It's all right. I just didn't know how to handle so many presents, so I hid under the table until I could come to terms with them. That, plus so many people!"

"You'll have to get used to it," my husband warned.

"I don't have to get used to it right now. Well, mostly. I have to tolerate turning the hotel into a circus, though. I'm going to French braid his snakes." I bounced on my toes. "He'll look wonderful with French braided coral snakes. And unlike him, his snakes like it."

"They like it because you cuddle with them and don't fall over dead if they bite you."

"That does help. I've figured out they have to bite something now and then or they don't feel well. His serpents give a nudge and a hiss when they need to bite. Yours whine."

Quinn sighed. "Do you want me to work on that? We have ways of draining our venom, you know—ways that don't involve you being bitten."

"Why would I want you to work on that?" Had my gorgon-incubus doohickey lost his mind? I frowned and considered him. "Are you feeling okay?"

Quinn's parents snickered, and his mother caught me in a hug and pulled me in the direction of the crowd loitering around waiting for the demonstrations to begin. "Ignore him. He's not happy unless he's fussing about something. I was warned my children would be weird. My fathers did their best to prepare me for that reality, but nothing prepared me for Sam, and his sisters are something else, too."

"I haven't even met his sisters yet," I replied. "When can I meet them?"

"They're around, probably trying to seduce strippers in a different hotel. One of them got the bright idea to start a competition."

My eyes widened. "To seduce strippers?"

"Samuel got the lion's share of angelic tendencies. His sisters are wicked little seductresses, probably to balance out how goody-goody Sam became."

"Mom," my husband complained. "My sisters are not out seducing strippers, are they?"

"They really are. I can't even blame them. We went to a strip club and got a very pleasant surprise. Vegas has some nice men. How could I deny them? They wanted to enjoy the local offerings. It's not *my* fault you're the only one of my children who has decided marriage is interesting."

According to Quinn's sigh, his family would break him sooner or later. "I can't believe you brought my sisters to Vegas. They'll take it over, and once they get bored, they'll probably destroy or sell it because they have nothing better to do, and there's no adult supervision here to convince them it's not a good idea to sell or destroy an entire city."

"Don't say such mean things about your sisters. It's your father's fault they're so randy. It's a gorgon thing."

Quinn's father shrugged. "Says the daughter of an incubus."

"Well, that didn't help matters any, that's for certain. How did you turn out so angelic, Sam? Where did I go wrong with you?" Without waiting for her son to reply, Quinn's mother dragged me through the crowd, who wisely made way for the insane woman on a mission. What her mission was remained a mystery, but I'd find out soon enough.

THREE

I don't know what I did, but I'm
sorry.

QUINN'S MOTHER dragged me to a mat placed disturbingly close to the canal's edge and shoved me in the general direction of my husband's grandfather, who kept me from falling on my face or plunging into the water.

"I don't know what I did, but I'm sorry," I whispered to the gorgon.

Archambault Quinn patted my shoulders. "My little grandson's mother is energetic, and she shares certain tendencies with her angelic father. As such, she is hoping all of her eligible offspring start producing children in high numbers."

"Well, I'm married to a gorgon-incubus doohickey, so if she's expecting anything less from her son, she's even crazier than I am. Considering how often I ask to fight for the right to claim baby gorgons, I don't even know what she's thinking. I'm concerned for Sam's sisters, though. His mother said they were out to seduce strippers?"

The gorgon pointed to the other side of the canal, where an entire gaggle of dark-haired, tall, and beautiful women bounced behind a cordon the hotel had set up to keep people from falling into the water. "She lies. Those are his sisters. The younger ones are with my bride, who would rather not see me fight with you, as she'd be torn over joining in. As she doesn't know if she wants to fight with you or defend me, I suggested she take care of the younger girls."

My eyes widened, as they were all feminine versions of my husband. "They certainly look like they could seduce any stripper they want."

"And they have their fair share of incubus genes, so they're quite adept at finding men when they want them. Thanks to those genes, they'll likely become surrogates for hives, as they have inherited tendencies from both sides of the family. Little Samuel is unfit for such a life. His sisters are quite interested, if you please—or even if you don't. They didn't inherit any dignity from either side of the family." The gorgon sighed.

"What are we waiting for?"

"Local law enforcement to oversee everything. It should only be a few more minutes now that you've arrived."

I nodded, and as I had nothing else to do, I went to work greeting all of Archambault's serpents, noting most of them were primed to bite. "Is this demonstration to see how many times a coral snake can bite me before I start frothing at the mouth? Their sacs are full." The worst of the lot made a forlorn hiss and nuzzled my hand. "Look at him. He's going to burst if he doesn't bite. The poor baby. How could you be so cruel to him?"

"I'm sure he'll get his chance to bite you soon enough. You wanted a fight, and since I can't petrify you, I came prepared. I have arranged for a little angelic and devilish help on that front, however, as I'd rather you not literally froth—and it will allow some of the humans to experience a gorgon's bite without death being involved. There is paperwork for most humans, as the partners of those bitten must consent to a heightened chance of pregnancy."

I bet the Devil had participated in the creation of that scheme, making full use of the ten minutes his wife had taken her eyes off him. "Seriously? What did you do to your poor snakes?"

"Rather than your typical response to my venom, you'll find you'll become quite interested in my little grandson, rather irresistibly interested. I will cruelly win this fight through the unfair usage of your husband's body." The gorgon smirked with zero evidence of shame at the underhanded tactic. "Their venom production was modified to become a rather potent aphrodisiac partnered with a little angelic magic. I have been told if my bride does not get to enjoy the con-

sequences of this meddling, I will be very unhappy for the rest of my vastly shortened
life."

The Devil and his brother truly loved me
and wanted me to be happy. "Have fun, Archambault. For some reason I don't understand, I even like you, so I'd be sad if you got
kicked to death by your centaur bride."

"It would be a terrible way for me to go, so
I will make certain she enjoys a nip. I am
planning on inquiring for a confirmation my
serpents are all safe for her after our fight.
You will be given, frankly, a rather ridiculous
dose, so you return to your suite and stay
there for a few days."

My eyes widened. "For a few *days*?"

"We are planning on taking your whelps
to the Grand Canyon and several state parks
while you are occupied. They need to be socialized more and learn more about how to
interact with other gorgons, so it will help on
that front while you get to enjoy your time of
rest."

If I got a full dose of all his snakes and
their venom, there would be nothing restful
about the next few days of my life. I rubbed
my hands together and smiled. "How does
this little demonstration work?"

"As the whining would be incredible
should I actually bruise you, I will demonstrate my various defenses with some stoner
bait before I do the same demonstration with
you, showcasing your various immunities.

There are a lot of people who wish to undergo petrification. It's usually barred without a special permit, but the hotel opted to get the permits required. You will not be asked to handle any of the cleaning required, as there are CDC recruits who need to learn."

Score. "This just keeps getting better and better."

Archambault chuckled. "You will particularly like the part where you will get to beat on me to your heart's content to showcase how durable gorgons are. I will lecture the humans on why it is unwise to do everything you will surely do, including braid my serpents."

"French braids, and I'll make sure they all get their appropriate attention and can bite as needed."

"They are being more patient than usual, although I've found they do enjoy when they can bite you. And you, insane woman you are, like it."

"Well, each type of snake venom is different, and I react to it differently. Darryl's snakes hurt like hell and itch, so I really don't like when he bites me. Yours is like getting a little drunk without the hangover."

"Ah, I understand. The lack of hangover appeals to you, as you cannot indulge in vices without paying for it in unfortunate ways."

"It really does." My husband, who had his mother hanging off his arm, hauled her over while his father laughed. "Grandfather, please tell my mother you're not going to kill my wife during a demonstration."

"My toxin has been modified, and even then, it just makes her drunk. There's nothing to worry about, my precious little one."

I couldn't tell which one of the precious little ones Archambault addressed, but I figured we all classified to him, allowing him to indulge in his vague tendencies to his heart's content.

Quinn's mother sighed. "Tell this son of mine he should be fighting instead."

"If he fights and gets bitten, he may spontaneously combust. I do not think giving the grandson of an incubus an aphrodisiac is a wise idea."

That caught my husband's attention. "Who did *what* to your snakes?"

"There are those present who wish to experience being bitten by my snakes. As my bites typically kill a human, my snakes underwent a minor adjustment for the day. Instead of lethal neurotoxins, their venom is now a rather potent aphrodisiac. You can thank your uncle. I believe it was his idea, although he had some help from his brothers to implement it."

"Is it weird that I love the Devil?" I asked. "He's just pure fun wrapped up in complete and total naughtiness. Plus, he likes cindercorns!"

Quinn bowed his head. "You do not need any aphrodisiacs, Bailey."

"Like hell I don't." I went on guard and warded my husband away with two fingers. "Stay back, fiend. You shall not pass or take away my playtime with your grandfather. Back, you!"

"You ran across the entire United States because you weren't getting enough sleep, my beautiful. This would not help with that problem."

"I do not need nor want help with that problem today or for the next few days. Babysitters, Sam. We have babysitters. *Babysitters.*"

My husband laughed. "If you're really sure. You're biting off more than you can chew, but I'm not going to stop you if you really want to participate in this insanity," he warned.

"We can open presents while you're catching your breath," I taunted, well aware he'd view my words as a challenge and do his best to make sure he won.

When he won, I won, and once we returned to work, we would have limited time where it was just us, and I intended to enjoy every minute of it. Of course, I expected he'd make me pay for mouthing off.

What a way to go.

"You're playing with fire," Quinn warned with his sexiest smirk.

Evil man. "I can play with the cranky gorgons if I want to, and you can't stop me."

Archambault rolled his eyes, and his coral

snakes jockeyed for position to win the rights to get in petting and cuddling time with me. To make the serpents happy, I took my time greeting them all, giving them kisses on their little noses.

"She's going to teach everyone it's a good idea to kiss gorgons if she keeps that up," my husband complained.

"They will be educated on why this isn't a good idea, do not worry. It will involve some young human lady wishing to have a good evening with her gentleman getting a nip on the nose for her troubles. Then I will teach them only members of a gorgon's family may be so familiar with us."

"Bailey would be pulling that crap even if you weren't my grandfather," my husband replied.

While he was right, I sighed over his insistence on spilling my dark, dirty secrets.

Somehow, probably from overexposure to my husband, I'd developed a keen enjoyment of cuddling up to gorgons and their snakes. "Just no bile I have to clean up, please."

"Bile is definitely unpleasant, and I'll just stay back here, if you please," my husband said, taking enough steps back his grandfather couldn't spit on him even if he tried.

"It's not like your dirty secret isn't already out, you know. Janet saw you."

"I really did," the cop in question said, and she wormed through the crowd and waved at me, dragging Amanda, my self-defense instructor and another cop, along with her. "I have brought a sacrifice."

"You brought a walking bruise generator," I grumbled.

Amanda grinned at me. "We'll be back to making bruises in January, never you fear. I was recruited to be the referee, and I get to direct you in offensive tactics to conquer your grandfather-in-law."

I liked the sound of that, but as I didn't want to get nipped by a snake prematurely, I continued making sure all of my grandfather's snakes were content. "Just call him my grandfather, as it gets to be a mouthful if we try to keep everybody straight. Quinn's family is crazy, second only to the craziness that is my family. And he's only partially crazy, because his family's craziness starts with his grandfather. Mine started at conception. I have decided I'm the best parasite."

"You're hardly a parasite," Janet replied.

"Oh, I'm not just a parasite. I'm the *best* parasite."

My husband sighed and bowed his head. "Just because your human parents are assholes doesn't make you a parasite, Bailey."

"I'm the *best* parasite, Quinn. I successfully inhabited the womb of my host, leeching all of her nutrients until birth, where their attempts to get rid of me were thwarted by my badass self. I am the definition of what it is to be a parasite. Non-beneficial to my host, totally beneficial to me. But I was somewhat benevolent. She survived pregnancy. I didn't burst out of her stomach or anything." I gave the final coral snake a kiss before striding to my husband and prodding him in the chest. "And now I'm leeched onto you, and you can't get rid of me."

"We have a mutualistic symbiotic relationship, and as such, you do not get to maintain your status as the best parasite," my husband countered. "You're now a symbiont, as am I, as I am your partner in our mutualistic symbiotic relationship. You're a former parasite, and I will consent that during your reign as a parasite, you were a most excellent one. But now you're my symbiont, and I'm pleased you're stuck with me forever."

My eyes widened as my husband went for the throat, using science to flirt with me. I turned to Janet and pointed at him. "Do you see this?"

"I do. It seems he has transcended all other men, figuring out how to woo you with scientific terminology. You're blushing." Janet snickered. "He's not wrong."

"How are you feeling?" After having been petrified and kidnapped, it amazed me the woman had come out to a demonstration involving gorgons and a general petrification free-for-all.

Janet heaved a sigh and glared at Quinn. "Chief Quinn is making me undergo several rounds of petrification tonight until I learn to dodge better."

"Quinn! You are not going to do anything like that to Janet."

"Yes, I am."

"No, you're not."

Janet smirked and walked over to Archambault, introducing herself to the former gorgon king, and rather than continue to argue with my husband over the thinly disguised torture of our cop under the thin guise of proper training, I observed.

Amanda patted my shoulder. "It was her idea, but she appreciates you care for her. She hates how easily they got the jump on her, and she wants to see if she can build a resistance. She'll be one of the demonstrators. She's also being paid a bonus by the CDC for participating, so she's quite happy. Not only is she getting transferred to join us, she's getting a really nice paycheck out of this."

"No biting!" I reminded my gorgon grandfather's serpents, as the little rascals would do just that if they thought they could get away with it. "I swear. His family is a zoo, Amanda."

"Says the fire-breathing unicorn."

"I really can't talk, can I?"

"You really can't." Amanda grinned. "And add in your inclination to rescue animals from dumpsters, you are the queen of the zoo."

"Being queen means I rule the zoo, and I'm all right with that."

"I feel like I should protest, but as the king of her zoo, I can't really complain." Quinn extracted his arm from his mother's hold, came to me, and gave me a kiss before turning me around and marching me to his grandfather. "Go get bit already. I have found the changed situation to my liking, and you seem to think you'll have enough energy to unwrap presents by the time I'm finished with you."

Evil, evil gorgon-incubus doohickey. "I am not going home until I have unwrapped my presents."

"I'm still trying to figure out how we'll get all of our presents home," he admitted.

"I'm not above asking the various relatives who can teleport to help move everything, otherwise, we hire movers to drive across the country for us." I escaped from his hold and stepped onto the mat, stretching as I'd been taught so Amanda wouldn't have extra reasons to bruise me when we resumed our lessons. "Apparently, I'm here to get bit," I informed the gorgon.

Archambault chuckled. "Someone thought about what my bite will do to you and found the situation pleasing. He probably won't even notice if you get a few bruises now. Well, he might notice, but he won't care."

"Let's get this show on the road, old man. I don't have all night."

The gorgon smiled and shook his head. "Patience, little granddaughter. The humans need to be lectured, then you'll have your turn. Only then will you get to drag my little grandson to your suite."

"Quickest beatdown of your life, old man," I promised.

"You are so amusing."

A CDC REPRESENTATIVE handled most of the lecturing, and Janet was petrified through exposure to Archambault's gaze first before she was exposed to his bile, which did a good job of convincing most of the spectators they didn't want to tango with a gorgon unless they had no other choice. I wrinkled my nose at the smell, only assisting the fledgling CDC reps with the cleanup job after the entire lot of them managed to become stone through improper handling of the substance.

As Janet lacked a significant other and had no interest in taking a random hookup to her room for the night, she didn't get to experience Archambault's bite. The number of volunteers would forever amuse me, and I suspected the gorgon's poor coral snakes would be exhausted by the time the night was over. As a few too many of his snakes had overly full venom sacs, I got to rumble with him first.

I could handle an overdose. He wasn't sure if regular humans could. With Amanda coaching me, I got to practice several tosses, one of which actually dropped the gorgon flat on his ass. I blinked, as did he.

Confused over how I'd floored the man,

who weighed a hell of a lot more than me, I stared at my instructor, pointing at Quinn's fallen grandfather.

"That's supposed to happen when you do the toss correctly, Bailey."

"He weighs like a bazillion pounds, Amanda. The bastard probably turns his legs into stone just to screw around with me."

Archambault chuckled, got to his feet, and brushed off and straightened his clothes. "That time, I had not. This is a good time to mention had I been less on my guard, I would have made use of most of my defenses after that."

"Thank you for not doing that," I replied, and as I felt bad I'd startled his coral snakes, I apologized to each of them.

"My little granddaughter is very considerate towards our serpents," the gorgon said, directing his attention to the curious crowd. "This is generally a wise approach, as they are individuals despite being a part of my body. Should you become friends with a gorgon, it is considered polite to ask if you wish to touch. Not all gorgons are able to maintain control over their serpents. In fact, I am not controlling any of them. She has built a relationship with each of them."

Movement in the crowd drew my attention, and while I kept cuddling with Archmabault's coral snakes, I indulged in my curiosity.

A tall man with an oddly familiar face and

a scowl eased through the people, and when he wasn't trying to escape in the general direction of the lobby, he shot glares my way. For once in my life, I hadn't done anything to offend anyone in the hotel. While I lacked my phone, Archambault had his in his pocket, and he unlocked it with a few taps at the screen when I held it out.

"As a general rule, picking the pockets of a gorgon is a good way to get petrified. My little granddaughter has problems with asking before snitching things, like my little grandson."

That made people laugh, and their jostling did a good job of keeping my target around long enough for me to snap a picture of him. Annoying someone hadn't been part of my plans, and I took a few more pictures of the crowd to get as many faces as possible before I emailed and texted the pictures to myself and returned the phone to the gorgon's pocket. "Thank you. Sam didn't want me to break my phone. And I really would. If I had it on me, I would've fallen right into the canal. By default."

"Never fear, little granddaughter. I will help you into the canal soon enough."

Quinn would enjoy peeling me out of my wet clothes, and I doubted my poor jeans would survive. Some sacrifices needed to be made. "You better put your phone somewhere safe, as I'll be doing my best to take you with me when I go."

"I'm not worried about my phone. It's waterproof."

I scowled. Turning to my husband, I pointed at his grandfather. "Hey, doohickey! Why does *he* get a waterproof phone?"

"Your new phone is waterproof, Bailey. Did you not read the box when you bought it?"

Oh. "My phone needs to be better than his phone."

"You're going to get bit if you don't pay attention to him."

"Why'd you make me leave my phone upstairs if it's waterproof?"

"You would inevitably crack the display roughhousing with my grandfather."

While true, did he have to announce it to the entire crowd? Before I could voice my opinion, one of the coral snakes nipped my finger. I yelped and tried to pull my hand away, but the little bastard dug his fangs in deep. "Now you're just being rude!"

"This is a good reason why you shouldn't turn your back to a gorgon *or* point at one," Archambault announced. "Unlike mundane snakes, mine generate venom at a significantly increased rate. In addition, my snakes continue to deliver venom for however long they bite. Had she been a standard human, she would be convulsing and frothing at the mouth, and her death would be counted in a matter of seconds at the dose she's currently experiencing. I've won, Bailey. You may as well accept your defeat."

Like hell I would accept defeat. I abandoned waiting for Amanda to give me directions, pounced on my gorgon grandfather, climbed him like a maypole, and went to work attempting to braid his damned serpents while they all took turns trying to sink their fangs into me.

In addition to venom modification, someone must have added a numbing agent, as the bites lacked their normal stab of pain. "You should ask for them to keep that anesthetic, Archambault. Normally, that stings a little."

"Ah, yes. You can thank the angels and archangels for that. They felt it would ruin the fun if it actually hurt to be bitten. The holes will close sooner than you anticipate, too. As we're in the season of their heightened power, I'm sure their benevolence may bring forth extra gifts, too."

The only gift I needed was the ability to keep clamping my legs around the gorgon's chest and having free rein to braid his coral snakes, who settled into our ritualistic game. I won when I dodged being bitten, they won when they bit, but as their bite packed the perfect punch, I made a show of dodging their bites while braiding them. "These poor babies have so much venom. You're a bad gorgon, not taking care of them better." I rested my elbows on his shoulders to make sure I stayed put while I worked, catching his serpents and weaving them together. Each time I caught one, I offered my arm as a reward for being good while I braided him. As was our way, they behaved once captured.

I gave it ten minutes before I was so hopped up on their venom I'd consider attempting a seduction of my gorgon-incubus doohickey in public.

To demonstrate his strength, Archambault strolled around the mat with no evidence my weight bothered him. "It is worth noting that gorgons *can*, in some circumstances, do dry bites, but this is rare. Should you be in a relationship with a gorgon, and you're invited to play with our snakes, as my little granddaughter is currently doing, they will do fangless nips rather than actual bites. You should never engage in such activities with younger gorgons, as it is a skill that must be mastered. When available, most of us carry antidotes in case of an accidental bite, or we petrify a bitten victim to allow time for rescue personnel to administer a treatment."

As I could see a bunch of idiots testing their luck because they could, I said, "The treatment for petrification reversal and the antivenin is usually around five thousand dollars. It requires a lot of neutralizer, an identification of the venom used, acquisition of the antivenin if available, and the services of an angel or a high-level practitioner if an angel isn't available. Practitioners are cheaper, but they're not as reliable about purging toxins of a gorgon's potency. More often than not, such a bite leads to death, but gorgons are particularly careful around their brides—or their permanent surrogates. There are contracts for surrogates, and any costs of care are included as part of their compensation. If such a thing interests you, you can either approach a gorgon or inquire with the CDC."

"And now, for a more practical demonstration of a gorgon's strength," Archambault announced before grabbing hold of my legs right above the knees and peeling me off, despite my best efforts to stay put. The instant he had my legs unwound from his body, he bent over and tossed me over his head into the canal.

I shrieked, landed with a splash, submerged, and flailed before my ass hit the bottom. I scrambled to the surface, glaring at the bastard while I tread water, as the canal was just deep enough I needed to swim. "That was just rude!"

"So, shall we begin the meet and greet? The CDC representatives will determine order, but please leave any valuables you do not want to get wet. I find throwing humans into the water to be quite entertaining."

What a jerk. I sighed, swam to the nearby ladder, where my husband met me, his smuggest smirk in place.

That smirk worried me. "What?" I asked.

"I'm just waiting for the aphrodisiac to start kicking in so I can fully enjoy my conquest."

When Quinn went on a conquest, I became the conquered, and I enjoyed every moment of it. "Apparently, it's slower onset than I thought. Probably because they don't want to turn the Canal Shoppes into a sex party."

"As I do not share, I approve. Did you have fun?"

"I tossed him!"

"I have several pictures of his expression when your pretty little self knocked him flat on the floor. They are now priceless treasures, and I have determined I need to reward you for good behavior. I've been informed if you ruin my new suit, I can have it replaced as part of my uncle's wedding gift to us. I know how you can get with buttons."

And shirts. And pants. And anything else getting between me and a close look at his skin. "You have the best uncle."

"That shirt looks great on you when wet," my husband commented, making no move to help me out of the canal.

Considering he likely had an excellent view of my cleavage, I couldn't blame him for that. "I'm sure it has nothing to do with your position up there."

"It has everything to do with that. I'm hoping you slip a few times. That will teach you to let my grandfather toss you like that."

"Oh, come on. He has arms of steel. There

was no way I was able to keep my hold on him. Give me a break."

"More like stone, but that's fair. Was your pride stung, my beautiful?"

I held up my bitten hand, which didn't bleed nearly as much as I thought it should. "No, but my hands and arms were."

"I have noticed you were given a rather high dose of his venom. The angels are likely making sure his venom doesn't kick in until the victims are somewhere more appropriate."

"Victim is not the word I would use. The blessed. The receiver of great gifts."

"The soon to be incredibly frisky."

"Yes," I purred. I scrambled out of the water, grabbed hold of his hand, and dragged him towards the nearest set of elevators. "Merry Christmas to me!"

FOUR

Are you ready to surrender?

AFTER AT LEAST four days of being under the influence of the venom, I decided I would need the help of an archangel to restore me to being a functional human rather than a fire-breathing unicorn turned succubus with a taste for gorgon-incubus doohickey. Quinn wouldn't stop smirking, not that I blamed him.

He ruled our hotel suite, I was putty in his hands, and I hadn't come close to exhausting him. In the four whole days we'd kept each other company, we hadn't opened a single damned present, I could barely move, and I wanted to drag my rather happy husband back to bed. Again.

"Are you ready to surrender?" Quinn asked, his tone amused.

Through a feat of extreme willpower, I'd managed to keep my hands off him for thirty minutes, long enough to eat a meal. I'd lost track of the time, the day, and anything else important. I'd lost my sanity along the way, too. I'd only eaten because he'd insisted on it, getting dressed and refusing to remove any clothes until all the food on my plate disappeared into my stomach.

"We could go back to bed," my mouth contributed.

Damn. My mouth was going to get me killed one of these days.

"We could, but we have presents to open."

"If you want me not taking you back to bed long enough to open presents, you need to tell your grandfather to turn this off, or I'll kill us both. Or at least me. I might not make it." Well, I'd probably make it back to bed, but I'd have to crawl to get there.

"I'm not even tired. Incubus," he reminded me.

Evil, evil gorgon-incubus doohickey, using his sinful body against me in the best ways possible. In my last gamble to restore sanity, I replied, "I don't know if we can keep the children pawned off on your grandfather much longer."

"That's not a problem. They're having a good time, and they've never gotten to interact with other hives before. They'll be fine. Once you fully surrender, I can help with your little problem, not that I view it as much of a problem. You purr in your sleep, you're warm, and I enjoy tiring you out."

I narrowed my eyes, and it sank in I'd

married a gorgon-incubus doohickey. "How much of my problem is your fault?"

"Right now? All of it. The venom only lasted six or so hours. After that, I was enjoying myself. Why not encourage you to show more of your wild side? I've been having a great time. How about you?"

Evil, *evil* gorgon-incubus doohickey! "You're going to pay for that."

"I'm sure you'll try to make me pay for making you among the happiest of women alive. Is it my turn to be fed steak and grapes in the tub?"

His smirk drove me wild, and I debated if he needed his clothes. As it was one of his favorite sets of pajamas, which he tended to put on in the mornings before getting ready for work so he wouldn't prance around the house naked, I restrained myself. "Okay. You win. I surrender. I seem unable to overwhelm a gorgon-incubus doohickey. But I am expecting a really good reward for surrendering. You might talk me into feeding you steak and grapes, but honestly, I have problems. I'd probably make the steaks and eat them before bringing them to the tub."

"You really would, too. Your surrender is sweet, and it only took you four days," my husband teased, and he kissed my cheek. The delicious incubus influence he liked tossing around eased to something I could ignore if I wanted. "I'm leaving a little going, as if I totally remove it, you'll probably fall asleep on me, and that would rob you of time to open presents. Four days is apparently *my* limit on how long curiosity can eat away at me before I need to know what is in all of these boxes. I might perish if I don't find out what is in all of these presents."

"We absolutely couldn't have *that* happen, now could we?"

"Absolutely not." My husband strutted across the suite, which was overwhelmed with presents, and he went to work sorting through them. The only places without presents piled everywhere were the bed, the couch, and in the bathroom, with narrow pathways linking them. "I got a present for you, so you get to open that one first."

Damn it! "But I didn't get anything for you."

"You ran through the snow as a unicorn to adopt an ocelot for us. As I like cats, that counts. Sure, Avalanche is really your kitten, but I pretend she's mine when you're not looking."

As my gorgon-incubus doohickey did an excellent job of making my common sense dribble out of my ears, I made a mental note to thank our various relatives for putting up with us at our worst. "Please thank your relatives for watching over our pets."

"Already done. Anyway, our pets are with our kids, as they would whine without the pets around."

"We've lost our pets to our children, haven't we?"

"It seems so. I'm strangely okay with this. They've been really careful with them, too. There have been no accidental petrifications. Apparently, their father impressed upon them Daddy and Mommy time was sacred, and my grandfather somehow convinced them you needed an entire week's worth of Daddy and Mommy time."

"Your grandfather is the best grandfather."

"All of them are, and I'm happy to share them with you, although you'll find you have tolerable grandparents now. Ra didn't want to overwhelm you, so you'll meet your grandparents gradually. Honestly, I think Ra is more worried you might be ambushed the instant the rest of your family learns of your existence. Your mother remains a mystery."

"Because of the moon phase."

"Right. Apparently, when she has been around, she's been dragging your father off somewhere, and nobody is brave enough to disturb them."

I giggled. "Hopefully they are not indulging during any possessions this time."

My husband found what he searched for in the pile and returned to the couch, placing a red-wrapped gift on my lap before sitting beside me. "Yes, I will continue to pretend I'm actually helping you with any technical stuff you may ask when you want attention and don't know how to ask me for it."

Busted. "Perkette snitched on me, didn't she?"

"You have been thoroughly caught, but I will indulge, just please stop checking out weird porn on my laptop. Or any laptop. Please."

I snickered. "I wasn't really watching them. I was looking for ideas. They're not even all that good. Most of the time, the poor women look bored. You just made the best expressions, so I had to find weirder things to blurt out to see what you'd do."

"Maybe I should make one of your presents a promise to endure one or two instances of your insanity a month, especially as I now know you were badly trying to get my attention."

"But your expressions are the best!"

"Just my expressions, huh?"

Double busted. "What you do after you make those expressions is also the best. I win from top to bottom. And in the bedroom. Or, if I had found a particularly naughty kink, somewhere on the way to the bedroom."

He bowed his head and sighed. "Children are going to make our adventures far more restrained."

"Babysitters," I reminded him.

"We can't get a babysitter every time I want to take you to bed, Bailey."

"Quinn, I love you, but if we went to bed every time you wanted to take me to bed, we would never leave bed. We'll somehow survive."

"But are you sure?"

As always, he made me laugh. I took my time admiring the pretty paper on the package, debating if I wanted to go through the ritual of trying to determine what was in it before tearing my way inside.

"You shouldn't shake that one. It's heavy plus you might break it."

"Do you read minds now?"

"No, I just know that look in your eyes. That's the look of a naughty little cindercorn about to destroy something."

Busted yet again. Without any reason to delay, I tore into the paper to discover two laptop boxes stacked on top of each other, taped together to give the illusion they were a single package. Neither had their original shrink wrap, and upon investigation, I discovered he'd marked one as for home and one as for work. "I'm still going to use yours because I can," I warned him.

"I bought your personal one aware that would likely be the case. However, you'll be able to play games on it with me now, rather than sigh sadly when I'm playing a game and you want to play, too."

Damn. At the rate he was busting me, I'd have to find a pair of handcuffs so he could handle the matter properly. "I can't help but notice one is labeled for work."

The laptop reminded me I had a bunch of

pictures to sort through to see if I could remember why I'd recognized the man in the
crowd or what I might have done to
annoy him.

"We still have a few days before the kids
are back, and now that you've surrendered, I
thought we'd try to get a head start on
teaching you what you need to know and investigate Morrison. To the limited degree we
can. I'll teach you our systems, go over the
rules and regs, and I'll set you loose on the
budget. It could use your magical touch."

"Isn't the budget for the year already set?"

"Yes and no. We can make adjustments if
we need to, but the commissioner will need
to get it approved, then it'll have to pass
through the city government, and depending
on the budget issue, it might get bounced up
to the state level. This year's was particularly
bad. We took a lot of cuts, but we're supposed
to be doing more work. We *do* have authorization to do program fundraisers, but we
haven't figured out how to pitch it to the
commissioner, who has to get the final ap-
proval for the specifics. Some things we're
not allowed to do fundraising for, like our
staff budget. However, we *can* do fundraising
for new K-9s, domestic violence support programs, animal rescues when animal control is
overwhelmed, and community outreach. We
need to do a lot of PR; while our precinct is
generally okay, mismanagement and poor
training has been an issue. Holding our

precinct at a higher standard only does so much good. But that's what the commissioner wants, especially after Morrison's less-than-legal activities."

"Have you been sneaking in work, Mr. Samuel Leviticus Quinn?"

He grinned at me. "I'm an incubus. I don't need nearly as much sleep as you do, especially after spending hours making you happy. As I wanted to make sure you were getting enough sleep, I worked when I wasn't cuddling with you. I set your work laptop up while you were asleep, and I mostly set your home one up, installed some games, and otherwise got it ready for you to customize to your preferences. I got laptops for the children, although they're heavily restricted, they'll only be able to access the internet when we're supervising them, and they're meant for education purposes. My grandfather has been helping me set up a schooling plan for them. They're far more advanced than most gorgon whelps at their age, but they're behind on some of the basic survival techniques. That's part of why my grandfather has them for another few days—possibly up to a month. We need them able to defend themselves and have better control of their abilities. Beauty is a biter, and Sylvester will reflexively petrify, although it's tiring for him. My grandfather is concerned that the circumstances of their birth has damaged their development."

"And their rabies treatment?" I scowled at the thought of what had brought the pair of gorgon whelps into our lives. If I got a hold of whomever was responsible for attempting to weaponize rabies, I'd bring them to justice one way or another. With my track record, justice would involve a quick death during some brawl or another, but I could handle that.

It beat leaving them out to hurt or kill others, and enough people—and animals—had perished already.

"That wouldn't have helped matters any, and while their father paid out for a miracle before his death, there's only so much an angel can do, and the angel would have only helped because of a perception of injustice."

"The rabies infection would have been a part of an attempted murder," I guessed.

"That's my thought. They're children, and any angel would have wanted to right that wrong."

"But their mothers? What about them?"

"It's miracle enough the whelps survived a round in a glass coffin, Bailey. Gorgons are magic. Everything about them is magical. Their mothers would have died in the coffins from that much exposure to neutralizer. I suspect part of the miracle was them surviving through treatment in the glass coffin. But they may have survived because of how they were born. I haven't been brave enough to ask."

I struggled to imagine Quinn being afraid of something like the answer to a question. "Why are you afraid to ask?"

"There are some gorgons who would risk cracking their children's eggs if they think they can create another Beauty or Sylvester."

I sucked in a breath. "That's horrible. But *why*?"

"I suspect that may be why Audrey wanted you in the first place. To conduct experiments just like that. Your immunities would make you the perfect surrogate for that sort of thing. Had you been their mother, you wouldn't have died bringing them into the world—and the other child may have survived, too. I won't be surprised if you are asked to carry a cracked egg in the hopes the shell would heal or the child might survive as a live birth."

It never failed to amaze me how much gorgon society could amaze and repulse me at the same time. Worse, I couldn't see myself saying no, especially in the case of a cracked egg where the whelp might survive. "How often does that happen?"

"Not often. Broken eggs usually kill the whelp immediately, and it's rare an egg will crack without being fully broken. Beauty and Sylvester were likely banged together during conception and their eggs cracked but didn't break until a few weeks later, when the eggs would have started to grow. The father would have known when he'd attempted to retrieve the eggs. That probably finished breaking their eggs. His bride must have loved him—and them—very much to have wanted to try to carry them to term. The human child was likely from superfetation—conceived after the whelps, usually by a matter of days or weeks. Human embryos wouldn't be able to survive the rigors of petrification, and gorgon whelps are born able to petrify."

"Thus the third child died along with their mother."

"Right. A cracked egg happens every few years, and even then, one in ten might make it if the surrogate is willing to attempt a live birth. Cracked eggs rarely survive, so the surrogate willing to take the risk would have to be flown in immediately. Gorgon magic would allow the woman to carry the whelps to term, though—or for however long was necessary. It's never really been tried before. Most gorgon fathers make the difficult decision to save their bride or surrogate."

"But Beauty and Sylvester are proof it can happen."

"That's right. Their mother must have fought hard to try to bring them to term. Most gorgon males just won't risk losing their bride. The brides are often the heart and soul of a hive, and losing her hurts the whole hive."

"If the bride has a cracked egg, won't she get upset if somebody else takes over being the surrogate?"

"It would be better than losing her child, I would think—and most surrogates wouldn't survive after month six or seven. The petrifications would be too taxing."

"Like what happened with their mom."

"Exactly. Beauty and Sylvester are very lucky to be alive."

"How many women are like me? Who don't get petrified by gorgons?"

"There are no other women like you, Bailey. There are some resistant women, but they'd probably die, too. If the petrification doesn't kill her, their venom would."

My eyes widened. "Do you think their serpents...?"

"Think? No. Know? Yes. I had the toxicity reports pulled from her autopsy. It showed lethal amounts of their venom in her bloodstream. Infant gorgons have weakened venom, but they likely bit her internally countless times during the stress of being born. That's the only defense they have, and they had no way of understanding what was going on."

"We're never telling the kids that. It's bad enough they're convinced their petrification killed their mom..." I couldn't imagine how much it must have hurt. "Their mother was truly amazing."

"The petrification certainly didn't help, but their snakes were the actual cause of death. Make no mistake. Their mother wouldn't have survived either way. And yes, it takes an amazing woman to do that. She refused to give up until her babies were born."

My poor little children. "But I could save eggs like theirs, couldn't I?"

Quinn sighed. "Assuming the eggs were left in the surrogate until the transfer, and if it isn't during your period. Gorgons plan for when their surrogates are at peak fertility to make certain their magic takes hold. In theory, if you wanted to take over being the surrogate, the hive male would retrieve the egg or eggs in question, hand them over to me, and I'd handle implanting them. It would not be a very comfortable process for you, especially if the eggs are more than a few weeks old. A little magic can help with that, though. Then you'd probably endure a pregnancy from hell, and the delivery would be complicated."

"Complicated? It would be full of sharp, pointy teeth!"

"Yes. Then there's an issue of the little gorgon having even more mothers than normal, so we'd end up with another child around. The child's father would not want you to be excluded, the bride would probably fawn all over you until the day she dies, and don't get me started about what the gorgon mother—or mothers—would do. It would be a mess."

"That doesn't seem highly problematic. We'd just have play dates with all the kids. At the rate we're going, is anyone going to notice an extra gorgon whelp running around under our feet?"

"Probably not," he admitted.

"Just make it clear I'll cut the dick off any gorgon who deliberately cracks their eggs. And I'm unavailable for any other gorgon nookie."

Quinn chuckled. "If being an emergency surrogate is something you want to do, I can register you with the CDC for specifically that exception. I'll give you a full list of when a second surrogate might be needed, and you can pick the options that you like best. They're all post fertilization, so that's not something I mind."

"As you'd be the primary participant, at least as far as I'm concerned."

"That's right."

I pointed at my flat stomach, which wouldn't show any signs of pregnancy for at least a few months. "What stage does this become a no fly zone for such efforts?"

"No gorgon male will use a pregnant surrogate. It's too dangerous for the unborn, and it goes against their general beliefs. Brides are precious—and even the paid surrogates are, for the time she's carrying their child, effectively their bride and precious. They won't risk the unborn. However, I'd just ask my grandfather to verify if it's safe, which would override that. But until we see how you handle pregnancy in general, this is only a theoretical discussion. I fully support the idea, but it needs to be done safely for you *and* all children involved. And that said, it's so rare it might only happen once every twenty or thirty years."

"Because most cracked eggs break?"

"That's right."

"Even if it doesn't happen, I'd still feel better if we could."

"Then we will. And now that we've detoured from the main point, if we can't get to the bottom of the rabies issue, gorgons will have a lot more problems than the rare cracked egg."

Right. "My father had a few suggestions."

"If your father is offering advice, it would be wise of us to listen. What did he tell you?"

"He told me that I'd be a lot happier with the situation if I dealt with three key things, including activities on your ex-wife at the time of and before she'd decided to be a cheating asshole, the rabies problem, and Chief Morrison and his whereabouts. There was also someone in the crowd at the demonstration I want to look into. I took a picture of him. I was supposed to start this earlier, but for some reason, I got distracted."

"I am your ultimate distraction when I want to be."

He really was. "Do you think my father realized I'd be busy for a while?"

"I'm sure he was aware I would be despoiling his daughter thoroughly. I was quite enjoying myself thinking about the things I'd do after making sure you'd eaten enough to be appropriately energetic for my plans. That was entirely on purpose."

"You're pure evil."

"I love you, too."

I grinned at that, separated the laptop boxes, set aside the laptop marked as for work, and freed my new toy from its packaging. "I'm proud I didn't run from the altar. Or throw up on you. Or do anything even more humiliating than what I babbled."

"As always, you were perfect."

"No, you're perfect. I'm just really lucky. And jealous."

"I love your jealousy. To answer your question, I have my dress uniform with me."

I stilled, staring at him with wide eyes. "What does a woman have to do to get you out of those pajamas and into your dress uniform?"

Quinn chuckled. "Ask, but only after we get some work done. Try not to destroy my dress uniform when you get your hands on me, as I'd rather not go in for a fitting before we go back to work. Did your father give you any hints on where we should start?"

"He's mostly concerned about rabies, as I have a reputation. It involves me rescuing animals from dumpsters. If people didn't leave animals in dumpsters, I wouldn't fetch them."

"It would be good for my blood pressure if you stopped rescuing rabid animals from dumpsters, but I understand why you won't stop. And Blizzard is a good puppy despite the fact you acquired him from a dumpster. Well, he's as good of a puppy as a husky can get."

"And he was only a little rabid. Do you think Blizzard and Avalanche are okay with the children? How about Sunny?"

"They're fine, Bailey. Our pets and our children will be back soon enough, and I'm sure they miss you. I'm not sure where to start with the rabies outbreak." Quinn sighed and leaned back against the couch, muttering something under his breath. "Under normal circumstances, I would assign an investigative team to gather the base information, and I'd be available if they needed me. I've worked some investigations, but only as time allows —which isn't as often as I want. So, we're going to have to make this up as we go, especially since we're not in New York. If you have any ideas, now is a good time to share them."

"Tracking the health records for rabies treatments is the first thing to come to mind. There'd likely be a surge of rabies cases, probably in wild animal populations. That would create a surge of rabies treatments in the general area where they were developing the virus, especially if they're trying to make it more contagious." I opened my new laptop to discover a password prompt. "What's the password?"

"Something you wanted for Christmas."

"Suit model!" I typed the phrase in, and as Quinn liked secure passwords, I exchanged the space for an underscore, substituted letters for numbers, and hit enter. To my delight, the system unlocked. "Not only did I get the suit model for Christmas, I'm getting pictures. And I got the naked model, too. That's one of my favorite models. But most importantly, there were *several* photographers around while you were wearing your suit. One of them will surely give me pictures of you just for me. And Perkette has my back. Oh! We should ask Perkette for help with rabies tracking. I bet she already has good data because of her work." I chuckled, as the laptop was already linked to Quinn's phone for internet access. "Is the hotel's internet too slow for you?"

"I've seen faster turtles. I'm spoiled, Bailey."

"Sure, sure." I tapped in a search phrase for rabies outbreaks, my brows rising at the ridiculous number of results. Adding the year didn't help. As the general internet refused to be of use, I logged into the backend of the CDC, chuckling I hadn't lost access to their databases yet, and did a search for rabies treatments. "I should probably be doing work on my work laptop, but this one is *mine*."

"For the record, if you want a new computer or phone at any point, all you need to do is ask."

"I was fine before."

"Only because you kept stealing mine."

"That was half the fun, Queeny." I considered what my father had said about the timing of my husband and his cheating ex-wife. "My father thinks Audrey is more significant than we might appreciate. As such, your job is to look into recorded gorgon matters from when you met her, before she met you, and up until she started being a cheating asshole. That way, I won't interrogate you again with stupid questions and reminders I made your life a living nightmare until you were able to wisely ditch her. I think my father may be right about one thing he told me, though. She was totally a training program so you could cope with the disaster I tend to be."

"You're not a disaster, Bailey. That said, I did learn a lot about tolerance, patience, and keeping my cool while married to her, that is for certain. No, she wasn't a good wife, but I also wasn't the ideal husband for her, either. Frankly, after a year or two, I think we had equal disdain for each other. Honestly, even without your help with that, the marriage wouldn't have lasted much longer. You just made it a lot easier for me to get through the paperwork and take minimal financial losses from my stupidity."

"You weren't stupid, Sam."

"Oh, I was. I was young, tired of being treated like a stud, and she offered a loveless marriage. She did her fair share of treating me like a stud, but since I had agreed to marry her, it seemed fair."

"All she gave you was a loveless marriage with a side of bad sex." I frowned, considering my husband. "Well, bad sex for *you*. I can't imagine you being capable of not doing your best by your partner. The whole incubus thing."

"That whole incubus thing is why we ever had sex at all," he muttered, shaking his head before reaching over me and snagging my work laptop. "I'm borrowing this because I'm too lazy to go get mine, which is buried somewhere under the presents."

"It's gone forever. Goodbye, laptop. Rest in pieces."

"The presents aren't that heavy. Well, most of them. I'm sure my laptop is fine."

As trudging through the CDC's database gave me a headache on a good day, I downloaded every rabies treatment record for the past ten years, dumped them into a spreadsheet, and groaned at the eighty thousand records, amazed the laptop and the program could handle so many results. "Rabies is even more of a problem than I thought. Looks like eight thousand on average a year that have been reported to the CDC in the past decade."

"And who knows how many cases weren't reported to the CDC," my husband muttered, shaking his head. "Now I understand why the other chiefs told me I'd appreciate the shit I dodged before being dumped into my rank."

"At least I had *some* training before being thrown at you."

"Yeah. You're definitely better trained than I was before I became a cop. Actually, I think you're better trained than most of our cops. You just have unconventional training, and you're missing some of the fundamentals. That's something we're going to have to address once we're at the station. I want to revamp our training programs."

"Do you have any say over training programs?"

"I have a lot of control over what supplementary training courses my cops go through after they're out of the academy. I'm thinking I will see if we can hire one or two extra cops so we can have an hour of supplementary training as a part of every shift. I also have some concerns about our gun handling. I'd like to see Amanda run more cops through unarmed training. General gun usage has been down, so there are concerns of inappropriate use of force."

"I'm going to regret having a salary, aren't I?"

"Matching work shifts," he reminded me. "That means more sleep for you, my beautiful."

"You're just making me walk the walk after talking about how good I am at budgeting."

"You're not just good at budgeting, Bailey. If someone told me you were a goddess of budgeting, I would believe them. I've seen what you've done with our household budget. And not only do you handle the budget to save us money, you do not shirk on the quality. That is very important—we can't afford to shirk in terms of quality and services, so the budget is a very careful dance."

"The budget doesn't have enough in it for coffee," I warned him.

"That's easily solved. We will put a tip jar on the eighth floor and make a note that all tips go to buying coffee and low-grade pixie dust for the station. You're going to keep your pixie-dust license, and we'll make a system to help make sure the cops are level-headed during stressful shifts. I already encourage them to get a low-grade dose on the way to work. Our job can get pretty damned stressful, and the dust dulls the edge."

"You've done work performance tests, haven't you?" I accused, as my husband would do just that to make certain his cops were in the best health possible.

"Absolutely. Getting rid of ticket quotas helped *almost* as much as encouraging pixie dust."

"What is the deal with ticket quotas anyway?"

"Revenue. I had ticket quotas removed from all Manhattan precincts, and general performance of the cops increased fairly significantly; they were able to worry about more important calls and catching dangerous

drivers. Once upon a time, we were also responsible for issuing parking tickets, but we
lobbed that over to the city level. Last I
checked, they had community service
workers handle issuing standard parking
tickets and checking meters."

"Efficient."

"It saved us a fortune." Quinn admitted.
"Unfortunately, how we saved ourselves a
fortune is going to make our search even
more difficult. While the police will help aug-
ment animal control as needed, we don't keep
much in the way of records unless it's a notable instance."

"Like the Chief of Police's wife being
caught with her ass sticking out of a dumpster while being slobbered on by yet another
rabid puppy?"

"Precisely. Don't forget about the one with
distemper."

I sighed, as that poor dog had been too far
gone to save, but I'd stayed with him the entire time before being carted off to be treated
for rabies, distemper, and any other disease a
dog might pick up on the streets. "They had
to put that one down."

"I know."

"I guess I can't turn into a unicorn and
burn any assholes behind the rabies outbreak,
can I?"

"However much I would enjoy helping
you do just that, we can't. It's tempting, but
we're the good guys because we *don't* do that

unless required."

"That ex-cadet deserved to be squished like a grape. He was going to hurt you."

"That is an excellent example of when it's acceptable to ram all six or seven hundred pounds of your unicorn self into somebody. However, next time, please try to avoid being poisoned with ambrosia."

"I didn't do that on purpose."

"I can handle being poisoned with ambrosia almost as well as you can, so try to remember that next time."

I wrinkled my nose and went to work properly labeling my spreadsheet, creating a pivot table, and getting statistics on rabies infections by year and state.

Vermont came in at the top with six thousand rabies cases, and with a frown, I filtered by year, discovering a surge in rabies cases in the state six years ago. When I filtered by species, I discovered most of the victims of the virus were raccoons with wolves nipping hot on their heels. "Hey, Quinn. How many wolves live in Vermont?"

While Quinn worked on a search to find out, I adjusted my filters to include the month, discovering a pack of a hundred and fifty wolves had been found to be rabid in a single month in the state.

"According to the Vermont Fish and Wildlife Department, the state can likely sustain no more than a hundred wolves spread across several packs. That's a rough estimation. According to this, there are currently two packs in the state. One has twelve known members, and the other has eight."

"Six years ago, in March, they found a hundred and fifty rabid wolves. The same month had a thousand rabid raccoons."

"Where the hell did Vermont get a thousand rabid raccoons?"

"How the hell did they *catch* a thousand rabid raccoons?" I added the locations, and sure enough, there were clusters of rabid animals. I pulled up a map of Vermont and plugged in the name of the town closest to the largest cluster. "Long Lake's rural area has a population of around seven hundred, but there's almost ten thousand people if you combine all of the surrounding towns, villages, and hamlets." I filtered to add a column to get a number of how many citizen-killed animals had been reported to the CDC. "Apparently, Long Lake residents take rabies seriously; they killed eight hundred rabid raccoons and asked animal control to deal with the wolves, all hundred and fifty of them that had moved in. Maybe hunting the eight *hundred* rabid raccoons? How many wolves can eight hundred raccoons feed?"

"Considering how much Sunny can scarf down for breakfast, I'm going to say not as many as you would think."

"Don't say such terrible things about my puppy. Sunny is the best puppy. So is Blizzard. We have the best puppies."

"And I'm going to guess our new wolf will also be your best puppy when she's ready to come home with us."

I grinned at my husband. "Absolutely. She can become a little pack with Sunny and Blizzard. Blizzard is a wolf trapped in a husky body."

"I have no idea where we're going to find a house big enough at a decent distance from work to have an entire animal sanctuary, but it looks like I'm going to have to figure that out. Is it only raccoons and wolves on your list?"

I checked, and once I determined some people had been infected, I checked their treatment status, relieved to discover everyone had been successfully cured. "A few humans, but they were treated. No deaths."

"Gorgons?"

"Not in Long Lake." I restored the sheet settings, filtered by species, and selected gorgon. My eyes widened.

According to the CDC, over three hundred gorgons had been reported as infected with rabies, and according to the treatment status field, there were precisely two survivors. Cringing, I included the name field, and sure enough, I found Beauty and Sylvester listed. "Three hundred and sixty-seven gorgons have been infected with rabies, and only two have been listed as successfully treated, and they're our kids." I checked the other records. "There are twenty gorgons listed as actively being treated, so that number may go up. How are gorgons getting infected with rabies, Quinn?"

"That is a very…" With a frown, my husband grabbed his cell phone, dialed a number, and held it to his ear. "Grandfather, ask Beauty or Sylvester what their hives fed their snakes, please."

I blinked. While I slipped Quinn's serpents bacon and other treats at a shameful interval, he made certain I didn't overfeed them, and once a week, they were fed a proper meal. The details on the proper meal turned my stomach, but we made a trip to a butcher once a week for chicks, which he cut into several pieces and fed to his cobras.

They ate everything, including the feathers.

"Okay. Thank you. Please tell the children we love them, and we'll see them as soon as they've finished their basic schooling with you." Quinn hung up. "Feeder mice."

"Can mice get rabies?"

Quinn made another phone call. "Police Chief Samuel Quinn with the NYPD. I need to speak to someone regarding rabies infections in rodents and small mammals, please."

While he waited to speak with someone, I continued my search through the data, making a list of places in Vermont with higher-than-usual infection rates.

"Hello. Is it possible for field mice, feeder mice, and rabbits to become infected with rabies? Specifically, can captive mice or rabbits be infected? Let's assume they aren't killed by whatever rabid animal attacked them."

Whomever Quinn spoke to had a lot to say about rodents and rabies, and I watched the play of expressions on my husband's face with interest, which ranged from annoyed to surprised. At the end of the speech, his surprise darkened to disgust and anger. "Can you provide me with a list of suppliers for feeder and lab mice and rats, please? Email it to me along with the names and numbers of any relevant contacts. Thank you."

Quinn looked like he wanted to fling his phone across the room, and having witnessed him do such a thing before, I snatched it out of his hand. "You will not fling this phone. You can have it back when you promise to behave yourself."

He sighed, and he slumped against the couch. "Yes, mice and small rodents can get rabies, but they're usually killed by the rabid animals that attacked them, so transmission to other animals is exceptionally rare. Grandfather said most gorgon hives use feeder mice, as they're cheap, readily available, and do not offend humans as much as chicks or other small animals."

"And you use chicks because of your wings."

"Right. Magic helps with that, but chicks are a better choice for my serpents. I have a deal with a butcher and an egg farm; whenever they have an incident with a rooster, the male chicks are frozen for me. They try to prevent that from happening, but it does happen from time to time."

"That's where you get our eggs, isn't it? I noticed you didn't get ours from the grocery store."

"Right. I get them before processing, too. That's why we can keep them on the counter."

"Gorgon-incubus doohickeys require a great deal of specialized care. Do wolves eat mice?"

"Yes."

"So, the mice could have been used to spread rabies in other animal populations?"

"That wouldn't explain a *thousand* rabid raccoons in a town in a month."

I went to a search engine and searched for rabid raccoons in Long Lake, and to my astonishment, I found only one relevant result, which claimed there had been an unusual surge in rabies in the area, but that it had petered out quickly. "Only one news site reported about it that I've found during a quick search."

"You'd think a rabies outbreak of that level would hit the news. There were more rabid animals in town than people." Shaking his head, Quinn retrieved my work laptop and resumed searching the internet for any clues that might help us. "I'm going to end up calling my grandfather back and telling him to have all feeder mice sent to a lab for testing."

"You should, especially from the hives with deaths. And pull their purchase records to find out where the mice came from."

"I'll need my phone back for that."

"You may have it back, but you may not throw it. The only thing you're allowed to throw is me, and only if you're throwing me onto the bed."

"Don't cry when you get what you ask for later," my husband promised, accepting his phone back and calling his grandfather to begin the tedious process of learning if the feeder mice were infected with rabies and who might be behind the outbreak.

I returned to churning through the CDC's data in search of more clues on when the rabies outbreak had begun, so we might bring a permanent end to it.

FIVE

You're stuck with me, so you better
like me.

WHEN HONEST WITH MYSELF, I had severe
workaholic tendencies, something Quinn
first attempted to resolve through the
strategic placement of presents on my lap.
When I worked around the box, he stole my
new laptop, closed the lid, and hid it among
the gifts.

I gaped at him. "But I was working on
that."

"You were. Now you are unwrapping
presents and spending at least an hour doing
something not related to identifying the key
states probably somehow associated with the
rabies outbreak. Once you have opened some
gifts, I'm throwing you on the bed and having
my way with you. Should you have energy
afterwards, we will resume working. I need
to digest what I've learned, and I've discovered you're rather beautiful when intently
working. As I'm just a man, I have reached
my threshold of patience. Now, open your

gifts." To establish dominance and make it clear I would be doing what he wanted, he piled more presents on my lap. "I will bury you in presents if you don't start unwrapping some of these."

"That's quite the threat. Open presents or be buried in them." I peeked over the pile, wondering just how we'd gotten so many gifts. "Why are there so many presents, Quinn? I don't get this."

"People like you."

I narrowed my eyes. "People like me? Like who? I mean, Perkette. She counts. Perky likes me, I guess. You're stuck with me, so you better like me."

"I love you, which is far more than merely liking."

"I love you, too, but this is an excessive number of presents! Nobody likes me this much."

"Tiffany is responsible for at least six of the gifts. I put one of hers on your lap already. Arthur got us a present each, as he was concerned you might rupture something in your head if you got more than that from them."

"In addition to the like ten other gifts they got us on Christmas morning. I'm glad I had done my shopping early, and I owe your relatives for fetching the presents. I didn't even offend either one of them, but I'm concerned over how much Perkette liked the miniature flasks. They were a prank. I think she now wants to do miniature experiments. We still need to get stuff for the kids."

"Bailey, I bought them almost an entire bookstore each when I found out they like to read. Apparently, Beauty wants to cook, so we're going to have to potentially remodel our kitchen—or make sure our new house has a good kitchen. You've been showering them with affection, candy, and giving their snakes treats whenever I take my eyes off you. They're not suffering from a lack of gifts. And anyway, my grandfather took care of the toy shopping, as he's better at picking age-appropriate toys for gorgons, although ours are ahead of the curve in some ways."

"But they need the basics. They need a bedroom, and they need clothes, and they need bookcases, and they need toys."

"It'll be fine. They're going to share a room until they're in their teens anyway. Sylvester will be wired to protect his sister until his sister picks her new hive. If we try to separate them, he won't be able to sleep and will suffer from anxiety. I invaded my sisters until I was a teen because of those base instincts. Let's just say my sisters were grateful when I moved out."

"Are they aware you're a gorgon-incubus doohickey?"

"Yes and no."

"They've never seen you? As a gorgon-incubus doohickey?"

"They think I'm a shapeshifter who can

become a gorgon, and as I did not want to be sacrificed to my sister's gaggle of friends, my parents opted against telling them about the active incubus portion of my heritage. They know I have the genes just like they do, but I'm careful. What they don't know about they can't talk about."

"And you didn't want anyone knowing you're a gorgon-incubus doohickey."

"That cat is out of the bag now, though. All the cops know, so it's a matter of time I'll be fully exposed."

"You can expose yourself to me whenever you want."

My husband chuckled. "I'm still amazed you were able to keep your hands off me for so long."

"It was horrible. I *hated* when you came to my work, but damn did I love watching you go. And then you went off with Mary on the worst shift of my entire career as a barista. Also the last day of my career as a barista. I don't miss that job, but damn it, I want to know why nobody showed up for work."

"I know. After the divorce, I kept getting some seriously mixed signals from you. I thought I was going mad. I'd go to your work, you'd play me cold, and when I'd leave, you'd go hot and…" Laughing, he shook his head. "You're something else."

"Hot and lusty and pissed off because I was hot and lusty and you hated me."

"Yes, I hated you. Utterly hated you," he replied in his most sarcastic tone.

"Do you know why Mary didn't return to work? It's been driving me crazy."

"You didn't ask her?"

"I haven't spoken to her since I wrote a bitchy note I was quitting, and then I got bombed with gorgon dust, then you happened. I need to get another little yellow dress."

I'd let him decide for himself what I meant by my statement.

"That dress won't last ten minutes," he warned.

The first little yellow dress hadn't lasted much longer once the incubus part of his heritage had come out to play, although I hadn't known then he was more than just a human with a high magic rating.

"I know. That's the best part." I laughed and rubbed my hands, eyeballing the presents on my lap. I picked up what could only be a lingerie box and tore into the paper. Chucking the lid onto Quinn's lap, I plucked off the tissue to reveal a lacy bra and panty set. "Oh, look. Someone likes you, Sam." I seized the bra and held it up, marveling how little there was of it. "Someone likes you a lot."

"I obviously need to send that person a thank you card."

I tossed the lingerie at him and checked the box, uncovering a card. I opened it to discover a gift certificate to an adult store. "Apparently, I'm being sent to a store for naughty things for our enjoyment. Do you think you can handle such an adventure, Mr. Samuel Quinn?"

"That box must be Tiffany's doing, as she definitely knows your sizes, and she'd find the idea of either one of us trying to go into an adult store to be the best entertainment money can buy. As a matter of fact, I can handle such an adventure. I'm not supposed to use real handcuffs on my wife, although I tend to ignore that rule at my leisure."

Whee. "It's a date." I placed the gift card onto the coffee table and tore into the rest of the presents, and it didn't take me long to determine someone had blabbed to the world what my sizes were, as I wouldn't need to buy any lingerie for at least a year, even if my gorgon-incubus doohickey destroyed a piece every day. "Is this normal?"

"When I married Audrey, we got four toasters, three waffle makers, more pots and pans than any couple needs in their life, and a lot of towels and sheets. Do they like you or me?" Quinn picked up a particularly skimpy set in red and held it up. "Are they trying to tell us we need to relax? This is going to be a challenge. Knowing how much this stuff costs, I'm going to have to be careful. How are you supposed to wiggle into this without damaging it?"

"I have no idea. Maybe you're supposed to help me into it before helping me out of it?"

My husband narrowed his eyes. "We're going to need a babysitter that night."

I ran out of gifts and went to work flattening all the boxes to make more space. Frowning, I considered the issue of Mary and none of my co-workers showing up the day Audrey's brother had brought me a bomb loaded with gorgon dust. "I wonder if that might be a good place to start with this investigation. Is it possible Audrey and her brother worked together to make sure I was on shift that day to give me that cell phone? I mean, I'm convinced she wanted to test my immunities, and that grade of gorgon dust was perfect for her needs. So that makes sense to me. But how did they get to my co-workers? Why did they all abandon their shifts? Was that ever investigated?"

My husband frowned, directed his attention to my work laptop, and tapped at the keys. "That's a good question. I don't remember offhand if we investigated your co-workers extensively. We usually don't question people who aren't on a shift during a crime unless we have reason to believe they're somehow involved. I do remember looking into McGee's financials and not finding any ties to your workplace. That was one of the first things we looked into. For all credit cards and bank accounts we accessed, there was no record of him having been there prior. He disliked using cash for much."

"He used cash to buy his coffee. It was a twenty, and he didn't want any dust, so I had to break a big bill for a small order, and that sort of thing is fucking annoying. He tipped more than he paid for the coffee, too."

"How much? Do you remember?"

"He put a five dollar bill in the tip jar."

"Odd." Wrinkling his nose, Quinn reviewed something on the laptop. "No, none of your former co-workers were questioned. I'll have that rectified." He grabbed his phone, dialed a number, and waited. "Hey. It's Sam. I need you to pull up the original file for the gorgon dust bomb incident at my wife's former apartment. It'll be listed under Gardener. I need a pair to head over to her former workplace and question all of the employees, including the owner of the shop, Mary. We need to know why they didn't show up to work that day. Get as much information as you can on it. You might need to get on the phone with the Queens chiefs for more information on the file, as we only have a partial record. If you need approvals, get ahold of the commissioner and tell him I'm pursuing an old lead for a live case. If anyone gives you trouble, have them call me." After listening for a moment, he sighed. "Yes, that's a good point. Tackle anyone in the stations who has gone to her former workplace and question them, particularly about the McGee family and any noticeable weird behavior by the employees. I'd like to get to the bottom of the gorgon dust incident. While we're at it, reopen the files about 120 Wall Street and do another review of everything we have on it. I want a brief on my desk in a week. I'll swing by to pick it up, so call me when it's ready. Is there anything important I need to know about? Good. How is the new pair working?"

While Quinn chatted, I returned to my rabies case tracking, making a list by city or town to get an idea of where outbreaks had happened, leading up to when New York and the surrounding cities and states had become the epicenter of infection reports.

He hung up, set his phone down, and glared at it.

"No throwing your phone," I rebuked.

"I was only thinking about it a little."

"Temper, temper. What has you worked up now?"

"That was Paul Rudani, one of the more senior cops in our precinct. A detective. He usually works on the tenth floor, but he's working on our floor until we're back. He wants to question you."

"Well, yes. That makes sense. It's a questioning session, Quinn, not torture. I didn't do anything wrong, so it's no issue. And if there's something I know that's important for the investigation, it's worth the time. What's the problem?"

"He can be a little ruthless."

"Isn't that a good thing during a questioning session? He wouldn't do a very good job if he bit his nails and fretted over hurting my fragile little feelings."

"He has zero idea of personal boundaries during an interrogation. It's something we've been working on."

"I'm not seeing the problem."

"He will ask you about my visits to your workplace. Extensively."

I loved my husband, but sometimes, he confused me. "And then I will extensively tell him you have a rap sheet of incinerated panties. Mine, for the record. I will even think I shouldn't say that, but then it'll fly right on out. And then I'll start complaining how it's your fault for daring to walk away from me. The view is pretty divine. You were put on this sweet Earth just for me. Maybe Audrey was like a set of training wheels? To be honest, I can't ride a bike, so I'm not really sure."

"You can't ride a bike?"

I stared at him. "Do you think my asshole parents would spend that sort of money on me?"

"Damn it." Slumping against the couch, my husband sighed. "He's good at his job, he just doesn't really understand how to be sensitive on certain matters. I don't want you to get your feelings hurt because he can be harsh."

"Well, he'll find out you are hot and bothered me, so I'm not particularly worried about that. I mean, it's a good thing you're hot and bother me, as the infection spread to you, so now we're married."

"You're not a disease, Bailey."

"No, I'm not an infection. I'm the best parasite!"

"Symbiont."

"Parasite."

"You're going to tell him you're a parasite, aren't you?"

"If I'm going to be embarrassed during an interrogation, I'm taking him out with me when I go."

"You're something else. Did you find out anything while I was being scolded about personal involvements in an ongoing investigation?"

"Yeah. New England is definitely the epicenter of this rabies problem; while the Long Lake outbreak is the highest in number, Vermont trended upwards in cases starting eight years ago. There was one smaller outbreak in Maine, and two in Massachusetts prior. There's no way of knowing if they're related to the Vermont outbreaks, but we definitely need to make a trip to Vermont and Maine to have a look. Do you think we can get around the personal involvement issues?"

"I think I might be able to, although we'll have to link everything we're doing with the gorgon dust and rabies outbreaks. Because of my heritage and your immunities, it makes sense for us to work the investigation; it would be potentially lethal to others, where we're only mildly inconvenienced at most. We will be strictly warned off about the Morrison issue, but if we can happen to connect the dots to him from the gorgons he worked with, accidents happen."

I'd observed Quinn often enough to recognize the accident wouldn't be an accident at all, and that my husband would use every weapon in his arsenal to make certain ex-Chief Morrison would never bother me again.

I doubted Sariel would even have to undergo extensive questioning, especially as the bastard would skip out of town to dodge conviction.

Morrison lacked ethics like that.

"So, we look into the rabies and the gorgon dust issue, figure out how they're related, and figure out if the 120 Wall Street incident was also connected to that mess. I mean, it probably was. It was the same grade of gorgon dust, wasn't it?"

"It probably was from the same batch. Gorgon dust is not commonly manufactured, although we have no idea if they were making multiple batches. That's possible, especially since we saw evidence of dust production in that gypsum mine."

"But that was a new batch, wasn't it?"

"Probably the replacement batch, and the

hive was infected with rabies to get rid of them. That's my suspicion."

"Do you think that male gorgon was that hive's male?"

Quinn shook his head. "No. A gorgon male would never treat his fallen like that."

I pondered what had happened in the gypsum mine up until I'd taken a rather unexpected trip to where the Egyptian pantheon dwelled away from the mortal coil. "That asshole recognized you."

"I have no idea who he was, but gorgons are aware I exist, as I'm the current prince of my line. My father is king in name only, although he's definitely embraced some elements of gorgon society. When he gets tired of staring contests and dealing with pissed gorgons who can't petrify him, he'll pass the title to me."

"And since you're a shapeshifter, you'll be justified in having it?"

"And should we have a son, he'll probably pick up more of my traits than yours, so he'll be the next prince of the line. Sons are rare for gorgons."

"You could control that, you know, Mr. Samuel Quinn."

"I could, but maybe I like the surprise."

"If I want a son, if you won't self-manipulate to do your job appropriately, I will bring your uncle into it."

My husband's chuckle was enough to curl my toes. "I'm not even going to battle with you over this one. Why don't you surprise me when you decide we should have a boy? Otherwise, we'll probably get girls constantly. My grandfather and his brother have over thirty older sisters, although it was unusual that they were in consecutive hatchings. There were no other boys from their parents. Then it was really unusual my grandfather had my father fairly early. I suspect my uncle or one of my grandfathers had something to do with my birth, truth be told."

"Because your father is consistently producing sisters for you to spoil?"

"Spoil? You mean flee from at the earliest possibility. My sisters are *vicious*. The only reason I haven't been ambushed is because I've been hiding in here with you. I'm hoping they go home before I have to face them."

"Do you love or hate your sisters?"

"I love them, but I am severely outnumbered, and they lack mercy. When we were young, I appropriately defended them. Now? I run away so I don't need to be rescued from them. Sometimes, I consider warning the gorgon males they will bring in true predators should my sisters decide to become brides. Gorgon males like to think they're the kings of their harems, but the brides are really the rulers."

"I definitely noticed your grandfather is the definition of hitched and whipped, and that your grandmother is the primary culprit.

His other wives are more reclusive. Have I even met them?"

"No. You probably will at Easter. His hive is rather large, and his wives are closely bonded. They hate leaving anybody at home, so they either all go or they all stay. Add in the whelps, and getting everyone moved around is quite the challenge. But, we can help with that moving forward, as we can babysit sometimes to give them some space, although we'll have to recruit some help from other hives."

"How many whelps does he have right now?"

"Twenty or so, all girls."

My mouth dropped open. "*Twenty?*"

"They're all six, too."

"*All* of them are six?"

"My grandmother is getting older, as is my grandfather, so that's their last clutch. He won't accept another bride at this point in his life, nor does he plan on cultivating any new wives. This clutch is from his youngest wives. That's just how it goes. That's why my father is the current king of our line. Grandfather wants to spend the rest of his days doting on his children, his wives, and his bride. My father handles the diplomacy, and my grandfather shows up to help remind the other gorgons of my father's authority. My father has it easy. The hives don't tend to push because my grandfather may be retired, but he's still spry, and I have a far shorter temper than my grandfather does."

"Big, scary gorgon-incubus doohickey." I grinned at him. "We just need to find out who has been hurting the gorgons, brutally kill them, and go about our business. Babysitting for him sounds like fun!"

"I should be telling you that we shouldn't brutally kill the guilty, but I'd be quite the hypocrite if I did that, as that's precisely what I'd like to do if I get my hands on the fuckers."

My husband would. "I'll try not to brutally kill them if you try not to brutally kill them. That whole day in court thing."

"We'd be saving the court system a lot of money," he muttered.

"I'll just ask Sariel really nicely for a favor to close the case quickly. Really nicely. Extremely nicely. I'll tell him it's cheaper to help the court system than it is to pay for or handle my rabies treatments. Until this is solved, I'll be working on my world record for most times a single woman can contract and be treated for rabies."

"That reminds me. That CDC rep wants you to not get treated for rabies the next time you rescue some animal from a dumpster, and if you're positive, they want to see if you can purge the disease like angels do."

"But will I get to keep the animal?"

"We can discuss that when it happens." According to my husband's resigned tone, he understood we'd have a new pet when the time came for that experiment.

I had severe issues with dumpsters and wanting to keep the animals I found in them. "I have the feeling this is going to happen even without the help of a dumpster. What if *you* contract rabies?"

"Standard treatments can work on me. I *am* concerned about the food supply for their snakes, though. Most eat feeder mice."

"So, we look into the mice situation, figure out why your family's gorgons haven't contracted rabies and other local hives *have*, and start there. Where does your grandfather get his mice?"

Quinn blinked. "Huh."

I stared at him. "What?"

"I bet he's been catching them with extermination groups, as the whelps are young and need to learn to hunt mice if they're unable to get to a supplier. That is an example of what gorgon young are taught. Beauty and Sylvester must have been fed feeder mice, where my grandfather's hive would have been using live-caught mice and rats." Quinn snagged his phone and dialed a number. "Sorry to bother you again, Grandfather, but have you been teaching the whelps how to hunt for mice? Excellent. Thank you. Have you been catching and freezing the excess? What is your general supply right now? How long have you been doing live hunts? Okay, thanks." Shaking his head, my husband chuckled. "Yep. They've been live hunting mice, and he's been taking his wives out for group hunts before that because it's a fun family activity. They petrify the mice, take them home, neutralize them, dispatch them, and then freeze them. They've been doing this for years. Apparently, he made an agreement with several exterminator groups to help handle swarms of rats and mice. They do eat rats, too—they just cut them up before freezing into pieces small enough for their snakes."

"And so your family dodged being infected because they weren't using a regular supplier."

"And I bet my cousin does the same thing. They just have to dish out for the neutralizer, and that's cheap enough compared to buying vast quantities of feeder mice. Better yet, the neutralizer would purify the wild rodents of most problems, including rabies. They just stack the statues, spray the whole lot of them, and then prepare them for eating later."

"Let's open the rest of our presents, then we'll make a to-do list, and get this show on the road!"

I wanted to begin the rest of my life with my family while keeping them safe. Maybe some of my life's problems couldn't be solved with a liberal application of fire, neither rabies nor gorgon dust could survive through me.

SIX

Are you sure about that?

MANY OF THE gifts involved clothing in some shape or another, including a mix of pretty lingerie, baby clothes in various sizes, and a disturbing number of fuzzy handcuffs for my enjoyment, which provided a rather strong hint everyone had rightfully assumed I'd fall prey to my husband. Constantly. Or I'd enjoy using handcuffs to catch him.

Also rightfully assumed.

"According to the number of baby outfits and general supplies here, we are not having twins. We're having octuplets. Or even more. This is way too much for two babies, Sam."

"Except the diapers. There will never be enough diapers." The diaper packs cracked us both up, and a small fortune in baby poop containment devices waited by the door to be sent home via various teleporting family members. "Storing those until the babies arrive will be amusing, but at least we won't have to worry about getting most things for their first few weeks of life."

"And we won't need to worry about getting a baby stroller, car seats, baby cages, or toys. There were only two bags, though. We're going to need more bags. We need to stash emergency supplies for the babies in our cars."

"You got several gift cards so you can pick out your own bag," he reminded me.

"I think they forgot weddings aren't baby showers, Sam."

"I think they did, too. Almost. The lingerie and handcuffs leads me to believe they were actually aware they were attending a wedding." My husband chuckled, fetched a pair of red fuzzy handcuffs, and spun it around his finger. "And I don't have to worry about using my work cuffs on you now."

Whee! "Gorgon-incubus doohickeys are the best doohickeys."

"I'm certainly glad you think so. I did order new tack for you, but it won't be ready for a while. I also put in official orders for your work tack, which will be ready soon, as that was a rush order so you can work. I'm going to have to get measured now, too."

"Do I get to ride you?"

"Obviously."

"Is now a bad time to say I don't have any idea in hell how to ride a horse *or* unicorn?"

"You'll be trained, as you'll have to possibly ride on mounted patrols. Or if we're required to ride in a parade."

"No parades."

"We're chiefs, Bailey. We can't avoid the parades, especially if the civilians demand one."

"But why would anyone *demand* a parade?"

"They like to show us off during the Christmas parades. This year is the first year since I started I *didn't* ride in the parade, but apparently, we got an announcement of our wedding instead. I refused to watch the videos, as I saw no need to embarrass myself."

"Oh, great. Now *everybody* knows we're married?"

"So it seems."

"Okay. I can live with that. The world now knows you're claimed. I can handle this like a mature adult."

My husband grinned at me. "Are you sure about that?"

"I will *try* to handle this like a mature adult," I corrected. "I didn't even run for the bathroom this time."

"While claiming your life was over because how dare anyone believe you're an affectionate fire-breathing, meat-eating unicorn capable of love," he teased.

"I'm so bad at this."

"You're exactly what I want and need in my life, so you're going to have to get used to it, Mrs. Samuel Quinn."

"Mrs. Samuel Quinn definitely sounds better than Mr. Bailey Gardener."

"It really does, but I'd tolerate it for you."

"I successfully got rid of that name, and you will not bring it back. No. I refuse. I'm still mad I can't change the name on my birth certificate. How rude is that? And I can't even get a new one issued with the proper parentage on it because they cap out at three. Why can't I get an exception? Gorgons have one."

"There are also enough gorgons to make it worthwhile to set up birth certificates for their offspring, whereas you're a rather unique entity."

"Just because the good parents had to get creative doesn't mean they should be excluded from my birth certificate. Then my birth certificate wouldn't be such a shitty document."

"I see you have embraced your divine parentage with full enthusiasm."

"He climbed under a table, Sam. For me."

"It's worth mentioning I would happily climb under the table with you, too. I even considered it at the reception, but the cops apparently wanted to talk with me. Well, us, but they found you climbing under the table to get some breathing space refreshing and amusing. You didn't miss much beyond some snarky commentary about how I'm slow, it was about time, and questions if you'd make them coffee."

"It's good to be wanted."

"Well, you make the best coffee in Manhattan. Or anywhere, really. I can't even lie, my beautiful, but I miss your coffee and can't wait to go home so you can reward me for my excellent behavior. With coffee."

"Obviously, learning how to make good coffee was my ploy to catch your attention."

"It was quite successful, although you really caught my attention by disliking me from the start."

"You're a sucker for punishment."

"It's not a punishment if I like it, Bailey," he reminded me.

I loved my gorgon-incubus doohickey. "Did we get anything we can use immediately?"

"You got that really nice red leather notebook with organizer." Quinn rummaged through our gifts until he located it. He handed it to me before digging out one of the fancy pen boxes we'd also received. "You'll definitely like it, as it has pockets, a place to put your new pen, and it'll fit nicely into that tote someone gave you."

"Oh! The tote." I joined my husband in searching the gifts until I found the black leather bag with extra-long adjustable straps. "I can wear this as a unicorn. It's magically fireproofed, and it can withstand up to napalm, Quinn."

"It's like someone had it made with you in mind," he replied with his most wicked smile.

I bounced back to the couch, took the pen, which was made of some dark, lustrous wood, and tested the leather notebook to determine it fit in the bag with room to spare. "Oh! I bet my gun will fit in here, too. And my wallet, and I bet I could fit something for lunch in here, too."

"Bailey, do you really think I'm going to let you pack lunches when I can take you out to eat most days of the week? We can have dates every day if we do that. Anyway, we both got those weird bento boxes we can use if you really want to take lunch to work."

The idea of daily lunch dates with Quinn hadn't crossed my mind, and I stared at him with wide eyes. "But won't that be expensive?"

"Salary," he reminded me.

I blinked. "Oh. I can afford lunch dates now, can't I?"

"You could afford lunch dates before, Mrs. Millionaire."

Right. Outside of buying an excessive number of coffee machines for the station, I had barely touched the money I'd received as my danger pay for leveling 120 Wall Street so the gorgon dust infecting the building couldn't spread. "I guess I can, can't I?"

"You're brilliant with budgeting, Bailey, but you can afford to come to lunch with me. And trust me when I say this: you'll be grateful to escape for even half an hour on a bad day. Our job isn't easy, and I doubt it's going to get easier. It'll be good for us, because we'll be working together. It'll be hard, but it'll be good."

Things worth doing were often difficult. "What else should I put into my bag if lunch doesn't need to go into it?"

"Your laptop will fit, as will your phone. I might have to get one for myself, honestly. It looks really convenient for when we're sporting four hooves and a fur coat."

"We'll test drive the bag looking into this gorgon and rabies problem. Did you get a bag or something?"

"I have a manly messenger bag which is also immune to fire-breathing unicorns, but I don't know if the strap is big enough to get around my neck when I'm a cindercorn."

"Show me!"

Like my bag, which was designed to accommodate me while a cindercorn, Quinn's was black and fireproofed to survive my wicked ways. His was a little wider and lacked the third strap meant to keep it snug to my body and prevent the bag from getting in the way of my legs. "Mine isn't quite as elaborate as yours."

"We can add a third strap to yours, and it'll be fine. My third strap can be removed, too. All we'd need to do is add a clip to secure it to your saddle if it's not being worn around your neck. Honestly, the strap should be fine as long as it's snug enough on your neck so the bag can't bang into your legs. The handles on both look sturdy enough we can carry them in our mouths if needed. We're nose breathers, so it's not like we need to open our mouths when we run. We'll fiddle with it until it works."

"Mine will definitely fit gloves, bags and any other tools we'll need if we find anything that might count as evidence. We're going to have to work on your evidence handling skills, Mrs. Cindercorn."

"It's not my fault the bomb squad hadn't swept better. If they hadn't left a bomb up there, I wouldn't have played around with the evidence. Or pulled the wires. Or decontaminated the exterior. Basically, don't do anything I did with that bomb, and I'll be mostly okay."

"Sadly, you're right."

I stuck my tongue out at him before resuming my exploration of my bag, stuffing both of my laptops inside because I could. "This is nice!"

"Before we leave, we can go make use of your gift cards, too. One of the group gifts should have enough for a new leather coat if you want one."

I sucked in a breath, as leather coats fell into the domain of wishful thinking unless Quinn showed up with one and tricked me into wearing it. "For me? But it's your card, too!"

"As my cops know what style of leather coat I like, they bought the coat. You watched me look it over for ten minutes, remember?"

Oops. "I was busy looking at you and not your coat," I confessed.

"Obviously, I'll have to attend to your special needs after we go shopping for a new coat for you. Get dressed, grab your new bag, and we'll do just that. Leave your laptops here, as we're going out to play and not work, but you should check to see if the image recognition request you put in on that photo has processed yet. It probably hasn't, but there is a chance it's done."

I obeyed, checking on the photo I'd taken during the demonstration. "It's marked as eighty percent complete."

"Give it another few hours and it should be good. There were a lot of people in the picture. Fortunately, it's an automated process, but it takes time to run everything. The software will even separate out all of the faces so we can see who might be who—and if there are multiple matches, we'll get a list. It really helps streamline some elements of investigation."

"That is so cool."

"Wait until you have to put in for fingerprints or a DNA analysis. Things get far less cool, and sometimes, it can take days for the database to churn through everything and get results. The good scanners are outside of our budget."

"That's a pity."

"It really is. Go get dressed, and I'll see about making arrangements for getting us home in a hurry. I'm sure I can cut a deal with my uncle."

"No deals."

"Bailey, we can't just demand *everything* from him without giving something back."

"He can have nice Easter and Christmas presents. No deals!"

"Bailey."

"Unless the deal fully benefits us while sending us home, no deals."

"We have to make deals with demons and devils as part of our job. You're going to have to get used to it."

"But we have special niece and nephew privileges, so we don't need to cut a deal. We're family, and he likes us."

"I'm going to tell him that, and if he laughs at me, you're going to owe me."

"As long as the owing happens in our bedroom, at home, I'm all right with this."

"You're absolutely wicked."

I smiled. "I really am, aren't I? I'm definitely the devil of this relationship compared to your angel."

"And when you're around, it seems my angelic side goes and takes a nap. I'm not your gorgon-incubus-angel doohickey, after all."

"That's true. But you have black feathered wings. Your angel is just a little naughty is all."

"Later, I'll show you naughty," he promised.

Nice. I skipped to the bedroom to get changed so we could get to the naughty portion of our day.

I FELL in love with a leather coat on display in the window, and its price tag broke my heart. "The gift card isn't enough."

My husband chuckled. "The gift card covers most of it, and I'll cover the rest because you saw it and it made you happy. I will insist you try it on first. That's me being selfish, by the way. You're sexy in black leather."

"But it's expensive."

"Yes, it is." Quinn caught me by the arm and dragged me into the store, and before I could stop him, he flagged down the first employee he saw, pointed at the coat in the window, and told her every damned one of my measurements from the waist up.

Somehow, knowing he had as many issues as I did helped a little. While I spluttered, the woman checked the coat in the window, nodded, pulled it down, and brought it to me. Before I could open my mouth and protest, my husband robbed me of my stuff and held the coat open for me, so I could wiggle into it.

It was a lot heavier than I expected, beating the super thin leather coats often up on offer.

Heavy meant expensive. Heavy meant I might not need to replace it anytime soon, too.

Expensive wasn't so bad when I didn't have to replace my precious jacket for a long time.

"You've been teaching your uncle some tricks, haven't you?" My face flushed from embarrassment while I tried the coat on, which fit like a glove but better. To my delight, the coat had pockets everywhere. The pair of pockets on the inside could even carry a small gun, keys, *and* a wallet. The exterior pockets could carry enough to be worth their while, too. "It has *pockets*," I breathed.

The employee, a younger woman with bright blue eyes and a ready smile, giggled. "All of the pockets zip closed, too. There is even an anti-thief layer between the liner and the leather. It won't stop someone from cutting through the layer, but it will stop most knives."

That caught my husband's attention. "What is it made of?"

"We use a quarter inch of Kevlar beneath a layer of micro-weave polyethylene."

"It's bulletproof." Quinn considered my jacket speculatively. "Raise your arms, Bailey."

I obeyed, and to my delight, my husband frisked me, patting my coat down. "Should we be doing this in public?"

The store clerk laughed. "He's just confirming the fit in a hands-on fashion."

No kidding. "Do you like it, Quinn?"

"Like it? I love it. Do you have a second one in this size?" Quinn tugged on the coat.

"We have two more of them."

"I'll buy all three, and give me one the size up, too."

"That's too much!"

"Bulletproof," he replied.

I frowned, wiggled out of his hold, and checked his coat, which was made by the same designer. Like mine, it was heavier than I expected. "Does this one have Kevlar, too?"

"It does," the clerk replied. "That's one of our other models but in the same general line. They're new this year. Both also have a layer of RFID-blocking material built into the liner."

"Do you have them in this size?"

"Of course."

"If you're buying me more than one jacket, you are matching me jacket for jacket," I informed him. As I could see them being highly useful for our line of work, I'd do my best to ignore the huge hit to our bank account buying them.

I couldn't put a price on Quinn's safety, and I had no reason to believe he didn't feel the same way.

"Done." My husband shucked off his jacket and showed the tag to the woman, who nodded and went off to fetch our new apparel. "I had no idea it was bulletproof when I was looking it over. I noticed it was stiffer than I expected, but the cut works well with it."

Yes, it worked very well on my husband. "Isn't it illegal to wear body armor when committing a crime?"

He laughed. "In many states, yes. It is. Let's look for ass kicker boots for you while we're here. Looks like we've been sent to a place with a focus on leather." With a sly smile, he pointed across the store, where a selection of boots designed to come up to right below the knee waited for me to admire.

Some had heels, some didn't, some had belts and buckles, but my new favorite pair had buttons up the side, which cleverly disguised a zipper for easy wearing. I hurried over, grabbed them, and checked their size, pouting when they were too small for me.

The clerk returned with the coats, which she carried to the counter, and when she spotted me staring at the boots, she walked over. "What size do you wear?"

I told her, and she shook her head. "I don't have those in that size, but I have something similar in the back that might work. We haven't shifted the product lines, but since we're doing it tomorrow, I bet my boss won't mind selling a pair a little ahead, but I'll have to ask her. Give me a moment."

I put the boots back and examined the rest of the store's offerings while my husband amused himself at the counter with our coats, reading over the labels. A purse with a stylized unicorn stamped into the leather caught my eye, and it bore a striking resemblance to a cindercorn, especially in the presence of claws on the hooves and the thick, fluffy coat.

It was red, and the unicorn was black, and I carried it over to my husband. Reminding myself I could afford the purse, I set it on top of the pile.

Quinn blinked at it, and then he blinked at me before staring at the purse.

"Mine?"

"Why is that a question?" my husband asked with laughter in his voice. "I was just surprised you actually got something for yourself without me having to coax you into it." He picked up my treasure and looked it over, his laughter growing when he spotted the cindercorn on it. "This was obviously made for you."

The woman came back with a pair of boots, and she grinned when she spotted the purse I'd picked. "Oh! That one is one of my favorites. The boots I pulled out of the back have the matching buttons. We have a product line with the two main species of unicorns. There is a pair of gray winter boots with white unicorns on them, a pair of red winter boots with the dark unicorns on them, there's a winter parka with a white unicorn on the front and the black and red ones on the back, and some other accessories."

"Cindercorns," my husband prompted. "What else do you have?"

"We have some polo shirts, riding breeches, a pair of riding boots, and gloves. All of those have it in both styles."

"Men and women's styles?"

"Yes, we have both. Those are custom made, so you have to be fitted for everything, but we can do the fittings here and ship, or you can pick them up."

"Your uncle can pick them up for us when they're ready," I announced.

"You like bossing him around, don't you?"

"No. I *love* it."

Quinn laughed. "All right. We'll need to be fitted. If you like those boots and they fit, get them, Bailey. It's not too expensive."

"Then let's try the boots on, shall we?"

"Most expensive gift card ever," I muttered, following the woman to see if the new boots fit. Like the pair I liked, they had buttons, and true to her claim, they were decorated with tiny cindercorns. The cindercorns were also stamped onto the top of each boot. "Quinn, Quinn, look at these!"

"Ah. Those must be one of the sets of riding boots. You better get three pairs, and we'll use one for your horseback riding lessons, leave one at work, and the third pair can be for at home. And we'll get you a pair of the standard unicorn boots, too. Actually, two pairs, that way one can stay at work."

"That is too many boots."

"It is not too many boots," my husband replied.

"You must really like unicorns," the clerk said, her tone amused.

My husband smiled. "Guilty as charged."

"But how can it not be too many boots?"

"Because I said so."

I frowned, staring at the boots on my feet. I tested them out around the store, liking the way they felt. "They're really nice."

"And they look great on you. Do you want to wear them out?" Quinn asked.

I hesitated, but then I nodded.

The clerk carefully removed the tag and carried it over to the pile of jackets destined to come home with us. "If you'll come this way, we'll get you measured for everything, and I'll see what we have in stock in your sizes, and everything else will be custom made for you. I'll need a phone number and email address we can use to contact you when your order is ready."

Quinn spotted something near the purses, and a moment later, he returned holding a wallet and coin purse with the cindercorn stamped on them. "It seems this store knew you would one day come to Vegas and pre-pared its shelves just for you."

I laughed, grabbing the wallet out of his hand and admiring it. "This is so cool!"

"There's a keychain, too."

"We need seven of those."

"Seven?" I blurted.

"Two for the kids, two for the kids on the

way, one for me, one for you, and one as the spare set of keys."

Huh. "Babies need keys?"

"They will in a few years."

"Oh? You're expecting?" the woman asked.

"We're expecting twins. It's still early, so she's not showing." Quinn smiled, and he kissed my temple. "I'm pampering her now, and after the little ones are born, she tends to have trouble keeping her weight up, so everything should fit shortly after."

"It's true. He tries to feed me everything, and I just refuse to gain much weight. I expect he'll have me at a doctor every other day because he's a worrier."

Quinn sighed. "Once every two weeks to begin with."

"Let's just get measured before I run out of here or embarrass myself further, Sam."

"You're fine. You haven't done anything embarrassing."

"Yet. I haven't done anything embarrassing *yet*."

"Why would you even think you're going to do something embarrassing?" he asked in an exasperated tone.

"Well, I'm breathing, aren't I?"

I loved his patience-worn sigh. "You're something else."

THE RAMPAGE through the store left us with more things than we could carry, so I made use of my new phone, debating which family member to impose upon. After a ten-minute debate with myself, I tapped the button that would call my father, the one I actually liked.

"Bailey," my father greeted. "How are you enjoying your time with your husband?"

"It's going great. We have zero respect for money, and we bought a lot of stuff. They have *cindercorns* on clothing at this store. Mostly, I wanted to see if I could abuse my daughterly privileges for help getting all of this stuff to our room. We rampaged. And apparently, Quinn is a standard-sized man, so they had most of the stuff for him in stock, and I'm a fairly standard-sized woman, so they had a lot of my stuff in stock, too."

My father popped into existence in a flash of sun-yellow light, and I hung up, as there was zero point in talking on the phone to someone standing right next to me. I showed off my new boots. "Look!"

My father peered at the design on my new boots. "That is an admirable representation. Did she complain much, Samuel?"

"Only that I bought too much of everything." My gorgon-incubus doohickey regarded our collection of boxes and bags with a raised brow. "She isn't wrong, but she would have put everything on display without ever wearing any of it if it was the

only set she had. The new jackets are bulletproof."

"Excellent for your line of work. I approve. You definitely require help getting this
to your home. When do you plan on returning to New York?"

My husband smiled at me. "As soon as
possible, honestly. We have some matters we
need to take care of before she begins her
training and comes to work with me. To
handle that matter you discussed with her."

"Prudent. I will handle the matter of your
gifts and taking these to a safe place for the
moment, and I will teleport you home where
you belong."

"I'll need my laptops! And my box."

I didn't want to tell the store's employee
my handguns were in the box, so I stared at
my father and hoped he did the thought-
reading thing and determined that I needed
to go home and sniff—and possibly eat—the
roses.

My father chuckled, snapped his fingers,
and flicked his hand in the direction of the
counter, and both of my computers appeared
on the glass with a soft thump, along with the
important box of my weapons. A smaller box,
which contained my ammunition, also appeared, as did my badge.

"Your dad is pretty cool, Sam, but my dad
is so much cooler than your dad."

My gorgon-incubus doohickey snickered.
"I can't even argue with that one, so I won't,

my beautiful. Put your computers in your bag and grab your boxes. It seems we have a short trip home ahead of us."

I did as told, making sure everything fit, and I put my new wallet, keyring, and coin purse in, too. To make sure it didn't get put in storage, I slung my new purse over my shoulder with my other leather bag. I gave my new jacket a pat down, giving a nod when I confirmed everything was where it belonged. I picked up my badge and tucked it into my pocket. "Okay. I'm ready."

Ra turned to the store employees, who gawked at him. "If you would please watch over their things until my return, it would be appreciated."

"O-of course, sir."

"Ra," he replied.

"The *divine?*" she blurted.

Ra seemed to enjoy being recognized a little too much, and I rolled my eyes while he preened. "The same. I shall return momentarily."

Unlike others, who seemed to need to touch to make the teleportation happen, my father chuckled. One instant we were in the store, and the next, we were standing in knee-deep snow in front of Perkette's house. "Oh *fuckshit!*" I squealed.

My father laughed. "My gift to your husband, so he might enjoy pampering you to his heart's content."

"I might hate the other in-laws, but you

more than make up for them, Ra," Quinn announced. "And since I have a set of keys and the alarm code, I can check on their house while fetching our car."

"Yes, you will need your car, of that I am certain. Drive safely, enjoy yourselves, and call your mother after the moon goes up, Bailey. It's now strong enough for her to manifest. Please do tell her I will see her in the morning; we can cross paths for a little while then, but only for an hour or two."

An hour or two beat not at all, so I nodded. "I'll do that. Thank you."

"Now, I need to go reassure those humans. That will take a while. I will take care of making sure your hotel room is handled and all of your things are in safe keeping. I'll bring them over when your mother can manifest during the day." My father vanished in a warm yellow light.

"Should I be worried he knows where Perky and Perkette live?"

"That sort of meddling and snooping is child's play for a divine. When we buy a new house, we need to make sure we have enough garage spots for all of our vehicles. We're going to need an SUV for the kids for certain."

"Not a van?"

"We'll probably have two SUVs, and one will be large enough to pull a small RV."

"Or we could get a big truck for the RV."

"Big trucks don't have enough seats for

the kids. We're starting with four plus our fosters."

"Fosters?"

My husband slapped his forehead. "Damn it!"

"Damn it? What did you *do*, Quinn?"

"I agreed to foster three gorgon whelps, a boy and two girls, over the summer. To be friends with Beauty and Sylvester. Fostering whelps is super easy; they want to prove to their father and mothers they're old enough to be fostered, and so they do their best to behave, because if they don't, they may not get fostered again. It's a rite of passage for them."

"And we get to host them?"

"While visiting my grandfather's hive will be good for Beauty and Sylvester, having fosters around will better integrate them with other gorgons. You'll be fairly heavily pregnant by then, so they'll want to help you. They're taught to always help the brides. I meant to talk to you about it, but I completely forgot with everything else going on."

"Merry Christmas to me!" I wanted to rub my hands together to warm them, but I settled with bouncing in place. "It's fucking cold, Quinn. Do the thingie to get into the garage."

Chuckling, he retrieved his keys and pressed the button on one of the fobs, which opened the garage door, revealing his beloved red convertible. He pressed a second button on a different fob, which made something inside the house beep. "I'll go do a walkthrough of their house and make sure everything is okay. Why don't you get the car started so it can get warmed up?"

I stomped the snow off my new boots in the garage, set my box on the hood, and unlocked the car before placing my guns and ammunition in the trunk. Quinn entered the house through the garage door and disappeared inside. By the time the convertible blew hot air, he returned, closing the door behind him.

"Everything okay?" I asked.

"Everything's fine. I checked the faucets just to be sure, too. I'll text Arthur to let him know we stopped by." Quinn got behind the wheel and smiled at his car, giving the steering wheel a fond pat. "It is getting to be about time to retire this, isn't it?"

"How long have you had it?"

"I got it right after I got promoted. I figured I'd use the bonus they shoved at me to get something just for me. The engine is going to blow out sooner than later, and honestly? I'm impressed it has lasted this long. We'll go shop for something sporty we can both drive when we have a babysitter to take the kids."

"Are you sure?"

"I am. The maintenance bill on this one is horrific, and I was planning on shooting it between the headlights when the engine blew anyway. Tell you what. When I've been really bad, we'll take the car out somewhere, and it

can have an accident involving two cindercorns."

"Or we could keep it for one of the kids."

"When the kids earn a car, we'll get one
for them *they* want, not an antique that'll cost
them a fortune to keep up."

I eyed the convertible's dash. "Does this
car count as an antique?"

"Not particularly. I doubt it'll be worth
much of anything ten years down the road."

"Why is it cold?" I complained, hunkering
in my seat. "Mistakes were made, and we
made them."

"Silly cindercorn. You're not going to
freeze to death, I promise. I'll warm you up at
the house." His phone rang before we had a
chance to leave the garage, and sighing, he
checked the display before answering, "Chief
Quinn speaking."

A moment later, his eyes widened, his
mouth dropped open, and he spluttered.

I stole the phone out of his hand and said,
"The other Chief Quinn speaking. What did
you just tell my husband?"

"Hello, Chief Quinn. I'm Chief Barfield."

"Oh! Peter? It's Peter, right? You're in
charge of Queens."

"I am. There was an attempted arson at
your house."

"A what at where?"

He repeated himself. I tapped my finger
against my husband's phone. "What's the
damage?"

"Surprisingly, there's very little damage. Some of your rose bushes have seen better days, the brick and the door and window framing will need some repair, but the structure was otherwise undamaged. There's one cracked window. One of your neighbors noticed the attempt and called it in and made a scene, which scared the arsonists off. They knew you weren't home, but it seems the arsonists were unaware you were not back."

"Give us five minutes. We're basically right down the street. We just got in."

"But you were just in Vegas? I was speaking to some of your officers earlier."

"My father—the not sucky one—teleported us over to the Perkins residence so we could retrieve our car. We'll be there in a few minutes." I hung up and handed my stunned husband his phone. "If you can't pull yourself together, I'll drive, and there is nothing scarier on this planet than a cranky cindercorn who hates the cold driving through the snow."

"Who is idiot enough to try to light a chief's house on fire? The stupidity is just…" My husband grunted and ran his hands through his hair. "Remind me to send a gift to our neighbors."

"Some asshole burned the roses!"

My husband sighed. "That death certificate is going to have some interesting notations when you find out who burned our roses. First, if the roses can't be saved, we will replant them. Chances are, it just burned the covers for them and the plants are fine. I'll just have to get new covers on them."

"Some of the brick was trashed, a window needs to be replaced as it was cracked, but the house is otherwise fine. How did *that* happen?"

"I can explain that. I fireproofed the house, my beautiful. You're a cindercorn. You snort fire. You watched me work with the fireproofers all fall to make sure it was suitable for you and your fiery ways. Some of the time, you were a unicorn, and you rolled around on your rug so nobody would take it from you. It'd take a lot more effort than some gasoline tossed against the side of the house to do much damage."

Oh. Right. "You did it when you replaced the fireplace. And I was rolling around because you stole my fireplace!"

"For five whole days while a better one was installed."

"Five days without a fireplace should be criminal."

He laughed. "I'm fine. I was just stunned someone would really be *that* stupid. I have a few ideas who might try to burn our house down."

"I have a *lot* of ideas." I pointed at myself. "Not the most likable unicorn on the block."

"But you are the best unicorn on the block."

"I'm the only unicorn on the block, Queeny."

"I'm sure you'll learn to cope with your status as the best of unicorns."

"Sample size of one, Queeny."

"Doesn't change anything for me. You're the best of unicorns."

"You are a biased and unreasonable man."

He smiled. "For you, yes."

How did he always win our discussions like this? I sighed and made shooing gestures with my hand. "We need to go check on the roses, and then I need to plot some fucker's murder if they hurt the roses!"

"Just don't tell the reasonable cops that, Bailey."

"I'll try to contain my runaway mouth for once in my life."

"I feel I just asked for a miracle."

What a jerk. Despite myself, I grinned. "You really did. Less talking, more driving."

"But what if I like talking with you?"

How dare he win again? "I raided one of the lingerie boxes when I got changed, but you can't personally explore my secret clothing choices until we deal with the cops and the roses."

Quinn eased the convertible out of the garage, parking long enough to close the garage door and rearm the alarm system. "I should protest how easy I am to manipulate under these circumstances, but I find I am highly motivated to deal with the cops at our house so I can explore your secret clothing choices."

"Just don't destroy them, else I'll have to wear the little black set that went with the yellow dress," I warned.

"That threat needs a lot of work, Bailey. Your secret clothing choice's days are numbered, and its doomsday clock is ticking."

"Such a tragedy."

SEVEN

Does that really say cindercorn
under species?

Cop cars filled our driveway and somewhat
blocked my view of the house, but I could tell
one important thing.

My favorite of the rose bushes, the one
with beautiful big red blossoms, had been
scorched to ash with a few straggler branches
left.

I wanted to cry over its loss, and Quinn
kissed my cheek. "It'll be okay. Yeah, the bush
isn't going to recover from that, and some of
the others don't look good, either, but the
house is okay, and we're going to be moving
anyway. We couldn't realistically take the
bush with us. I'll get you new roses."

"But that one was special."

"I know. You looked like you wanted to eat
every last blossom on it the first time you
came home to me. I know what variant it is,
and I even know who the grower is. I can
probably get the same strain. It'll just take
some time to grow is all. I'll ask my grandfa-

ther to come over and see if he can do anything for it. Maybe we can transplant what's left of it in a pot and take it with us. If anyone can help a rose plant survive that, it's an angel."

Quinn parked in front of the cordon blocking part of our street to make sure the fire truck and cops had access without curious folks getting too close. Heaving a sigh, I got out of the car and strolled over to the blockade.

I didn't recognize any of the cops barring the way to my house.

"Sorry, ma'am, nobody can come closer."

I debated my options, grabbed my badge out of my pocket, and flipped it open, showing him my shiny new identification card. Then, as I could be a mature adult when I wanted, I waited.

The cop read my badge, and he raised a brow. "Does that really say cindercorn under species?"

I checked my card, and sure enough, I was listed as a cindercorn in addition to being human. "Oh, cool. Sam, Sam! Somebody put cindercorn on my badge."

"Yes, Bailey. That's because you're a cindercorn." My husband pulled the same trick I had with the badge.

"You're both Chief Quinn?" the cop blurted.

I spotted Chief Barfield, stood on my toes, and waved at him. "Peter!"

He waved back. "Let them through, Benjamin. They're the real deal. Mrs. Chief Quinn just joined the force. We nabbed her from the CDC, and she's our new top bomb specialist."

The cop held up the cordon tape. "Sorry about that, ma'am."

"I have trouble believing it, too, so don't worry about it." I ducked beneath the tape and strolled to Chief Barfield, pocketing my badge before holding out my hand to shake with him. "See Quinn's new jacket?"

"I do. It's damned nice. I know because I helped buy it. I also contributed to your gift card."

I laughed. "Bulletproof!"

"You get to be the guinea pigs on the leather jackets with the Kevlar and anti-theft stuff built in. Well, sort of. When we heard about them, we decided to check out what the civvies were getting. Those things are nigh indestructible, so it's likely all of our undercover cops will be getting them. We're in talks with the company to have special designs for law enforcement."

"Did the commissioner put you up to that?"

"He really did."

"Nice. I lost count of the number of them Quinn bought because once he realized they were bulletproof, I needed them all. I made him buy the same number for himself, hoping to deter him. That backfired. Thanks, though. It's really nice."

"You're welcome. So, here's what we know. A white male, a little taller than you, dark hair and eyes, parked in your driveway, got out, and looked to knock at the door. We aren't sure if he actually knocked or if he was doing a ruse. He splashed gasoline over the front of the house and the bushes, returned to his vehicle, and did the same with three more cans of gasoline. Your neighbor noticed because she was coming home from grocery shopping. She spotted him right as he lit a match and tossed it on. He ran for it, and she blew through three fire extinguishers in the time it took the fire department to arrive."

I scowled, got out my phone, and hit the internet to pull out a picture of my human father. "Was it Valorie?"

I could see Valorie, a ripe seventy going on sixteen in her mind, diving right into trouble and handling the problem herself. Of all our neighbors, I liked her the most.

She always came over with a rose and an apple when she spotted me out and about as a cindercorn.

"Yes, it was Valorie." Chief Barfield took my phone and whistled for one of his cops, who came over. "Run this over to Mrs. Valorie and ask if this is the man she spotted lighting the fire."

The cop took my phone and headed for my neighbor's house.

"When did the fire start?"

"Two hours ago. I opted to wait to notify you until I couldn't push it off, as I knew you were enjoying your honeymoon."

"Appreciated. Can we go into the house through the back door to retrieve some things while you check the front as a crime scene?"

"We've done all our evidence gathering, so you can use your front door if you'd like."

My husband regarded the charring on the brick and the melted frame around the door, and he sighed. "I wonder if it'll open like that."

"Dowry brought the spare key over and disabled the alarm for us so it'd stop squealing, so yes. It still opens. He left an hour ago."

"The commissioner has a copy of our house key?" I asked.

"He has a copy of all the police chiefs' keys. We're targets, and it lets him investigate if something goes wrong." Quinn wrinkled his nose, retrieved his phone from his pocket, and dialed a number. "Hey, Grandfather. Some asshole torched Bailey's favorite roses. Are you willing to check if the bush can be saved? I'd rather my wife not start crying because her favorite rose bush can't be saved today. Yes, we're at our house, and yes, somebody really did try to torch it. The roses are the only real casualties." Quinn hung up and returned his phone to his pocket.

A moment later, Sariel appeared, and for a

headless being, he did an excellent job of clucking his tongue. "That was quite rude."

"I know." As the archangel might be able to save my precious roses, I trampled through the snow covering the yard, discovered the gasoline and fire had turned the sidewalk to ice, and landed on my ass. "Fuck."

Quinn followed at a safer pace, kept his feet where it hadn't been turned to ice, and hauled me to my feet, waiting until I caught my balance before brushing the snow off my clothes. "You all right?"

"If I had any pride, it would be destroyed and in need of CPR, but as I seem to embarrass myself daily, I appear to have emerged intact."

"God, I love you so damned much."

I stared at him with wide eyes.

"Try not to wrap your head around his adoration today, little granddaughter. You will give yourself a headache to go along with your chill." Without any sign of there being ice on the sidewalk, the archangel crouched beside the roses, brushing away the charred ruins of the fabric Quinn had covered them with. "I can save these, my little grandson. Do go get some pots. You have some in your basement for your project, do you not?"

"Pots? What pots?" I asked. "What project?"

"I was hiding pots in the basement so I could plant some new roses for you. I'll be right back. How many do I need to bring?"

"Hmm. Six," the archangel replied. He pointed at one of the bushes, which hadn't taken much damage. "That one should be covered, but it will recover without other intervention. The others will have to be put into pots for the winter and brought inside to be cared for. It could be transplanted as well, if you wish to keep all of your front rose bushes."

"I'll bring ten pots," Quinn replied before skating to our front door. I giggled at the dance he did to stay on his feet while fighting with the keys, but unlike me, he made it inside without falling.

I counted bushes, frowning. "But there are sixteen bushes."

"Six of those were planted when he was married to that other woman," the archangel replied. "The ten were planted before his marriage to her, and the one you like best is among those. He wants to take those bushes with him because they're special to him. The other six will look nice along the walkway as they are."

"Okay. That's fair. The bushes will be okay?"

"I will help them heal from the damage. I will face the scolding for inappropriately using my magic, I am certain."

I reached for my phone, sighing when I realized I'd given it to a cop to see if my asshole father had tried to burn my house down. "I'd call my uncle and start shit because I can if I hadn't given my phone to a cop."

The archangel held out his hand, and a cell phone appeared. "Here. I would be burdened with guilt if I were to bar you from starting trouble."

I accepted the phone, scrolled through the contacts until I found Lucifer's number, and tapped on the screen.

"Stealing from Sariel now, are you?" the Devil answered.

"I am. Some asshole burned our rose bushes trying to burn down our house, and I wish to stir some shit. Who is better at making sure my precious roses don't die? An archangel or the Devil?" Because hanging up tended to light fires under asses, especially under egotistical asses like the Devil's, I did so and returned the phone to Sariel. "I'm a very bad niece. And granddaughter. I'm sorry."

"You have done nothing wrong. You didn't steal anything, as I gave you my phone willingly, and you did nothing more than issue a challenge. It is my fault I will play the game."

The Devil showed up, and he wore another one of his beautiful suits. Smiling, I kissed his cheek, as I'd learned he liked affection almost as much as archangels, gorgons, and the other oddities in Quinn's family. "You need to stop wearing suits I want to see Sam wear. When you wear suits, I wonder if Sam will wear it better."

"This one he'll be spectacular in, especially if he's displaying his wings for you."

My eyes widened at the thought of my husband wearing a suit while in his gorgon-incubus doohickey form. "Oh. Oh, *my*. Please?"

"Invite my wife over for some of your coffee. Coffee is life for her, and she likes it iced with cream and sugar."

"I make a mean iced coffee."

"That was a factor in establishing this bargain with you."

Oh, well. I'd just cope with the scolding when Quinn found out I was making deals with the Devil to get him in a wickedly sexy suit. "I hope she likes kids, because we'll be outnumbered and surrounded."

"She loves children."

Well, then. "Deal. Bargain struck!" I held out my hand to seal the deal. "I'll even give her back sometimes, although with the number of kids we have around, you may have to bargain with me to get her back."

The Devil frowned.

"You lost that one, my dear brother. Now, for the matter of the roses." Sariel pointed at the one with the best blossoms, big, red, and delicious. "This one is her favorite, and it is the first she sampled when she came home to my little grandson for the first time, so it is quite special for them both."

The Devil crouched beside the roses and touched the charred branch. "Did you see?"

"I did. She heard the description already."

"It's totally something my asshole father would do, and he's not smart enough to do the job right. I mean, the house is made of *brick*."

"And has been fireproofed to my little grandson's standards," Sariel added.

I wrinkled my nose. "Yeah, that didn't help matters for that asshole at all. Now I'm wondering if we can fireproof our poor roses."

Valorie emerged from her house, and it amused me how the cops scrambled to make sure the older woman didn't fall making the hike over.

"I love that old woman," I confessed.

The Devil chuckled. "She loves you as though you were hers. She is a sweet woman who has no place in one of my hells, although don't tempt me into bringing over one of my devils. He might be able to keep up with her."

Sariel smacked the Devil with his wing. "Do not play matchmaker right this moment. She is slated for elsewhere."

"But she'd make such a fine little demoness," the Devil complained. "Don't ruin my fun."

"If you hurt my roses even more than they're already hurt, I will teach you both the true meaning of pain and fear," I warned.

To my amusement, the archangel and his brother turned their attention to the poor plants. Aware I might eat snow or bruise my ass again, I slid along the sidewalk.

Chief Barfield intercepted me at the end and kept me on my feet. "Your husband would kill me if I let you fall. Stay in the snow and off the ice, you."

"Valorie!" I waved at the old woman, eye-balling how to reach her. I opted to take the long way around, crunching through the snow until I reached the street, which had been questionably salted.

"Welcome home. How did you enjoy your trip?" she asked, coming towards me. I met her at the halfway point, and accepted a hug from her, as she'd trained me well. "Your poor roses."

"They better be fine," I hollered at the archangel and the Devil.

Valorie held up my phone. "This looks a lot like him, yes. Who is he?"

"The shitty father. It turns out I have more parents than normal, and the Gardeners are the shit ones. The other pair is far cooler. I'll bring them over so you can meet them. Was there a woman with him?"

"Yes. She was driving the car."

I took my phone and pulled up a picture of my mother. "Her?"

Valorie huffed. "Looks like her to me."

I stomped through the snow to Chief Barfield. "It's a case of the asshole parents trying to make my life miserable yet again. My mother was driving the car while he was trying to torch the house. And since they'll lie their asses off, I'll just request an angel now to verify their guilt, just in case there was some practitioner up to some pretty bad tricks. I can email you information on them, once my roses are taken care of."

The chief chuckled. "I can tell where your priorities are. Still, until we bring them in, it's not going to be safe here."

"We were just swinging by for some things before resuming our vacation," I admitted.

"That will work nicely. Check in with us daily. Normally, I wouldn't ask such a thing for a pair on vacation, but Dowry is concerned for your safety."

Wrinkling my nose at the added complexity, I thought about it for a few moments before nodding. "Sure. We can do that. Just let you know if there's anything weird and call if we find anything amiss?"

"Exactly so. Dowry will want you to check in with him, too, but since you live in my jurisdiction, I'd like you to keep in touch with me, too."

"Sure, I can text you both or call as needed." My husband came out of the house, and I spotted several large ceramic pots in the entry. "He's being excessive again."

"He is so good at being excessive," Valorie commented. "When it comes to you, he takes the little things to extremes."

"He really does. He looks really good in that jacket."

"And that's my cue to go warm up in my

house while you admire your scenery. Send over some hot cops to question me," she ordered before heading home.

I bit my lip so I wouldn't laugh until she disappeared into her house. "Did you hear that, Chief Barfield? Send over some hot cops to question her."

"I'm not sure I have any sufficiently hot older cops capable of withstanding her wily ways."

"Sacrifice one that deserves a good woman before the Devil starts sending his minions over to seduce her. He really will, too."

"I might have an older gentleman who has been a widower for a while, and I'll send some of the young, fit men to learn how to question a friendly old woman." The chief snickered. "You're going to turn Manhattan upside down."

"I really will." Aware I would fall on my ass again if I got anywhere near the icy sidewalk, I trudged through the snow and observed my husband, his uncle, and his grandfather conferring over the roses. To my shock, Sariel manifested a shining sword out of the air and eyed the ground. "Don't kill my roses! Swords are for stabbing. Don't stab them, they're already having a bad day."

All three shot glares at me, and I stomped my foot. "No traumatizing my roses."

The archangel sighed, flicked his wrist, and turned his glowing sword into a shovel.

"I'm not going to stab them, my little grand-daughter."

"That poor sword is going to file for its retirement or put in a request for a new owner."

"It's a sword, not a living thing," Sariel stated before going to work digging up the abused rose plant. Once freed from the ground, he handed it over to the Devil. "*He* will whine sufficiently less should you be the one abusing your holy fire."

More fire? I crossed my arms over my chest and kept a close eye on my uncle.

"Your cindercorn is positively cranky this morning," the Devil said, taking the rose bush and walking to the house, completely ig-noring the ice. The ground steamed in his wake, and I realized he cheated, melting it so he wouldn't slip and slide.

"What did Chief Barfield have to say?" Quinn asked, examining the gaping hole where the rose bush had been. "Can I hire you to be my gardener, Grandfather? That would have taken me an hour to dig out."

"No. I'm only doing this because my little granddaughter would cry if her roses couldn't be saved."

"Her roses?"

"She loves them more than you do, so they are hers, and you just get to enjoy them, too."

Hah. I slated that as my victory, and I pointed at the Devil, who worked at putting my poor plant in one of the pots. "And that one is my *favorite*."

"The roses will be fine, Bailey."

"I showed pictures to Valorie. Of my asshole parents. She thinks it was them. I already told Chief Barfield to request an angel for verification when they're brought in for questioning. Practitioners could trick people with their likeness, and I'd rather have the truth than jump to conclusions. But, let's face it. My asshole parents would do just that. Maybe we should ask the uncle over there about adding some extras to their future accommodations."

"I could work something in with roses," the Devil replied, coming out of the house and brushing his hands together. "I'll take the roses home with me while you're vacationing and care for them until your return. That will prevent any future trouble, and my wife enjoys caring for the underdog."

"I'll call her over for coffee when we're back, and I might even give her back," I replied.

"You're evil," the Devil informed me.

I giggled.

My husband regarded me with narrow eyes. "What have you done, you sneaky woman?"

As I looked forward to whatever punishment my husband would concoct, I announced, "I cut a good deal with the Devil, so

I get to invite his wife over whenever I want, and I might even give her back."

"And you yell at me about bargaining?"

"But she likes coffee, and I make the best coffee. And she likes kids."

"She wants you to have another one of my suits, and I may have told her this specific suit works very well with wings."

It didn't take my husband long to figure out what I had in mind. "I'm going to let this slide once, Bailey."

Victory was mine. "Okay. What do you want to do about my asshole parents?"

"I'll let Barfield deal with that problem. Once we get the roses moved inside, we'll gather what we need for our trip and resume our vacation."

"I can go start the packing while you manly men—and angel—handle taking care of my roses," I offered.

"I'm going to need your coffee for this," Quinn announced without any shame. "I have gone weeks without your coffee, and I will surely perish if I do not get any."

I loved him so much it hurt. "I'll make extra coffee just for you." As I'd get scolded if I fell again, I waddled to the door, gave my favorite rose's new pot a fond pat, and began preparing for our adventure to Vermont.

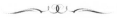

I DID my best work on making coffee while my eager husband hovered, the equivalent of an excited puppy while observing me make his precious brew. As such, I went to work scouring the house for clothes suitable for a hike into Vermont, discovering I needed to do a better job of shopping for winter clothes. As promised, I snagged the lacy black bra and panties Quinn loved best, and I dug through my box of spare clothing to retrieve several other sets just like them I'd found in different colors.

I grabbed enough clothes for him, selfishly selecting what I enjoyed him wearing the most.

Once we had what we needed for the trip, I went into our home office, which had our filing cabinets, book storage, and a small table two could work at when necessary. Fortunately, Quinn kept immaculate records, and he had receipts from the day he'd turned eighteen. Not only did he have his old receipts, he labeled them by type and month, making it easy to sort through. As I had no idea when he'd married Audrey, I started from the very beginning, rummaging through his life before we'd met.

The receipts told a startlingly sad story of him working and doing little else. I found the title and purchase agreement for his car, discovering he'd bought it used and had financed it for five years. It hadn't had many miles on it when he'd gotten his hands on it.

It cost significantly less than I'd expected it to.

I would have thought his promotion would have earned him something better—or at least with a much higher price tag.

Once Audrey came into his life, his spending habits changed—and his work hours increased a terrifying amount. Then, starting shortly before he'd come storming into my life, his financial story changed again.

He established a budget for coffee, and he established folders dedicated to his coffee habit.

Most of the receipts came from my work.

"What an obsessive man," I murmured, making sure I put everything back exactly as I found it before eyeballing the filing cabinet Quinn constantly glared at. It took some trial and error, but one of the keys he'd given me for the cabinets opened it.

Apparently, Audrey McGee hadn't bothered to claim her financial records following her divorce from my Quinn. Unlike my husband, her records were haphazardly kept, marked only by tax year, which would make life interesting for me. Like Quinn, she'd kept records from when she'd turned eighteen.

I bet he had a lot to do with that, as he hated sloppy records, and he'd insisted I gather as much of my records as I could, although napalming my apartment had given me a clean start.

The most current filing cabinets blended

our lives, and the rift between Quinn and Audrey became more apparent every minute I snooped through her life.

I grabbed my new leather travel totes designed for hanging file folders, unwrapped them, and lined four of them up on the table. I had no idea why Quinn thought I would need ten of the damned things, but they were the same as his but in a different color.

As my gorgon-incubus doohickey might burn his when he found out Audrey's files had contaminated them, I loaded her entire filing cabinet into them, discovering I needed all ten to fit her messy paperwork. Wrinkling my nose, I hauled the whole lot downstairs to discover the Quinn family had gone and done something excessive again.

Instead of the ten planned rose bushes, a collection of thirty took over our living room, meaning the archangel, the Devil, and my husband had rescued every damned rose plant we owned, including the six he'd planted when married to Audrey and the ones from the back yard.

Men.

"You three are excessive," I announced.

The Devil grinned at me. "He began to fret you might miss the other roses, so we rescued them all. I recommend you build a greenhouse in your next home specifically for your roses, and then you can plant new roses outside to add to your collection."

Oh, I liked that idea. "Please tell my husband all roses are edible roses."

"They are. You can even eat non-edible ones to your heart's content. That is one of the benefits of your line. You could chug nightshade without issue. Sure, you'd get one hell of a high and an even worse hangover, but it's not going to kill you."

"No, you may not chug nightshade," Quinn stated, and according to his tone, we would have an epic fight if I even thought about it.

"Cut me off spaghetti, and we will have problems, you."

The Devil laughed. "Your tomatoes are safe, and so are your greasy fries."

I glared at my husband until he threw up his hands. "Bailey, I'll have a heart attack if you start fiddling with poisons."

"Stay away from my sauce supply, you."

The Devil chuckled, and he slapped his hand to the side of the pot containing my favorite of the roses. "I'm going to head home. Enjoy your vacation, and when you decide on where you'll live, I'll bring your roses back."

"Thank you." I crouched next to my roses and patted them. "Be good until you come back."

Before I could make even more of an idiot out of myself, the Devil disappeared and took the roses with him. Sariel straightened, stretched his wings, and rubbed his hands together. "With that handled, I shall head home as well. Try not to get into too much trouble, you two. I'll be in the heavens for a while, so I might not be readily available. Reception is questionable depending on *His* mood."

Before I could thank him, the archangel vanished.

Quinn closed the door and heaved a sigh. "That was exhausting."

"Physically or emotionally?" I could fix the physically exhausted aspect. Gorgon-incubus doohickeys responded well when showered with affection, and mine particularly enjoyed when I showered him with affection in the shower.

"I'm going to say both."

Score. "You can tidy the bathroom while I finish what I'm doing, then we can catch a short nap before we head off."

"I won't need a nap at that point, you saucy woman."

"Well, I will!"

"You can nap in the car."

Double score. "Find us a rental SUV so we can leave your precious car in the garage while we're gone. We won't have the space in the trunk for everything I've packed."

"Okay. I'll take care of that and pack."

"I already packed for you. Selfishly."

I loved his dark, sinful chuckle. "You're something else."

That I was. "Just hurry it up. We don't have all day, and I forgot to schedule in time for a shower."

EIGHT

I hate the stupid.

LIFE NEVER WENT TO PLAN.

The shower revitalized my husband, and I admired him while he strutted around the house, waiting for the rental company to pick him up so he could finalize the rental and bring the vehicle back so we could hit the road. I made his coffee, chuckling at his restless energy. "Be careful driving."

"I will," he promised, accepting his travel mug and giving me a kiss. The doorbell rang, and he grabbed his wallet from our coffee table. "This could take up to an hour, but hopefully not that long. If the assholes come back, remember you are a meat-eating, fire-breathing unicorn and act appropriately."

I translated that to mean I should put on my fur coat for a while and play guard unicorn. "Okay."

Quinn left, and I went upstairs to grab the stash of grade-A transformatives I kept taped to the bottom of my nightstand. I'd have to order a new stash from the CDC, but the grade-A was easier for me to transform through, and I struggled less reversing back to human. I stripped, folded my clothes and put them in a bag, and swallowed the pill.

Ten minutes later, I carried my bag downstairs in my mouth, set it with the rest of the bags for the trip, and stretched. As there was no reason to not enjoy myself, I sliced open the box of long-burning logs with a claw, picked one up, tossed it into the fireplace, and used my horn to open the flue so I wouldn't fill the house with smoke.

While I liked it, my husband adamantly did not enjoy my adventures with the fireplace and a closed flue.

I snorted to light the log, settled on my favorite rug, and admired the flames, keeping an eye out the window for anyone suspicious.

Within twenty minutes, most of the cops left, leaving one unmarked car parked across the street with a pair inside, keeping watch on those coming and going. As I'd made a large travel Thermos of coffee, I got up from my spot and grabbed the handle in my mouth, which was positioned on the top specifically so I could carry it while a unicorn, and eased through the house to a window, hitching a lift on a sunbeam to get outside without having to bother with the door. Snorting fire over the chill, I trotted across the street, making use of my claws on the ice to keep from slipping. The cop on the passenger side rolled down his window when I approached, and I thrust the Thermos at him, which he accepted.

"No dust but good coffee," I told them, giving a swish of my tail. I stomped my hooves to keep warm, and as that worked, I pranced in place and bucked, giving my mane a good shake, too. "Idiot par-rents no un-der-stand I un-nee-corn."

"Seriously? I'm Troy, and my partner is Lucas, ma'am." Troy handed the Thermos over to Lucas. "We were asked to stick around until you leave, as our chief seems to think the perps might come back to finish what they started."

"They are that stupid." I pricked my ears forward over how well I'd managed to talk despite the cold stabbing away at my fur. "Keep Thermos. It old one. Have new one inside." We'd just gotten it before I'd gone on my road trip adventure, and it was still in its box. "Give good excuse to get out new one. Odds idiot par-rents coming back to house?"

"Pretty high. They made their attempt in broad daylight, which smacks of general desperation."

"But why? Makes no sense. I leave them alone? They go away, I happy. Very happy."

"It's not uncommon with abusers. They seek revenge when the gig is up, and people like them value their reputation. We've been doing groundwork on them as part of the investigation. According to the briefing, they're part of a somewhat influential vanilla family."

"Yes. Hate magic, hate magic users. Hate any-thing diff-er-ent from them. Me diff-er-ent."

"Well, yes. You're in a class of your own. You need a high rating to qualify for your job."

"I hate the stupid," I complained, hanging my head.

Troy reached out of the unmarked car and gave my shoulder a pat. "We all do. It's so annoying."

I raised my head, and as Quinn kept telling me the cops liked when meat-eating, fire-breathing unicorns nuzzled them, I bumped his fingers with my nose.

He scratched my forehead below my horn, and I settled in to enjoy the attention.

"That silver car matches the witness description," Lucas announced.

I cracked open an eye to regard the vehicle coming down the street. Sure enough, my idiot, asshole parents were in the vehicle. "So damned dumb," I complained. "At least no can burn roses now. Or house. Fire-proof house. So stupid."

Both cops reached for their firearms, and I got out of their way, stepping back and flattening my ears.

Smart people would have noticed the irritated black and red unicorn snorting smoke standing beside a suspicious looking vehicle most would believe to be an unmarked cop car, given even half a second to examine it and its occupants. Rather than utilize one of their limited brain cells, my parents pulled up alongside my house. Rather than go the gasoline and a match route, they'd gotten a Molotov cocktail, which they flung in the direction of the big picture window.

Had my father had a stronger arm or better aim, I might've been worried, but he hit wide and low. The bottle shattered on the brick, and the sticky substance caught aflame.

My poor house.

I pivoted and trotted along, eyeballing their vehicle. My mother, who was driving the vehicle, continued down the street as though nothing happened, and after she passed Valorie's house, she sped up.

Did the assholes really think I would just let them try to light my house on fire *again* without doing anything about it? I bucked, kicked my heels, whinnied, and charged down the street. Within a few strides, I hit top speed, making use of my claws to maintain traction on the slick roads. When I caught up with the vehicle, I calculated the distance to the hood of their car, jumped, and landed hard, slamming all six hundred plus pounds of my weight on the plastic and metal.

The car came to a rather abrupt halt, and I yelped, crashing to the icy asphalt. Scrambling to my hooves so they wouldn't run me over, I blew flames at the vehicle.

Troy and Lucas joined the party, their firearms out and ready, trained on my idiot parents.

My mother seemed to believe she would be able to get her car on the move after having an angry unicorn bash the hood in. On closer investigation, not only had I bashed the entire front end of the car into the ground, I'd broken the axle, as both front tires pointed in separate directions.

Wow. I regarded the destruction with interest.

"I broke it," I informed the cops.

Rather than pay any attention to me, the cops began barking orders, directing my ass-hole parents to get out of the vehicle with their hands up.

Amused neither seemed to care I'd trashed my parents' car, I amused myself circling them, snorting smoke and fire to keep my body temperature up. Sometime after the cops had read my parents their rights, a black SUV with a rental car sticker came down the street.

I bolted for the house, dug at one of the holes left from moving my roses, and tried to hide in the frozen ground. "Not here!"

Down the street, the cops laughed at me.

I didn't blame them.

My husband parked the rental in our driveway, and I hunkered down, attempting to escape his wrath.

"I can see you, Bailey. You don't fit."

Damn it. "Not my fault!"

"The unicorn-shaped dent in the hood of that car is definitely your fault, unless there is another unicorn hiding around?"

"May-be?" I turned my ears back and showed him my teeth. "They start it!"

"Now that I can believe, especially as it seems the side of the house has been lit on fire. Did they use a Molotov cocktail?"

"May-be. Okay. Yes. Do you think Mol-o-tov cock-tail tast-ee?"

"Go lick it and find out."

I scrambled out of the hole, scrambled to the side of the house, and gave the fire on the brick a lick. Whatever they'd used tasted peppery with a solid punch of diesel and some other accelerant. "Die-sel! Tast-ee!" I enjoyed the flames tickling over my fur, and I went to work licking everything off our house.

"Just try to leave the broken glass alone. Don't step on it or cut your tongue. I'll give Barfield a call."

Within twenty minutes, the cops were all back along with a single fire engine. The fire fighters stood around and did nothing while I handled the cleanup, and when I finished my treat, I burped. With a claw extended, I tapped on the broken glass. "This part no tast-ee, Queeny."

My husband joined me on the front steps

of our house, shaking his head at the damaged bricks. "A few inches to the left, and we
would have had a charred interior, and even
then, it wouldn't have done much damage."

"Not much damage because Queeny the
best husband and fireproof house."

He rewarded me with a stroke of my nose.
"A wise man adapts to his wife's special needs,
and my wife's favorite treat is napalm. Did
you enjoy your snack?"

"Very tast-ee. Not as good as nay-palm,
but good. Peppery. Die-sel plus some-thing
else." I considered the taste. "Blue gel stuff for
hot plate things."

"Methanol blue," my husband replied.
"Easy to get, a good enough gel, and would
help keep the fire concentrated enough to
light the house up—if I hadn't fireproofed it."

"Par-rents very stupid."

"Yes, they are. Did you really have to total
their car, though?"

"Cops would have put bullets in car and
may have shot idiot par-rents. May-be earn,
but my way bet-ter. No par-rents shot, only
car damaged. No tell nice father or mother
about this? They be upset. Very upset. Might
smite."

"Smote, my beautiful."

"Might smite," I replied in my most
solemn tone.

"You're incredible."

I nuzzled his chest before using his
shoulder as a headrest. "Think they get bail?"

My husband wrapped his arms around my neck and held me. "I don't know. Are you all right?"

"Fine! Got tast-ee treat, smoosh their car with my not-fat ass. Gave cops coffee. Their Ther-mos now. I make more cof-fee in new Ther-mos!"

"The pair was across the street?"

"Yes. Can walk across street by self. I talk with them, give cof-fee. Then par-rents come. I stop them. Did not want to lose to car. Lost to trans-port once. That hurt, no do that again. Fell off car when stop, but no hurt me. Did not burn car."

"You did great, Bailey. Not quite to regulation, but we're allowed to use force to stop a vehicle in situations like this, and you did so with no damage to anything other than their vehicle. I don't even think you damaged the road."

"Leave some holes in asphalt. I blow fire for fixer people and help ree-pair in spring. It cold. Open door, puh-lease? Keys inside. I ride sunbeam through window to say hello to cops. No sunbeams in house. I go change. Talk hard."

Quinn kissed my nose before letting me into the house and giving my rump a slap. "Go enjoy your fire and catch a snooze. I'll be a while sorting this mess out. Since you went through the trouble of lighting it, go enjoy it."

I had the best husband. "I love Queeny."

He smiled at me.

NAPS by the fireplace were the best, especially when my sneaky husband lit a proper fire and cranked the temperature in the house so I wouldn't get cold. By the time the cops finished with him, the sun had set. I woke to Quinn running the brush over my coat while talking to someone on the phone.

"He asked her to call you, but she's sleeping in front of the fireplace. Cold weather isn't great for cindercorns, and we had some excitement earlier. No, no. Everybody is fine, so please don't worry. Ra wanted her to tell you that he wanted to see you in the morning while the moon was still up. As soon as Bailey gets up, we're going to resume our vacation. All right, I'll let her know, and I'll try to have her call you tomorrow night."

My mother. Ra had put her number into our phones, but I'd figured out early on the phones only worked when they were active. I hadn't quite figured out the specifics. Magic worked in mysterious ways, and I'd learned not to think too hard about some of the odder impossibilities—like why I couldn't call my father when the sun shone brightly on the other side of the world.

Before I could notify Quinn I was awake, he hung up, and then he smacked my rump with the brush. "Up, my beautiful. I need coffee, and your machine refuses to give me good coffee. It laughs at me."

I whinnied a laugh, rolled, and scrambled to my hooves. "Mother okay?"

"Ah, caught part of that conversation, did you?"

"Some."

"She's fine. I opted against notifying either of your parents about the incident with the assholes. The last thing our house needs is an angry divine coming over and raining hell on a pair of assholes."

No kidding. "Go change, make coffee," I promised.

"While you were sleeping, I printed out all of the old banking information I had on Audrey's accounts."

"You have her bank info?"

"She had me go over her accounting work because she's hopeless with money, so she dumped all of her transactions into a spreadsheet for me. I never deleted it. Technically, because she never asked me to delete the files, it's legal for me to have. Even after our divorce, I helped her with her paperwork. She wasn't exactly a bad woman."

"She just not stay loyal."

"Right."

"You ruined me for other men. Tragedy." I shook off and stretched. "Go change now. Then coffee. Then we run away in rented SUV. No more assholes try to light things on fire?"

"We have a pair of cops parked in our driveway to discourage anyone from trying anything stupid. Oh, that reminds me. I saw Valorie flirting with the cops. In our driveway."

"Do we have older, single hot cops?"

"Bailey, we're not playing matchmaker for our neighbor."

"Why not? Else your uncle may get her."

"Maybe we'll play matchmaker for our neighbor, although it depends which devil he has in mind for her."

"I worry for world. We may destroy it. Bring ruin."

"Or marry everyone we know to demons or devils." Laughing, Quinn kissed my nose. "Go get changed, lawbreaker."

"I such bad cop."

"You'll learn. Just try to keep your general lawbreaking ways somewhat contained for a change."

"Break a few laws once..." I muttered while my husband laughed.

REVERSING BACK to human took a lot out of me, and if Quinn wanted me going anywhere, I'd need a lot of coffee. Some days, I regretted not having a coffee maker capable of brewing my dark brew a pot at a time. It took me almost half an hour to fill the new Thermos and both of our travel mugs with coffee, and as I was not a complete monster, giving the cops outside their fair share, too. I even gave them a light dose of pixie dust to make their night a little happier.

"House sitting isn't precisely prestigious, but it's not so bad you need to dose the cops with pixie dust, Bailey."

"It's cold, so it is that bad."

"You realize we're going north, right?"

I heaved a sigh. "Unfortunately. I might freeze to death. What will I do if I freeze to death?"

"You're not going to freeze to death. I did go over your winter clothing, and we're going shopping specifically to make it so you don't freeze to death. Get that pretty little ass on the move. I'll take the coffee out to the cops, but it's time to load up the SUV and leave."

"You're way too energetic."

"It's your fault. You're just so good to me."

"Keep talking, gorgon-incubus doohickey. That's how you get dragged into a shower at a hotel."

"Strangely, I figured that one out on my own." Quinn took the older Thermos he'd stolen from some of his cops at work outside to the cops on duty so they could enjoy a warm drink while I cleaned my beautiful machine, polishing the stainless steel to a shine.

I hadn't quite finished when he returned, and he wrapped his arm around my waist and dragged me out of the kitchen. "Hey, I wasn't done!"

"Your baby will be fine without having every inch of it washed four times before we leave." To make it clear it was time to go, he hauled me out of the house, took me to the SUV, and shoved me into the front passenger seat, buckling my seatbelt for me. "Stay, you."

Pouting earned me a kiss. He gave me his phone to play with while I waited, and I opened my favorite puzzle game and went to work trying to beat a hell level determined to drive me insane.

In his typical, efficient way, within ten minutes, he had the SUV packed to his liking, and he'd brought everything I'd packed, plus his own contributions. "It's a good thing your grandfather has the kids, as they would not fit right now," I observed.

"They really wouldn't. I wasn't sure how long we'd be doing this, so I may have over-packed while you were napping. You were too peaceful to disturb." Quinn gave me my new bag with my laptops, and he handed my new cindercorn purse to me, too. "Your guns and ammo are in the new purse."

"They're both new."

"The one bag isn't really a purse."

"I am using it as a purse, so it is a purse."

"Is that how purses are defined? If it is a bag you use as a purse, is it a purse?"

"Well, if designers would give us more pockets, we wouldn't need purses, so they deliberately keep the pockets on pants small so we need purses. Your day comes, Quinn. One day, the manufacturers will realize men can use purses, and pockets will go extinct."

"That's pretty fucked up, Bailey."

"So is trying to buy pants with pockets when you're a woman."

"I'd offer you my pants, but they look better on me than they would on you, and I would hate if we were to both suffer because you wore my pants."

Damn. "That was a good one. Do that again, but with something else. I haven't been put in my place enough for one day, apparently. Encore, encore!"

"It's a good thing you hadn't run out in front of your parents' car, as if they'd hit you, I would have probably burned down the whole street with some help from the Devil."

"That's not quite what I was aiming for, but for once in my life, I had completely thought that through *before* I jumped on their car. I remembered. Transports hurt. Cars probably hurt less than transports, but I figured I would prefer landing *on* their car rather than being squished *by* their car."

"I'm not sure how I'm supposed to argue with that, Bailey. That's what you're supposed to do. Good job. Also, I took the liberty of loading in my ex-wife's banking records onto your work laptop so you can play with that while I drive. As you went through the effort of digging out her paper records, too, I also loaded in the digital version of the files, although I don't know if there's anything missing. She built the digital version after I showed her how. Honestly, if she's hiding anything, it should be easy enough to find. We'll just cross-reference the digital records and the paper records. Call me a fool, but I trusted her with the paperwork when, perhaps, I should not have."

"I would say love makes people do stupid things, but I've come to the conclusion love wasn't a part of that relationship, so I can't give you a free pass on that. But to be fair, you need *all* of the patience to put up with me, so she was a suitable teacher for patience."

"I don't think you need me for coming up with zingers tonight, Bailey. That was a good one. Do I get an encore?"

"No, but you'll get dragged into the shower at the hotel. Does that count?"

"As a matter of fact, yes. I have us booked into a decent hotel two hours from here, and the staff knows we'll be late. I asked for them to prepare dinner for us, so it should be ready when we arrive. I figured you'd want something quiet tonight. Tomorrow, I'll try harder to appropriately dine you, although you do not get to partake of any wine."

"They better not take away my coffee."

"I have no idea if coffee is in the diet of pregnant cindercorns. Since most women wouldn't find out they're pregnant for at least another two or three weeks, I think it's safe to say your coffee is safe for at least that long, but I'll ask my grandfather and uncle. They probably know more about cindercorns than

anyone else. I mean, I've been ordered to re-
serve most of my venom for you, so it's obvious you don't play by anyone's rules. Cobra
venom? Typically not safe for pregnant
women. Compared to that? Coffee's nothing."

I did the math. Quinn's cobras plus me
being bitten by Quinn's cobras equaled a fun
time. "I don't know who gave you that advice,
but I will be very upset if you make your poor
snakes sit around with uncomfortably full
venom sacs. You better bite me daily. Right
after dinner, every night. After we've sent the
children to bed, of course. But we'll make
sure they know they can read for an hour before lights out."

"Better give them two hours, as one hour
is not sufficient time to appropriately care for
my cindercorn."

"That sounds reasonable. Should we call
and check in on them?"

"I'll call at the hotel to make sure they're
fine. It's customary they don't speak with us
directly for the most part. That helps make
sure they understand my grandfather and
grandmother have full authority over them
while in their care. It's a gorgon thing, which
he'll be teaching them. They'll probably cling
when we get them back, but that's also
normal—and doubly so in their case. Since
they're with a familial hive, they won't feel
abandoned, so don't worry. Family is pretty
important to gorgons, and they're probably

overwhelmed with how much they need to learn right now."

"I can work with that. Drive, my gorgon-incubus doohickey. I'll fight with numbers and see if I can make sense of them. The next time you gas up, you can hand me the first of the files, so I can start matching things, too, assuming I haven't found anything interesting by then."

"You have a deal. But no homemade napalm today, even if I stop at a gas station with diesel."

"That's just mean, Quinn."

"You'll survive."

NINE

Ew, ew, ew.

THE INSIGNIFICANT, with new knowledge, could become significant in the blink of an eye, and Audrey's financials told a chilling story. Lacking any reason to suspect his ex-wife, there was no reason for my husband to become suspicious over some—no, a lot—of the transactions in the spreadsheet.

However, understanding there might be a link between her, Chief Morrison, and the gorgons who'd kidnapped Janet changed the way I viewed her receipts.

Three years before her questionable marriage to Manhattan's Most Wanted Bachelor, Audrey McGee had made weekly trips to the Hamptons. Those had changed to monthly trips to the Hamptons, although where she went remained fixed. Making use of my phone, I determined she'd gone for coffee at a shop several blocks away from the primary police station serving the rich and famous in the area, the perfect place for her to meet someone.

Most times, she returned home the same day, but before her marriage to Quinn, she'd stayed until morning more often than not, filling up at a gas station not far away.

How odd.

Near the end of their marriage, her forays to the Hamptons became weekly again, and she tended to go to the gas station several hours after the coffee shop. Sometimes, she went to the pharmacy. The purchases at the pharmacy baffled me until I checked the price of condoms and got a match on a common brand.

What a bitch.

Grabbing my phone, I went through my options and finally texted Janet, asking if she was aware of where Chief Morrison lived.

She replied with an address in the Hamptons.

I checked the address compared to the pharmacy to discover it was a quarter of a mile away from where the chief lived.

Ew, ew, ew.

I thanked her, wondering what to do about what I'd learned.

If Audrey had been involved with the batch of gorgon dust production, which seemed obvious to me, considering she'd become a gorgon and had been found with a batch, how did she relate to Chief Morrison?

More importantly, how did Chief Morrison tie into the gorgon dust problem?

Considering Morrison was likely guilty of aiding and abetting gorgons into kidnapping a police officer, how was he tied to the rabies problem?

I worried Audrey's activities might give me the clues I needed. I returned to her financials and filtered out all transactions from New York and focused on when she left the state.

Sure enough, I found several trips that took her through Vermont, Maine, and Massachusetts.

"Your ex-wife is quite the character," I told my husband.

"Yes, I had figured that out, which was why I asked for your help divorcing her. I really should have just tipped off an incubus. That would have done the trick."

I spied an exit sign with a gas station ahead, and I pointed at it. "Stop there, because I do not want you to crash the rental."

"That doesn't sound promising. Did you find something?"

"I think so."

The exit led to a full-fledged rest center with several restaurants, enough gas and diesel to make a life-time supply of home-made napalm, and a visitor's center, one that was miraculously open. "Oh! We should get stuffed animals for the kids, then we'll talk."

"Sure." He parked, and I shoved my laptop

into my bag, and hurried for the gift shop in case it was about to close. I searched for presents for our kids, debating how best to break the news to Quinn.

They had stuffed cindercorns, and I stared at them with wide eyes, my mouth hanging open.

Quinn spotted them, laughed, and reached up to take two off the shelf, and then he retrieved two more, which he handed to me. "Two for the whelps, two for the twins, and I should get two for us so we can play with the kids."

He did just that, and after a moment of thought, he grabbed the remaining stock.

"That's too many."

"It's not enough. I've been warned, Bailey. We're the kind of parents who will inevitably have more kids because we love children. And two are for us."

So much for sane purchases. I pointed at the white unicorns on the neighboring shelf. "Grab a few of those, and we should get new travel mugs."

On his way to the register, he snagged a black and red blanket to add to the pile. "You'll get cold."

"While true, you're being excessive again."

"Leave me to my excessive ways, woman. Go grab some candy and some jerky so you can appease your carnivorous ways."

Giggling, I obeyed, joining him at the register and adding to the pile. While he paid for everything, I headed for the bathroom so I wouldn't be bothering him in thirty minutes, taking the time to tame my hair and pretend I wasn't a hot mess of a woman.

When I emerged, he waited for me burdened with a ridiculous number of bags.

"You bought more stuff, didn't you?" I accused, wondering how we'd make it all fit in the SUV.

"Maybe."

"You're crazy, Quinn." He'd be angry within five minutes, so I didn't complain about spending extra money, settling with taking some of the bags from him and helping him carry everything.

To my amazement, it all fit in the vehicle with room to spare.

"This is a pretty good pitch for buying an SUV," my husband admitted.

"We should do that. Buy an SUV, that is. If we need a break from the investigation because of frustration, we can shop for one."

Quinn got behind the wheel. "All right, my beautiful babbling brook. What has you so nervous you didn't mind spending extra money in the gift shop?"

"Busted," I admitted, getting into my seat and digging out my laptop. "I followed the money and found a few coincidences I don't like very much. And at some point, the coincidences stack up to the point where is it really a coincidence?"

"When there are that many coincidences,

it's probably not a coincidence at all. That's
something we look for during investigations.
Coincidences happen, but when they're
stacked repeatedly in a way that fits the evidence, the likelihood that it's a coincidence is
slim. What do you have?"

"Judging from receipts, Audrey was pur-
chasing condoms at a pharmacy disturbingly
close to Chief Morrison's home, and she was
going to a coffee shop near the copper shop
there—and filling her car up at a gas station
nearby. I had Janet tell me where Morrison
lived, as it seemed odd she was going to the
Hamptons every week for years. Then she
married you and only went once a month.
Near the end of your marriage with her, she
was going back weekly again. This was going
on for years before she married you, by the
way."

"With Chief Morrison?"

"I suppose it could be another cop that
happens to live near his place, but she was
definitely visiting someone in the Hamptons,
and I bet she was buying condoms. The receipts I have don't say *what* she purchased,
but I did some searching on the internet, and
one brand costs the amount she was consistently spending when tax is included. There
are very few restaurant purchases, so
someone was buying her dinner or feeding
her. Likely before or after one of her trysts."

"If you look on your laptop in my folder,
you'll see a folder with my name and date

tracking as the file name. That has my records of when she was cheating on me. Do the dates line up?"

I opened the file, and it didn't take long for me to match up most of the dates. "Most of them." I checked the other dates, and several over a short period of time coincided with one of her trips to Maine. "She went on a trip to Maine once."

"To visit family." According to his tone, he hadn't bought that line when she'd originally gone, either. "When she told me she wanted to go, I'd already guessed she was going to meet someone for yet another tryst. But with Chief Morrison?"

I checked the locations in Maine against the rabies records in the CDC database, and I went through the hassle of checking distances between where Audrey had gone and the largest concentration of infected animals, discovering one location was within twenty minutes of where she'd gone. More importantly, the rabies outbreak began three weeks after her departure, which was the baseline time for animals to begin showing symptoms of infection. "Or someones. Not far from where she went, there was a severe rabies outbreak. It infected a small group of wolves, some raccoons, a couple of skunks, and a lot of bats. There was one infected fox that showed up a month after the largest cluster, likely as a result from being bitten by or eating an infected animal if I had to make a guess."

"Let me see if I understand this. Audrey, long before she even met me, was possibly seeing Chief Morrison, who likely allied himself with gorgons to kidnap Janet long *after* my divorce from Audrey."

"And was probably banging her the whole damned time. Except for that bit where she was playing you. Or something." Crap. "I mean, she may not have been playing you?"

"Oh, she was playing me as much as I was playing her, Bailey. We didn't get married because we loved each other. We got married because I got tired of being hunted by a bunch of women, and she promised she wouldn't need much attention and liked my looks."

"Have you been checked for any diseases? Maybe we should both get tested. You know, just to make sure. Because now I'm utterly creeped out."

"I have been tested several times, and with a few notable exceptions involving pixie dust, I wasn't sleeping with her. Definitely not often."

"That's probably a good thing. But at least it looks like she was using condoms?"

"Let's confirm that, shall we?"

"Good thought."

Quinn retrieved the files from the back, and we spent twenty minutes searching for pharmacy receipts. Sure enough, she liked buying condoms from the pharmacy, and the times the amounts hadn't matched, she'd purchased a few other products for her evening adventures—likely with Chief Morrison.

Ew, ew, ew. "We're going to that hotel and eating dinner, after which I'm going to begin an exhaustive therapy session with you. Also, with you as an exception, her taste in men is absolutely disgusting."

In record time, he returned the file folders to the back of the SUV, got behind the wheel, and started the engine. "I love the way you think, Mrs. Samuel Quinn."

"What? You're hot in that jacket."

He smiled. "Well, I'm certainly glad you think so. You're not so bad yourself."

I regarded my laptop with a sigh. "This is a mess. You really should quality check your wives, Sam. I mean, you did an excellent job of getting rid of the first one, but you may have jumped the gun on the second one."

"If you say so, Calamity Queen."

"See? That right there is evidence you need to at least make sure you're marrying a quality woman. I'm a disaster on two and four feet."

"You picked me, and I'm not letting you talk yourself out of how perfect we are for each other. I heard you very clearly, Bailey. You wanted to know how you could make the bastard marry you, so I helped you figure that out."

He really had. "It turns out you're not really a bastard, your parents are really nice, and I even like the rest of your family despite their oddities." I sighed. "My mouth always gets me into trouble."

"You're perfect for me, and that's all I care about. I *should* have quality checked Audrey a little better, but realistically? Because of her, I now have you. That means a lot to me. Life won't be perfect, but while you're a disaster on two and four feet, you're *my* disaster on two and four feet. So, we'll go figure out why and how the hell Audrey had gotten into so many messes, put an end to the rabies and gorgon dust issues, and start the rest of our lives without that looming over our heads. Will we find out everything? Probably not. But I'll sleep better at night knowing we stopped two dangerous threats to humanity."

"That sounds like a plan to me."

"Good. Now chin up, work your magic with numbers while I drive, and prepare yourself. I need therapy. I'm terribly distraught and in dire need of your love."

"And you say I'm something else, Quinn."

"Well, you are."

"Kettle," I accused.

"But I'm a very happy kettle, my beautiful pot."

I rolled my eyes and focused on the spreadsheets, wondering what other secrets they hid.

QUINN MADE up for lost time through a mix of driving a little too fast for my comfort and refusing to stop until we reached the hotel, resulting in us arriving right on time. As promised, dinner was ready shortly after our arrival, and rather than worry about rabies, gorgon dust, and Audrey McGee's long-lived treachery and betrayal, I spent the rest of the night with my husband.

The evening was quiet, and I wondered what storm lurked in our future.

When morning came, I woke first, tiptoeing around the hotel room to let Quinn sleep, a rarity thanks to his genetics. I tidied and packed, and when I ran out of things to do, I ordered breakfast for both of us and resumed my work chasing after information on Audrey's activities with Chief Morrison.

As a public figure, people took pictures of police chiefs often, especially when they went out into public unexpectedly. While my husband's looks made him a common target of photographers, Chief Morrison oversaw the protection of the rich, which offered him a certain amount of prestige.

With Audrey's receipts as a guide, I scoured the internet for evidence of the woman's wrongdoings. As I expected, Chief Morrison was popular with newspapers in the Hamptons, leaving me to wade through hundreds of pictures of the asshole. Restricting my search by date helped, and after an hour of searching, I began uncovering photos of him with Audrey in the background.

Not only was Audrey in the photos, so was the idiot cadet I'd squished like a grape for threatening my husband.

Then, like some omen determined to ruin my day, I found a picture of Audrey with the person I'd recognized at the demonstration. That got me on the move, and I bounced onto the bed to wake my husband.

With startling speed, he caught me in his arms and dragged me down onto the mattress. "Wicked woman, sneaking out of my bed while I slept. I should discipline you for not cuddling me awake."

Damn it. I didn't want to work when he talked like that. "I love you, but I found something important."

That woke him up, although he didn't release me. "On a scale of one to ten, can it wait an hour?"

"I'd worry about it the entire hour," I admitted.

"All right, my beautiful. I'm up, I'm up. What did you find?"

Someone knocked at the door, and I wiggled free of his hold. "Breakfast!"

He chuckled while I hurried to retrieve our food, carting the trays to the coffee table, doubting I'd ordered enough. I tipped the gentleman, thanked him, closed the door, locked it, and fell upon my food like a starved beast.

"It's like watching a shark, but instead of blood, you're attracted to maple syrup."

"And it's not even the real stuff."

"How is that not criminal?"

"I will eat your pancakes," I warned.

"Like hell you'll eat my pancakes, you wicked woman." The threat of losing his breakfast to my gluttony got him out of bed, and he wrapped in his robe before joining me on the couch. "What did you find?"

"Remember that guy I wanted to run the facial scan on?"

"I do."

"I found a picture of him with Audrey, that cadet I squished, and Chief Morrison. I did a search and checked by dates, matching them to when she went to the Hamptons. I found enough pictures of her with Morrison to generally confirm she was seeing him. I think I even found a picture of them in the coffee shop together."

"You're right. She has really horrible taste in men."

"Well, she had the right idea with you, but she was too stupid to figure out what to do with you when she had you. I'm smart. I know exactly what I should be doing with you. I do wish we'd brought our pets."

"Actually, I think I'll have them fetched for us—or at least Sunny. We might need her."

Crap. "I don't want to be shot with more ambrosia, Quinn."

"That is not my idea of a good time, either,

but I've learned where you go, trouble follows —and ambrosia is serious trouble."

That it was. "I could go for some napalm, though."

"When can't you go for some napalm?"

I took my time thinking about that, nibbling on a piece of bacon. "Whenever you take your shirt off?"

"Why is that a question?"

"Why did you ask me such a hard question? It's napalm! Napalm is so much better than ambrosia."

"You get hungover, Bailey."

"But before the hangover, napalm is life." I devoured the rest of my bacon before demolishing my pancakes. "Okay. I'm ready to work."

Quinn stared at my empty plate. "You're not still hungry, are you? Are the twins already rising up to turn my beautiful cindercorn into a ravenous beast?"

"The twins have not been around long enough for that yet. I'm not even at the weird smells or morning sickness phase yet. That nonsense starts in a week or two, and then you can spend the rest of this pregnancy convincing me they aren't trying to kill me."

"They're not trying to kill you, Bailey."

"But are you sure?"

He regarded my stomach with interest. "I know people we could ask."

"The archangel, your uncle, or other?"

"All of the above," he admitted. "But my

uncle seems to be the one obsessed with unicorns, so I'll start with him."

"Do you think it'll be safe for our puppies and our most vicious huntress to come with us?"

"Sunny will be fine, and we'll be careful with Blizzard and Avalanche. I'd really rather Sunny come with us, and I'd rather not separate her from Blizzard—and Avalanche whines if Blizzard leaves her."

"But what about our babies? They're with our babies."

"Beauty and Sylvester will understand. They're already unusual. Gorgon whelps usually aren't allowed to have any pets until they're at least twelve. It's too much of a risk to the animals. I'll just tell them the pets need to be trained. Gorgon whelps understand training, so they won't think twice about it. Training our pets isn't punishing them, and they know this."

"They're so different from human children, aren't they?"

"In a way, but it's necessary. Don't feel badly about it, Bailey. We're protecting our children this way."

I scowled but nodded. "We are. And this whole rabies thing has hurt our family enough."

"That's right. And if we can sink Morrison with his involvement in the rabies outbreak, we'll nail him on multiple murder charges."

"If Morrison runs from bail, do you think

they'll tell us?" I asked, allowing my insecurities to come out, so I wouldn't bottle it up and have it explode out later.

Time—and Quinn—had changed me.

For the most part, I loved the woman I'd become since tumbling into his life.

"Probably not," he admitted. "With my heritage and tendencies, they—mostly meaning Commissioner Dowry—will believe I'll do anything necessary to protect you, which is correct. I will. You've already demonstrated you'll do whatever is necessary to protect me. By neglecting to tell us, they stop us from pursuing the matter personally."

"Except we are. Pursuing the matter personally, that is."

"We are, but we are doing so in a questionably acceptable fashion. We are using only resources publicly available or already have in our possession. We'll have to avoid looking at the facial recognition results to make that stick, but since it hadn't processed when we last looked at it, we can get away with a technicality on that score. The CDC rabies resources will look innocent enough. I mean, there's no reason to think Audrey was involved with that."

"Was she rabid?"

Quinn sighed. "Yes, she was. Her hive sisters, too. She was likely infected at least a few weeks before she kidnapped you, too. The surrogate was also treated for rabies. The whelps are all fine, however. Fortunately, most diseases don't transfer from surrogate to egg."

"What happened to her? That poor woman."

He smiled at me. "Her prince has a brother who was without a bride. Last I heard, he introduced himself to her, claimed her whelps as his own, and has been coaxing her into taking her rightful place as their mother. She'll be fine. Last I heard, she wants to meet you, as you were the one who helped save the eggs and keep them warm until they could be taken to my grandmother."

"That's good. So, if Audrey was involved with both the gorgon dust production and rabies, how is she connected to the incident at 120 Wall Street? What was the real purpose of that incident?"

"That's a very good question, and it's one we're going to have to find the answer to, I think. Initially, I thought it was a distraction from another incident, a raid on one of the CDC warehouses."

"For what? Which warehouse?"

"High-grade neutralizer."

I cringed. "That stuff isn't cheap."

"No, it's really not. And it was a large enough operation that it needed a big distraction."

"120 Wall Street was a pretty big distraction, yes." Quinn picked up a piece of his bacon and held it up. "This is 120 Wall Street. Using gorgon dust would have made every police chief in the area converge on the site. If everything had gone to their plan, making some assumptions about their plan, it would have severely crippled a majority of the NYPD, who showed up to help with crowd containment and to resolve the bomb threat. By disguising the dust as bile, if it hadn't been for you and your recognition of how it differed from actual bile, things would have played out a lot differently."

"Manhattan would have become a city of stone."

"And the high-grade neutralizer capable of possibly reversing some of the damage would have been unavailable, as it had either been stolen or destroyed during the warehouse raid."

I faked my saddest sigh. "I ruined all of their plans. How utterly tragic."

"Such tragedy," he agreed with a grin. "Not only did you ruin their plans, you thoroughly crushed them beneath your hooves while you were high on napalm."

"That hangover was so bad, Quinn. So bad. Is that orange drink you gave me magic?"

"Only in part. Once I realized you were as interested in me as I was in you, I helped make you forget all about the hangover while the medication did its work. I rather heavily influenced you."

"Oh, look. More tragedy. I got influenced by my gorgon-incubus doohickey. Not only are you the best husband, you are the best hangover cure." As he insisted on holding his bacon up where I could snatch it out of his hand with my teeth, I did so. Once out of his hold, I went to work making it disappear into my stomach where it belonged. "Meat-eating unicorns require a lot of bacon in the mornings."

"I have noticed we go through a pound of bacon a day in the morning for some reason. I think my favorite time was when you went downstairs one night while a unicorn to steal a package of bacon. You cooked it on the porch by snorting on it."

"Desperate times, desperate measures. My bacon provider was sleeping on the job."

"It was three in the morning. Why did you change into a unicorn then, anyway?"

"I got itchy."

"Itchy?"

"Yeah. Itchy. Transforming stops the itch. It takes a few weeks without transforming for the itch to start up. I got itchy, and after I popped a pill, I got hungry, so I stole some bacon and helped myself." I giggled at the memory. We hadn't been married all that long, and I'd still felt like an intruder in our home. "I've gotten better. I check to see if you're actually asleep before raiding the fridge now."

"You don't have to check if I'm awake if you want a snack, Bailey."

"But if you're awake, you're part of my snack." Well aware my remark would rile my husband up and make him hungry for more than breakfast, I took my laptop and sat on the bed so he could finish eating without falling prey to me and my wicked ways. "Once we're back, you'll have to suggest that someone go through Audrey's financials from after her marriage with you, up until her death. That might help us pin down her involvement with 120 Wall Street. Also, I really hope they don't build another concrete cake. That building always pissed me off. It's not edible."

"You thought of 120 Wall Street as a concrete *cake?*"

"It's the tiered top. It reminded me of a damned wedding cake each and every time I saw it. Then I'd get hungry, and that'd piss me off even more because I could barely afford to make ends meet, and there was no room in my budget for cake."

"I see I'm going to have to learn how to bake cakes for you."

Some women wanted roses and diamonds. I got the roses, but instead of the diamonds, I'd gotten a man willing to learn how to do new things for my sake.

No one had told me love could hurt so much as a child.

Then again, love had never been a part of my childhood. Coming to terms with that helped almost as much as my husband's willingness to be patient with me while I figured out how to navigate a world where people actually wanted me in it. I still embarrassed myself when I became emotional, but I got a little better every day about not running away and learning to face my new circumstances.

"Do you think my father would mind bringing Sunny, Blizzard, and Avalanche?"

"He seems like the type to enjoy flouting the rules as much as he can, as he views the world as his, so I don't see why not. You can also ask for advice about our kids if you want. He's been around long enough he can probably help on that front, too."

"But he's probably with my mother right now."

Quinn checked the time, and then he shook his head. "The moon set about twenty minutes ago."

My poor parents. "Tonight, don't let me go to sleep without calling my mother."

"I called her on your behalf, so don't worry. She seemed happy. You'll get a chance to talk with her tonight. You needed the rest yesterday, and you were stressed enough after the incident with the assholes."

"Think we should tell my father?"

"I'm sure he already knows, so confessing would show him you trust him. That said, if the assholes are wise, they'll never bother you again."

"Okay. I'll call him. Are Beauty and Sylvester too young for pets, really?"

"If they'd been brought up traditionally, I would say yes, but they weren't. We'll have to take some care with their snakes, but our pets should be fine. We'll have to train them and the children so everyone gets along well."

"Okay." I got my phone and dialed my father's number.

"Bailey," my father greeted. "How are you this morning?"

"I'm good. The asshole parents tried to torch the house, but they didn't anticipate Sam's overprotective tendencies and inability to handle things like a normal man. They damaged my roses, but his uncle and grandfather saved them. We're on vacation, except in reality, we're working. I wanted to ask you if you could bring Sunny, Blizzard, and Avalanche over right after we get checked out. And possibly cart off an obscene number of unicorn stuffed animals my husband bought for the kids."

"I would be honored to do that for you. I can take the stuffed animals to your little ones as well, that way they have something while they are being taught by your grandfather."

"Oh. That's a great idea. Thank you. Thank you for the suggestion about looking at Audrey before she married Sam. It was very helpful. I learned a lot."

"It was a small thing, but I am glad you found the advice useful. Your mother told me she talked to your Sam last night, as you were indulging in a nap in front of the fire. You definitely get that from me."

No kidding. "I may have jumped on the assholes' car and totaled it. I'm not all sorry about that. Sad, really. I make a lot of mistakes, but I learn from those mistakes. I've gotten smacked with a transport once, so I jumped on their car rather than in front of it."

"Wisdom reveals itself in strange and disturbing ways at times."

"Sam was telling me that gorgon whelps don't usually get pets until they're twelve or so because they can be dangerous to animals. Do you know of any pets that might be safe for them? To help teach them responsibility?"

My father chuckled. "I would be honored to handle that matter for you. With your blessings, I will discuss the matter with your grandfather, and I will introduce them to possible candidates. That will keep them amused until you have made a safe home for them. A suggestion, if I may?"

"Of course."

"Recruit your children to help you with your search. They are smart, and I can provide them with supervision and the machines they need to do this. It would help them feel a part of the hive and home."

I wondered what my life would have been like if only I'd had my divine parents rather than my asshole ones during my childhood. I would never know, but my children would find out. Changing the past remained outside of the realm of possibility, but I could secure a bright future for my children. "Can you handle that matter and tell them you're doing it on our behalf while we handle the dust and rabies situation?"

"Of course. I will recruit your mother to help as well. She is more nurturing than I am. I will come with your animals as soon as you are checked out, so that the hotel will not be displeased about animals in their facilities."

"Thank you." My father hung up before I could embarrass myself, and I set my phone on the coffee table. "My father is going to arrange for pets for the kids, and he's going to take two of the stuffed animals to Beauty and Sylvester so they have them while we're handling this matter. He'll bring Sunny, Blizzard, and Avalanche over after we check out."

"That sounds good. Go check the facial recognition database to see if you can get an identification on that man you spotted while I grab a quick shower, check over the room, and get dressed. I'll leave a change of clothes out for you so you can grab a shower while I'm making sure everything else is ready."

"Sounds good." I went to the laptop, opened the portal to access the NYPD's system, and checked on the status of my picture, which showed as complete. I clicked to look, scanning through the names of those captured in the image. I struck gold halfway through the list.

According to the notation, Alexander Hautlin was the illegitimate son of ex-Chief Morrison. Hautlin's mother had, a year after his birth, disappeared under mysterious circumstances, leaving Morrison as the sole caretaker of the boy. Rather than raise his son, Morrison had sent him to boarding school, where he'd spent the entirety of his childhood.

I wondered about Hautlin's last name. Had his mother wanted to erase Morrison from her son's life? Had Morrison known about his son before her disappearance?

"What's the matter, Bailey?"

"The guy I recognized is Morrison's son. According to the NYPD's file, Morrison had him sent away to boarding school. I don't know why I recognized him, though." I wouldn't blame Haultin for having looked annoyed.

I'd probably made a mess out of his life.

"I bet you I know who knows," my husband muttered, his tone dark. "My grandfather would have removed any memories surrounding Morrison he felt would disturb you."

"More than I'm already disturbed?"

He scowled at me. "Bailey."

I grinned. "Yes, Sam?"

"You're a wicked woman. Please marry me."

I giggled. "Considering I already told my father I'd probably make you marry me every year until we worked our way through every family tradition in our confused family lines, I suppose I must."

"You suppose?"

Smirking at him, I closed my laptop lid and headed for the bathroom. "You have thirty minutes in the shower to present your argument."

"As you wish, my beautiful."

TEN

Do you think my tendency to be
excessive comes from my father?

As promised, my father appeared, and he had all three of our pets with him. I took Avalanche from his arms, and the ocelot kitten purred and tried to nurse off one of my knuckles. "I'll give you some milk soon, little baby," I promised, setting her on the front seat and closing the door to keep her from escaping.

Sunny and Blizzard greeted me, washing my face with their cold, wet tongues.

"I took the liberty of teaching Sunny how to detect the rabies infection by scent. She will sit and bark twice if she detects the scent. Should she detect gorgon dust or bile, she will sit and bark three times." My father handed me the leashes, claiming two of the cindercorn stuffed animals from the SUV and tucking them under his arm. "I will return shortly."

He disappeared.

"Do you think my tendency to be excessive comes from my father?" I asked.

"There is no thinking involved on this one, my beautiful. I know it comes from your father. Your mother is the one who blurts embarrassing things, too. It seems you somehow managed to inherit many of their mannerisms."

"Parasite!" I sang out, and I rewarded my puppies with kisses on their noses.

"Symbiont."

"I'm definitely a parasite. I'm the best parasite. I managed to steal from the good parents, too."

"Symbiont."

We argued over which type of thieving organism I was until my father returned. Ra listened to our debate, which mostly consisted of reciting our opinion at each other while our pets watched in bemusement.

"You are both parasite and symbiont," my father announced, gathering up the bags of goodies we'd purchased at the gift shop and filling his arms before he disappeared again. It took him three trips to gather everything we didn't need so the puppies and kitten could fit in the SUV with their supplies. "You have made a good choice leaving your children in the care of a strong hive. They will be safest there. Should you contract rabies—"

I stared into my father's bright eyes. "You mean when, right?"

He sighed. "When," he agreed. "When you ultimately manage to contract rabies again, seek out alternative treatment methods. You do not wish to switch off your children's immune systems so early in their development. Make use of that archangel or his brother. Both can handle that situation without testing them so early in their lives. I recommend the highest grades of transformatives for your general transformations, as that will ease the way for your children and adapt them to shapeshifting while in the womb. By the time their nervous system develops, the process will no longer be painful for them, should you indulge several times a week for the next few weeks."

Score. "We're going to need to hit up the CDC for more pills, Quinn. I'm out of the good ones."

"Okay. Anything else we should know about her diet moving forward? How about my snakes?"

"A wise man does not interfere with a pregnant woman's desire for conquest. This is an ancient truth. Their venom will not hurt your children, and it will help them develop their immune systems. Variety, however, is encouraged. As my daughter enjoys checking on gorgon snakes, issue invitations for gorgon children to visit. This way, your children can socialize while my daughter is bitten by the various serpents of the visiting hive. That will satisfy those requirements. I have already handled speaking to the CDC regarding the appropriate napalm to be dispensed to her. Do not be alarmed when she seeks out snowbanks to nap in."

"Me? Snowbanks?" I blurted.

"You will find pregnancy is full of adventures. You have already seen evidence of this. Were you not outside with little issue?"

"This early?" I poked my flat stomach. "You two are *trouble*."

My husband laughed. "As long as I don't lose my ability to coddle my wife, I don't mind adventures."

My father chuckled. "I will leave you to your work. Try not to create more trouble than you can handle." Without another word, he vanished.

"I like that he didn't even bother telling us not to create trouble, he just asked that we keep the trouble manageable." I herded the dogs into the back, and Avalanche climbed over the center console to join her canine friends, snuggling against Blizzard's side. The husky went to work grooming her, and I took pictures of them before they could grow up on me. "Where do you think we should start?"

"With some harebrained speculations and making use of some contacts. I'll make some phone calls. Listen and take notes on your laptop. You're about to get your first real introduction to gorgon subterfuge."

"Gorgon subterfuge?"

"Yep. With the gorgons being targeted for eradication through rabies, they're not going to sit still and let it happen. Now that the gorgons are aware it's malicious rather than natural, they will defend themselves. I'm going to attempt to manipulate how they defend themselves to benefit our investigation."

My eyes widened. "Is this what you do at work all the time? You manipulate people?"

"Sometimes. Other times, I have to figure out what the greatest evil is and deal with it. For example, there are multiple mafia groups operating in New York. Some have been heavily invested in sex trafficking and enslavement. Another group is more involved with your more stereotypical local crimes and crime organizations. Which group do I dedicate the most resources on?"

"I'd *hope* the sex trafficking and enslavement group."

"Yes. That is one of the simpler decisions to make. Things get complicated, especially with highly established crime operations. Not long ago, we made use of tip-offs from a crime network in a different city to bring down a large portion of one of those rings. That's definitely a shade of gray in terms of the law, but it essentially meant I could let one fish go to catch more dangerous fish and get those off the streets."

I blinked. "Are you saying you cooperate with big-time criminals, Sam?"

"That's exactly what I'm saying. Every time we take out a ring, a new ring will start operations, and we always have to consider who will do the most evil. While we'd like to catch them all, we simply can't. And some of the criminals I've worked with are fairly ethical."

"How can a criminal be fairly ethical?"

"They pick their targets with care, do not threaten the average civilian, and keep to the spirit of certain laws. There's a good example of this in a gang in Miami. They essentially target some of the more hardened criminals the cops down there can't get off the streets. The gang's actions fit the crimes, so the cops don't tend to work too hard at taking out the gang. You don't want to be a serial killer in Miami right now. The gang takes a brutal stance against mass murdering scumbags there. When caught, they turn up. In pieces."

Ew. "But they don't get a trial."

"That's part of why the gang has been left alone. I figure they're former law-enforcement, pushed out or retired from old age. They're taking all of the general steps to prove guilt. There's no trial, but they're not just slaughtering people. Some of them are registered bounty hunters and mercenaries, too, so if there is a hit out for one of these criminals, the gang will get involved, gather the evidence, and collect the bounty, which funds their activities legally."

I got into the SUV, dug out Avalanche's bottle, and twisted in my seat to give her a drink while Quinn set up her litter box on the floorboard. The ocelot abandoned Blizzard long enough to eat before returning to her furry throne. "I'm sorry I stole your kitten."

"I'm not. I view her as a sufficient reward for you. You've earned her after having climbed into how many dumpsters rescuing sick animals?"

"A few too many," I admitted. "And there will be more. There are dumpsters I have not yet sufficiently explored in my quest to save every helpless animal on Earth."

"You can't keep them all."

"I would have to take over the Earth to keep them all." I considered the probability of successfully taking over the planet. "That seems like a lot of work. I'll practice with my new job and reevaluate my stance on world domination later."

My husband stared at me with wide eyes, his mouth hanging open.

"Taking over the planet while pregnant might be stressful on the babies, so I have to wait until after they're born at the absolute earliest. Don't worry so much, Quinn."

"Well, I wasn't worried before, but now I am."

I giggled, wiped out the interior of the bottle, and used the erasable marker to jot a note reminding me to clean it properly before using it again. "You're so easy."

"I don't know who taught you to be so wicked lately, but keep doing it."

"You know, that's a really good question. My husband, who keeps encouraging me to be more vocal and not worry about when I do stupid shit, couldn't *possibly* have something to do with it. My husband, who rewards such behavior using his sinful body, couldn't *possibly* hold any responsibility at all."

"I have done a pretty good job if I do say so myself. You should reward me for a change."

"You are so full of it, Mr. Samuel Quinn."

AFTER BOOKING a hotel for us in Maine, one that could accommodate our eclectic collection of pets in exchange for offering the other guests a chance to meet and greet with them, Quinn took over our investigation. He began his share of the work after connecting the SUV to his phone so he could call using the vehicle. "Call Thomas of the Orlando hive," he ordered.

The phone began to ring, and the sound came out of the vehicle's sound system.

"Thomas," a man with a nasally voice answered.

"It's Samuel. My bride is listening in. We have some questions for you."

"Good morning. Congratulations on your promotion, Chief Quinn."

"Thank you," I replied.

"How can I serve?" Thomas asked.

"We're technically on vacation, but we're trying to look into the rabies outbreak and the latest incident of gorgon dust production. You tend to be well-connected, so I wanted you to find out if you could approach the hives about a missing woman."

"A woman?"

"A woman. We have reason to believe that former Chief Morrison, who served in the Hamptons as part of the NYPD, may be involved with the rabies outbreak at a minimum. As I'm of the opinion the dust production and rabies outbreaks are connected, I need to find out more about who he has been working with and why. He has a son—"

"Michella Hautlin's boy. Human hatched. She was infected with gorgon dust at the start of her pregnancy, and she fled with her egg to Chicago, where she was taken in by a vampire hive. She's still in Chicago with her vampires. She's a propagator, so she can't mingle with humans. Vampires are immune to infection, as are the older incubus and succubus that work with them, so she's cloistered with them. From my understanding of the situation, an incubus recovered her egg and helped her care for him until he hatched, but he hatched human rather than gorgon. She has several children now with incubi and succubi in Chicago, although she doesn't have a gorgon male. We have been building a case to assist in your efforts, especially when word spread this Morrison, the father of the boy, might target your bride. Morrison has several daughters through other women, most of whom disappeared under similar circumstances. I suspect they are statues somewhere, but this is only speculation."

"Jesus," my husband whispered. "Does the boy have a gorgon mother?"

"We don't believe so. We are of the opinion she was infected with gorgon dust after the boy's conception, and the potency of the dust was such it partially converted her boy into a gorgon, in that he was hatched. He is not contagious, and if he can embrace his other nature, we haven't heard of it happening. I suppose he may be a hybrid."

"Alexander," I said, determined to humanize him despite my awareness he could be his father's ally. "He was at our wedding. Well, at the demonstration. I thought I recognized him."

"He looks similar to his father, an unfortunate enough thing for him. You likely spotted the resemblance. The boy often shows up where there are gorgons in public. It is our nature—possibly his. He would be drawn to a family unit because gorgons are not solitary creatures, and Morrison is not precisely a nurturing individual." Thomas grunted. "Alexander has not created any trouble for any hives, and he has made himself useful from time to time. He is known to rescue whelps from trafficking rings and returned them to their parents."

My eyes widened as the memory of

playing with the gorgon whelps flared back to life, and one of the boys had looked strikingly similar to Alexander Hautlin. "He's the boy from the time my parents tried to dump me with a bunch of gorgon whelps. Traffickers tried to grab them. He was the one who took the lead on petrifying them. But he was a gorgon, not a human."

"Perhaps the dust has made him a shapeshifter, and he wisely hides his form, much like you do, Samuel."

"That doesn't match the NYPD's record on him going to boarding school," Quinn stated, and his expression darkened. "But the NYPD's databases have been wrong in the past."

I huffed. "Or he wasn't in school when that happened. Remember, Morrison's close friends with my parents. It wouldn't surprise me if he had been in on the attempt to get rid of me from the start."

"And then he would have known about your immunities and would have wanted you for his projects. Assuming he's involved with the dust production and rabies," my husband speculated. "How does that sound to you, Thomas?"

"It sounds like your bride is wearing a rather large target on her back."

"No kidding. Remember Winfield?"

"Yes. I heard he came to a rather abrupt end."

"He pointed a gun loaded with ambrosia at me."

"Well, that was rather stupid of him."

"My bride, while in her fur coat, took offense to that. She squished him like a grape. Her words, not mine."

"I popped him like a grape. But he was also squished. He deserved it. It was his fault. If he hadn't threatened you, he would have survived for at least five more minutes. And that gorgon. Well, maybe not. He looked at you wrong."

"My bride becomes very offended when rival males look at me wrong. It makes enrolling her into challenges quite difficult. We try to leave the other contenders alive," my husband said in an amused tone.

"I better get to fight at least once, Quinn."

"Not until the twins are born and you are no longer breastfeeding."

I shrugged, as I couldn't see myself seriously fighting when worried about their milk supply. "That's reasonable."

"You are expecting twins?" Thomas asked.

"We are. Fostering your children won't be a problem. The chances our children will inherit her general immunities or my general abilities are rather high. Beauty and Sylvester are currently with my grandfather learning how to socialize with other gorgons. Their education has been unique. If you can, begin teaching yours how to read a little early, as our whelps are voracious readers. You may want to inquire if your whelps would like to learn how to cook, as Beauty will be starting as soon as we move into a new home. Ours is not sufficiently sized. We'll also have pets in the house, so we can work with your whelps on that as well. Sunny, my wife's wolf, should be capable of handling defensive whelps, but our other pets are mundane in nature."

"I will begin their lessons immediately. When would you like to begin their fostering?"

"Bailey?"

"As soon as we have space for them is fine with me."

Quinn smiled at me before focusing his attention back on the road. "I'll get back to you on that as we start our house search. Do you have a contact we can reach in Chicago about Miss Hautlin?"

"Yes, of course. I will text you with the information, and I will warn him you will be calling. I have a relationship, as he sought out my advice regarding her. She misses humans."

'Bailey?"

"There is no reason we can't take the kids to visit her and her family, especially if she can help us sink Morrison."

"I think you will find her an eager participant in your investigation. She hates him with a burning passion. She only gave up her son because she was terrified she would infect him."

That poor woman. "But he's already

gorgon enough he won't be infected, will he?"

"It would be a mercy for him to be infected. He straddles two worlds without being welcome in either."

Damn it. No wonder he had looked annoyed. The poor man likely wanted what we had, a caring family and a sense of belonging. "The chances he's allied with Morrison? There are pictures of him with his father and Quinn's ex-wife."

"His hatred for his father is an equal for your love for your husband, I suspect."

Huh. "Damn. He'd light him on fire while still alive and screaming, and he'd take his time about it while roasting marshmallows, then."

My husband snickered. "I love you, too, Bailey."

"I can help him with the fire part. I'm really good at making fire, and my father said I need to transform several times a week to keep the babies happy and healthy."

"Your father?" Thomas asked. "Surely not that Gardener man?"

Sam laughed. "No. Ra. Her other father. She's the daughter of a quartet. It might be worth informing the hives that her divine parents are very protective. Her mother is Menily, a moon goddess. A guardian divine from a tribe somewhere in the western United States, from the little I know about her."

"I will pass the word. Her father being Ra

explains much, especially about her willingness to engage in challenges for whelps. It is
her nature."

"She does like conquering. Mostly me,
though. Oh, well. So much tragedy."

Thomas laughed. "Continue your con-
quests without fear, Lady Quinn."

"Oh, look. He thinks I'm a lady. Boy, do I
have him fooled."

My husband snickered. "What can you tell
me about the Chicago vampires?"

"Ernesto Saven."

With a low groan, Quinn took one of his
hands off the wheel and rubbed his temple.
"You have got to be kidding me."

"I'm sorry, Samuel. I know you dislike
when you must deal with him."

"Do you know what happened the last
time I had to talk to him?"

"I believe he asked if you would work his
brothel for a few weeks, to overcome the
grief of your divorce from that woman. He
sent you flowers and a succubus, although he
did not request the succubus seduce you,
from my understanding of the situation."

"She hugged me, because Ernesto is convinced there are no circumstances in which I
would strike a woman, so I had to deal with
accepting his affection. The succubus loved
tormenting me. She left without doing anything nefarious beyond insisting she hug me
every other damned minute. Making up for
my ex-wife's lack of affection, in her words."

I burst into laughter, as I could easily imagine my husband being grumpy a succubus was attempting to comfort him. "Sam? At a brothel? He'd die of mortification before he made it through the door. He's an angel, Thomas. A real one. He's just a little naughty sometimes. And anyway, his snakes get nippy, so they'd have a lot of bodies at the brothel, and that wouldn't work well at all."

"A little naughty?" the gorgon asked, his tone a mixture of amused and astonished.

"It's the black wings. They suit him. He's shy, so he doesn't pose as often as I'd like. But those snakes of his are nippy, randy little bastards."

"She processes their toxin in a unique and fully beneficial—for her—fashion," my husband muttered.

If Thomas kept laughing so hard, I worried the gorgon would perish. Even his snakes joined in, hissing a storm.

"Let me guess. They are a stimulant for her."

"Of a variety," my husband replied in his most dignified tone. "Saven is really the vampire?"

"He is. Do you think other vampires would be so willing to take in such a danger?"

Quinn heaved a sigh. "No. You're right. I'll call him. I have his number unless he changed it on me again."

"I will leave you to that, and I will begin calling around other hives for more information, especially in terms of seeking out others who were infected with gorgon dust. Hautlin is the only known propagator, although she is not the only victim."

"Talk to my grandfather about the victims. It will help him feel useful in his retirement, and it's an effort he can get behind. I'll deal with Saven and see about integrating that poor woman with some hives and at least have her be able to visit with others."

"On it." Thomas hung up.

Quinn grunted. "Call Ernesto Saven."

The phone rang three times before an amused voice answered, "Well, well, well. If it isn't Police Chief Quinn. It has been a long time since you have graced me with your company."

My husband rolled his eyes. "Mrs. Police Chief Quinn is with me, and you're on speaker phone."

"I had heard you acquired a treasure. A good day to you, Mrs. Chief Quinn."

"I thought vampires slept during the day."

"I am old, and the sun no longer bothers me as it once did. Has she been bitten yet to check her resistance, Samuel?"

My husband muttered curses. "Not yet, but if you were to bring the gorgon lady in your care to my residence, I'd permit you to see how Bailey reacts to vampires, but not until after the birth of our twins."

I narrowed my eyes, wondering what my husband was up to.

"I see congratulations are in store. Excellent. However, I had not mentioned my lady to you. How did you learn of her?"

"We are investigating the production of gorgon dust and the utilization of rabies as a weapon. We stumbled upon her son, and the NYPD records stated his mother had disappeared. I inquired with a gorgon, who directed me to you, mentioning your lady is cloistered. As my wife cannot be infected with gorgon dust, she can do no harm to me, and our children should inherit the same abilities as my wife and I, it might be prudent to arrange visitations so she can socialize. Her children would likewise be welcome."

"I have tried to suggest she mingle with the established hives, but she is frightened. She thinks they will blame her for another's sins."

"Well, I'm hoping to make that problem disappear completely. I'm tired of fetching my wife out of dumpsters to rescue rabid animals. It costs me a fortune in treatments. Add in that two of our children, who are gorgon whelps that we adopted, lost their entire hive to this mess…"

Silence fell, save for the steady clicking of a pen. Ernesto sighed. "I loathe when the machinations of men make the young suffer."

"As do I."

I kept quiet, wondering what other secrets I might learn about the vampire with more compassion than many men.

"You want information from Michella."

"I want to hang Morrison from the rafters," my husband growled. "After cutting him open and allowing crows to feast on his entrails."

Ew. "That is gross, Sam."

"Warranted, however," the vampire said. "Let's barter, Samuel."

"I'll bite," my husband announced. "Remember that NY mafia group annoying you?"

"With unfortunate clarity."

"Task force reassignments happen at the end of January, and I will leave a note for my wife informing her they deal in human trafficking and the illegal, unwilling sex trade. A pregnant, cranky cindercorn in charge of said task force will give you the results you want in a rather short period of time. If anyone can ferret the bastards out, it's her. In exchange, you will help us eradicate the dust producers and find the source of the rabies outbreak. Be careful with your gorgon, Saven. They've been infecting feeder mice."

"Feeder mice? Interesting. We do not feed her snakes feeder mice. She has milk snakes. They prefer worms, so we just go above at night and dig for her if our supply is low. In a pinch, we will go to a bait store, but that is rare."

"She has no venom? How is she with petrification?" Quinn asked, his tone sharpening.

"Her ability to petrify is practically non-existent, but she is highly contagious. If you have someone who wishes to become a gorgon, you go to her. But she lacks the defenses of other gorgons. Even her bile is impotent."

"Damn it. How does she infect someone if her defenses are nil?"

"Blood transfer, like lycanthropy, or extreme contact to her bile. It takes a lot of bile to pass on the contagion, however. Her snakes can infect her victim as well, so she's not precisely without all defenses. When her snakes bite, it takes several hours for the infection to take hold, after which petrification occurs. In a week, the new gorgon will reverse to flesh. None of those she has infected are contagious."

"How many has she infected?"

"There is a hive of twenty members who have undergone the process. They were all willing."

"Snake species?"

"Kingsnakes except for the male. He has Oenpelli pythons."

"Never heard of them."

"They are endangered and may go extinct. They are found in Australia. They're constrictors. His snakes are gray, but sometimes they change colors somewhat."

"How are his petrification abilities?"

"The hive is aware of its weaknesses and hide. I will have them tested for rabies and treated as necessary. They do use feeder mice and rats. I helped them get supplied from local pet stores."

"Good. If they are not infected, get them vaccinated."

"There is a vaccine for gorgons? For rabies?"

"Yes. They dislike being treated as animals, but after seeing hives wiped out, most hives are vaccinating against it. They started a few weeks ago. If Chicago doesn't have a supplier for the vaccine, call the CDC and put in the request. They will send a nurse, and you will need to give them the count of gorgons needing to be vaccinated. If the hive has a surrogate, she will need to be treated."

"The hive has an arrangement with my succubi as needed."

"How is their reproduction rate?"

"The females produce one or two eggs per clutch, and their survival rate is fifty percent."

"That's low."

"I'm aware. But the whelps that do survive are healthy, at least so far as we can tell. They have five, ranging in age between a year to three years old."

"Have they been socialized?"

"No."

"Gorgons are social, Saven. My grandfather can educate the hive's male, and Michella can socialize with my family, who is at no risk of infection. There's no reason she can't socialize with other gorgon hives as long as the hive's bride isn't present. There is no reason to isolate her."

"She isn't isolated. Her company just isn't

at risk of infection, nor are they gorgons. She
has been invited to meet with the hive she
helped to create, but she did not ask to be the
way she is now."

"You think Morrison forced her?"

"I know he forced her."

"He is to be put on trial as it is, so if you
can provide evidence and submit it anonymously to the CDC, that would be useful."

"The CDC? Not the NYPD?"

"CDC. My wife is involved with the
charges."

"I see. I have some contacts. I can ferret
out more of his wrongdoings that can be
filed. Limitations may be an issue."

"Do what you can."

"I shall. Are there any other matters you
wish to discuss, Chief Quinn?"

"Actually, yes. I'd like you to do some digging on the Gardeners. My wife's human parents. More importantly, I want to learn about
their involvement with Morrison and if they
might be related to these incidents. Anything
you can dig out on them, I want it. Submit
any illegal activities anonymously, please."

"As you are helping mine, I will help
yours. I'll be in touch," the vampire promised
before hanging up.

"And that is your first taste of the murky
waters of law enforcement," my husband announced. "How did you like it?"

"I'm feeling a little cranky, honestly. That
poor woman!"

"This is a case of embracing the enemy with morals we know rather than encouraging unknown entities. Ernesto is a lot of things, but he fits a specific place in the criminal world. If his operations were to stop, who would take his place? Better to have a cooperative enemy we know than an unknown entity filling the void. Ernesto plays the game well. He toys with the police where he lives often. It's a game for him. But there are some things he just doesn't do, so he remains."

"And how does that sweet little angel side of you like him?"

"Honestly? I'd let him babysit the kids. No one would reach them with that vampire on guard. That hive he's caring for? Probably the best defended hive in the United States. When he gives his word, he means it. That's what I like about him. Sure, he's a crook, but he's an interesting crook with morals. I can live with that. Would the FBI sink him if given a chance? Or the CPD? Or the NYPD? Sure. But that's part of the game. You'll get used to it."

"I will?"

"You will. If Ernesto decides he likes you, he'll come visit, like it or not," Quinn replied in a rueful tone.

"When was the last time Ernesto visited you?"

"About two months before the 120 Wall Street incident. Don't be surprised if we have a fanged visitor, and he enjoys toying with his prey, so he'll have some fun with us before he raids our kitchen and complains I don't stock the right ingredients for his culinary adventures. That time, I swear he brought half his brood, and they all love annoying me."

"Why do I have the feeling I'm going to like this vampire?"

"You are pure evil and enjoy my suffering, that's why."

"And yet you can't get enough of me."

"It just happens the pure evil who enjoys my suffering is beautiful and perfect for me. It's a burden I happily carry. But you are definitely being evil today. If you like Ernesto, I'll have to let him into my house and act like I like it, and that ruins the fun."

"You like making him think you hate him, don't you?"

"Absolutely."

"So he comes back to visit because you play pretend that you hate him."

"Basically."

"Are you saying you like him and act like you don't so he'll come visit you?"

"That sounds about right."

Men. "You're an idiot."

He laughed. "Love you, too, Bailey."

Shaking my head, I resumed my search for the clues that might lead us to where we needed to go and put an end to the rabies and gorgon dust threats once and for all.

ELEVEN

Have I ever told you I love it when
you're being sneaky?

I COMPILED a list of addresses based on
Audrey's receipts, and we began our search at
one she'd visited several times before her
marriage to my husband. The navigation
system in the SUV had trouble locating the
address, but with a little help from an actual
map, I found the place at the end of a long,
winding road in the mountains of Vermont.

According to Audrey's files, the last time
she'd visited had been five years ago, and
judging from the decrepit state of the bed and
breakfast, she'd been among the last of the
guests to visit it. Had I not known better—if I
hadn't seen so many gorgon statues over the
years—I would have believed the pair of
women flanking the road had been art.

"We didn't bring neutralizer, Quinn." The
oversight annoyed me, especially as I owned
an obscene amount of the sparkling substance. "Do you think our relatives will kill us
if we keep asking them to carry things

around for us? You know, super powerful divines relegated to fetch duty. I bet they could wave their hand and make all of these problems of ours disappear, and we use them to teleport our pets and stuffed animals around."

My husband stopped the SUV between the statues and got out of the vehicle, careful to keep from banging his door into the woman.

Someone had dressed her like a Greek goddess before petrifying her, and her expression implied she'd been drugged with something, probably pixie dust, to force her cooperation. The clothes, likely through some form of practitioner magic, endured the elements.

Most petrification victims had startled or disgusted expressions depending on which defenses the gorgon used. I followed his example, careful not to lose my puppies or kitten or damage the statue nearby while getting out. The ocelot pounced on the statue's feet.

Sunny sat down and barked three times.

I rewarded her with a pat on the head. "Good girl."

"Bile or dust," my husband stated with a scowl. "Her nose must be really sensitive to detect it from the stone."

As I didn't want Blizzard or Avalanche to be exposed, I put them back into the SUV and kept Sunny on a short leash. "Call the CDC and request a delivery of neutralizer. There's no way of knowing how long these people have been like this, and I'm the most qualified to get them safely reversed back to human without potentially spreading more of the contagion. And however much I like your gorgon-incubus doohickey form, I know you're shy. I'll scout the place with Sunny while you get a team here. Make sure we have jurisdiction. Just tell them we were visiting blasts from the past. That's not a lie. We're just visiting someone else's past is all."

"Have I ever told you I love it when you're being sneaky?"

I smiled despite the severity of the situation. "No, not really. I'm not usually the sneaky kind, am I?"

"You're really not. I'll take care of getting the neutralizer and help for the vics. Take your gun, unleash Sunny, and let her guard you."

I retrieved my Glock, checked over the weapon, and set Sunny's leash on the hood of the rental. "Stay close, Sunny."

My puppy obeyed.

Someone had gone through a lot of effort transforming the bed and breakfast into a garden filled with statues of women posed to be Greek goddesses, and one of the victims was a gorgon, one who'd been killed before being turned to stone, one of the human women posed in triumph with a sword, heavily rusted from exposure to the elements.

Dark, old stains marred her clothes, and a

few tears in her modern shirt revealed where she'd been stabbed through the chest. The stone beneath preserved the killing wound.

I took care not to touch anything, walking around the building and counting victims before returning to my husband.

He hung up his phone while I approached. "It'll take an hour or two, but a team is on the way. What did you find?"

"A murdered gorgon. She's been petrified, and one of the women has been posed to coincide with her statue. I believe she was petrified after she'd been killed. All the clothes look to be in good condition, so probably a practitioner helped with that. The sword is probably the murder weapon, and one of the statues is holding it."

"Damn it. How do you know she was murdered?"

"There's a big hole where it looks like she was stabbed in the chest, and the stone is likewise damaged. It's near the heart, so it was probably quick. Even as a statue, she looks pretty dead to me."

"All right. Step one is to fully photograph the scene. This place has been abandoned long enough there's no chance in hell we'd get any useful footprints, but try not to walk anywhere else you haven't already been to limit the damage to the site. Take pictures of everything, and I'll show you how to upload them as evidence into the system once we have a few moments. Get a good face shot of all victims, and we'll try to do a black and white facial recognition scan. It looks like this got significantly more complicated than it already was." My husband let out his breath in a gusty sigh. "It's as good a time as any for you to start learning the ropes."

"I never thought I'd say working with bombs seemed a lot easier than this." I dug in the back for my holster, strapped it around my waist, and stowed my Glock before arming myself with my phone. "Whose bright idea was it to make *me* a cop again?"

"Personally, I'm grateful Clemmends had it out for you and wanted to dump you with the NYPD. You have far superior co-workers now."

That I did. "What a dick. You should have let me light him on fire and shove our marriage license down his throat, though."

My husband chuckled while he made his own preparations, which included arming himself and zippering up his new bulletproof jacket rather than show off his resilience against the cold. I pouted over his ability to tolerate snow and the brisk wind better than I could, regretting I hadn't gotten a scarf, gloves, and the little things that helped make the outdoors during the winter almost bearable.

Within twenty minutes, I'd freeze my ass off, and I deserved to be mocked for my failure to plan accordingly. "Hey, Quinn?"

"What is it?"

"I need scarves and mittens and gloves and a cute little hat to keep my ears warm, assuming I survive this. Winter is bad for cindercorns. There's no fire. No fire anywhere. I'm going to turn into a block of ice before the team gets here."

"Check the back of the SUV in my black leather bag. I anticipated your special needs."

Huh. I really did have the best husband. I checked the back, and sure enough, there were several pairs of black leather gloves that would fit me, several scarves, and a winter hat meant to keep my poor ears warm. I bundled up, muttering over how phones were evil and I'd have to wear the pair without fingertips in order to take the needed pictures. "We need an actual camera, one that doesn't need me to touch a screen to operate."

"Normally, we have one as part of our work kit, but we'll get one of our own just in case. Until the team arrives, you'll survive using your phone."

"But will I?"

"You better."

THE GORGON WAS the only victim I believed to be dead, but I struggled to comprehend how seventy-three women had been left as statues for so long. Fortunately, none of the statues seemed weathered, which offered some hope they would survive being returned to flesh. While I took pictures, Quinn handled running the facial recognition software while keeping Blizzard and Avalanche company in the SUV.

When I finished documenting everything I could, I returned to the vehicle to watch him.

"Have I told you today you're beautiful and smart?"

"Not sure," I replied. "I could probably handle being told again. I haven't had time to recruit the entirety of a mental health department to resolve my self-esteem problems."

He snorted. "You're smart and beautiful. I wouldn't have thought to go this far back in Audrey's records despite having them, and I probably wouldn't have thought to come to some little bed and breakfast, as I would have assumed it was just yet another location of one of her trysts."

"It looks like a lot more than that. What have you found so far?"

"A lot of missing women, the newest of which is six years ago, so they've been here a while. The oldest is from eleven years ago."

"Long before you married Audrey."

"Bingo. The real question is how do these women connect to Audrey or Morrison? If they connect to them. They might not. However, considering Audrey became a gorgon and killed her brother when he refused to go through the process, I'm starting to think this is far more than a mere coincidence."

"Audrey had weak snakes, too. Like Michella."

"And she was just as impotent, so that tells me that the batch of dust, while registering as high potency to the scanners, didn't have sufficient magic to create strong gorgons. Perhaps it's got a higher infection rate?"

"Easy to infect, hard to destroy." I wrinkled my nose. "Which supports my general decision to torch 120 Wall Street. I really thought Yale would kill me for that stunt if the CDC didn't get me first. In other news, that hangover *really* sucked."

My husband shot me a glare, which promised retribution in some form or another. As his favored form of retribution involved trying to convince me I had value, I expected to enjoy every minute of it. "Without your napalm order, a huge number of weak gorgons may have been created, and they would have become easy targets for gorgon trafficking—and they would have become excellent pets for the wealthy. They would have fetched a high price on the black market."

"They wouldn't have been able to defend themselves." I regarded the nearby statues with a frown. "How many of these women do you think were infected?"

"None of them. They would have reversed their petrification on their own if they'd become infected. Whoever did this probably dosed them with pixie dust to make them cooperative, had them pose, and then exposed them to the gorgon dust to see if they would become infected. Infection rates are typically low. But, considering there were at least two infections from this batch of dust, it's not the normal one-in-a-thousand rate."

"But why kill the gorgon they had? Do you think that one was infected, too?"

"No, she's probably a natural gorgon. Gorgon males are usually the ones killed and used to create the dust, so she would have been killed for sport or to force the male to cooperate. The females can get quite vicious trying to defend their hive, and she wouldn't have been useful to the dust producers." My husband shook his head, checking something on his laptop. "Honestly, I'm impressed we have reception at all out here. I'm not getting any hits on the gorgon, so chances are the entire hive was wiped out. The hive was probably small, with one male, two or three females, and no whelps. Hives with whelps tend to be poor targets for schemes like this because the male will fight to the death along with the females, and they want the males alive."

"But they just need the bodies for dust production, right?"

"The most common method of dust production involves the gorgon victim being alive at the start of the process, and then the decaying body used to strengthen the dust. It *is* possible to make the dust from just the bodies, but the dust is typically impotent and incapable of infecting others with the virus. You can view that type of dust as potent bile. If they took a male, they would have killed his females first to demoralize him before they began the batch of dust production—or held them hostage to force himself to be a more willing sacrifice."

"Like that gorgon prince where we killed Audrey." Technically, Quinn had done the killing, but I'd been there causing trouble, so I accepted my share of the responsibility for his ex-wife's demise.

"Exactly right. He wouldn't have done that unless he was trying to save his bride, his wives, and his children. That much of his sacrifice didn't go to waste. He lost his wives, but his bride and youngest whelps survived—and his sole surviving daughter."

"The little whelp was his?"

"Yes, from his previous hatching. She's with her grandfather's hive now."

"Do you think she would get along with Beauty and Sylvester? They have a lot in common."

"We can inquire for fostering. And yes, they do. I'll call about fostering her after we're back and we have a chance to talk with Beauty and Sylvester."

"Maybe we should have requested napalm."

"They're bringing a few cups for you. They'll have you purify the statues with flame before we use neutralizer on them. You'll torch the entire exterior, and then we'll do an investigation of the interior. They're going to dome the building so you don't light it on fire, and they'll do a secondary dome around the garden so you can be a happy little pyromaniac. Hopefully, you can neutralize this batch of dust without harming the victims."

I had my doubt on how effective that would be, but I would do my best. "Should I shift now?"

"If you want. You can poke around while sporting your fur coat if you think you won't get too cold. And if you do get too cold, I'll enjoy warming you up tonight."

"Can you warm me up tonight even if I don't get cold?"

"That was my plan," my husband admitted with a shameless grin.

"Gorgon-incubus doohickeys are not precisely complicated to care for, which is a good thing, as I'm not sure I could deal with a high maintenance man. I only have lower grade pills with me."

"They're bringing a supply of the high grade pills, so don't worry about it this once. It's not that you can't take the lower grade transformatives, the higher grade ones are just better. But at this stage? You can get away with a lot—or so says my grandfathers. All of them."

"Has anyone told you that you have too many grandfathers?"

"On occasion."

"I have more grandfathers than you do, so I can't really say anything. But we have too many grandfathers."

"We really do. Try not to light anything on fire before the CDC arrives, but if you went inside and had a look while a unicorn, you shouldn't do any harm. Just don't step on anything that might be evidence."

"You could ride me inside and tell me what's evidence and what isn't evidence."

"I didn't bring your saddle, Bailey."

"You don't need a saddle to ride me. You're not going to hurt my back."

"I was less worried about your back, truth be told. Your spine is more pronounced than a horse's underneath all that fur, though I wonder if you being at a healthier weight has helped with that."

Oh. I thought about that, and I winced at the thought of a sharp spine to the groin. "You're right. You're banned from riding bareback unless it's an emergency. Should such an emergency occur, I will have to nurse you back to good health. We should check and decontaminate the statues first, anyway. If we have time, then we'll investigate the building."

"To be fair, I'm not really a fan of riding regular horses bareback, either. Saddles are useful things."

"I don't know how to ride a horse," I reminded him.

"You'll learn how to ride on a cindercorn, I'm afraid. I'm very jealous, and I don't want my wife riding a horse when—"

I lunged across the vehicle and clapped my hands over my husband's mouth. "We do not pervert my future horseback riding lessons with your gorgon-incubus doohickey naughtiness!"

My husband laughed and kissed my hands. When I released him, he said, "Okay, my beautiful. I will try to limit my jealousy and inquire with my uncle on how to shapeshift into a regular horse, too. Especially when you're first learning, I'd feel a lot better if I'm playing at being a horse rather than put you on a school horse. Some of them have opinions."

"If you say so."

WITHOUT ANY OTHER sources of fuel to work with, I ate an obscene amount of underbrush before running around the garden and bucking to elevate my body temperature enough so I could begin the tedious process of checking the victims for anything of use before burning the contaminated clothing off them and prepare them to be treated with neutralizer and returned to flesh. My husband joined me as a cindercorn after locking our pets in the SUV with the window cracked open and the engine running so they'd stay toasty warm while we flirted with dust contamination.

I suspected the dust had been exposed to weather for long enough Sunny had detected the residual scent, which in such low concentration wouldn't be able to petrify most people.

"Pretty stallion," I observed after having lit several statues on fire enough to destroy the contaminated fabric. "Remind me to thank uncle. He make you pretty stallion."

"Well, I am part incubus, Bailey. The whole point is to be irresistibly attractive."

"Ir-res-ist-i-bly attr-act-ive, all for me. Like this math. Other math suck."

Quinn laughed. "I'm sorry he hasn't helped you with your English, though."

"So rude you talk good."

"I know. You can punish me later over it."

I bucked, careful not to hit one of the statues. "Much punish!"

"You are such a one-track mind."

"Your fault you gorgon-incubus doohickey."

"I don't mind taking the blame for this situation."

Of course he didn't. He enjoyed whenever I became frisky. Or friskier. Could anyone blame me for falling for his charms? I couldn't be blamed for falling for perfection. "Just no show other lady-ees your per-fec-shun. Comp-e-ti-shun bad."

"You're so jealous." Quinn nipped my

shoulder. "Show me how to help so I can be shapeshifted back to human before the CDC arrives, especially if you don't want to share me with others. I'm pretty sure half of the CDC's evaluators are women."

"Check clothes, light clothes on fire, but not big fire. Little snort. Little snort ignites clothes. Several little snorts may be needed. Big snort might hurt statue. Stone okay against little snort, might melt in big snort."

"I'm going to need some help with this, Bailey. Show me a big snort so I know not to do that."

I eyed a large patch of snow a safe distance from the statues, charged it, and exhaled, snorting a large burst of flame at the patch, which sizzled and evaporated in the intense heat. I then gave a small snort, which was enough to ignite the air in front of my nose without sending a big column of flame billowing at the ground. "This little snort. That big snort."

"That is a very big snort," my husband agreed before giving a little huff, which was like my little snort but smaller.

"A little harder, not much harder," I prompted.

He obeyed, and he gave a little snort with the appropriate amount of flames to light the clothing on fire.

"That good, do that on statue after nosing through the fabric. We look for things not cloth. Like sharp pointy things. Or wallets."

"For some reason, I don't think we're going to be finding any wallets, Bailey."

"Can dream."

"Sure, my beautiful. You can dream. The facial recognition system is working on the photographs now. We might have results before the CDC gets here with the neutralizer."

We made it halfway around the house, taking turns torching the statues, when my husband came to a halt, turned his head, and snorted flame at some snow in a big enough cloud I recoiled, flattening my ears. "What? What?"

Quinn snorted again before turning his attention to one of the statues. "I know her."

Shit. "Guess no need to look at com-pu-ter then. Who is she?"

"She's one of Audrey's friends, the daughter of a New York senator. Her name is Kendra. A nice enough woman, tends to prefer a vanilla way of life, but she was always pretty open about practitioners, general magic usage, and even pixie dust usage, so she's not precisely like your asshole parents."

"How long Kendra missing?"

"I wasn't aware she was missing. She doesn't live in Manhattan, and while she was a friend of Audrey's, I didn't see her often. Please be careful with her. She's nice enough —and her father is actually a pretty decent man for a politician."

"You get praise from politicians for this," I warned. "You dislike praise from politicians."

"Hey, you actually said that without having to sound it out carefully. Good job, my beautiful. See? You're already getting better with English with practice."

"You bad in-flu-ence."

"Bad?"

"Very bad," I replied in my most solemn tone. "Naughty, even."

While my husband chuckled and re-warded me with a nip on the shoulder, I took care of checking Kendra's clothes for any-thing important and flammable, discovering a pouch tied around her wrist. "Find thing!" Careful not to gouge her with my teeth, I gnawed through the leather and dragged off my prize, clawing through the string until I could peek inside.

The smell informed me I dealt with gorgon dust. "Rude! Dust. No gorgon-in-cubus doohickey ex-posed." I picked the pouch up in my teeth, went to a deeper patch of snow, and set the pouch down. "Both make big flame on it. Big flame make it go away. Big snort. Extra big snort. Actually, me make biggest flame. You watch, admire my biggest flame."

My husband joined me, pawing at the snow-covered ground with a clawed hoof. "Use that column of fire you eliminated that gorgon with," he suggested.

"Must run fast and get hot to do extra big fire. That is biggest flame? May-be."

"I will make sure the pouch doesn't escape while you go run."

I tore off and did several circuits of the garden before skidding to a halt near my husband and blowing as much flame as possible at the pouch. Blue fire burst from my nose and engulfed the pouch, which vanished in a flash of white before the blue overtook it and eradicated the pouch and reduced its contents to a fine powder. "Pow-der!" I pranced in place and snorted more blue flame. "All gone, now ash."

"I'll shift and bring Sunny to see if she can detect any dust," my husband said before trotting off in the direction of the SUV.

I snorted more flame at the smear in the smoking ground. "Dust no like blue flame!"

"Better safe than sorry," my husband retorted.

I pawed at the ground before eyeing Kendra's statue. "You make shit choice in friend. Audrey no good. Me introduce you to nice people, you do better next time. Me better friend than Audrey."

The statue didn't reply, and already bored waiting for Quinn to return, I rolled on the ground and kicked my hooves. When that didn't help alleviate my boredom, I played in the snow to learn if cindercorns could build snowmen.

To my dismay, hooves did not work well for packing snow into vaguely ball-shaped objects, although I could make ice statues using little snorts of fire on the piles of snow I made and carving it with my claws. By the time my husband returned, in his human form, I'd crafted a small ice sculpture of a cindercorn.

Well, if I tilted my head to the side and squinted, my artwork almost resembled a unicorn of some sort.

"What are you doing?" my husband asked, keeping a firm hold on Sunny's leash.

"Bored, bored, bored," I complained, shoving more snow into a pile so I could try to carve another ice sculpture. I snorted little flame, waiting for it to partially melt and freeze over before layering on more snow. "Sunny no bark!"

My puppy sat and regarded me with one ear flicked forward.

Damn. Even my puppy recognized I was more than a little crazy.

"That's a good thing. Apparently, pregnant cindercorns are rivals of phoenixes for heat and flame generation. I'm not going to allow them to study this, for the record."

"Left no dust for them to study." I snorted, checking to make sure my flames no longer glowed blue before resuming my work checking the statutes. I discovered no more pouches, and I took care to be gentle with burning away the clothes covering them. "No be per-vert. Go to car and not look at pretty women not me. Cuddle pets. Make CDC bring me pink pow-der."

"I think everything will be okay. Come on, Sunny, before Bailey gets jealous enough she bites chunks out of me. I'll see if I can get an identification on any of the other victims and look into Kendra's case, assuming there is one."

"Good luck. Enjoy in-ter-ro-gay-shun later. Ex-wife stupid."

"That she was. Be careful. If you want to roll around in any other snowbanks, do so near the SUV, please."

"I check statues, do more flame to make sure extra safe. You stay out of dust, Queeny!"

"I'll be careful," he promised.

TWELVE

That sad. Beating gorgon
males fun.

THE CDC ARRIVED before I could investigate the decaying bed and breakfast. I sighed, staring at the convoy of vans, water tankers, and trucks destined to make a mess of my day. After ten such vehicles parked behind our rental, I opted to hide in the nearest snowbank, doing my best to burrow into the snow.

There was not enough snow on the ground for me to hide well, and I sighed at the unfairness of it all.

"Bailey, what are you doing?" my husband asked.

"Hiding."

"I can see you."

"Hiding," I repeated, and as he could wear flame at his whim, I huffed in his general direction. My flames didn't even come within a foot of him, which earned me a raised brow. "Hiding!"

"Bailey, you're being ridiculous again."

"Kick snow. Help hide."

"I'm not burying you in snow, Bailey. The last thing I want is you getting sick because you decided to become one with your worst enemy."

"Mean!"

"Chief Quinn?" an older man asked, approaching us. The suit stood out compared to the other sensible CDC folks, who wore protective gear.

My husband sighed and turned. "That's us. We've already dealt with at least one source of gorgon dust, and we have burned the clothing on all of the statues to remove any remaining residue. We're both immune to dust, but you will want to use a high sensitivity scanner to make certain we have destroyed all remaining sources. We have not gone into the building yet."

"Excellent. I'm Alan, and I'm an FBI-CDC liaison. I see your wife has already made use of transformatives. We have a note to provide a higher grade? I only had a short briefing, but I was asked to request her assistance with any bile or dust removal."

"Normally the lower grades are fine, but she's pregnant, and the higher grade is better for her and the babies."

"Babies is plural. Twins?"

"Twins. Shapeshifting is also good for them, and she's to be rationed napalm, and her immunities need to be used so our children properly develop them as well." My husband smiled, crouched beside me, and scratched under my chin. "It seems pregnant cindercorns appreciate snowbanks. Her internal body temperature seems higher than normal, too. She was snorting blue fire after a short run around the gardens so she could dispose of the dust. One of our dogs is trained to detect dust, and she couldn't smell any when she was finished with the contamination."

"Interesting. Would you consent to non-invasive testing? Honestly, we haven't had any records of a cindercorn foaling in over a decade; the surviving cindercorns, outside of yourself, are very old and are no longer of breeding age as far as we can tell."

Huh. I'd known the wilds were in trouble, but I hadn't thought they'd been in *that* much trouble. "That sad."

"I'm all right with non-invasive testing, but only if you reward her with a cup of napalm afterwards for good behavior."

I had the best husband, and with a happy sigh, I rested my head on his foot. "Queeny best."

Smiling at me, my husband patted my shoulder. "All right, my beautiful. We have to work for our supper, and the sooner we handle this, the sooner we get to our hotel for the night."

"Why did you come here, anyway? This is pretty remote."

"It's somewhere my ex-wife liked, and I

wanted to show it to Bailey. She's often curious about my life before I met her. We weren't expecting this at all. We have one positive identification on a victim, though. She used to be a friend of my ex-wife's, although judging from the situation, that friendship has expired. I was unaware Kendra had gone missing. Audrey hadn't mentioned anything. Here's the bigger problem—"

Huh. My husband could lie with the best of them, and if I hadn't known better, I would have believed him.

"Wait. Kendra Thames? The senator's daughter? There was a note that she had a relationship with Audrey McGee, and that was in the files I was reading over on my way here."

Well, that rabbit hole was a deep, dark place—and it worried me that the FBI or CDC had already begun investigating Audrey's connection to others, like the poor woman stuck as a statue. As my big mouth would make a mess of things, I nosed at my melting snowbank, sighing over my general misfortune.

The one time snow didn't bother me, my hot coat made it go away.

Quinn scratched me behind one of my ears, and I focused on enjoying his affection. "One and the same. Her statue is intact, and my wife has taken care of the base cleaning. Between the two of us, assuming the weather hasn't done irrevocable damage to her statue, we should be able to restore her. I have the facial recognition software trying to identify the rest of the victims. There is a gorgon who was mortally wounded before petrification. There is a slim chance she was petrified before death, but it would take an intervention to save her if she's still alive. We may want to deal with her first."

I nipped Quinn's ankle. "May-be alive?"

"Maybe, but it is unlikely, and if she is, it would be very expensive to get the care to keep her that way. That damage is lethal."

"We ask angel, we pay bill? Too much tragedy. May know things? Don't want to kill her. Thought maybe already dead."

My husband sighed. "I love your compassion, Bailey. We can ask, but even if we're willing to pay it, she may be too far gone to save. It may not be our choice."

"It's worth inquiring," Alan said, digging his phone out of his pocket. "In cases like this, angels sometimes refuse payment, but as you're willing to pay the bill, I see no reason to not ask. As you say, she may know something—and I won't kill someone unnecessarily, either."

"Sad if we let her die, Queeny."

"I have no problem if you want to spend your money that way, Bailey. It's your money. But if we end up with a gorgon who lives with us for a while because she has no hive, I don't want to hear any whining."

"She become second mom for our whelps

until we find her hive," I countered. "She be like house sitter. Live-in maid gorgon! Oh, oh, she can be a live-in nanny. We have many gorgon whelps needing a gorgon nanny to help care for them. We have many pets, need extra hands. Then we ent-ter-tain gor-gon males who be good hus-band for her. We be guardians for her until she fly from nest to new hive. Like a grown child we feed and care for."

My husband laughed. "All right. If you want to try that, and she can be saved, we'll take responsibility for her. And whelps around are good for gorgon women, so that'll help ease her transition. We have no idea how long she's been a statue."

"Or why she made statue." I sighed, lurched to my hooves, and shook the snow out of my coat. "Sad for gor-gon. We give her hugs and pur-pose."

"Just be aware there will be a lot of gorgon males coming to interview her if we do this, and you can't tell them all no because you're picky. She does get to decide which hive to make her home."

"But can we beat the males?"

"That's not how it works."

"That sad. Beating gorgon males fun. Gorgon males durable."

"I see your wife's reputation of causing trouble with gorgons is not unfounded," Alan said.

"Don't worry about it. She loves gorgons.

She's even forgiven my idiot cousin, although she'll probably give him a hard time for all eternity because she finds it amusing."

I did, and I bobbed my head to accept responsibility for my general inability to handle life like a normal adult. "We help gorgon first?"

Alan tapped on the screen of his phone and held it to his ear. "I have spoken to Mr. and Mrs. Chief Quinn about the situation, and it seems there is a gorgon female who may still be alive but is critically injured. They have offered to pay the bills for angelic intervention if it is possible to save her, and they have offered to take responsibility for her until she can be placed with a hive." Alan spent several long minutes listening. "All right. I'll handle the rest of the situation here. One of the victims has been identified by Mr. Chief Quinn, and it will close a rather old and complicated case. We will need a full FBI team for this. It's definitely a crime scene, and there are a lot of people in need of assistance. Bring a lot of clothing, blankets, and perhaps a bus."

"Maybe two buses," I said. "Many statues."

"Ah. Mrs. Chief Quinn suggests two buses, as there are a lot of victims. That may allow them to have space if needed. Send three just to be sure. I'd rather have three quarter-filled buses than create additional problems for the victims. Send some nurses and ambulances in case they're needed. I'm going to begin my walk around while the practitioners seal the building so we can make sure the victims can be removed before we purify the zone." Alan hung up. "We've already gained authorization for the use of napalm as needed, and we have the tanker if we have to make the high-intensity grade. We do ask you attempt to limit how badly you become intoxicated on it, Mrs. Chief Quinn, especially with the number of victims we have to work with."

"Should not need much nay-palm. Site old, only one source contained dust so far. Should be okay. One cup bribe for good behavior nice?"

My husband chuckled. "You'll do just about anything for napalm, won't you?"

"So good! No blame me."

"And on that note, I'll go get the meters." Alan left, heading for one of the vans parked behind our rental.

"Think angel save gor-gon?"

"Well, I think even if the angel can't, we know if there was a way, we would have. You'll go to bed knowing you did your best."

"What we do with gor-gon if she live?"

"That's easy. I'll call in someone to teleport her to my grandfather and our whelps, and they'll integrate her with his hive. She looks too young to be a candidate for his hive, so he'll be a good temporary guardian while we put an end to Audrey's schemes."

"Too bad Audrey dead. Kill her again. And again. Bad Audrey."

"Do you need therapy, Bailey?"

I flicked an ear. "Therapy in bed?"

My husband sighed. "I meant actual therapy."

"But why would you do that to some poor therapist? What therapist do to you? Would need army of therapists to fix me. Don't need. Could use bed therapy?"

"And you call me insatiable."

"Is your fault. You good and warm and nice and stuff." I bobbed my head and gave myself another shake. "Much stuff."

"Is that all I am to you? Good, warm, nice, and *stuff*?"

"Yes." I whinnied my laughter and trotted after Alan. "Check our babies."

My husband obediently headed for the SUV to check on our pets while I followed after the FBI-CDC liaison, who talked to several people in protective gear at his van. "Do meter reset before testing for this dust. It is hard to scan, use clean meter. Set highest setting. It high potency, but odd. We think high infection rate but weak actual potency. But it shows high potency on meter." I pricked my ears forward at my tongue's cooperation. "Sorry for talk strange. It hard. My Sam better, but he shy."

"Yes, we were made aware he can shapeshift to be a cindercorn for your amusement due to his incubus genes, although he is not one whereas you are."

"I weird. Good par-rents make me cindercorn, but I cindercorn because an-cess-tor also cindercorn! Comp-lee-cay-ted."

"According to your file, you're com-plicated."

I whinnied. "True! Ask hus-band. He con-firm. I comp-lee-cay-ted. If you worried about dust, I carry meter by strap and check."

"Actually, I'll take you up on that. This model of scanner can create a map of the zone you scan, and you can just walk with it, and it will record the area around you. It will have a ten foot range, and it's smart enough to be able to handle overlapping zones, so you can just take a walk and get a full scan."

"It dee-tect statues?"

"Yes, it will pick up the magic on the statues."

"I walk while you do tech stuff. Will take time, explore whole garden."

Within a few minutes, Alan set up the scanner. Rather than make me carry the meter in my mouth, he strapped it around my neck. "Ignore any beeps and alarms and keep walking. It's designed to keep you from step-ping in dust, but as you're immune, should you be contaminated, we'll fill up a bucket of napalm for you and have you go on a run and burn it off. If you're producing blue flames without napalm, you won't have any trouble decontaminating with a little of your favorite barred substance."

"I go find dust! I no roll in dust, but I find it so I get nay-palm."

"I'd prefer if you found no dust, honestly."

"Already find dust once. Destroyed that. Dust here, find where."

"I hate that you're probably right."

"Am often right, but I sad I right. Dust bad. No burn statues more. Crystal coffin if needed, but no burn statues more."

"We'll do our best for the victims," Alan promised.

ACCORDING TO THE METER, the building was a gorgon dust nightmare, and it would be flooded with napalm, lit on fire, and reduced to ash before the sun set. As the only being capable of going into the building without facing some sort of mishap or another, I was volunteered to handle the search.

The pesky CDC reps wanted to know what was inside the building before they restored the humans to flesh.

Muttering curses that made my husband laugh, I trudged into the structure armed with multiple cameras, several of which were tied to me, including a pair around my barrel. I wanted to gnaw through the straps and rid myself of them, especially as they'd been secured tight enough to keep the cameras from shifting. The cameras amused me, as they were attached to stabilizing arms to make certain those outside got a full view of the building before I destroyed it.

I made it all of ten feet inside before I found the first gorgon corpse, likely a female judging from the earrings beside her grayed, decaying body. According to the meter around my neck, she was a source of at least one dust contamination. "Ew. She all rotted."

Rigging a headset to a unicorn took some work, but they'd sent me inside with one, and Quinn sighed. "That's dust decay—not quite the same as the dust we're worried about. While it can cause petrification, the probability of it causing an infection is nil. Rather than putrefaction, gorgons erode down to a dust-like state following death."

"Female magic less potent, make less potent dust?" I guessed.

"Essentially. Some females are strong enough to be candidates for dust producers, but most humans have no idea how to identify it—or process a female's body into dust. That's something gorgons would rather not have studied."

"Duh. No want to be ex-per-ee-ment. Me feel this way, strongly."

He grunted. "Right you are. They're going to start erecting the shield to keep the dust around the building before giving you a good napalm supply. Try not to get too drunk this time, and try to stay outside of the building once it starts to collapse. Do your full walk-through. If you find evidence we need to recover, we'll set up a crystal coffin inside the shield and have you place the objects inside for decontamination."

"Okay." I made use of a claw to poke through the gorgon's clothing, finding a decaying leather purse with a wallet inside. After some work, I uncovered several credit cards and her identification. "Have cards. See on camera?" I did my best to position myself so the camera dangling around my chest could get a good view of her name, her picture, and her relevant information.

"We have it," he confirmed.

"Not even bother to take purse. Just leave her on floor." I pulled her clothes away from her body to reveal broken bones in her chest, similar to the statue outside. "Like poor woman outside, but truly dead. Stabbed in chest. Bones broken."

"I see the damage," my husband replied. "Keep going."

The stairs creaked under my weight, and I flattened my ears at the thought of plunging through the weakened wood, but I made it to the second floor, discovering five more gorgon females, all dead from traumatic damage to their chests. "Why kill them like this?"

"I don't know. It's definitely weird."

Like with the other bodies, they had their purses with them, and I dug for their identification.

Not all of them had gorgon listed as their

species. "Dust change, they murdered after change?"

"That's definitely a possibility. I don't know why they would kill them after going through the trouble of infecting them, though."

"No co-op-er-ate. Like me no co-op-er-ate with stupid bitch."

"That's possible. Audrey lacked patience on a good day. And considering she was less than sane by the end *and* rabid, it is what it is. Get the identifications you can, and the CDC will notify any living relatives."

"Sad no burial."

"I know. It's just too dangerous. Look for any paperwork while you're up there," Quinn ordered.

All-in-all, someone had done an excellent job of cleaning the place out, leaving nothing but bodies, empty rooms, and decaying furniture. I checked every room, and in the bathroom of the largest bedroom, I discovered a gorgon male, and the meter squealed a warning. "Oh. Poor male."

He'd been left bound after death, and someone had beheaded his serpents. Dust filled the tub around him.

"And that's the real deal. Alan is processing the meter data now to see if we can get a match on the 120 Wall Street dust—and the stuff that'd been in your apartment. They did a full sample diagnosis on the stuff out of your apartment before destroying it, and the meter reports from 120 Wall Street indicated it was the same batch, so if this matches, we'll have some damned good evidence. Does he have his wallet?"

"Don't see wallet. He in rags, very rotted. Tied up. Why do that to his poor snakes?"

"I don't know."

Fuckers. "Want to find bastards and burn them!"

"I know. Chances are, the women you found were members of his hive, which should make it possible to identify him. Go finish checking the building, then we'll light it up and help the rest of the victims."

I sighed, did one last circuit of the upstairs and ground floor before heading into the building's basement.

Save for a rusted metal cage filled with bones, it was empty.

I examined the skeleton, pondering at the skull shape. "Big dog? Wolf?"

"Likely a wolf," my husband replied. "Too long dead to be of use for us telling what killed it."

I placed my bet on rabies. I did a circuit of the basement to discover decaying scraps of paper. "Oh, paper!" I nudged them with my claw until the camera, with some help from the flashlight, could snap video of the text. "Very sturdy receipts. For big dog food, rodent food." I nudged the pet store receipt out of the way, uncovering several invoices for medical equipment beneath the dust. "Oh, this weird."

"Flip it over to see if there is anything on the back," Quinn requested.

I obeyed, discovering handwritten notes about disease progression, eating habits of several test subjects, and some cryptic notes involving months and days but no years listed. "This very weird, Queeny."

"It is. Check for anymore papers. The CDC is getting nervous, and they want to get onto the napalm portion of your day."

"They no hurt statues?"

"The statues close to the building have been safely moved, and an angel has arrived to assist. I fear we've been sent an archangel that's not my grandfather, and the archangel is rather miffed. It turns out archangels have zero problems with picking up statues and moving them to a safe location. Without magic. Everyone has been thoroughly intimidated. He's seen the gorgon, and she's been moved a safe distance. Judging from the blindfold being carefully tied into place and the hoods for her serpents, he intends on saving her."

At least there would be a little hope amidst the tragedy. "Thank angel for me."

"I'm sure we will, with our wallet or some form of horrific bargain."

"Archangels bargain?"

"When it suits them."

Ugh. "Naughty angels, always making

trouble." I explored the basement, but I found no more pieces of paper. "Want paper in coffin or let burn?"

"Let it burn. We have what we need on video record. The neutralizer would ruin it anyway, and there's enough dust in that building to become a major problem if it isn't destroyed. Try to stay outside of the building when it collapses this time, my beautiful."

"I try, but no make promises. May not keep. Nay-palm's fault. It tay-stee."

"Just try not to give me a heart attack this time, Bailey."

"That promise can make. Will try best!"

"That's all I can ask for when it comes to you and your favorite treat."

THIRTEEN

Cindercorns are not supposed to like being wet.

I LIMITED my napalm consumption to enough to make my coat burn and ignite the thick, sparkling gel.

It seemed wrong to indulge while at the equivalent of a funeral.

It took me less than five minutes to ignite the napalm, and I helped reduce the building to ash and rubble with the help of a few larger snorts, which did an excellent job of flash-frying the structure so the napalm could do its job better. None of the CDC's equipment survived the inferno, which burned blue-white until the napalm finished its work. Unlike in New York, there were no tones, and the CDC wasted no time hosing the rubble down with neutralizer.

I listed my enjoyment of being sprayed down as a perk of early pregnancy, and I snapped my teeth at the spray whenever it came close. Taking a firehose of neutralizer to the chest knocked me right over, and I snorted my shock the blast had managed to do more than thump into me. Whinnying, I pawed at the barrier to get at the naughty stream.

The archangel joined me inside, and he laughed at me. "I have been asked to check on you, as cindercorns are not supposed to like being wet."

"Want!" I replied, thumping my shoulder into the barrier to get at the hose.

"I can see that." The archangel vanished, and a moment later, I got my wish, and several hoses smacked me at full blast. I rolled around in the pink, sparkling fluid, which steamed around me.

Being wet worked so much better when my coat refused to cool down.

Once I had a nice puddle to keep me amused, the CDC resumed dousing the smoking building until they switched to regular water to continue cleaning up the site. The shield dropped, and I bounded into the snow, dropped, and rolled.

The snow melted, and I lunged to my feet for a deeper patch to cool off my coat.

My husband approached and observed with a raised brow. "Are you feeling okay?"

"So hot," I complained, doing my best to burrow into the snow-chilled ground. "The babies make me insane, like cold?"

"You were already insane, Bailey."

Oh, wow. I stopped and stared at him. "Oh, that burn *good*. Reward you later."

He smirked. "Love you, too. Are you ready to shift back to human? If so, they'd like to confirm you burned the dust out, and they have a big blanket for you so you don't get chilled while getting dressed."

"Big blanket so they don't get show, you mean."

"That may have factored into things. I've been told I'm unreasonable when it comes to you."

"Yes, that right." I rolled to my hooves, braced, and shook out my coat, which steamed. "I did good, only had few bites of nay-palm."

"Much to the astonishment of the CDC. Then again, after the second chomp, your fur went blue-white hot and the napalm began combusting when it came in contact with you. They are speculating pregnant cinder-corns run as hot as phoenixes."

"Me the best cindercorn."

"That's not hard when you're the only cin-dercorn below the age of several hundred to a thousand years old. Or so says Alan."

"I young like filly!"

"Come on, my beautiful. They want to scan you and check your temperature before you shift."

I trotted over to Alan and pranced at a safe distance while he played with his meter before holding it out. I tested a snort to dis-cover I blew blue-hot flames still. "Use area scan. No meter survive that hot. I melt it.

Over two thousand degrees because blue not orange."

Alan nodded, adjusted the meter, and held it in my general direction. It remained silent. "Great job, Bailey. Stand still while we try to get a temperature check on you. Snort when I hold up my left hand, please."

I waited for his signal and snorted on command, pleased with how hot my flames remained.

"You're exhaling at just below three thousand degrees. Your internal body temperature is higher, and your coat temperature is moderating to a safer ninety degrees. If that isn't magic, I don't know what is."

"Cin-der-corns best unicorns."

"Just agree with her," my husband suggested.

"I'm having a difficult time coming up with any reason not to," Alan admitted, and he retrieved a blanket from his van. "Once you're changed and dressed, the archangel wants your help with the gorgon. Wear clothes you don't mind having to burn. He has informed us she will be defensive."

"I just wear blanket," I announced. "No ruin nice clothes with bile and blood. Yuck."

"Can't say I blame her. If you get some rope, we can make cleanup a snap." My husband tossed the blanket over me. "Try not to roll in the snow while human. You won't like it nearly as much."

"Pets okay?"

"They're enjoying a nap in the rental. Fortunately for us, the CDC has spare gas with them, so they'll fill up our tank before we leave."

"Run out of gas would suck."

"Yes, it would."

As there was no such thing as privacy when a full CDC team was in attendance, I forced myself to reverse back to human, a process that went faster and better than I expected. As warned, I didn't like the cold nearly as much as when a cindercorn, and I jumped into Alan's van to escape the snow. "Fuck! Shoes, Sam! Shoes!"

My husband dared to laugh at me. "I told you that you wouldn't like the snow nearly as much when human."

"I already said I'd reward you later."

Alan handed me a pair of rubber snow boots and several pairs of socks. "You'd be upset if you ruined shoes you actually liked, so ruin these. Those have already seen more than any one pair of boots should ever see, so they would appreciate being retired."

"Poor boots." I pulled on the socks and stuffed my feet into the boots, which were several sizes too large. "And now that I'm oddly dressed, let's get this show on the road. It's going to take all day to deal with that many statues. Time's wasting!"

THE ARCHANGEL PRESSED his hand to the gorgon's wounded chest, and the stone re-formed until no evidence remained someone had stabbed a sword through her. "I cannot take the memory of her injury from her while she is stone, and doing so might erase what you need to learn. As such, she will be hostile. I will do my best to limit how much damage she can do, but I can offer no more than that."

"You've done so much already. Thank you."

"It is an honor. It is rare we can help like this. Most simply do not ask. She is not human."

"But she didn't deserve this."

"No, she did not. And that is why I can help. Your willingness to pay for the work was also a key factor."

"Right. How much do I owe you?"

"Nothing. It was your willingness to do so that mattered. It would unbalance things if we were to require payment, for you will have paid too high of a price for what you do now and will do in the future. You have made her life your responsibility, and that is a far higher price to pay than any money."

"Is that why Beauty and Sylvester were saved?"

"Their father would have paid far more than he had, and they were all he had left. But yes. The money their father paid will find its way back to his children, for we knew even then he would not live long beyond their survival."

Oh. "But you, as in your fellow angel who saved them, couldn't say that. So you took the money knowing what would inevitably come?"

"Yes. Please do not cry, for it will alarm your husband, who does not handle such things well."

"He really doesn't." I sighed, double checking the hoods on her serpents, her blindfold, and doing a full inspection of her statue to make sure there was nothing else wrong with her. "Alan?"

"Yes?"

"What's the best grade pixie dust you have on you?"

"We have the good stuff."

"Give me a vial and make sure everyone stays out of the way. If she's too happy to see straight, she'll be a lot less likely to harm anybody. You should get lesser grades for the rest of the victims, too. We may as well make this as pleasant as possible."

"That ploy will work well," the archangel stated.

I tapped my temple. "Sometimes, I remember I have a brain and decide to use it."

Alan headed off for his van at a jog.

My husband sighed. "I'm going to the SUV until you're done. Make sure they decontaminate you thoroughly. The last thing you need right now is me on a pixie dust high."

"Wait. What? No. You take that back, you fiend. I absolutely do need you on a pixie dust high."

The archangel's laughter chimed. "However much I like your grandfather, I am siding with your wife on this one. She is very deserving of you, should you be under the influence."

I smirked. "See? Even the archangel agrees with me."

Muttering curses, my husband stomped off towards our rental.

"He's just mad because it's a felony, no matter how much he'd enjoy me committing a felony tonight. Really, Sariel got to him a little too young, making him such a goody-goody. It's just a little felony!" I hollered at my husband's departing back.

Alan returned carrying a metal case, which he handed to me. "It's not a felony if someone in the CDC gives you the sample for your use. Since you didn't go on a napalm bender and did such a good job with the dust removal, I see no reason I can't slip you a vial of some dust so you can enjoy your husband's company tonight. I'll give you one grade below the best, so he might stand half a chance of remembering it in the morning."

Hah. "You and I are going to get along just great."

"They told me you were difficult. I suggested they just failed to speak your language. I figured a reward system might work, and considering your husband's special genetics? I could be talked into adding a line to your file that you're highly motivated into being able to use samples of high-grade pixie dust on your spouse in recreational fashions following testy work like dust removal to limit the consequences of your exposure to napalm."

"Hold that thought." I took the case, popped it open, and whistled at the selection of dust samples available. The vials of the top-grade dust alone could enslave the entirety of a football stadium. "Damn, they sent you over here prepared, Alan."

"I have another case just like it locked in the van, and I also have sedatives and ambrosia in case they're required. We will not discuss the phoenix feathers we brought just in case."

"It's like the CDC learned from its mistakes. I'm impressed." The last thing I needed was to set loose another phoenix and be responsible for more mass destruction. For some reason, where I went, things became either irrevocably broken or lit on fire. I plucked out one of the highest grade vials, giving it a shake to check on the pixie dust's consistency, which matched my expectations. "How close to the moon am I sending this gorgon?"

"All the way there. That's fresh from one of our most potent contacts, made this week."

I whistled, as even trace amounts of the

dust would be enough to enslave somebody—or turn my husband into a sex fiend. "I'll just keep the empty vial for my amusements tonight if this stuff is that fresh. That little should make him able to remember it. Maybe."

"I'll make sure you have the right neutralizer on hand so you can keep your husband somewhat contained."

I smirked, observing my husband open the SUV door to be pounced upon by a wolf, a husky, and an ocelot. Somehow, he kept the animals from escaping, although I worried they might lick his face off by the time they finished with him. "It seems he's being disciplined by our pets for leaving them alone in the rental for so long. Deserved. All right. Time to get to work. Make sure you have neutralizer on hand. I'll need a low enough grade of neutralizer it won't neutralize the pixie dust while reversing petrification for this."

"I've a batch about to expire with me, and having heard about your general inclination to use near-expiring batches, you can even take the bag with you when you leave in case you need it. You have a habit of finding trouble."

"I really do."

With Alan's help, I dragged the fifty pound bag of neutralizer over to the statue, held the vial of pixie dust between my teeth, and mixed the neutralizer with some water to create a paste. Normally, people worked head down to begin the process, but I smeared the neutralizer between my hands and started with her feet and legs, giving her a brisk rub to begin restoring her to flesh. When I made it to her chest, I popped open the vial of pixie dust and shook it out on her face before dumping the rest of it over her head.

Unfortunately for me, very little of the dust remained in the vial, and I sighed over my misfortune.

"I'm not sure that's the appropriate handling of pixie dust," Alan observed, backing a safe distance away. "Also, I commend you for somehow managing to get it all out of the vial. I'll provide a proper vial for your evening entertainment, as that little left won't do anything to anybody."

No kidding. I sealed the vial and tossed it on the ground before taking the neutralizer scoop and burying it. "It's perfectly appropriate. It's all in her nose, so once she starts breathing, she's not going to feel a damned thing. Just don't try to give her snakes a kiss until she's gotten cleaned up. You'll be fine."

"I was not planning to give her snakes a kiss."

"Just get permission before you kiss them. The little bastards like attention. We'll have to check their venom sacs once she's somewhat coherent." I resumed spreading neutralizer up to her neck to beneath her chin, pleased when color began returning to her cheeks. "Showtime."

As I didn't want to be covered in gorgon bile, I got out of the way and waited.

Within a few minutes, she stood on her own, and her snakes reared back, hissing their discontent. The gorgon breathed, and within moments, her body relaxed and she sat on the ground, swaying back and forth. The swaying worried me, and I regarded the archangel with a frown.

"Don't worry. Between the influx of divine magic and the high dosage of pixie dust, she is a little sleepy. That will fade in a few minutes. She should be coherent enough now for you to speak with her and remove her blindfold."

Alan handed me a pair of sunglasses, and at a curt order, everyone turned so they wouldn't get a dose of her gaze.

I took care with removing her blindfold. "You'll be all right," I promised, carefully untying the blindfold and putting the glasses on her. "What's your name?"

"I'm Annie," the gorgon replied in a sleepy voice. "I had a bad dream."

I cringed. "Well, the bad dream is over. There are humans nearby, so you need to be careful with your snakes and your gaze, okay? If you feel sick, let me know."

Gorgons couldn't really control their bile production if they were truly startled, but like humans, I'd learned they could get sick, too.

Their vomit just took a hell of a lot more work to clean up.

"I feel okay. Better than I should. What a horrible dream."

Damn it. I wanted to lie to her, but I couldn't bring myself to do it. "It probably wasn't a dream, but you'll be okay now. Were you part of a hive?"

"Oh, no. That's when the nightmare began."

Okay. If she wanted to insist it had been a nightmare, I'd work with that. I sat down in front of her, and I began the tedious work of removing the tiny blindfolds from her snakes, who joined Annie in her pixie dust haze. "How did the nightmare begin?"

"Humans stole me from my father's hive. I was old enough my father no longer kept as close of an eye on me, and I stayed home one day when he took my younger sisters out. I was old enough to stay at home alone. My father hadn't found a new hive for me yet, but he showed me favor by leaving me alone. It was my first time."

Poor Annie, although I couldn't help but feel relief the tragedy wouldn't worsen.

It hadn't been her hive to die.

While it wasn't much, I'd cling to the silver linings I could.

"Can you tell me your father's name and where he lives?"

Annie frowned. "He's Father. But I can tell you where our hive lives." To my surprise, the address was in a mid-sized town we'd passed through on the way to the bed and breakfast, a quaint little place I hadn't expected to be the home of a gorgon hive.

"Alan?"

"I'll inquire," he replied, heading off to his van.

"My father will not be happy. I'm too old."

I grunted. "Don't you worry about that, Annie. My husband will speak to your father about making arrangements. Were you old enough to help care for your younger sisters?"

"Oh, yes. Father taught us early."

"Well, that's perfect. I'm fostering some young whelps this summer, and you can help take care of them until you're settled and some nice gorgon men have a chance to meet you." I expected she'd get an offer fairly quickly, as the males would want to garner favor with Quinn regarding Beauty.

I sometimes hated gorgons as much as I loved them.

"But you're human."

"I'm immune, and my husband is the son of a rather human gorgon king."

Her eyes widened. "You are a bride of the Quinn family?"

I stood and pointed at the SUV. "You are so much trouble, Samuel Leviticus Quinn!"

Apparently, the SUV had a window open, as my husband got out of the vehicle and strolled over, and our pets romped through

the snow with him, all wearing their har-
nesses and leashes. "What did I do now?"

"Does every gorgon on Earth know about
you and your wicked ways?"

"Well, I'd say not on Earth but definitely
around here." My husband chuckled, staying
a safe distance away. "Introduce me to your
new friend."

"This is Annie. She was stolen from her
father's hive. Alan is trying to contact him."

"I better go help. Stolen, you say?"

"She says she was."

"That'll make this easy. Check over her
snakes. At least one or two of them need to
bite." Quinn pointed at one of the serpents,
who sure enough, had bulging venom sacs.

"Oh, your poor snakes." I cupped the ser-
pent's head in my hands and examined her.
"I'm immune, Annie, and we don't have a kit
handy, so it's okay to bite me. What type of
snakes are these? I haven't seen them before."

"Kraits. They're venomous."

"I'm immune, so let's get your poor babies
dealt with. What sort of toxin?"

"Neurological, which induces paralysis.
I've only had one test done, but my father was
worried because I can kill humans quickly."

"Well, don't you worry at all. I'm a champ
at this, and your babies can't be comfortable."
To encourage her, I tapped my finger to the
snake's snout, and after a few encouraging
prods, I earned a bite. "There you go." I pet
the snake with the other hand. Once she let

go, I gave another nudge, and the second bite came faster and harder. It took four bites for the venom sac to empty enough for the snake to be comfortable.

I'd feel that later, although to my relief, her venom didn't induce immediate itching.

Most of her snakes needed two or three bites to clear out their venom sacs, and I wondered how long she'd been held hostage without her snakes being able to bite that so many of them were in such discomfort.

I assigned all blame to Morrison, and I'd add in a few extra kicks or stomps if I ever got a hold of the bastard.

"That feels a lot better," Annie admitted after I finished becoming the dumping ground for her snake's venom. "You are really a bride of the Quinn family? But you do not look like the bride."

"Ah. Audrey. Let's just say she's a cheating bitch and landed herself a divorce for her inability to stay loyal to a man who cannot tolerate disloyalty."

"Vile," Annie muttered.

It amused me the gorgon had such deep feelings over loyalty to be cranky over it while under the influence of the best pixie dust on Earth. "I agree, but it's no concern. Audrey won't be bothering anyone again."

"No? But she…"

Hello, intel. "But she what?"

"She had plans. She wanted me to help with them, because I was an unwanted gorgon female. I refused. That's when the nightmare ended. She ended it." Annie touched her bare chest, which lacked any evidence she'd been stabbed with a sword. "Oh. I thought she did."

No, she had. "Audrey stabbed you? Is that what you're trying to say? Or shot you?"

"Stabbed. She had a sword. She said all who failed to do as she wished would fall to her sword. She was a little crazy. She claimed she was the new queen of the Quinn hive." Annie giggled. "She had no idea the Quinns were even gorgons. She spoke of them as if they were all human. That confused me."

"What a fucking moron," I muttered.

"I didn't correct her. She seemed unhinged."

"That she was." I made more of the neutralizer paste and went to work cleaning the pixie dust off Annie's face. "You were badly injured and turned to stone, which saved your life. One of the CDC's representatives is trying to get a hold of your father, but I'm fairly well versed with gorgon customs at this point, so you'll probably go home with me in a few weeks, and in the meantime, I'll ask one of the Quinn hives to have you as a visitor. Sam and I adopted two whelps, and they're learning how to survive better, as they had odd schooling. You'll join them for now." I eyed the archangel. "Do you accept contracts to teleport?"

"I can offer you teleportation services as

needed for this situation, as it would be uncaring to not make certain the healing has fully restored her. I can also send word to Archambault Quinn about his impending guest and her circumstances so he can make preparations."

"If you please could, I would appreciate that."

"It shall be as you ask." The archangel vanished.

"Did I die?" Annie asked.

"No, you didn't die. You were just hurt really badly. Everything will be better now."

That much I could promise.

EVERY TIME I thought I understood the depth of gorgons, they managed to surprise me.

If I were to judge gorgons by Annie's father, there was no species on Earth more capable of love or grief. I hated keeping them separate while Quinn did his best to comfort the distressed male until they could be reunited.

Detoxifying her of the pixie dust took time, as did making certain all of her snakes were healthy. Once I finished my work, I wrapped her in a blanket and handed her over to her father, who wept and held her as though she were a child.

I guessed, to him, she'd always be his little girl despite the culture that demanded he send her off to a new hive now that she'd grown into a woman.

My husband ignored any potential risk of pixie dust contamination to kiss my temple. "Your left hand looks like it went through a meat grinder."

"Her poor snakes all needed at least two or three strong bites, and they were in pain. And they pack a punch, so we'll have to be careful. I assumed she was infected with rabies, so I gave her the first dose of neutralizer while handling the dust contamination. My hand will be fine in a day or two. You'll just have to amuse yourself pampering me, as I'm temporarily unable to use my left hand for much."

"Good call on the pixie dust, by the way. If she'd been distressed when her father showed up, it would not have ended well."

"I may have some intact skin still on my left hand if he needs to bite to work out his nerves."

"He'll be fine. He'll take her home for a week, and then we'll take her to be with Beauty and Sylvester until we've handled our business here. I'd rather send her to my grandfather now, but she's her father's first born."

"Oh, that poor hive."

"He learned the hard way why we take the precautions we do. He gets the right kind of closure, which you'll find is a rare enough thing in our line of work. Normally, we do not adopt every victim, so don't get into that habit."

I scowled. "I don't see why we can't."

"Bailey."

Damn. I loved when my husband growled at me.

"We need to deal with that other woman. Kendra," I said, determined to give the gorgon some time to comfort and protect his daughter. "How long do you think it'll take before he calms down enough he can be approached?"

"At least an hour. The CDC can handle him. This is more familiar territory, as the CDC is often who rescues gorgons from trafficking situations and handles reuniting them. Of course, this is different from normal, but it's familiar enough territory for them."

"All right. I'll start with her, and we'll see where we get. I bet she didn't want to cooperate with Audrey, got exposed to gorgon dust, and joined the statue garden when the dust didn't infect her."

"I'm not making any sort of bet, mainly because we'd be betting on the same thing, and that doesn't make for a very satisfying wager. At least she'll be easy to deal with."

"Really?"

"I wasn't really friends with her, but she was sensible enough. At least she had been when I'd known her. Had I known she'd disappeared, I probably would have started looking through Audrey's files to see if I could find anything, though."

"And ended up Audrey's gorgon plaything," I muttered.

"However much I love your jealousy, you don't need to be jealous. Even if she'd snorted gorgon dust and become one before our divorce, I still would have divorced her. And because gorgon law is far stricter than human law, she probably wouldn't have survived the divorce proceedings, because gorgons do not cheat. Not in that sense. Gorgons are polyamorous, but they're loyal to their multiple partners. I just can't handle that sort of lifestyle, especially because gorgons will change loyalties fairly often."

"They're loyal while engaged in a relationship, but they'll shift relationships often."

"Right. That doesn't really work with me."

"You don't say?"

My husband glared at me.

I smiled.

"Okay. You win. I love you, my beautiful. Try not to turn our house into a menagerie more than it already is. Remember, for every species we bring into the house, we have to be certified and trained in their care."

"That's so weird. Like, we can produce humans, gorgons, cindercorns, or possibly others, and we don't have to be certified for them, but the instant we adopt a wolf, we need to be certified. Wolves are easier than humans or cindercorns. Feed them, don't let them eat people. Treat for rabies as appropriate. Cuddle or avoid cuddling as required."

"It does bother me, at least a little, that we are somehow qualified to care for young, defenseless tiny humans, gorgons, cindercorns, and some others without certification, but wild dogs with a domestication problem require certification."

"It's the domestication problem." I shrugged. "I like certificates. I have many. I collect them. And for some reason, people keep putting me in classes and expect me to collect yet another certification. I am the queen of certifications."

"You really are."

"I'm not certified to be a cop yet, yet here we are. For some reason, people expect me to go to work and do cop stuff starting in January. You should make me flash cards to teach me how to be a cop. I'm not ready to be a cop. Unless you're putting me on the bomb squad. I was born ready to be on the bomb squad. I get so many delicious explosives when I work on the bomb squad."

"You also get shot. From my understanding of the situation, in the ass."

I frowned, thought about the times I'd gotten shot, and realized I had stopped a round with my rump at least once. "Right. They give me fancy gear to protect my head and important bits from bullets. They didn't have a lot of spots left to shoot me after that. I mean, somewhat. If a bomb went off, the gear didn't last long. But that *usually* didn't happen."

"That usually not happening implies it did happen."

"Well, explosions just annoy me a little. Don't make such a big deal out of it. It's just a few bombs."

"We're going to have to have a talk about your enjoyment of bombs."

"I wouldn't call it an enjoyment. We just have an explosive relationship, and it tingles nicely."

My husband sighed.

KENDRA THAMES HANDLED her freedom from petrification better than most of the victims. I believed there needed to be limits to how calm and collected someone could be upon learning she'd lost years of her life to her friend's treachery. She wandered through the gardens while the CDC kept an eye on her and I finished helping the other victims.

Quinn stayed at our rental, waiting until I finished my dirty work before bringing me clothes so I could change out of the blanket, which I tossed in a pile with other contaminated materials destined to be burned.

When Kendra spotted my husband talking with me, she approached and said, "You picked a really shitty woman to be your wife."

I twitched, scowled, and put my hands on

my hips, staring at my husband while waiting to see what he would do.

"Her shitty behavior played a major factor in why I divorced her. Had I been aware you had gone missing, I would have had this place looked into a lot sooner."

Did my husband like or hate the woman? I couldn't tell. He'd seemed concerned when he'd identified her, but he'd gone icy cold.

"Really." Kendra looked my husband over. "Never thought I'd think this, but the years have done you wonders. Damn, Sam. You're looking good."

That earned her a raised brow. "Thank you. Anyway, I'm not at all responsible for what Audrey did, but I would have worked to resolve your disappearance had I known. As you may not have noticed, love had nothing to do with our marriage, which ended in divorce after I gathered sufficient proof she had been cheating on me. Anyway, she's dead."

"Finally bit off more than she could chew, did she? What finally got her? I'd guess one of her jilted lovers—or her main fling. Not you, that is. You're one of the good chiefs, and you don't play that game."

He did, but unless my husband informed her of his heritage, I'd keep my mouth shut.

Well, mostly. If she ticked me off, I'd have to start blurting something about his prowess and hope she got uncomfortable enough to leave.

"She opted to become a gorgon, and she

kidnapped someone else's bride. As such, she was put to death according to gorgon law. Let's just say she wasn't bright, and she got a better end than she deserved."

Kendra sighed. "I told her not to fuck around with gorgons. Gorgons make our worst laws look like child's play. She said she'd come up with some way to almost guarantee someone becomes a gorgon, and she wanted to test it on me. I refused. She tested it anyway." The woman checked her hands. "Well, it doesn't look like I've become a gorgon at least. Not like that poor woman over there."

"She's a natural gorgon. Her name is Annie, and that's her father. She was taken from his hive."

"Oh." Kendra had the base decency to grimace. "Then that was quite rude of me. I'll apologize to her later. I thought she was one of the willing experiments. Still, your wife? Well, ex-wife? Pretty shitty."

"Yes, she was. You picked a pretty shitty woman to be your friend."

The pair looked at each other and burst into laughter.

I contemplated the various ways I could make my husband pay later.

"Who is your girlfriend? She looks ready to blow her top."

"She's always a little cranky," my husband said, and without looking at me, he held out his arm and waggled his fingers at me. I considered biting him—or transforming into a unicorn and sitting on him.

I heaved a sigh and stepped closer, holding out my hand to Kendra. "I'm the nice woman who fixed your petrification problem, as I'm immune to gorgons and their various tricks."

Kendra shook with me, looking me over. "You're Bailey Gardener, then. I've heard about you. Audrey mentioned something about you corrupting her husband. In the next breath, she'd rant about how you'd be the perfect bride for her hive."

Wait. I had corrupted him? I considered Sam with a raised brow. "I'm not sure I'm all that good at corruption. She's not wrong about the perfect bride for gorgons." I stared my husband in the eyes. "Right?"

"You did just fine with your corruptions."

"Are you trying to be confusing on purpose, Sam?" I asked. Why hadn't he fessed up to being my husband? Did he want me to show him how jealous I'd get in a heartbeat?

Oh. Right. My gorgon-incubus doohickey liked when I became jealous. Sighing, I shook my head at his antics.

"It is one of my joys in life. Don't worry so much. Kendra likes when I'm difficult. I'm just acting normally for her. If I acted like we were best friends and showed too much concern, it might freak her out. Now that I've confused you both, I get to enjoy the show while you two figure out what the reality of the situation is."

Rather than argue, Kendra shrugged. "The few times we've met, we have annoyed each other significantly. It didn't help I told him he would have been better off marrying me, and that I would have slept with him every night without complaint. I was honest with him. He'd married a snake. Audrey was a bitch, but my mother liked Audrey's mother and wanted us to be friends, so I was friendly. Little good that did me. If you get a recorder, I'll tell you everything I know about the bitch and her plans. Well, not that it will do you any good, seeing as she's dead. Deserved if you ask me."

"It's more that we're trying to figure out how often she was banging Morrison, his involvement with her plans, and how deep the rabbit hole goes," I replied.

Kendra regarded me through narrowed eyes. "You learned they were sleeping together? How?"

"Receipts," I announced with pride. "She liked buying condoms from the pharmacy near his house. We even figured out which brand from their cost. And since Sam knew when she was cheating on him, it was easy to piece together."

"How did you know?" Kendra asked.

I grinned while my husband squirmed.

"You're liking this too much," he complained.

"Well, yes. There is a very good reason for this. I know who—and what—I'm taking to a hotel tonight, and I really couldn't be happier about it."

"I'm confused," Kendra stated.

"My father is a gorgon king although he is categorized as a human, Kendra. My grandfather is a rather powerful gorgon. Archambault Quinn. Audrey was not invited to learn about that part of my ancestry. My mother is the product of a triad."

Kendra's eyes widened. "Oh. So you're part angel."

"And part gorgon."

"Most importantly, he is also part incubus," I announced. "Add angel and incubus genes together, and he's a walking loyalty detector among other things. Because of that, he knew exactly when his bitch of an ex-wife cheated on him."

"Huh. So her gig was up before she'd even started it, really."

My husband nodded. "I started tracking her infidelity early, and when I tired of her and her home pregnancy tests, I asked Bailey to gather evidence. She's been dubbed the Calamity Queen for good reason, as she's exceptionally good at finding things while disasters happen around her. She doesn't even cause most of the disasters. She just stumbles her way into them. Bailey acquired the photographs I needed to proceed with my divorce. Audrey and I had a civil divorce, she walked away with a lump sum of my choice, which was lower than the half she would have received had she not been cheating on me."

"It looks like you got a slow screw, too."

"Not at all." As I hadn't played his game earlier, my husband snagged me around the waist and pulled me close. I did my best to wiggle free, but he opted to use his unfair manly strength to pin me to his side. "Now that we've done the customary dance, this is Mrs. Police Chief Quinn, my wife and future mother of my children."

"Future mother? Oh! Do you mean you'll be having children? I guess it *has* been a long time. I'm happy for you, Samuel. I knew you liked children, but I just couldn't see you having any with Audrey."

"I couldn't, either. Hell, I couldn't even take her home to most of the family. She met my mother and father, and they played stupid. The rest of my family hid."

"Smart of them, really."

I strained against Quinn's hold on me. "Did you put steel bars in your arms this morning?"

"No, I just like you where I have you, and I'm willing to show off to keep you where I have you."

"I believe he's attempting to, in a rather odd fashion, show me you have a different relationship with him than he did with Audrey. With Audrey, he could barely tolerating touching her. You've made your point, Samuel. Honestly, you were never the type, and I just never understood what you saw in her."

"I didn't see anything in her. That's why I married her. She kept the other sharks at bay." My husband released me, although he captured my right hand in his. "We're actually honeymooning, as our first was rudely interrupted. By Audrey."

"How?"

"She kidnapped Bailey."

Kendra winced. "I'm sorry, Bailey. By the time she turned me into a statue, she'd become cruel. Had she not, I would have exposed her. She'd caught a gorgon male. I think she wanted better dust—dust that could guarantee someone would become a gorgon. The dust she had hadn't worked on her other chief."

My husband sighed. "You mean Morrison."

"Yeah, him. Watch yourself around that man, Samuel. He's bad news, and he was using Audrey as much as she was using him. Of that I'm sure. I don't know why he wanted to rule a gorgon hive with Audrey, but they were up to something—and they were willing to kill to accomplish their goals."

We'd already learned that lesson, and I worried what else we would learn from those who'd been petrified and left to become mysteries.

FOURTEEN

You want to eat sea bugs?

I LEARNED two important things about Kendra Thames: she trusted nobody, and she hated Audrey with a passion hotter than my flames.

Upon realizing she attempted to keep everyone at a distance, things went smoother. I could only guess the events leading up to her petrification had left scars, and I could only hope the CDC would help her adapt to having her life put on hold.

Of the petrified victims, one needed to go to the hospital for additional treatments. I added the woman's failing health to the list of Morrison's crimes. If I got my hands or hoofs on him, he'd come to a quick end—far quicker of an end than he deserved.

My temper frayed, and to keep myself from doing something I would regret, I took my turn keeping our pets company in the rental until the CDC gave us permission to leave. Sunny and Blizzard opted to nap together in the back while Avalanche slept on my foot. With the pets napping off their hard day, I worked at trying to find more information on the rabies outbreak in the CDC's records.

My effort proved futile, and I figured our next stop would be the address in Maine that Audrey had visited several times before we headed to Long Lake. After having found so much tragedy at the bed and breakfast, I feared what we would learn at our next destination.

I appreciated Kendra's willingness to confirm some of our suspicions, but those confirmations would dump us straight into a mess. With a police chief being confirmed to have been involved in mass kidnapping and murder, the entire police station in the Hamptons would come under fire.

Nobody believed for an instant that Morrison had participated in such extensive schemes without at least some of his cops being aware of it—like that stupid cadet I'd squished like a grape. Worse, I wondered if that idiot had been planted to hinder the 120 Wall Street efforts. Janet had done a good job of reining him in.

I suspected her ability to rein in Morrison's puppet had landed her in trouble as much as her relationship with me.

Rather than Morrison taking over Manhattan, I worried we'd be sent to his former turf to clean his operations up. But with my involvement with Morrison, would we be given jurisdiction? I didn't even know how to find out. A headache brewed behind my forehead, and I contemplated texting my husband and whining until we were set free.

I wanted to get to our hotel and call my mother. What was she like? Had she enjoyed her brief time with my father? How did they schedule their time? Did they keep a calendar of when the sun rose and set and when the moon happened to be around?

Could they possess people outside of their general times of influence?

I had questions, and sometime, after I got to know my parents a little better, I would ask them.

In the meantime, I would wait. The CDC ultimately decided when we got to leave, I vowed to keep from whining to my husband or bothering our pets.

I deserved a cookie or some cake for my good behavior.

When the boredom became unbearable, I leaned the seat back and caught a nap, something I didn't get often enough. The heat being turned off woke me, and I growled curses at the lost warmth to discover my husband taking the keys out of the ignition. "Hey, that's rude. I was napping with that on."

Leaning across the seat, he smiled and kissed my cheek. "We're getting gassed up so we can get on the road, my beautiful. You slept through the rest of the festivities, and all three busses have left. It's just us and the CDC reps with the extra gas at this point. I changed our hotel reservation and asked our angelic visitor to teleport one of the vics to the hotel we were going to use. The CDC is picking up that tab, as she's one of the more delicate of the women. Morrison had gotten ahold of her."

I cringed. "Poor woman. Will she be okay?"

"She should be. The archangel is staying with her until he's confident she is in good hands. Right now, she's a suicide risk."

"Please tell me this would prevent his bail if he hadn't already dodged town."

"Let's just say there is a country-wide warrant for his immediate arrest, and should he resist arrest, lethal force has been authorized. The archangel has offered to take the burden from the victims and has confirmed that what we suspect is likely less severe than the crimes actually committed."

"What a fucking dick."

"You won't hear me arguing with that. Are you hungry?"

My stomach growled at my husband. I poked at it. "Apparently, according to that, I'm ravenous, and may someone have mercy on those who get in the way of me hunting for my dinner."

Chuckling, Quinn straightened and closed the door, talking to Alan while one of the remaining CDC reps filled our tank. Several minutes later, my husband slid behind the wheel and restarted the engine. "Do you want the good news or the bad news?"

"Janet is going to be investigated because of her association with Morrison and her presence at 120 Wall Street," I guessed.

He raised a brow. "Did you put that into the good news or the bad news category?"

"Bad, as it means I'll have to beat off the investigators to get them to leave our cop alone. Essentially, upon thinking about it, I came to the conclusion that it is probable Morrison sent that idiot cadet to make a mess at 120 Wall Street, but he made a mistake in sending Janet, who wasn't tolerant of the asshole cadet, so she mitigated the problems he could have created. Basically, their presence at 120 Wall Street implies there is a link between Morrison and the gorgon dust incident *and* possibly the warehouse incident."

"The bad news is you'll need to be questioned about their behavior."

"I don't see how that's a problem. The cameras caught everything, and the CDC has a copy. I'll just support what the camera says. This is not bad news. It's only bad news if they want us to do it, say, tomorrow morning when I have other plans."

"In a week. They want to do some more investigation first."

"I can work with a week from now. Am I right? About that potential link?"

"It's the most plausible possibility we have right now."

"What's the good news?"

"We're good to go and the moon has risen, so you can call your mother. I'll drive while you talk, and then we'll eat, make plans for tomorrow, and work from there."

I retrieved my phone. "That sounds like a good plan. We're in New England. We should go find somewhere with seafood. Lobster!"

"You want to eat sea bugs?"

"I do not merely wish to eat sea bugs, I wish to conquer them all, escorting them to my stomach with the help of offensive amounts of garlic and butter. And I will expect you to kiss me afterwards, no matter how much garlic butter I consume." I leered at him. "I hope you like garlic, Quinn. In vast quantities."

"Just because I didn't want garlic toast once doesn't mean I hate garlic."

"That's what you say now, but I shall put this to the test when you feed me delicious sea bugs coated with garlic and extra butter."

"Is there a reason you haven't asked for sea bugs in the past?"

"We were not in the land of sea bugs, and Manhattan clam chowder is disgusting. New England clam chowder is the one true clam chowder, and I swore I would have lobster in Maine—or somewhere near Maine but north of New York. Vermont counts. Ish. Why did I swear this? I don't know, so don't ask me that."

"I see you like your clam chowder creamy, and you have been convinced the only good lobster is one from New England?"

"Yes."

"You're something else, Bailey. But if sea bugs are what you want, sea bugs are what you shall get. I, on the other hand, shall pray for steak. Fortunately for you, we aren't too far from New Hampshire, which in turn isn't *that* far from Maine's border, so I might even be able to get you sea bugs from Maine. But I shall pray for steak."

"Wuss," I teased.

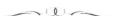

TO MY ENDLESS AMUSEMENT, while my mother answered the phone and did her best to talk to me, she was busy volunteering at an animal shelter in Florida, the pets wanted dinner and they wanted it now, and she couldn't handle fending off a bunch of starving kittens while managing the phone.

I took mercy on her, laughed, and told her to call me back when she had a few spare minutes, with a reminder that if I happened to be passed out, my gorgon-incubus doohickey would love to speak with her. I hung up, shook my head, and smiled. "I see the relentless drive to help animals in need is genetic."

"I am utterly shocked, I tell you. Shocked." My husband chuckled. "While I am not quite the traveler my ex-wife was, I can tell you there is a good restaurant that serves the sea bugs you desire about an hour from here, along the New Hampshire-Maine border. It's part of a hotel, so we should be able to have dinner and go to bed shortly after. However, you'll have to contact the hotel and see if we can stay there because of our menagerie."

"CDC certifications for our pets are useful in moments like this." Within ten minutes, after regurgitating their license numbers, giving them a contact for the CDC to verify we were legally allowed to possess an Egyptian wolf and an ocelot, and promising to otherwise adhere to the rules of their establishment, I had reservations for us. Then, because miracles could happen, the hotel was able to book us in for dinner at the sea bug place, too.

Once I disconnected the call, I dropped my phone on my lap and clapped. "I handled that like an adult!"

"You really did. It's like my careful training program has begun to bear results. You have successfully become an adult, Mrs. Samuel Quinn."

Damn. My husband was on a roll. "I don't know what has gotten into you today, but I really like it."

"After witnessing me eat spaghetti, you

would think you would understand how much I enjoy garlic."

"Unless it's in toast format," I complained.

"And now that I know I can rile you up by refusing food with garlic in it, I will use this to add spice to my evenings as required. I win this round, Bailey. I especially win, as you then try to find things to cook containing garlic, and not only do I enjoy your culinary escapades, I get fed along with a fun show."

"And you say I'm something else."

"You are, but that's exactly how I like you. As you will fret unless it's addressed, what is bothering you about today beyond the entirety of the situation?"

"I mean, the entirety of the situation definitely bothers me, but Kendra seemed weird."

"Kendra suffers from some mental health problems. She doesn't really mean harm, but she goes through some pretty dramatic phases. She told me she liked when people just went with the flow, so that's what I do with her. Audrey always kept trying to put her in little boxes."

"Audrey was shit."

"She was."

"Terrible taste in women, Sam. So terrible."

"It's like you want me to take you to our hotel room and go through intensive corrective therapy."

I spent all of half a second thinking about that. "Yes, please."

He laughed. "Don't worry about Kendra. She's no threat to you, no matter how open she is about her past interest in getting in my pants."

"I had noticed that."

"She's psychotic, but she's a fun psychotic. That said, I have no interest in her getting in my pants. Some days, I did regret I hadn't accepted her offer, as she would have made a far better wife than Audrey. I mean, when being honest about it? I would have at least been much happier on the incubus front, as Kendra is a lot of things, but she's not a cheater."

"I can't even argue with that, but I'm glad I didn't have to compete with a woman who would happily take you to bed every night."

"I'll admit, a few years ago, she was really good for my esteem. I couldn't stand Audrey, and I had done a pretty good job of giving my self-esteem a beating."

Huh. I struggled to imagine my husband struggling with any form of self-esteem problem. "Obviously, you need intensive corrective therapy tonight after I get to eat as many sea bugs as possible. Maybe we should invite her over for dinner once this settles down. Surely we have a single cop in need of a loyal albeit psychotic woman."

"I'm not against having her over for dinner. It would be good for her, but we'll both need a refresher on how to handle certain mental illnesses. It's not her fault, and I'd rather not have dinner become something emotionally scarring for her."

"I'm good with that. Does she need a doctor or anything like that?"

"Well, if she does, I suspect we'll be neck deep in making sure she gets the treatments she needs. I never asked if her problems needed to be treated, honestly. I didn't want Audrey to get the wrong idea."

What a bitch. "She would get upset if you inquired about someone's mental health?"

"Then, and even for a while after our divorce, I really thought she wasn't a terrible person—just incapable of loyalty. I was wrong about a lot of things."

"Don't feel too badly about it, Sam. I was convinced you utterly hate me."

"I never did understand that."

"Well, I had ruined your marriage."

"I literally hired you to ruin my marriage because it was an awful marriage and I wanted out of it."

"I was the reason you divorced."

"Bailey, you're being ridiculous again. When you had brought those pictures to me, I wanted to hug you, spin you around, and take you home with me. You far exceeded my expectations. I never hated you. You drove me insane because you always and relentlessly put others in front of yourself, and that was terrifying for me. Once I'd started loving everything about you, I worried that your tendencies would get you killed."

Those tendencies almost had. "Why had you gotten a little yellow dress and those lacy black panties, anyway?"

My husband's face flushed. "Yale had told me to go make myself useful, sent me off to get clothing for you after giving me your sizes, and had me go home after I'd done my share of the work. I saw the yellow dress, and it looked sweet and innocent. And then, well, I'm your gorgon-incubus doohickey, and the black lace gave me a lot of ideas. To be honest, they were bad ideas, but I was desperate at that point."

"Sundresses kind of do imply they're to be worn by a girl when in the midst of childhood innocence, don't they?"

My husband's chuckle promised sexy things on the horizon. "Your innocence in that dress lasted all of an hour at most."

"Innocence is overrated. Like, according to society, not having my virginity should have been this *really big deal!* But it wasn't. Like, life went on absolutely as normal. Well, as normal as my life gets. And why do men have no real care for *their* virginity?"

"It couldn't *possibly* be because virginity is a pointless societal construct... and it's easier to convince half the population her virginity is somehow valuable than it is to convince an entire society and hold everyone to the same standard. That, at least, is what my mother likes to say. Also, as this is now important, virginity is not a concept most gorgons really understand."

"Your cousin understood. Sort of."

"My cousin is an idiot. The only use virginity is to a gorgon is for making sure there won't be any jilted lovers in the wings to cause hives trouble later. No gorgon cares about who his wives or bride was or wasn't with before they entered the relationship. They just don't care."

"I'm still torturing your cousin for all eternity."

"And I am here to enjoy the show."

I smiled at that, as my husband loved when I stood up for myself, even over ridiculous things—like my hatred of cheap coffee makers named Suzy. "Can I ask a question?"

"Of course."

"Well, it's less of a question and more of a statement. I just don't understand Morrison," I admitted. "Or Audrey. I don't understand why they'd do this."

"One of the hardest things I had to learn as a chief is that I will never understand why. It's just not possible for me to understand why anyone would do as many criminals do. Logically, I can comprehend greed can drive people into theft, and so on... but this sort of sin against others is beyond my comprehension. It's just not my nature, and once I figured that out, I decided it was for the best that I didn't truly understand why. What matters is securing

justice for the victims, and I don't need to understand their motivations beyond linking
them with the crimes and working to make
sure the guilty are the ones who pay for those
crimes. That's not as easy as it seems at times."

"Because the guilty don't want to be
caught, and they'll do everything they can to
make sure someone else takes the fall for
what they've done."

"Precisely. And we're not infallible. We'll
never be. We will make mistakes. The best we
can do is try to undo the damage from the
mistakes we make."

"Do you think Annie will be all right?"

"Her father and his hive will do most of
the magic on that front. What they don't accomplish, we will."

"You're confident. Why are you so
confident?"

"Gorgons are, in many ways, much easier
to understand than humans. Their lives are
harsher, but their society is far more black
and white and easy to understand when
you're a part of it. It's not like with humans.
Her father won't care about what happened
to her while in Morrison's hands, nor will
her mothers or sisters. It just doesn't matter
to them. All they care about is the fact she
came home. There are crimes gorgons can't
abide by, but the victims are victims. They
are not blamed or devalued for having been a
victim."

I flinched, as humans often did devalue

victims—or worse, blamed them. "Humans can really suck."

"We can, yes. The only thing greater than a human's capacity for good is their capacity for evil. I learned to accept that long ago, however frustrating that reality is."

I considered my phone. "My mother was working at an animal shelter, Sam."

"Your mother is a guardian divine associated with the moon. She probably can't help herself. She probably climbs into dumpsters for rabid animals, too."

"I'll do it again!"

"I know you will."

"Will we ever be good enough, Quinn?"

"I don't know, but we'll do the best we can. We'll make that good enough."

AFTER SETTLING our pets in our room, Quinn took me to a seafood paradise. To my amusement, his prayers for steak went unanswered. He regarded the menu with a perplexed expression.

"Sam, are you allergic to seafood? Did I make you take me to somewhere that might kill you?"

Before I could panic, my husband laughed and shook his head. "No. Not at all. I'm not allergic to anything that I know of. It's the angelic genes. They tend to keep those with more than their fair share of angelic genetics from developing most allergies. Add in my gorgon heritage, and I'm pretty sure I could eat almost *anything*."

"Okay. Let me rephrase that. Have you ever had seafood before?"

"Not precisely." The skepticism in his voice made me giggle, and he glared at me over his menu. "My mother likes having fish as *pets*. I can't just eat the family pets. And none of my gorgon relatives like seafood. Some hives live for it, but the Quinns prefer land-based fare. And once I lived on my own, I just couldn't understand spending that much on sea bugs."

I giggled. "Sea bugs are delicious. Okay. Let's find you something you'll like." After a moment of looking at the salad section, I found one that would be close to his comfort zone. I took hold of his menu, tilted it so I could look over it, and pointed at the seared tuna salad. "This will be a good starter for you. Salad, a kind you like, and you'll have some fish to start with. It's seared, so it looked at some heat, and you can get a feel for if you'll like sushi or not."

"I'm man enough to admit I'm scared."

My phone buzzed on the table, and according to the screen, my mother had remembered to call me back. I snatched the device, and aware I was in a restaurant and couldn't be rude to the other guests, I answered, "Did the taming of the hungry beasts go well?"

"Everybody has been fed, watered, and cuddled," my mother reported. "Is everything okay?"

"It seems my husband's upbringing had a dire lack of seafood in it, so I'm rectifying the situation through making him try various sea bugs. I'm starting him on training wheels with some tuna on a salad, and he will enjoy some proper clam chowder with me. After the clam chowder, I think I'm going to get this big platter for two, so he has the most choice of sea bugs to try. He claims he's man enough to admit the strange new food scares him."

"Ah, yes. Don't blame him much. Gorgons are particular with their diets, and one of the brides in his family line was likely allergic to seafood once upon a time, and the entire hive will avoid the food the brides are allergic to. You don't have to worry about allergies with him, so feed him whatever you'd like. Your father and I have been learning things like that so we know what's safe to feed you both."

I had a mother who cared what I could eat, and I had a mother who wanted to burn my house down along with my poor rose bushes. It would take a long time to come to terms with the vast differences between my mothers—and my fathers were in two entirely different universes. "I'm sorry I wasn't able to talk to you before."

"You were asleep, and I do quite enjoy

talking to your Sam. He's quite the gentleman."

"He really is. His expression is really cute. The menu is baffling him."

"There's really no steak anywhere on this menu," he whined.

"The lack of steak is disturbing to him."

My mother laughed. "I bet it is. I spoke to your father this morning, and as he was aware you would be busy with important matters this morning, he suggests you should look into that woman's activities in Maine before you head to Long Lake. That will be an efficient way of handling the matter. He would prefer to just smite all that might be a threat to you, but that is not allowed. He is also working on a present for you, one he thinks you will enjoy."

"A present? What sort of present?"

"The kind where he meddles more than he should and decides to interfere when he shouldn't. I tried to talk sense into him, but he claims if all it takes is some random human telling an idiot you're going to be somewhere at a certain time to put an end to this mess, he sees no reason why not to pay some random human to talk to the idiot and make those arrangements. By the way, do make sure you're in Long Lake by noon the day after tomorrow. That would fall nicely into your father's manipulations."

"There are so many idiots, Mother. Which idiot are we discussing?"

My mother was quiet for a long moment. "That is going to take some getting used to."

Oh. Right. I had a mother I actually wanted to call my mother, and I'd just gone and addressed her as such without thinking about it. Oops. "To being called Mother?"

"Yes. Now I understand why your father was strutting around. I mean, he usually struts around, as he is very much like a peacock. I really do like birds, which is part of your father's charms. He's like a very warm peacock who enjoys showing off. But you must have called him your father. Now I understand his peacock ways."

"You like animals to a compulsive degree."

"That did not take you long to figure out."

"Sam is convinced I get my dumpster diving habits from you."

"I have been told I am not allowed to retrieve any animals from any dumpster. As a result, I spent all of last night checking dumpsters for abandoned animals. As soon as the moon rose, I resumed my search. I found a nest of raccoons, but I left those alone. They didn't need to be rescued. Your father should have learned by now telling me I can't do something is a damned good way of convincing me to do it. I'm going to find new dumpsters to explore tonight on my quest to find some pets to rescue."

Yep, she was definitely my mother. "I think Sam is resigned to how I will insist on rescuing animals from dumpsters, but he has told me I can't adopt *all* of the animals I rescue."

"That is a smart approach. For some reason, your father thinks I'll actually heed his various little warnings when it comes to rescuing strange animals from dumpsters. My first step is to find an appropriate animal to adopt out of a dumpster. Alas, I lack your ability to find your way with ease. That is a gift from your father, although I temper your abilities somewhat."

I pondered that. "He's the reason I can find my way, but you're the reason I can find my way efficiently?"

"That's right. Do you have any recommendations on how I might find the dumpsters with animals in them?"

"May my father forgive me, but go to Manhattan. There are many dumpsters. If you can't find an animal in a dumpster, you'll find plenty of them on the street. Just be careful. The rabies outbreak there is serious. My father probably snooped into how often I've contracted rabies from rescuing animals, so he is concerned we'll both become rabid on him. At the same time. That's a lot for someone to handle."

My mother laughed. "Yes, that is a concern for him. He's trying to figure out how to rid the Earth of rabies in an allowed fashion so you will be safe while rescuing pets from dumpsters. It will keep him amused for a while. Tomorrow night, I will be working on a project somewhere remote, so don't fret if you can't get a hold of me. Your father has protective tendencies, and he is not quite ready to handle all of the women in his life creating trouble at one time. We must ease him into us causing trouble together, all right?"

"I am game for causing trouble. I'm very good at causing trouble. It's one of my best skills."

Quinn heaved a sigh and bowed his head. "It really is."

"Since you missed that, my husband is coming to terms with just how honest I was by making that statement. But he acknowledged I am skilled in causing trouble."

"Poor Samuel." My mother laughed. "Please don't worry if you can't get a hold of me or your father. Your father is fretting, and when he frets, he spends every one of his moments where his light shines on you trying to mitigate the fates he dislikes. I told him you are his daughter, and it would take a lot more than some stupid human to do anything truly harmful to you. Just be a good girl and go to that place in Maine tomorrow and then go to Long Lake the day after, and plan to reach Long Lake in the morning hours. That should work best for what your father is trying to arrange."

"Okay. We can do that."

"Bring your darling pets with you, but

leave the kitten in the SUV. Your puppies will be most important."

"And you say my father tries to meddle," I teased.

"I am so much better at protecting things than he is. It is my purpose. I'm merely doing exactly what I should. Oh. That reminds me. Your father is quite upset over those mortals."

I sighed. "Remind my father that my husband's uncle has been making preparations for them, and if he wants to be involved, that's a good way to go about it. They're digging their own graves, so it's all right to just leave them be. I can handle those idiots myself."

"Yes, you can. Good girl. In case your father doesn't remember to call you tomorrow because of his scheming ways, we both love you. Now, I have more dumpsters to explore, for surely there are more animals out this time of night. And I might even adopt one just to drive your father a little closer to the edge of his sanity."

My mother hung up, and I giggled. "She's seeking out dumpsters so she can rescue animals, Sam."

"Yes, she was trying to do that yesterday, too. I'm surprised you dove right in on calling her your mother."

"She's nice. It was easier than I thought. Because she's nice. I figured I'd dive right into the awkward first daughter-mother conversation, but it wasn't awkward at all."

The waiter came, and my husband sighed, gave me his menu, and told me to pick for him, else we'd never eat dinner. Giggling, I went with my first plan, ordering him the kind of salad he enjoyed with seared tuna while I had a shameful number of tiger shrimp, one of which I'd save for him. I ordered us a cup of lobster bisque and a bowl of clam chowder each before ordering their most elaborate seafood feast for two. I ordered a pot of tea for myself so I'd feel fancy, and with a chuckle, my husband requested the same.

Once the waiter left, I raised a brow at him. "Tea?"

"I should ask the same, Bailey. You asked for tea, and you asked for it in such a way to lead me to believe you are excited to be receiving minty grass. Should I be concerned?"

"My coffee is better, I recently had my coffee, and I'd sulk if I had to drink inferior coffee. Anyway, I didn't order minty grass. I ordered spicy grass I plan to add sugar and cream to. It's like a dessert to go with my sea bug feast. I'm excited. You get to try something new, and I get to eat sea bugs!"

"I'm concerned the sea bugs will rise up and try to feast on me."

"You'll be okay. My mother said you're not allergic, so you can eat without fear. She thinks one of the Quinn brides, at some point, was allergic to seafood, and gorgons are obsessive compulsive."

"Gorgons really are, especially when it comes to the health and safety of a bride. Huh. I wonder who is allergic. Or was."

"We'll call your grandfather after dinner and ask. Then we'll talk to the kids about Annie."

"That's a good idea. We may have to get grandfather to do the talking, though. He's better about integrating new gorgon women into the hives. I don't want to accidentally traumatize them more than they've already been traumatized."

"Is it because of how they were raised?"

"In part. They're different. That's fine. We'll figure it out, especially after we've dealt with Morrison."

"I think my father is trying to herd Morrison to Long Lake for us to deal with. My mother said we would be wise to be there by noon the day after tomorrow, and that we should be nosy in Maine first before going there. Apparently, my father is interfering more than he should."

"Well, that doesn't surprise me. Your father is who he is, and he's always been known to push the limits. That's why he holds the position he does in the Egyptian pantheon. As long as he doesn't break certain rules, he'll get away with it. Since there are a disturbing number of pantheons with interest in us, I expect your father will get away with a great deal while on his quest to protect you. He'll protect me because if he doesn't, you might

cry, and I don't think your father is at all prepared to handle you while you're crying. I'm
not prepared to handle you while you're
crying."

I smiled, as my husband hated when anything upset me.

I might one day, with sufficient coaxing
from him, get used to that.

"I can't tell if that's your expression upon
realization you can easily control me through
the power of tears or if you're simply smitten
with my handsome looks and can't help but
smile."

"Can it be both? I am rather smitten with
your handsome looks, but if I'm honest, I'm
not sure I'm mean enough to fake crying to
get my way about anything. Unless you're refusing to come to bed. But that won't be fake
crying. That'll be real tears."

Upon the arrival of Quinn's salad, I observed with interest while he investigated his
appetizer. "This is deceptively normal in appearance, although there is partially cooked
fish on this. Why is the fish only partially
cooked, Bailey?"

"Because it's like the fish version of a
steak, Sam. Think of it as a very strange steak,
seared for your enjoyment."

"Enjoyment?"

I grabbed one of my shrimp by the tail,
dunked it in my cocktail sauce, and
chomped on it. "I am going to save you one
of my sea bugs for you to try. But you have

to eat your manly salad so you have strength for later."

"You are the reason you felt the need to run away and go on a road trip to escape my sexy ways. I am going to remind you of this often, mostly so you don't try to go on a road trip without me in the future. Road trips are much better when you're with me."

I couldn't argue with him, so I didn't. "Try your tuna."

While his expression remained somewhat skeptical, he speared a piece of his tuna as ordered and nibbled. He blinked, nibbled again, and when the fish didn't rise up to eat him, he took a proper bite. "I feel like I have been deceived my entire life, warned against the perils of fish. Though, honestly, the stench of fish in the microwave did a pretty good job of warning me away from fish."

"Microwaved fish is a sin. Fresh fish, seared for your enjoyment, is a delicacy to be enjoyed. Just watch out for bones. They're sharp and will poke you if you try to chew on them. I recommend you check for bones, even in a good place like this. Well, I'm assuming it's good. My sea bugs are tasty." As my husband had earned his share of my sea bugs, I dunked one into the cocktail sauce and deposited it on the rim of his bowl. "That is your prize."

"Why did you not talk me into trying this earlier?"

"You kept feeding me really good steak

and bacon." I'd considered lobster a time or two at the grocery store, except the price had done a good job of deterring me. "Seafood seems like extra special occasion restaurant food. I am saying that because I don't know how to cook lobster, and I wasn't spending that much on a lobster to ruin it."

"I have noticed you are infatuated with bacon."

"Especially when you make it."

"I'll admit, that makes being your personal chef so much better. You hover while I make it. And the things you'll do for a greasy burger and fries."

I licked my lips and indulged in another shrimp. "I've been told shrimp can be grilled, but shrimp were always too expensive for me to get."

"I see I will be bringing sea bugs into our home and questing to learn how to grill them for you. What other strange things are you going to make me learn how to cook?"

"I can tell you what not to cook. Restrain me if I ask for pickles on ice cream at any time. Pickles by themselves? That's okay. I can work with that. Ice cream by itself? I can definitely get behind that. But do not ever let me mix those two together. I don't care if I cry. Don't let me do it. Distract me somehow."

My husband grinned at me. "I'm not getting between a woman and her pregnancy cravings, Bailey. If you ask me for pickles on ice cream, I'm going to shudder from horror, but I'm going to provide it for you. That was the first piece of advice my father gave me upon learning you're pregnant. A wise man does not come between his wife and the pregnancy cravings, no matter how strange those cravings may be."

Crap. "That's terrifying. If you make it, I'll have to eat it, and that sounds *wrong*."

"It really does."

"Do you think we can beg Sariel for an aversion to make sure I never walk down that dark road?"

"That will be the first thing I do when we get home. I'm going to ask a rather odd question, so please don't think too badly of me."

"What?"

"How are we going to deal with Morrison if your father sends him our way?"

"Isn't it premeditated murder if we discuss how we're going to deal with him in advance?"

"He'll force us to kill him, thus making it a self-defense verdict, especially as part of his bail condition is to stay away from you."

"There's a restraining order?"

"Yep." Quinn shrugged and ate more of his salad, and I smirked when he eyed the shrimp on the edge of his bowl with interest. "I initially didn't want to tell you because it would worry you. If there's a restraining order, then obviously somebody believes he needs to be restrained. That somebody is my grandfather, because he was quite upset over what he found in your memories. He won't tell me, because he would rather I not be charged with premeditated murder."

"Which leads you to believe his actions were closer to the rape scale of things than not."

"I don't think you were raped, but there is a huge spectrum of things he could have done to you that all count as violations. If my grandfather believes it is best to bury it, then it's probably best to bury it. That said, you were most certainly a virgin when I got my hands on you. There is a reason people say virgins are extra special treats for incubi and succubi."

"You are so bad, Samuel Leviticus Quinn."

"I am. So, how would you like to bury him?"

"Big fire leaves little smear," I muttered.

My husband frowned. "We probably need to report he was dispatched if he attempts anything."

"Probably. But big fire leaves little smear, which in turn, is very little to clean up. I view it as reducing burial fees should anyone actually want that bastard's body."

"And considering how hot you're rolling, you won't have to work hard to make a big fire."

"But a big fire would be *so* much better with napalm."

"I should have known you would try to work a napalm bender into this somehow."

"I bet Perkette would give you the recipe for her special blend, and I could easily con the CDC into giving me the good neutralizer." I fluttered my lashes at him. "Pretty please?"

"You are so going to owe me for this, Bailey Ember Quinn."

FIFTEEN

I can't win this one, can I?

UPON LEARNING ABOUT ANNIE, Archambault Quinn did the equivalent of locking down Fort Knox, opting to take precautions to prevent his hive—or other hives—from further falling victim to the demented former police chief still on the loose. My husband rolled his eyes at the development, which involved his grandfather immediately doing a head count of his wives, his bride, his children, his grandchildren, and his great-grandchildren.

He hung up on us before we had a chance to ask our whelps what they were learning and check in with them.

I figured we could handle being a little lonely as long as they remained safe.

The lonely problem I resolved with a little bit of dust and a whole lot of lust, which did a good job of making us skirt the line checking out on time in the morning. Thanks to Sunny, we did wake up before our pets perished from their delayed breakfast, although the trio gave us dirty looks even after we fed them, let them walk around and stretch their legs, and otherwise shower them with our affection.

"We're late once with breakfast, and we're going to be in the doghouse for the rest of the day, Sam. I feel our kitten has taught them some tricks. That's feline disapproval in triplicate."

"Oh, no. Canine disapproval is a real and dangerous thing, Bailey. We have failed as pet custodians. We dared to make them wait for breakfast. Shame, shame, shame." Quinn did a check of the SUV, making sure everything was ready for our pets in the back before rewarding our animals with treats and the pettings they were owed. "Apparently, I sleep really well after that grade of pixie dust. When was the last time I slept in that late?"

"Good question. Obviously, the solution to my sleeping problem is to exhaust you so much even you're forced to sleep. Actually, forget that. We slept in. We'd be late to work daily."

"Think we'd be fired if we started sleeping in all the time?"

"Probably," I complained. "I'm glad you got sleep. You needed it."

"You needed it even more than I did. What did I have to do to get you on the move?"

I grinned. It had taken him dragging me to the shower to wake me up, and I hadn't gotten a hit of pixie dust, although I had enjoyed the consequences. "The next time we do that, we have pet sitters, babysitters, and a week."

"That sounds like a plan. So, where in Maine are we headed?"

I dug out the receipts for a second bed and breakfast Audrey had gone to, one with weird receipts. "Kennebago. There's a bed and breakfast there." I hit the internet to look up the place, and I grunted at the results, which implied the place had gone out of business at least three years ago.

"That fills me with foreboding. What sort of town is Kennebago?" Quinn asked.

"Tourist trap as far as I can tell. It has a lake. Currently, there are two resorts there, and they look fairly inclusive. I don't think there are any actual residents? Well, I guess there are houses here and there for those who run the campgrounds, resorts, and fishing holes. The bed and breakfast isn't near the lake, and it's off a remote track. According to the map, we'll be driving through the underbrush to find it."

"We'll park somewhere sane and walk. It'll be good exercise for us and the pets. And that way, we can at least claim we were hiking if we find more trouble."

I glanced at him. "Still going with the story you want to show me parts of your old life?"

"Well, that *is* true. This is a very important part of the story of my life, although I wasn't precisely present for these chapters. I'm just twisting the truth a little."

"A little?"

"Okay, a lot." My husband plugged the lake into the navigation system, revealing we had several hours of driving ahead of us. "That's not too bad, and the pets don't mind car rides."

"For which I'm grateful."

"Me, too. It's a good thing we didn't bring the kids with us, no matter how useful I think they would be helping us with research. Some things they don't need to see."

"Yeah. This has been horrific. Even if we had brought them, I would have called angels, devils, and demons until I found someone willing to teleport them to your grandfather once my parents had started trying to light our house on fire."

"That was really fucking stupid of them."

"And they came back for a second go at it!"

"That was exceptionally stupid of them," my husband agreed, and he smiled at me. "You handled that really well. But yes, I would have been sending them to my grandfather after that, too. I am sorry about your roses."

"They'll be fine. They're being cared for, but our next house will have a greenhouse for the special roses, and it'll be super fireproofed."

"Not just fireproofed, super fireproofed?"

"Well, I am the best cindercorn, and that

means you have to do super fireproofing. And I have two really shitty parents balancing the awesomeness that is my cool parents."

"Huh. When phrased like that, I guess your parental situation is pretty balanced, isn't it? You got the worst and the best with them. And you'll get the rest of your life with the good ones, which I think is fair after having to put up with such a shitty childhood. We will have to discuss sheltering our children too much. They do need to have a base understanding of how the world works."

"But we can wait until they're like at least five before exposing them too much, right?"

"We'll take care to make sure they understand early enough to protect themselves. We don't want our children so sheltered they're incapable of telling when someone is up to no good. And honestly, in our line of work? They'll get exposure early. We'll just have to make sure we show them the good in people, too. They'll see the bad more often than I'd like."

Right. "We are going to use the daycare near work, right?"

"As much as we can, yes. I like that daycare, and it would let us take our children to work with us and maximize how often we can see them. And it would let us do fun things with them after work every day. Once they're older, we'll look into schooling options for them, too. We'll have them make some of those decisions. I attended boarding school, mostly because of my ancestry. Safer."

"Because you're part gorgon?"

"Yes."

"There are boarding schools capable of handling gorgon-incubus doohickeys?"

"Well, they weren't really aware of my unique genetics, but they were capable of handling children with abnormally high magic ratings. If the kids are okay with it, we may send them. It's a good way to learn discipline. It's part of why I've done so well. The education met my parents' standards, but my parents augmented that a lot when I was home. It was pretty rigid, but that's what I needed at the time. Did I like it? Not really. Every minute of every day is controlled, but I learned how to handle that rigid structuring and monotony really well."

"That's important when you're a gorgon-incubus doohickey with shitty taste in women."

"You're so getting corrective therapy tonight for that one."

I smiled. "Until you reward me better for not making that comment, as long as we're not in front of the kids, I am so making that comment. Corrective evening therapy is a mandatory part of cindercorn care."

"All right. I see I did not think that one through properly. I'll come up with something properly motivating for you."

"Or you can continue your corrective

evening therapy tactics, which I thoroughly enjoy."

"I can't win this one, can I?"

"Nope."

"All right. Get on the phone with Tiffany and get me the ingredients for your napalm. After what we saw at the first bed and break-fast, I'm expecting trouble."

"If it's like the first bed and breakfast, the CDC will bring the napalm, in vast quantities, to us. Oh. Did the dust sample match? I passed out before the test results came in."

"It wasn't a match."

Damn it. "How'd it rate up in terms of potency?"

"Now that was a little more conclusive. It wasn't the match we were hoping for, but it had a lot of the same general properties. What we don't know is if that gorgon was a later or previous experiment. But they think his dust was manufactured in a similar method to the stuff used in 120 Wall Street."

"Is that enough evidence to add to Morri-son's charges?"

"Not quite, but we're getting there. Ideally, we'll find the original batch of dust, and we'll destroy it."

"What about that first batch I destroyed? Could it be that one?"

"No. That batch was traditionally manu-factured, and it would have been closer to what we expect from dust. Was it potent? Yes.

Was it the same stuff at 120 Wall Street? I really doubt it."

Damn it. I retrieved my phone from my purse and called Perkette, wrinkling my nose at the thought of having smacked right into another dead end with the 120 Wall Street investigation.

"You are such a bitch, Bailey Ember Quinn!" Perkette shrieked.

I blinked. "I am? I didn't do it!"

"True. Tell your husband he's a bitch!"

"Sam, Perkette says you're a bitch."

"Found out she's pregnant, huh?"

I giggled. "Can't have wine?" I guessed.

"Arthur popped a cork yesterday, and I ended up throwing up my lunch from last week. I spent all day at the damned hospital today. Was there *something* you may have forgotten to tell me?"

"Forgotten? No? Neglected to, yes."

"I am so fucking proud of you."

I laughed at her complete change of mood. "I'm not sorry, but you should be yelling at your husband. He's the one who lured you to his bed and did wicked, wicked things to you. It's his fault. I'm an innocent cindercorn. As innocent as a cindercorn married to a gorgon-incubus doohickey can be."

"Such a bitch," Perkette muttered. "First, one of you recruits a what to do what?"

"You may have been meddled with by an incubis, an archangel, the Devil, and a gorgon-incubus doohickey. Please don't do anything heinous to my gorgon-incubus doohickey. It's my own damned fault we're having twins."

"But seriously, Bailey? Quadruplets? Do you hate me?"

"I wouldn't call it hate. I call it correcting some unfortunate past events barring you from having entire flocks of children. Upon my close and careful evaluation of the situation, I have decided you want entire flocks of children. I recommend adopting a few to help boost your flock numbers. Adoption is great. I managed to convince Quinn we really needed to adopt a young gorgon lady yesterday. Her name is Annie, and she's coming home with us because she is too old to go back to her father's hive, so we're going to keep her until she's placed with an appropriately nice gorgon gentleman."

"Seriously, Bailey? Seriously?"

"Yes."

"Goodness gracious. I took you on a single road trip, and you evolved into a terrifying demoness capable of taking over the world. I am so proud of you. You hoodwinked me!"

"I think my gorgon-incubus doohickey did the majority of the hoodwinking. I'm innocent. I didn't find out anything until *after*. I'm just claiming credit because that is totally something I would do, given a single opportunity."

"You really would. Arthur was all smug with me yesterday. The bastard knew, yet he

made me freak out and go to the hospital because I threw up at the smell of *wine*."

"Wine isn't good for mommas."

Perkette wailed. "My drinking days are
done. Over. Gone, forever!"

"Only until after you breastfeed. Apparently, pregnant cindercorn care is ridiculously complicated. Sam asked me to call you
because he needs your napalm recipe. Pregnant cindercorns require it. I run really hot
and need the fuel to keep going. And when
divines tell my husband I should be rationed
napalm and poisons, apparently, he listens."

"Poisons?"

"That part is easy. I just play with gorgon
snakes until they bite me. We're adopting a
gorgon woman until we can match her with a
suitable husband, so she can help with that.
She was in a bad spot, and she's too old to go
back to her father's hive permanently. The
kids can also help once we get them back
from his grandfather. My gorgon-incubus
doohickey is only whining a little over how
his snakes don't get exclusive biting rights." I
regarded my left hand with a scowl. "Annie's
snakes had to do a lot of biting yesterday, so
I'm a pincushion. I had a left hand. It's now
full of holes."

"It sounds like you've had an adventurous
few days."

"Yeah. My asshole parents tried to light
our house on fire, and the fuckers hurt my
roses. They were arrested. My roses should

survive, but it is taking an archangel and the Devil working together to make that happen. Don't panic that we went into your house and took our car."

"I had noticed the alarm was disabled, and we did see footage of the Quinns having their way with our house. Do we need to come back from Vegas?"

"It's okay. We're playing around in New England. I made Sam eat sea bugs! He liked them."

"You actually got him to eat seafood?"

"Not only did he eat it, he liked it."

My husband sighed. "You were right. Sea bugs are delicious."

"I love when he tells me I'm right. Sea bugs *are* delicious, and I proved it to him. We had a really nice dinner last night. It included many varieties of sea bugs." It had also cost a small fortune, but while I'd floundered, my husband had paid the bill without missing a beat. Had pixie dust worked on me, I would have taken a dose to get over the excess.

I'd even been aware of ordering ridiculously expensive food, but I'd been so excited to feed something new to him I hadn't computed how much our gluttony would cost.

"Good. He needs some spice in his food life. So. Sam is the guilty party?"

"I fully support my husband's decision to create mayhem in the form of unexpected children. I was too busy conspiring for twins," I admitted.

"You were conspiring for twins when you haven't gotten used to having two children yet, so you thought you'd have me deal with quadruplets?"

"I support his decision!"

My husband laughed. "Just route the phone through the speakers, Bailey. I'm man enough for this conversation."

"If I hang up on you, it's my fault. Quinn wants to join the conversation."

"Okay."

After some fiddling and a few curses, I managed to make the vehicle do what I wanted. "Okay. There. Can you hear me?"

"Sure can. You're in so much trouble, Samuel Leviticus Quinn!"

"I volunteer my family to help babysit," he replied.

"You are no longer in any trouble," Perkette announced.

I laughed. "Are you feeling okay otherwise?"

"So far. I've been a moody mess, which is why I ultimately went to the hospital this morning. Apparently, being a moody mess is what happens when you have ovaries and a functional uterus you didn't have in November. Then my husband started snickering. That's when he assigned some blame to one of the Quinns."

My husband chuckled. "I'll accept a lot of the responsibility. Had I known you wanted children, I would have had the problem fixed long ago. Any incubus or succubus can do the work. I'm not as good at it, so I had Arthur ask my grandfather. My uncle helped. They actually started messing with you before Christmas. There's no guesswork on the conception date, if you'd like to give that to your doctors. That said, your real doctors have been preselected for you, and I'd like to see a human beat an archangel at the baby game, especially my grandfather, who will do just about anything for an invitation to babysit children."

"Can I thank you in a few days after I deal with a ridiculous number of tests? You know how tests make me when I'm not the one conducting them, Sam."

"You're welcome, Tiffany. My wife is innocent this once, though. She was too busy hoodwinking me for twins with my other relatives to be able to hoodwink you into having quadruplets."

"I'll come up with a suitable present. There aren't really any standard treatments for my problem."

"Outside of an incubus or succubus, and those are expensive."

"It would have been five million," Perkette replied. "I'd looked into it before marrying Arthur, and Arthur was okay with what we couldn't have, and well, who has that sort of money?"

I choked on my own spit. "It's how much for what?"

"It's five million for that level of miracle unless you get lucky and an incubus or succubus decides to take pity on you. I've never gotten lucky. That's pretty rare, but it does happen."

I grumbled curses. "That's insane."

"It is what it is. I mean, no ovaries is a pretty big stumbling block. I'm going to have to explain this to my mother. She's going to accuse me of having slept with the Devil. And then Arthur is going to laugh. I'll have to tell her no, I slept with Arthur, but the Devil *may* have involved himself, and that's just going to be an interesting discussion."

I dug out my personal laptop, booted it up, and opened the word processor. "So, Perkette. How exactly does a strong, manly gorgon-incubus doohickey make my favorite treat? I need napalm, and he wants to be able to make it himself. You know, in case we can't swing by the CDC and get them to give it to me."

"Despite her grumpy attitude about that, the CDC is allowing her to have napalm. I'd just feel better if I can make it myself."

"Well, which grade do you want and how expensive do you want her treats? I have varying recipes."

"Start me with a lower grade and work me up to better grades."

"Okay. This one isn't a terrible grade, it's cheap, and it's easy enough for manly gorgon-incubus doohickeys to make. Go to a camping store and get a big jug of the camping gel."

"Methanol?" Quinn asked.

"Yeah. Methanol gel. You can get the pink stuff, too. Either works for this. Mix that with equal parts diesel, a quarter part neutralizer, and hot sauce. The hot sauce is only because Bailey likes hot things and I thought it was amusing, so I added it. Once you have that all mixed together, seal it up in a container so the fumes don't kill you. I recommend you use a practitioner trick to contain the fumes. They're a problem with this mixture. Get some charcoal, grind it up or smash it, and add it to the mixture. Quarter part. Then add a quarter part of lighter fluid. Use a cup as a part, and that'll give her enough to cause some trouble and have a good time without the extreme hangover—hopefully."

"Napalm hangovers are the worst," I complained.

"Well, you be careful making that for her, Sam. It's toxic, and the only reason I get away with making it is because of practitioner tricks. If you can't do the tricks, I'll make several batches and put them in sealed containers for her enjoyment."

"I can handle the required practitioner tricks, so don't worry about that. How about the higher grade napalm?"

Perkette listed more ingredients, how much needed to be added of each, and the extra precautions needed to mix the stuff without asphyxiating in the process. "I rec-ommend against mixing it until you need it, unless you're really good at sealing in fumes."

"I'll be careful," my husband promised. "And I will ration out her treats in acceptable quantities."

"Good idea. Ah, bugger. I have to go back into the hospital gauntlet, where I'll get yelled at for my age in addition to the appearance of ovaries I shouldn't have. Wish them luck. If they keep pissing me off, they're going to need it!"

She hung up before we could say a word, and I saved the formulas for the napalm. "Maybe we should have given her a little more warning."

"Maybe a little, but I'm sure she'll be fine. That said, we better leave them gifts and bribes until she forgives us for meddling behind her back."

"Us?" I asked. "I think you mean you. I was too busy meddling behind your back to meddle behind hers."

"I'm sure she'll only make me suffer a little."

I laughed so hard I cried. "Sure, Sam. Keep telling yourself that if it makes you feel better."

ON HIS QUEST TO be the perfect husband, Quinn decided we needed burgers with fries, and he scoured Maine to find a takeout place suitable for my special needs.

The sad truth revealed itself upon our arrival at the fast food joint he'd selected.

My reformed fish-hating spouse had found a place with lobster rolls and burgers so he could indulge while pretending to cater to me. I raised a brow at the menu posted by the door. "If you think I'm getting a burger when sea bugs on bread are readily available, you're insane. Oh! Clam chowder."

"I wanted you to have the option for a burger if you wanted it, although I see my choice of making sure they also served sea bugs was sound. So, what would my beautiful like for lunch today?"

I checked the offerings again, and I gasped when I noticed the pet menu. "They have a menu just for pets!"

"We can dine in because it's a pet friendly establishment. That was also a factor."

I squealed and bounced in place, and Blizzard bounced with me, barking his excitement. Avalanche, as was her wicked way, pounced the husky's tail. "I was already resigned to eating in the rental until we made it to the hotel tonight."

"I thought this would give us a good chance to come up with a strategy."

"How are we going to come up with a strategy without knowing what we'll find?"

"I'm going to make some educated guesses." Smiling, my husband took Sunny's leash, and the instant he ordered her to heel and headed for the restaurant's front doors, Blizzard and Avalanche followed, doing their best to heel with Quinn.

Laughing, I hurried to catch up so the poor animals wouldn't try to strangle themselves heeling as ordered. To keep the pets happy, I shoved their leashes into my husband's hands. "We need to teach them to heel with the leash holder rather than the person giving the order."

"I find this oversight hilarious and endearing."

While my husband juggled three leashes and the animals, I strolled to the counter, which instructed us to stand in one place to order or wait to be seated. As I expected trouble, I got out our permits for our pets.

The hostess, a young woman with her pale hair captured in a ponytail, gasped when she saw Avalanche. "Oh, what a cute kitty! What breed is that?"

"She's an ocelot kitten." I held out the paperwork the CDC had given me. "I hope she won't be a bother?"

"Oh, absolutely not. Pets are welcome as long as they're legal. We keep the animals on this side of the restaurant, and we use some practitioner magic to keep allergens out of the other half of the restaurant. Will you need the pet menu?"

"We absolutely will need the pet menu. This is their first time in a restaurant."

The hostess smiled. "For two humans and three pets?"

"Yes, please."

"This way." The waitress led us to a booth, handed us the menus, and headed off, returning with three pet beds, which she put down on the floor at our feet. The puppies and kitten needed no other invitation and made themselves at home. "Would you like anything to drink?"

"Coffee, black," my husband requested, and he stared into my eyes as he did so.

"Spiced minty grass of some sort." Damn it. "Tea. I meant tea!"

"We have spiced grass, but it isn't minty," the hostess replied with a smile. "We have mint syrup if you'd like your spiced grass to be minty, however."

"Hit me up with a pot of the regular spiced grass, and because I'm really curious, a cup of spiced grass with mint syrup," I replied, meeting my husband's challenging gaze with a raised brow.

"I don't know what I just lost in that exchange, but take me for all your worth, because you won that without question," my husband stated as soon as the woman left. "Also, for the record, she thinks you're hot."

"Wait. She thinks *I'm* hot? Not you?"

"Yep."

I blinked, leaning over to catch a glimpse of the woman as she went to make our drinks. "You're not upset, are you? Does this bother your sexy incubus self? She's a woman. Didn't you say rejection hurts your pride?"

"I am more delighted because she sees you like I see you, and that is very gratifying. My sexy incubus self is rather pleased with this. Really, I'm very pleased, and you will be rewarded for being so beautiful tonight. I have zero regrets about this situation."

"She gets a huge tip when we leave. And whatever I think is huge probably isn't, so we need to double whatever number I try to put in as a huge tip." I giggled and ducked my head. "This might be a first."

"It is part of my extensive campaign to raise your self-esteem."

"You're very good for my self-esteem. I seem to have graduated from my initial knee-jerk disbelief to concern my sexy incubus might become unpleasantly jealous rather than delighted." I leaned towards him and whispered, "If I wasn't already the prey of a sexy incubus, I'd say she's really pretty."

"That is because she is really pretty," my husband replied with a soft laugh, and he checked on our pets. "Is Avalanche doing okay with her meats? I know you're giving some to her every day, but you don't usually give her a lot. She's still pretty heavily drinking milk?"

"She would very much appreciate some fresh meat from the pet menu, but she should still get her milk, and her meat needs to be in small pieces, so we should look at the kitten menu for her." I checked the pet menu, my brows raising at the wide assortment of meats and brands they kept for pets. "This is a pet paradise, Sam! They even have moose. Oh, they have edible bones, Sam. We need to get those for the puppies." I thrust the menu at him. "Are any of those bone types what you give them?"

He checked. "Yeah, these are good. I'll order a few extra for the road so they can keep busy while we're driving around and in the hotel room tonight. We'll get a box for them to go. It should keep them happy. Oh, I want you to do rabies treatments on them in a few days, just in case, and we'll do a round ourselves. No idea if we'll be exposed handling this, so I'd rather just pretend we will be."

I wrinkled my nose. "I will be sad if I flip off that damned marker again."

"And if you do, my grandfather will flip it back on, so don't worry about it. He'll want to check on you weekly anyway to make sure the babies are okay."

"It's going to be a constant stream of worriers, visiting and visiting and visiting. Make it clear if they visit, they babysit!"

"I can do that."

The waitress returned with our drinks, and we ordered for our pets first, which amused the woman. Once certain our furry friends were cared for, I ordered a salad to appease my husband's vegetable-eating ways to go with my sea bug roll.

It amused me when he ordered the same thing.

"I have learned when it comes to sea bugs, I should follow your lead."

"What is this strategy you want to talk about?"

"I've been thinking," he began.

"Thinking, now that's a seriously frightening statement right there. That's almost as bad as when I've claimed to be thinking. Do you know what happens when I think?"

"A slightly mitigated version of what happens when you don't think."

I would feel that burn for at least an hour. "Oh, wow. Do that again."

He laughed. "I swear, Bailey. You're the only woman I know who enjoys it when I fling zingers at you."

"That one was just beautiful. I need more of that, or I start thinking life is too perfect. But then those zingers make it actually perfect. I can't help it. I'm a glutton for punishment, and it burns better when you're the one handling the punishment."

Still laughing, he sipped his coffee. "It's not as good as yours, but I've learned there is no coffee as good as yours. However, this was made by someone who knows how to operate a coffee machine."

I held out my hands. "Sip!" He handed me his mug, and I took a tentative sip. As promised, someone with some skill with a coffee maker had made the brew. After a moment of thought and a second sip, I returned his drink. "You may go to the car and retrieve our Thermos, and you may pay the nice waitress to fill it for us. And you'll call your grandfather and find out if coffee is off the list of things I can have, because that is good enough I will drink it with minimal complaint it's not as good as mine."

"The highest of accolades," he teased.

"It's true! Less tease, more strategy. Although you can still tease while we strategize. I don't think I can handle a day without feeling the burn."

"We're going to play the flame game."

"The what game?"

"The flame game. Essentially, the goal is to burn Morrison in all regards. We must completely destroy his reputation at the same time we, if an opportunity happens to present itself, eliminate him as a risk. Ideally, we will figure out what his end game is so we can burn that to the ground, too. What we need to know is why Morrison and Audrey wanted to convert so many people into gorgons."

"That seems simple enough to me. Gorgons aren't protected by most of the human laws. They're considered second-rate citizens and have very specific ways they have to behave. They're executed if they don't follow those rules," I replied. "But if there are sufficient gorgons mass petrifying people, those laws would go second to the recovery of petrified citizens. However, if the infection rate is as high as what Audrey was hoping for, Morrison would be in a position to eliminate most Manhattan law enforcement, yourself included, as the grade of gorgons produced would not qualify to serve in any policing roles. The plan falls apart because of your rating and base genetics, which Audrey didn't know about."

"Right, because all of my official documentation lists human as my primary species, which is true."

"I'm listed as a cindercorn. Why is that allowed but gorgons aren't?"

"Probably for the same reason centaurs are allowed. Centaurs with the appropriate magical rating can serve as police chiefs, as they are not considered to be unfairly matched to humans. Gorgons have a lot of dangerous defenses, and despite their sometimes human behaviors and appearances, they are not humans. Centaurs look human enough despite their bodies being that of animals—and genetically, they are usually a majority of human genetics. Gorgons have no human genetics unless you're a mix like I am."

Oh. Huh. "Gorgons really don't have human genetics?"

"They don't have any human genetics. They just resemble humans. And yes, I will be having Beauty and Sylvester DNA tested. We don't know if being live birthed changed their genetics. They'll have legal protections if they have any human DNA instead of pure gorgon. It's not much extra protection, but even a single percent will make trafficking them a felony."

"It's not a felony to traffic gorgons?"

"No. It's a borderline misdemeanor. If someone were to be found guilty of three charges of trafficking a gorgon, then it would classify as a felony. Should the gorgon be a mix with any human genetics, it is treated as human trafficking, which is a felony."

I scowled, and I couldn't help but wonder if men like Morrison had been responsible for those shitty laws. "That absolutely fucking disgusts me."

"I know, I know. It's not fair. We have to pick our battles, Bailey. So, what we call the flame game in our precinct is a fairly simple concept to understand but rather difficult to execute. We typically work this angle with large-scale operations against crime lords and gangs. The idea is to make a multi-pronged attack to burn the culprits out. Stage one is to discredit the group in the eyes of the public. This gives law enforcement more room to work, as it's easier to do our job when the public isn't upset with us. In the case of Morrison, we need to thoroughly discredit him. Once we have connections established to 120 Wall Street and his various other ploys, that phase of the flame game will be remarkably simple. The next phase is to burn his current operations and discredit him through his past operations—and make certain those plans are thoroughly burned. Once again, this has to be done in such a way that the public sympathizes with law enforcement. Morrison was not disliked in his home turf, so we will need to work the Hamptons fairly hard, especially if we end up saddled with helping to handle Long Island in addition to Manhattan."

"That's too much work, Sam. Nobody can handle that much jurisdiction sanely." Quinn could barely handle his work with Manhattan as it was.

"Well, I'm glad you're able to see that with such clarity. What it would really mean is that instead of Manhattan, Long Island, and Staten Island working with independent chiefs, we'd ultimately work more jointly, in that the established chiefs would have connected jurisdiction. It's something we've talked about for a while but haven't implemented. Losing Morrison would put us short some chiefs, and this would let us better work the whole territory. That way, we could get a chopper to take us to anywhere in the general New York City and surrounding areas without having to do the dance we do now. If we burn Morrison sufficiently, we might be able to get that passed. Commissioner Dowry has been discussing it with the other commissioners to see if it's plausible. We'd probably become the voice for most of the New York City region. They like having me handle public announcements."

"Well, your ridiculous sexiness has something to do with that. Plus when you talk, it usually makes sense. Or maybe it doesn't make sense, but you're talking, so who cares if it makes sense? You have to be careful about that smile though, sir. That smile incinerates panties. Mine, for the record."

He grinned at me. "I'm aware."

Evil, evil gorgon-incubus doohickey. "Please tell me one of the phases of the flame game is to burn Morrison literally."

"Ideally, for my peace of mind, yes. It depends on if he violates his restraining order. If he does, you absolutely are within your rights to burn him. I'd also be within my rights to deal with him. However, I would likely go with petrification and allow the flame game to play out to its full extent."

"But he might do more harm if he lives."

"Bailey, I give his lifespan no longer than a week if he's sent to prison. He's responsible for the deaths of children. There is an angelic confirmation of sexual assault of a minor. While the worst of the worst end up in prison rather than out doing community service, they have limits. That? That crosses their lines. The instant he's put into general holding, he'll be dealt with. If he happens to be put in the same prison with those he's put away? It won't end well for him. Frankly, it would be more merciful if you used your biggest fire on him. That leads to the next job."

"Wait, there's more?"

"We do our best to set it up where nobody wants to try that sort of scheme again."

For fuck's sake. "You seriously think someone might copycat him?"

"Audrey and Morrison couldn't have been working alone. That bed and breakfast is good evidence of that. Whoever was running that place was aware of it. I suspect whoever ran the place we're going to next was also aware of it, depending on what we find. For all I know, Audrey really could have just been heading up there for a tryst. But after seeing the other place? I doubt it."

I did, too. "Do you think the CDC is looking into the previous owners of that bed and breakfast?"

"Oh, I know they are. They were already working on the investigation at the site. Having a liaison there was not a mistake. The FBI is getting involved, too."

"Because the incidents crossed state lines?"

"It's being flagged a terrorism event."

"Terrorism?"

"Gorgons may not be humans, but they're sentients, and while the law often does not favor them, the species lines were blurred, and this rabies outbreak is terrorizing gorgons. So, it's the FBI's jurisdiction, and they're working with the CDC. They'll work with us, too. This is the kind of case everyone wants closed as quickly as possible. They know people are dying, and if it goes unchecked, more people are going to die. I suspect they'll focus on the infected feeder mice to start with, while the interior staff does the groundwork on the bed and breakfast. Ideally, we'll direct the CDC over. Fortunately, it's easy to prove I wasn't involved with any of these."

"You worked seven days a week most weeks of the year." I'd guessed that much from looking over his papers and receipts. "You couldn't have been involved because you were in Manhattan working all of the time."

"That plus angelic verification, which I did after your apartment was bombed and the 120 Wall Street incident."

"Wait. You angelically verified that? But why?"

"I am an overbearing police chief who had a crush on you, and I am considered ruthless enough to napalm my future wife's apartment in a shameless ploy to make her move in with me."

My mouth dropped open. "You wouldn't!"

He laughed. "I know that, Commissioner Dowry knows that, everyone who knows me knows that, but any time a chief is determined to have personal involvement with a crime, we have to verify our lack of involvement. Morrison dodged that because he's a clever asshole—but his game was up the instant he had Janet kidnapped. He forgot when something happens to one of our cops, if *any* law enforcement officer questions the situation, the chief will be required to undergo angelic verification."

"You don't think he would make it through verification."

"I know he wouldn't. But the accusation involving you overrode his connection to Janet's kidnapping. Assuming he's caught, that'll be carefully scrutinized, but nobody had made the base accusation of his direct involvement. It was on the minds of a lot of people, but he hadn't been formally accused, and innocent until proven guilty still applies."

"Right. But we're piling up a lot of evidence, though it's circumstantial right now, isn't it?"

"The instant an angel verifies the truth from a victim, that's that. Angels cannot lie or they fall, and it's pretty damned obvious when an angel falls. As such, Morrison is already guilty of a felony and will lose his rank. How much more guilt is on his shoulders remains to be seen."

"All right. So, what do we do at this place we're going to today?"

"We check for evidence, and if it's there, we contact the CDC. If there's no evidence, we leave and head for Long Lake at your father's recommendation. I don't want to see what Ra will do to protect you, and the last thing we need is a divine breaking one of the universal laws because his daughter can't stay out of trouble. I expect there will be trouble, but at least it's sanctioned trouble, and your father can handle that. Surprise trouble that threatens you or your mother? Let's just say while Egyptian, the consequences of him breaking certain rules would probably help the End of Days come along in a hurry. Divine doesn't mean infallible, and he's pretty damned aware he's missed out on the entirety of your life so far. Anything that might cut your life short? He won't handle it well." My husband sighed. "Neither would I."

"It would be weird if you did. In other news, I don't handle threats to you very well, either."

"Oh, you handle them just fine. Except you tend to get yourself hurt in the process. And even when you don't get hurt, you find some way to scare the liver out of me."

I frowned. "Where do you think that asshole cadet got that ambrosia from anyway?"

"That is a very good question, and truth be told? I'm not sure it's one I want the answer to. The last thing I need is to have to face off against some idiot divine with a dire lack of common sense and ethics. The last I checked, the CDC was investigating to see if they were missing any ambrosia. Morrison has access to one of the CDC vaults, so chances are, he just stole it from there. That is also a felony, and that would become a critical part of the flame game should it be proven to be the case."

"Why? Because people don't tend to like when mere men attempt to become gods, or that there is a high chance of the ambrosia taking him out along with an entire city block out when he goes?"

"Mostly the general acceptance he would be taken out along with an entire city block. People don't like when assholes are willing to kill them for the sake of power."

"I agree with that. Can we make a plan other than don't destroy evidence, call people at the appropriate times, make sure our furry prince and princesses are content, and eliminate all threats to our children?"

"A plan for accomplishing those things would be nice."

"Quinn, look at who you're talking to here. Have I ever made a plan that actually survived to its conclusion?"

"You did pretty well with those phoenixes, although I would appreciate if you did not do that again. Phoenixes are really bad for my blood pressure. Your plan to run away from home went off pretty well, too. You made it to your destination and acquired what you set out to acquire."

"A full night of sleep is vastly underrated, Quinn. However, I would be content enough with maybe only two or three nights of those a week. It turns out I don't sleep all that well when you're not around, and that sucked."

"I will do my best to make sure your sleeping needs are met."

As I could interpret that in one of two ways, I eyed him.

He smirked.

Evil, evil, delicious gorgon-incubus doohickey. "You're a bad, bad man, Sam."

"I try."

SIXTEEN

I need you to zing me, Quinn.

WHILE I KEPT a close eye on our pets, Quinn went to the bathroom. Avalanche growled over her scraps of moose meat, minced so she could eat it without any difficulty. Sunny devoured her bones with startling efficiency, and Blizzard spent as much time playing with his bones as he did chewing on them.

By the time my husband returned, with his smuggest smile in place, I'd been completely bewitched by our animals.

"They're so cute," I informed him, pointing at Sunny. "She is a most fierce huntress of bones. Did we get her enough?"

He checked under the table. "That's a good amount for her to have, and we're getting plenty for the road, so don't worry. Your puppy won't starve. I see your other puppy is making a mess."

"He's really good at that. It's his special power, along with howling complaints should we dawdle and he needs to go out."

"He's surprisingly quiet for a husky and far less opinionated than I believed. The dumpster life must have toned him down."

"He's the perfect dumpster puppy, and he was only a little rabid when I rescued him. I still don't understand why anyone would dump a puppy like that. If I hadn't pulled him out of the dumpster, he would have suffocated in that bag."

"Before you get too emotional, he is fine, he's enjoying his bone, he's quite possibly tied with Sunny for being the perfect puppy, and he's going to have a great life, because he has you to care for him."

I found praise a lot harder to cope with than one of his burns. "I need you to zing me, Quinn."

"Was that too much reinforcement of why you're a good woman?"

"Yes."

"I'll think of something appropriate. A good zinger has to be properly set up and deployed for maximum enjoyment. That plus it's more fun if you're not expecting it. The shock on your face is almost as delightful as your enjoyment of a good zinger. You'll survive until the right moment comes."

"You're mean."

"Yes, I am so mean. I'm forcing you to practice your coping strategies when someone says something nice to you. I am the cruelest husband."

"Liar, liar, pants on fire."

"Please don't light my pants on fire. I know I'm tempting, but we're in a restaurant."

I giggled. "I'm not that bad!"

"Really?"

"I thought you were waiting to zing me."

"That wasn't a zing. It was a verbal caress and a warm-up for an actual zing, which will happen at a time of my choosing."

I loved my evil, evil gorgon-incubus doohickey. "So, about that coffee."

My husband showed me his phone, which revealed a text conversation with his angelic grandfather confirming I could enjoy coffee for at least a few more months, although I would be cut off five months into my pregnancy, as nobody needed a hormonal, caffeine-fueled cindercorn taking over or attempting to destroy the world.

Wow. The Quinn family had it out for me. "I'm going to feel that zinger for a while. That implies if I have any coffee after five months, I will be a world-destroying menace. Or the empress of the planet. Hmm."

"We were just talking about how a merged jurisdiction would be too much work," he reminded me. "You do not want to be responsible for the entire planet."

Right. "Okay, no coffee after five months, then. But if my spiced grass supply is limited, there will be severe problems."

"I'm sure we'll be able to take care of your special needs. When we hit the road, I want you to start phase one of the flame game while I drive. Build a document detailing everything the asshole has done, things we suspect he's done, and start organizing it in a coherent fashion. We'll turn that into strategic press releases and commentary one of our attorneys will use to sway the public in court. Skipping on bail means there will be a trial, he won't be in attendance, although he will have a public defender, and it will be open for the public so the judge can hear all of the accusations and determine how to proceed. That trial will exist because Morrison is a police chief being accused—and already determined guilty—of a felony. We can do this because of my grandfather and your willingness to go through angelic verification."

"We can burn him fairly hard right out of the gate, then."

"Right. My grandfather will testify during this to confirm his guilt, as due process does need to be maintained to a certain degree. This is our chance to layer on a lot of charges and help burn him in the eyes of the public."

"What about Morrison's son? Won't he go under fire if he's discovered?"

"We'll have to work to prevent that. Ideally, we'll be able to get a hold of him and put him into protective custody with a strong hive—and reunite him with his mother."

"That poor woman."

"She'll be okay. Saven is a lot of things, but

he has a surprisingly strong sense of justice. It's part of why he hasn't been taken out yet. It's hard to break the cycle when the victims walk away better for it. Yes, he commits crimes, yes, he's definitely a criminal, but the victims often get life-saving treatments they couldn't afford before becoming involved with his brood and their sex demons. He chooses his victims with care. It helps he also harshly deals with the criminals who step across the wrong line. If he keeps acting like that, I expect most law enforcement entities will continue to ignore him. The replacement would probably be far worse. And in some cases, he ultimately helps law enforcement."

"How?"

"He cleans house in his cities, and corruption in the force is a serious issue. That's also part of why I've been given so many responsibilities. My precinct doesn't have the corruption problems others suffer through."

"That is because you're one of those insufferably angelic types," I replied.

"I try."

"Okay. I can do that, especially if I will be armed with coffee. Did we have a second Thermos in the SUV?"

"We have three, plus we have several travel mugs from the gift shop. They had a cindercorn one I got you, so I'll get that filled for you."

"Cindercorns are the *best*. But why are there so many cindercorn products now?"

"Well, several months ago, somebody dusted 120 Wall Street with some high-grade gorgon dust, and a cindercorn mare, the most beautiful to exist, consumed a ridiculous amount of enhanced napalm, reducing the building to rubble. Upon finishing her hard work, she rampaged where a bunch of reporters could record her through the shield. She chanted wonderfully amusing love songs to her favorite narcotic, becoming a media sensation. Of course, New York opted to encourage the love of cindercorns, so you are now famous and a beloved force of destruction."

"Your sarcasm doesn't need any work. I thought you should know this."

He smiled. "Well, you asked."

"I'm on designer *purses*, Sam!"

"As you should be. You're the most beautiful of cindercorns, and you're all mine. But I am not entirely selfish, so everyone should be able to admire your badass beauty."

"You are something else."

"Finish your sea bug roll while I order treats for the pets to go and take care of your coffee needs. I'm also going to order you another sea bug roll for the road, as I know full well you're ignoring those last two bites because you don't want me to think you're still hungry despite having polished off everything else."

Damn. I picked up the last token bite or two I'd left because he tended to keep feeding me until I couldn't finish off my plate. "Better get me two," I mumbled.

"I'll get three so I can have one since watching you eat yours will make me hungry for more sea bugs, but I'll give you half of mine because I can't inhale food in quite the same quantity."

"You're the best husband."

"You deserve the best."

While I polished off every scrap from my plate and began the tedious work of convincing our pets they could finish their treats and bones in the SUV, after we put down a sheet to mitigate how much of a mess they made on the leather, my husband fetched the tools of coffee containment from our vehicle and ordered too much food to go, including the fries I'd drooled over but had skipped out on in favor of the healthier salads my husband liked.

I hid a twenty dollar bill partially under my plate, and then I repeated the process with my husband's plate, making sure he didn't catch me in the act of over-tipping, as he always tipped at the counter. Once I finished my naughty work of tipping extra, I gathered our pets' leftovers into the cardboard containers the waitress had left for us and joined my husband while the animals did their best to trip me.

"It'll be about ten minutes, my beautiful. Do you want to handle their walk while I finish in here?"

I nodded. "I'll make sure the snow is out of their fur before setting up their travel palace."

Walking the three pets involved a lot of leash dodging and untangling, and all three of them handled their business like champs, although I wished Avalanche didn't insist on burying hers, which added to the complexity of properly disposing of their messes. I almost made it to the SUV when Quinn came out of the restaurant burdened with several bulging bags with the waitress following carrying a tray with our coffees. "So much coffee," I breathed with wide eyes.

My husband laughed and kissed my cheek. "Try not to enter orbit drinking most of it. Retrieving you would take a lot of work."

The waitress laughed. "While I was making your coffee, he told me about how you had rescued two of your pets!"

I recognized the signs of hero-worship, as I indulged in such behaviors at least once a day with my husband. At a loss of what to do about it, I picked up Avalanche and held her out. "If I could have rescued her mother, I would have. This is a very lucky kitten."

Quinn opened the passenger side front door and put the bags on my seat before taking the tray from the waitress. "That is my wife's way of saying you should hold the exotic kitten and make friends with her. Avalanche loves people, which is a good thing, as she won't be a candidate for release back into the wild. Sunny was a gift from my relatives, although I have come to understand the gift is also a prank against her father."

"We have the best families, and their feuds are cordial, hilarious, yet surprisingly intense." Once the waitress had both hands free, I gave her Avalanche. "I found Blizzard in a dumpster outside of a police station, and he's quite possibly the best husky puppy on Earth. He limits his protests to when we do something particularly heinous. We were late with his breakfast this morning."

"That is particularly heinous," she agreed, and she smiled, cuddling with Avalanche, who was happy to work her charms as usual. "I'm Bethany."

"Bailey. He's Sam."

"He looks just like that police chief out of New York."

"That's because he is that police chief out of New York," I replied, unable to contain my giggles. "He's shockingly normal outside of work. He's recently taken up the mantle of tour guide for me."

Bethany's eyes widened. "You're her."

Uh oh. A thousand possibilities crossed through my mind, all of which involved me having been deemed a villainess or terrorist of some sort. "I'm her?"

"The cindercorn!"

Oh. I dug into my purse and retrieved my NYPD badge so I could show her my species label. "They even officiated it on my badge! It's new, and I didn't notice the designation until recently."

"She becomes very excited about her status as a cindercorn." My husband chuckled and herded Sunny and Blizzard into the vehicle. "She operates on coffee and spite."

"Spite? Spite? Tell that to my face, Mr. Police Chief Samuel Quinn!"

My husband turned, looked me in the eyes, and replied, "You operate on coffee and spite."

If I loved him any more, I would either faint or implode. "It's true, I really do. And possibly napalm. Her coffee is almost as good as mine, Sam. But no coffee beats napalm. But I can operate on napalm, and I resent that most do not agree with me."

"You definitely can operate on napalm. I've seen what you'll do for some napalm— and what happens after you get a hold of it."

Bethany giggled. "The news reports said you had a feud, but then the reports said you were married, and it was all confused. But you have a feud *and* you're married. Were the rumors not true?"

"About the pictures of my ex-wife?" my husband asked. When she nodded, he grinned. "They're absolutely true, and that's the story of how I fell in love with a trouble-making cindercorn who rightfully has earned her title as the Calamity Queen."

"I'm on vacation from creating calamities,"

I announced, bumping my husband aside to check on Sunny and Blizzard, who had passed out on the seat. "Oh! The poor babies must have been tired."

"It's exhausting work eating treats."

It really was. "Make sure Avalanche is nestled with Blizzard, or we'll have a concerto in the back seat when they wake up and things aren't to their liking." While Quinn talked to Bethany, answering her question with more patience than I could muster on a good day, I secured our coffees so they wouldn't spill and could be easily retrieved for refills down the road. "Get a card or something for this place, because this is now my favorite road trip stop."

"Why am I not surprised?"

As I'd already done enough to embarrass myself, I dove into my work to finish preparing for the next leg of our trip, discovering my husband had purchased six of the cindercorn travel mugs. "Really, Sam?" As we didn't need six, I snagged one and held it out to Bethany. "Apparently, my excessive husband thinks I needed six of these, so this is now part of your tip, because anyone who makes coffee as good as you do obviously deserves a cindercorn travel mug."

Quinn shrugged. "We have issues with coffee."

"Insufficient travel mugs will never be a problem in our household." As Bethany couldn't take the coffee containment vessel while holding Avalanche, I eyed her apron, discovered it had big pouches, and put it inside. "There! Now you can drink your coffee in style." I scooped up my ocelot, buried my face in her fur, and dove to the SUV, scrambling inside before I could make even more of a fool out of myself.

"She means thank you for the wonderful time, and she hopes you have a great rest of your day," my husband translated.

I caught a glimpse of the woman smiling and handing something to Quinn. "You're welcome, and thank you. Have a safe drive."

Once I had the door safely closed, I took off Avalanche's harness and eased her onto Blizzard, who slept on without a care in the world. Quinn got behind the wheel, started the engine, and snickered.

"I'm sorry. I made a mess of that."

"Was that because you forgot your usual tip sneaking and you became embarrassed or you genuinely saw the extra travel mugs and wanted her to have one?"

"I hid forty dollars under our plates," I confessed.

"I tipped her as though you were not going to be sneaking cash under the plates as you usually do, so she'll have a pretty good afternoon once she checks her tips. I also tipped the other staff separately after asking how many people were working."

"Oh, that was really nice of you."

"The kitchen staff don't get tipped often, and they did a great job on our lunch, so I decided to dip into my wife's not-so-secret tip fund."

Crap. "You found that?"

"Bailey, you have it listed in the budget as your tip fund."

Double crap. "You actually *read* our budget?"

"It's not much use if I don't read it, my beautiful. Your 'Convince Sam I Really Actually Love Him' fund is rather adorable, and I will deny its existence if I'm questioned about it. That said, I don't know what you have in mind for that fund, you sneaky woman, but I'm really looking forward to finding out."

Triple crap on a cracker. "That's the presents fund, and it's not just presents for you, but I figured maybe bribery was a viable tactic."

"I see I will have to continue corrective therapy sessions in the evening to convince you that you do not need to convince me."

So tragic, being invited to yet another corrective therapy session. "I really am the reason I don't get enough sleep. Goodbye, sleep. Did I really need sleep anyway?"

"I will take more care to monitor how much sleep you're actually getting, but I will do so in such a way you do not feel you're being punished while getting something you need, unless you want to go witness Tiffany brassault a bunch of cops in Atlantic City again?"

"After helping to raise quadruplets, will she even have enough energy to run away to Atlantic City?"

"Well, with that in mind, I'm thinking I'll make sure Arthur has four daily spots at the daycare. Fortunately for us, they're expanding, so we should be able to get spots. And if there aren't spots, I'll negotiate with the building owners to help them expand even more. It's job growth."

"Can I afford to take over the day care and expand it every time we have children so we don't displace anyone else's children?"

My husband frowned, put the SUV into gear, and began the drive to Kennebago. "Talk to me again after we're home."

"That wasn't a no."

"It's more I would need to check your stock performance and think about it. Could you afford the yearly pay of staff, insurance, building maintenance, and supplies? I think so. But could we afford to pay out the owner and hire them to manage it? That I'm not sure of. I *will* say that the owner would love not having to worry about the operational costs."

"Holding that thought until we get home." I dug out my second lobster roll and went to work putting it into my stomach where it belonged.

"I see my cindercorn is really hungry."

As talking would slow my digestion rate, I freed a hand and pointed at my flat stomach, blaming the twins for Quinn's careful cultivation of my appetite and providing delicious sea bugs for my consumption.

"I'm not sure you're far enough along in your pregnancy to increase your general ability to eat, but you know what? I'll let you get away with it. I accept the blame for your current ravenous state."

I bobbed my head and focused on my extended lunch, while debating the best ways to incinerate Morrison with my husband's version of the flame game.

IN ORDER TO convince my husband I could be a reasonable person when the situation demanded it, I made two documents. One, with a little effort and feedback from him, might provide information to the appropriate legal entities how best to charbroil Morrison in the eyes of the judge, the jury, and the people. The other boiled down to my wishlist of various crimes I could nail the bastard on.

Fact would drown my fantasies, but every single crime I could think of went on my second list, and some of them he might've even committed.

"Should I be concerned?" my husband asked.

"I love that you now ask me if you should be concerned rather than automatically worrying?"

"Forty minutes ago, after you inhaled your second lobster roll with alarming enthusiasm, it became suspiciously quiet in this vehicle. The pets are sleeping, and beyond the frantic typing of a woman on a mission to murder, it's been silent. I can hear myself breathe. You're not even giggling, and that level of intensity usually means you're preparing to either light something on fire or tell me something that will, inevitably, alarm me."

"Am I a giggler?"

"When you don't think anyone is watching or you forget you're with others, you absolutely are a giggler. I like it best when you giggle while you're reading a book. I'd get a lot more reading done if I kept reading instead of admiring you while you're lost in your book and giggling."

I paused working to regard him with a thoughtful frown. "I giggle?"

"Is that so hard to believe?"

"Well, yes. I have been rightfully accused of being a dour and depressive excuse of a human being."

"That was before you had a good reason to be happy, Bailey. You're happy now, and there's no reason for you to hide when you're happy. If other people want to be miserable, that's on them. You hurt nobody by being happy, so be happy. When you're happy, I'm happy."

"Well, you are a gorgon-incubus doohickey, and may the heavens forbid if you were to become unhappy."

"I suspect my wicked grandfather is behind all of this. Obviously, he made some form of arrangement for me to meet Audrey—"

"No."

My husband chuckled. "No?"

"That's on my wishlist of crimes Morrison has committed. He recruited Audrey to seduce and marry you specifically so he could collect dirt on you and defame you as a police chief. However, he did not anticipate your inflexibility in your ethics, resulting in Audrey being unable to gather the evidence *or* catch you in the act of cheating or whatever it is other police chiefs might use to discredit one another. As it is on my wishlist of crimes Morrison has committed, your grandfather cannot take credit for your decision to marry her."

"Huh. Do you have a list of plausible crimes?"

"I do."

"Move that wishlist item to your list of plausible crimes and motivations. Motive matters in cases like this, and if that motive is presented, the judge may request additional information from Morrison's cops—and also demand angelic verification. The innocent cops will be critical in the proceedings, as his character is on trial as much as his actions are. It absolutely is a factor if the court determines Morrison was attempting to corrupt or discredit a fellow police chief. That's a direct violation of our oath to our communities and those we serve and protect. That alone would lose him his job, as we're supposed to be the highest ethical standard among uniformed officers. We need to have sufficient circumstantial evidence to warrant additional investigation into Audrey's relationship to Morrison *before* my marriage to her. If we can prove a relationship, that becomes very good fuel for the flame game."

Huh. I copy-pasted the entire section involving my guesses regarding Audrey and Morrison into the more realistic list. "Done."

"As your first wishlist item is worth pursuing, give me your next wishlist item."

"That his son is the product of rape from a woman he forcibly turned into a gorgon, stripping her of her rights as a human so she would not be able to press charges against him."

"Move it to the other list. Both of those are crimes. Angelic verification should be requested on this one, so we need to confirm with her. We'll have to lean fairly heavily on Saven for that, but he probably has an angel or two who owes him a favor and can verify everything before the official verification. Angels can't lie, but that doesn't prevent them from instructing humans on how best to manipulate the truth through omission and careful selection of words. Cases like this trip angelic triggers."

No kidding. "Your grandfather is probably more pissed he has to be questioned as a witness than anything else, because it means he can't play that game this time."

"You're probably right. Next item on your wishlist?"

"He's rabid."

"Bring that up for questioning, because an angel *can* verify if he was, at any point in the past, infected with the virus or treated for it. That's something specific enough they might be able to search through the past without him being present."

"I really meant that he'd just fall over dead in a month or two after the disease progresses because he wouldn't be able to get the right grade of neutralizer to cure it."

"Unless he was behind the warehouse raid and had the neutralizer available," my husband replied.

"Which would make him complicit in a major felony theft and manipulating law enforcement through the 120 Wall Street incident." I copy-pasted that from my wishlist, too.

"Next item?"

"Noodles topped with sea bugs with some form of cream sauce for dinner. I really like sea bugs and believe we should find another restaurant tonight that will serve me sea bugs."

"If you want noodles topped with sea bugs, we shall look for noodles topped with sea bugs. Just don't forget to eat your other sea bug sandwiches before we quest for more sea bugs."

"You should eat your share of the sea bug sandwiches. And have some fries."

"I'm not feeding three, and it seems fair for the twins to get a sea bug roll each."

"Do I get to use that claim when I feel like overeating like some glutton?"

"Considering how infrequently you allow yourself to overeat like some glutton? Yes. Please. You have a horribly difficult time gaining weight, and you need to be packing on some extra healthy pounds right now. You know that pregnancy weight a lot of women complain about after the delivery?"

"I'm concerned for my back and feet," I admitted.

"With your metabolism, if I feed you salads for a week and ask you to keep up with me, you'll have lost all of that weight plus ten extra pounds."

"I'm a freak."

"You're a cindercorn, and I've been feeding you like you're a human woman. All shapeshifters have heightened metabolisms."

"Except you!"

"I do have a heightened metabolism, Bailey. I'm just feeding really well just about every night several times over."

Right. Gorgon-incubus doohickeys had specialized diets of delicious tasty woman, and I was on the menu most nights. Whee! "I'll have to exercise you extra to make sure you don't gain excess weight."

"I'm sure I'll be fine. So, after your noodles with sea bugs, what else is on your list?"

"All of my co-workers abandoned me the day Magnus McGee delivered that cell phone bomb filled with gorgon dust. We should check if Morrison was involved, as we do know his sister was the one who gave him the bomb and ultimately murdered him because he refused to participate in her games."

"Add it to the other list."

"These are supposed to be pipe dream additions, Sam!"

"I'm going to have to make sure you give me both of your lists on all future investigations, because these ideas are the exact kind we need when we're working on identifying a culprit or a motive. Thinking inside of the box is important at times, but creativity is also needed to go along with the understanding that we can't use sane logic on the insane."

"Oh. I was using insane logic on this list."

"And one of the main culprits? Insane. Keep going. Your ideas are good."

"My co-workers, though?"

"If the goal was to infect you with gorgon

dust, and Morrison was somehow linked to their inability to show up to work, then he is an accomplice in the gorgon dust bombing of your apartment. That is considered to be a terrorism event, as it was targeting someone who lived in an apartment complex *and* is a highly certified government contractor. Well, it could be flagged as terrorism, attempted murder, disruption of the peace, destruction of personal property, and a slew of other misdemeanors with a few felonies added in for good measure. As the dust found in your apartment matched 120 Wall Street, that would link Morrison to 120 Wall Street—and potentially make your former co-workers important witnesses. If anyone was hurt preventing them from going to work, then they're owed restitution from Morrison, too."

"This is excessively complicated."

"The cases I'm brought into usually are—otherwise, the detectives would have already handled everything. This would have been bumped to my desk if I hadn't become involved in other fashions. As it is, we're going to be severely scolded by the commissioner for using our vacation time to creatively put ourselves where we might find clues. He's going to see right through my ploy, but because we have receipts for these locations, he won't call me out on it—and even if he does, I'd just honestly claim I had wanted to close the book on that part of my life. Closure is important to him. He became a cop because his family never got closure on the murder of his uncle."

"That's sad."

"It is. That case is still open, and it's in our jurisdiction, so I'll leave the file out on your desk during a slow week so you can start poking your nose into it. He can't afford a wayfinder, and his uncle's body was never found."

"How does he know he was murdered, then?"

My husband smiled. "That is an assumption—one founded on his knowledge of his uncle, how much he cared for his family, and other factors. Nobody in the family believes that his uncle would have just left them."

"But amnesia could have happened."

"And that's exactly why that's some serious lack of closure for them. What if his uncle is still alive? Why did he leave? It's a nagging mystery that hurts his family every time the holidays roll around. So, I'll leave the file on your desk along with everything we have on the Dowry case, and we'll go from there."

"And if we don't like what we find?"

"That's sometimes one of the hardest parts of our job, Bailey. We often don't like what we find. But we'll decide then. Even the stories with an unhappy ending end that way for a reason... and sometimes, we give the families just enough for them to get some closure without the full story ever coming to light. It depends."

"But what if he was murdered?"

"Then we bring the killer to justice and give him closure that way."

"And if he ran away?"

"We find out why—and we get justice for him. Men like that don't run without a reason."

I nodded, and I retrieved the next sea bug roll out of the carry out box so it could fall victim to my anxiety and my hunger. "And if he was involved with an accident and has amnesia or something like that?"

"We involve his family and do what's best for everybody. That one is hard, because if he's having a great life now, it'll be tough to meld his old and his new life together, but it can be done. That's what therapists are for."

"Hey, Quinn?"

"Yes?"

"What do you mean he can't afford a wayfinder? Am I not a good enough wayfinder for him? He thinks I can do this cop thing, but I can't wayfind? I can do it, and I can do it better. And cheaper, since I'm not an asshole enough to charge him for having the magical equivalent of a temper tantrum while looking for something."

My husband laughed. "One disaster at a time, Bailey. One disaster at a time. If you want to help him find his uncle, I'm certainly not going to stop you, but I will set some ground rules for the investigation."

"I mean, we have a map in the back, and I'm pretty sure I saw you bring my junk for this. It'd take like five minutes. I'm fueled! Pull over."

"You want to do this *now*?"

"Well, why not? I can ask if he's dead, alive, or in danger, and get where he's at."

"Wait, you can *ask*?"

"It's usually yes or no questions." I hesitated. "You know those marbles from my apartment?"

"Yes. They're very similar to the ones in with your other wayfinding stuff. I brought them, as it would be a tragedy if you were to lose what's left of your marbles."

Oh. I giggled. "I'm going to feel that one for *days*."

"You really shouldn't be excited when I do that. It encourages me to keep doing it."

"But it was a good one. Do it again. See, I'm encouraging you to keep doing it, so you should keep doing it. You aren't pulling over yet. I can't do my wayfinder trick without my stuff, which is in the back. The very back."

"I'm not against looking into his uncle, but I am going to insist we wait until after we deal with Kennebago and Long Lake. That way, if you get a trail, we can act. Ideally, we would do this when we're in a position to have someone watch over the pets, as we can run as unicorns. Also, as you yourself say your wayfinding is a creator of disasters, we are not creating additional disasters to go with our current disaster. We are at maximum disaster capacity right now."

"It'll only be a little bit of a disaster. Come on. It'll be an *adventure*."

"We're already on an adventure."

"It'll be an adventure within our current adventure."

"I'm not sure we can handle our current adventure as it is. Please be sensible, Bailey."

Me? Sensible? I hoped impending fatherhood hadn't done irreversible damage to my husband. "Sam, why are you asking the impossible of me?"

"Oh, right. I guess asking you to be sensible was a little rough. I'm sorry. Try to be patient. You can use your wayfinder tricks to your heart's content as soon as we're done with this nasty business in Kennebago and Long Lake."

"Or I can just use my wayfinder trick to find the source of this mess and skip Kennebago and Long Lake?"

"Your father went through all of that work to arrange Long Lake, and it would be really rude of us to steal his thunder, especially since he's trying so hard to be the cool dad for you. We should go to Kennebago and Long Lake. If our date with disaster is a no show in Long Lake, then you can steal your father's thunder and find the culprits that way. For now, let your father satisfy himself.

The last thing we need is a divine who just found out he's a father snapping because his daughter got herself in trouble again."

"No take backs!"

My husband sighed. "No take backs. Just try to be *somewhat* reasonable should we need to use your wayfinder magic, okay?"

"So, when *did* the commissioner's uncle disappear, anyway?"

"Huh. Good question. It happened before I joined the force, so at this point in time, it's really unlikely you'll be able to find any good news. I'd have to dig out the file and read it over. That case has been considered dead in the water for a while."

I devoured the rest of my sea bug sandwich, rescued the final one from the container, and debated how best to separate it so my husband could have his share.

"Just eat the whole thing, babe. If you're that hungry, I'm sure I can stop and forage should I become peckish."

"I'm eating my feelings," I admitted. "They're frustrated, hungry feelings."

"Eat the sandwich, my beautiful. You need the extra calories. If you start gaining excess weight, then you can worry about nibbling on those salads you're convinced will rise up and get you."

"Well, if my salads had more sea bugs on them, I'd probably eat salad willingly more often."

"You're going to make me learn how to cook fish, aren't you?"

"You can use other types of sea bugs on salad, too."

"I demand evidence of this."

I laughed. "You just want to explore more sea bug options, now that you know they're open to you."

"I really do."

SEVENTEEN

You really are the reason you don't
get enough sleep.

WE NEEDED to use my wayfinder magic in
order to locate the 'resort' Audrey had visited
once upon a time. In the past few years, nature had done an excellent job of erasing the
trail. The snow was deep enough Avalanche
couldn't navigate through its depths without
disappearing, so my husband carried her
while I transformed and made the journey as
a cindercorn. Sunny and Blizzard bounded
through the drifts, and for the first time since
we'd started our trip, Sam let them off their
leashes.

"Is that good idea?" I stared at Blizzard,
who romped after Sunny.

I gave it five minutes before I needed to
chase down my runaway pets.

"Sunny will keep Blizzard around, and
Sunny won't abandon you. And if I'm wrong,
I'll put on my fur coat and help you track
them down."

"Such a nice stallion. Yes, put on fur coat. I like stallion."

"Tiffany's right. You really are the reason you don't get enough sleep," he teased.

I flicked my tail. "Fur coat?"

"Maybe later. Work first, indulgences after work and we have someone to watch the pets and kids. You may have to survive, sadly, for a while."

I could do sadly. "So much sadness."

Chuckling, my husband stomped through the snow, cradling Avalanche close while the ocelot snuggled against him. I kept an eye on our puppies, who bounded through the trees and ran back to us before running off again like furry lunatics. "Puppies so much fun."

"They really are. Your kitten is a little spoiled, too. She has decided it is nap time, and that I am present only to serve as her bed."

According to my husband's tone, there was nothing better than him being present only to serve as the ocelot's bed. "You love kitty! But my kitty. You tool of kitty, so you prop-er-tee. You best prop-er-tee."

Quinn chuckled. "I have no problems with being your property, especially as this means you're also my property, and I enjoy our joint property arrangements. And if you don't think you're my property, I will implement particularly intensive corrective therapy techniques tonight to reinforce my claim."

"Okay. You do that. After noo-dles with

sea bugs. Need those or might perish from sadness."

"As I can't have my wife perishing from sadness, I will do my best to get you noodles with sea bugs tonight."

I pranced in place and waited for Quinn to pick his way over the trail, following the glimmering path I'd created to guide us to our destination. Snow began to fall, and I dined on fallen trees to keep my heat levels up, although it didn't take much to snort blue flame. "Tiny terrors make me hot," I announced.

"Did you just call our children tiny terrors?"

"I snort blue flame with no effort. This is thing of true fear, terror for those who annoy me! They are the creators of blue flame. They tiny terrors. Very tiny right now. Do I get extra bite from Francisco for calling them tiny terrors?"

"Sure."

"Tiny terrors much trouble. Think we find some-thing here?"

"I hope we find something, else I'll have gotten a lot of exercise for nothing."

"Pets happy, not for nothing. They have much fun. This snow? This snow is fun! Only fun because tiny terrors. Usually not fun."

"I am grateful the tiny terrors turn you into a cold-loving cindercorn rather than a miserable one."

"Much misery without tiny terrors."

"I hope the sea bug populations can handle you and our tiny terrors."

"Me, too. No sea bugs would be sadness."

My magic led us deep into the woods to a clearing with several run-down buildings. Years of abandonment hadn't done the place any favors, although the structures seemed sound enough except for the roof of one of the smaller buildings, which had begun caving in. "That building no safe."

"We'll have to be careful when we check around that one, yes. It looks like your trail is going inside the main building."

I followed after my magic, which had gone for the route of least resistance, entering through a broken window, one too small for my mass. "Put kitten on back, I stand still, you go inside and open door like good Queeny should. Open door for lady."

"What lady?" my husband asked, although he did as asked, placing Avalanche on my back. The ocelot stretched, nestled into my thick fur, and resumed her nap.

"Best burn. So many burns today. Not sure how I will recover. You must help me tonight with recovery."

"We'll see." Smirking, he climbed through the broken window. The instant he made it inside, my magical trail disappeared. He headed to the front door, and careful not to dislodge my furry passenger, I followed. After a few minutes and some cursing, he opened it.

"The lock is rusted and the hinges were stuck," he announced, shouldering the door fully open so I could walk inside. "We'll have to detox."

"Gorgons?" I asked.

"They didn't even bother trying to hide it in this one. We'll need a scanner. I'm going to take the pets to the SUV and call the CDC. They left me with a meter, and it can scan the dust types, so if this is the original dust sample, we'll know about twenty minutes after I start processing it. Alan showed me how to do the test early. He seems to think you are the queen of finding trouble."

"I am the queen of finding trouble. I found you."

He gave me a round of applause. "That was well done. Soon enough, I will have you trained to do that intentionally more often than blurting things when you're nervous."

"Clever boy," I praised, stepping into the battered bed and breakfast.

Sunny halted at the threshold, barked twice, sat down, and barked three times.

"Oh, get rabies and dust. Sunny best puppy. Sam no go in. Out, out. Go get scanner. Only need one rabid person. Take kitten. We treat all pets tonight. No dust on pets."

Quinn scooped Avalanche off my back, leashed both of our puppies, and headed for the SUV. To make sure he didn't get lost, I gave a soft snort and stomped my hoof.

A pink, shimmering trail appeared, leading off in the direction of our rental.

"Good magic."

The entry seemed normal enough, and I followed Quinn's snowy footprints to get a better feel for what had unnerved him. I passed through a short hallway to a large, rustic sitting room, one meant to entertain many people.

Rather than entertained people, decaying barrels rested on the floor while the desiccated bodies of male gorgons hung from the rafters, dust trickling off their bodies to pool over the floor. A shimmering barrier kept the dust to one half of the room, although it, too, eroded from time.

Quinn had come within several feet of showing off his gorgon-incubus doohickey form, and I flattened my ears, counting the bodies, stomping my hoof at the brutality of their deaths.

Like the poor male at the other bed and breakfast, their serpents had been decapitated.

"Who?" I demanded, stomping my hoof again in fury over so many lost lives. Worse, the gorgons had been killed in a fashion nobody deserved.

The dust swirled, creating a haze within the dying barrier, which broke under the onslaught of new magic.

My magic, given life by anger over those killed, ignored its usual rules, spelling out the name of a man I learned to hate to a whole new level.

Morrison.

I resisted the urge to snort, which might erase the precious evidence of Morrison's misdeeds.

"Need proof," I whispered to the dust of the fallen, wondering if ghosts might truly exist. If anywhere in the world might have them, the lounge corrupted into a ghastly tomb surely counted as such a place.

The dust settled, erasing the bastard's name and leaving me alone among the decaying dead. I explored their final resting place, the gray clinging to my legs and trailing in my wake, its damp chill penetrating through my coat. The furniture fell to ruin like everything else, but several books on an end table endured despite the years. Taking care with my sharp claws, I flipped open the topmost title to discover a ledger.

No, not a ledger. A scientific log detailing the progress of the dust batch. Not batches, but batch. Names went with the fallen gorgon, which would allow me to find closure for their hives if they still lived. Quinn's grandfather would know. I memorized their names.

In the back of the book, I found the evidence I needed in the form of several receipts for equipment and supplies, and they bore Morrison's name.

However contaminated with the dust, it

contained the clues we would need to put an end to the man's plans, whatever they were.

The log only provided a step-by-step guide on how to make the dust, and its infection rate, a horrific 25.7%, ensured I would be burning the building to the ground to make certain the recipe and the victims never surfaced again.

"Bailey?" Quinn asked.

"Stay out. This master batch. Bad dust. Recipe here. Morrison name on receipts used in ex-per-ee-men-tay-shun and creation. Use scanner from window, but barrier broken. Dust may get out. Must burn, Sam. They tested. High infection rate."

"How high?"

"Twen-tee five per-cent."

"Did you just say it has a twenty-five percent infection rate?"

"Point seven. Plus point seven."

"Fuck."

"No kidding. Need napalm. Barrier. Around building. No let dust out. Make hurry. Bring big dozer to get tanker here. No let this stay. No big snort big enough for this. Must all burn. I stay in building, get information. Bring good cameras? I take pictures of all pages before burn. Done in few hours. Have names of gorgon, notify family."

"On it. Find what you can, and I'll make the rest of this easy on the CDC and just hand over all of Audrey's files so they can look over everything and do additional investigations.

But if this is the master batch, we should be near the end of this mess."

One could only hope.

AFTER SAM CONFIRMED we'd located the same dust found in my apartment and responsible for the devastation at 120 Wall Street, the CDC descended on the place worse than a nest of infuriated hornets. In good news, I was out of their reach, as they didn't want to send anyone near the building even in a hazmat suit. In better news, I would enjoy as much napalm as I could stomach to make certain I eliminated the entire batch.

Unfortunately, the discovery brought a cranky Marshal Clemmends my way with Professor Yale in tow. They stayed a safe twenty feet from the building, and my former boss opted to use a megaphone to bother me.

"Not deaf but will be if you keep using that!" I snorted flame at him, which did not impress the CDC's asshole head honcho in the slightest.

"I don't feel like ruining my voice yelling at you today."

How rude. I flattened my ears and snorted again. "Is not my fault I curious and most beautiful cindercorn, and we were hiking!"

"In the middle of a no-horse closed tourist town? Emphasis on the closed."

"Didn't know was closed, we wanted to

hike. Yes, hike. In snow, where pretty. This pretty!" I blew a larger flame, which glowed blue. "Except for the dust. Why not explore cool place left empty? Exploration fun! We honeymoon. Exploration, exploration!"

Professor Yale, who remained relaxed with his hands in his pockets, regarded me with interest. "You've really improved your basic speech, Bailey. Well done. However, I can't help but notice you're freezing and you seem to like it."

"Tiny terrors fault. Burn extra hot." I pointed my horn at my husband, who was chatting with Alan. "His fault. We adults, we make tiny terrors. Doc-turs make me unicorn at least several times a week. Good for tiny terrors. Also, need poisons."

"You do not need poisons, Bailey," my husband announced without even glancing my way.

"Do!"

"You need venom," he corrected.

Oh. "I need *venom*," I dutifully informed the old professor. "Many different gorgon venoms. Good for tiny terrors and their immune sys-tems. Very good. You help provide, yes? I stand in box and you use me to teach if you get me good venoms."

"Deal. I'll talk with the CDC and see what I can get for you. Has your honeymoon been going well?"

"It go well until we find bodies. We explore Queeny's past because he see things I not see before, and I never travel before him. His past full of sad things, but therapy may help."

"That's funny," Yale replied, shaking his head. "We have a slight problem regarding the equipment. That dust is too potent to risk, so we can't even bring it to you, and we were barred hazmat access."

"Put camera on stick give me stick, use longer stick to hand me camera on stick."

Clemmends grunted but headed for one of the vehicles they'd managed to use to traverse the trashed trail, attaching a cell phone to a selfie stick. "All right, Quinn. This is how this works. We have a controller for the app, and we'll take pictures while you hold the stick. You will accept me yelling at you with this megaphone without complaint while we record the images we need. We'll need to take a photograph of every piece of evidence before you have access to any napalm."

"Okay. Can do. Yale do controller while you yell?"

"That's the current plan."

With Yale handling the pictures, I had confidence the evidence would be appropriately gathered and handled. "Okay. Good. Other Chief Quinn help with cop stuff while I do this. No headset. No safe to put on head. Sad. Headset useful. Also, rabies contagion here. Confirm scanner, not sure where source."

"I'm going to guess the rodents infesting

the place. There's evidence of mice all around the exterior. We'll do treatments of all staff and animals we can catch to be safe. We have sufficient evidence of a connection between this and the rabies outbreak to bring it to trial. Once was a coincidence. Three times is not a coincidence," Clemmends replied, using a long pole and some string to deliver the selfie stick and phone to me. I grabbed the stick in my mouth and pulled it free.

Clemmends wisely dropped the pole, where it would join the dust batch in burning as soon as I finished my work. "All right, Quinn. Show me your stuff, and make it good this time."

With my mouth full of selfie stick, I couldn't tell him I was good all of the time, although I shot him a baleful glare before getting to work.

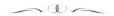

I BEGAN with the books on the end table, listening to Yale and Clemmends confirm each time they snapped a good picture of the text. The second book, which I hadn't checked, horrified me even more than the first.

It contained a list of names, when he had tested the dust on the victim, if they had become infected, and what he had done with their body post infection or failure to infect. I wanted to run out of the building and light my hooves on fire, for I stood on a mass grave.

I set the selfie stick on the book and trotted to the door. "This Morrison hand-writing?"

My husband, who worked with Yale and Clemmends at a folding desk on the other side of the cordon around the building, sighed and nodded. "I've seen it enough times to know it. Yeah. That's his handwriting, without a doubt."

"It good evidence?"

"It's good evidence."

"Squish him like mother fucking grape! Squish! Stomp! Burn! Stomp! More stomp. Make Morrison vintage wine with stomping. He kill many. Better I kill, do so quickly and with much stomping. Jail? He die. Maybe with soap in shower by angry burly man. This leave scars."

"And I now will never look at wine the same way ever again. Thanks, Bailey," my husband complained. "I liked wine until today."

I snorted. "You like sniffing wine and sip-ping here, sipping there. Leave wine to sips. You like sipping wine, and over entire night, you might finish baby glass. Not lose much."

"Ruthless."

"Can stomp to goo. Not make wine make goo. But would have goo on hooves, not pleasant."

"There's already a warrant out for his apprehension dead or alive," Clemmends stated. "Frankly, I don't give a shit if you deal with him, just turn the body into the FBI or CDC when you're done with his body and leave enough to be recognizable."

"Leave head intact but squish rest? That gross."

"You know what? Forget I said anything. Do what you want with him. We have sufficient evidence here to warrant excessive force, and if anyone complains, he is aware of the restraining order and shouldn't have been in your range to begin with, so it's his own damned fault for violating his restraining order."

"I like. Okay. Take stick, explore more. Shout extra loud if I go far and you need take peek-ture." I retrieved the selfie stick and phone, exploring everything room by room. Several more books and logs of evidence ate away an hour, and when I finally made it down to the basement, I only descended several steps before the sea of little red beady eyes sent me bolting back upstairs.

I ran to the window, dropped the selfie stick, and snorted blue flame. "No. No, no, no. Burn! Burn *now*."

"Bailey?" Quinn asked, raising a brow.

"Burn it to the ground!"

"Why?"

"Beady eyes. Millions of beady little eyes. In basement. They get me. Burn it to the ground. Now. Give me nay-palm. Beady eyes."

Professor Yale laughed, and he wiped tears from his eyes. "I'm guessing there's a rat or mouse swarm in the basement, she went downstairs, and the light from her flaming breath reflected in their eyes. Honestly, I would have run, too. Go around the rest of the place, and we'll start getting the hoses ready so you can deal with it. We shouldn't kill the rats or mice, though."

"Con-tam-ee-nay-ted," I insisted.

"If they're contaminated, why aren't they petrified?"

I squealed my alarm. "No. No gorgon-rat-mice doohickeys. No. No. No mutant gorgon-rat-mice doohickeys. No."

My husband sucked in a breath. "It can't be possible. Rats or mice couldn't be infected with the gorgon virus, could they?"

"That is something I'd like to test, but I'd need one."

"Gorgon-mice-rat doohickeys scary," I whined.

"You're a cindercorn, Bailey," Yale chided.

"Not mean gorgon-mice-rat doohickeys not scary."

"Rabid, too," my husband added with a wicked smirk.

Evil, evil gorgon-incubus doohickey. "You are still the best doohickey, but rabid gorgon-mice-rat doohickeys scary. What if infect humans? Much risk, say no."

Yale sighed. "However much I hate agreeing with her, it would be very difficult to get them contained without someone getting some sort of infection. Okay. Here's a plan. We'll do the sentient test. If they prove sentient, we get them out and contain them and try to help them. If not, they burn."

"Okay. Rabid gorgon-mice-rat doohickeys tested for sentience. How?"

"Simple. Go to the basement, ask them to line up, and pretend you're the pied piper. If they're sentient, we'll just whip up a barrier in the supply van."

"Many more than van fit."

"We'll worry about it after the test. Get the phone, please," the professor said.

I stretched my head out of the window, picked up the selfie stick, and set it somewhere safe before going to the steps, aware of the beady eyes staring up at me from the darkness. "Okay, gorgon-mice-rat doohickeys. Come if you want to not die."

The beady flashing eyes drew closer, and the swarm squeaked at me.

Fuck. "Come if you want to not die in nice neat line, no scary squeaks or eating cindercorn. I rare, so want to not die. Puhlease."

The beady flashing eyes continued to come closer, and to my horror, they did so in a nice neat line, and they stopped squeaking.

"Queeny?" I wailed.

"What's wrong?"

"The rabid gorgon-mice-rat doohickeys

un-der-stand English." I stood my ground despite the gorgon-mice-rat doohickeys coming
closer, obeying my command to form up in a
nice neat line. To test if it was just a freaky
coincidence, I unsheathed a claw and tapped
a row of ten spots in front of me. "Make lines
here. Go safe place, much food. Nice. Bath?
Like bath? Food? Good food. And help not be
sick?"

For rabid gorgon-mice-rat doohickeys,
they possessed a rather phenomenal ability to
coordinate themselves as a group, and within
ten minutes, I'd created a tiny legion of gorgon-mice-rat doohickeys organized into perfect little rodent columns. As I'd already
plunged into the deep end, I lowered my nose
to the first gorgon-mice-rat doohickeys.

The one nearest me offered a little rodent
kiss.

I led my gorgon-mice-rat doohickey army
to the window. "We adopt gorgon-mice-rat
doohickeys? We need new house, make basement for them, but a clean tidy basement
with nice house for them."

"Seriously? You went from terrified to
wanting to adopt them?"

I reached for the selfie stick and pointed it
at my gorgon-mice-rat doohickey army and
waited for the phone to click before setting it
down. "They smart, speak English. Good
little gorgon-mice-rat doohickeys. Probably
scared, probably hungry, probably sick."

Professor Yale sighed. "That demonstration passes the sentience test, Sam. There's no doubt. She talked to them, she lined them up, and they're following her. They might not be actually *speaking* English, but she had zero interaction with them before the test, and they understood what she asked of them. For all we know, they may be transformative victims. The logs stated they'd done some experiments with that."

"Fuck," my husband announced.

While unfair play, I stared at my husband and sighed. Longingly. With extra longing thrown in for good measure.

"Wow. She's giving you the mare stare on steroids, Sam." Professor Yale chuckled. "You can help be their temporary custodians once they are deemed safe for the general public. The first stop is to somewhere they can be treated for rabies, because my meter is screaming about it from over here, and it's the bad kind of rabies."

"Bad kind?"

"Airborne."

I froze. "It airborne?"

"We have confirmation this strain is airborne. It takes a long time to kill, but its death rate seems to be equal with the standard disease, and it can be spread through the air."

Well, that explained the high level of spread in Long Lake and similar areas. "How treat wild animals? All? Many ill?"

"Neutralizer and prayer," Professor Yale replied.

THE SUN SET LONG before I marched my army of rabid gorgon-rat-mice doohickeys to the trailer brought in to transport them to a care facility until they could be treated and helped as much as possible. Someone had gotten the idea to put down blankets, and after each of the little critters underwent a brisk neutralizer bath from volunteers in hazmat suits and given a few spoonfuls to drink, they were put inside to settle in.

Their trust in us to do the right thing hurt.

As I was undoubtedly contaminated with the dust, I waited by the building for the next phase, which involved a lot of fire and burning the entire resort area to the ground. All of the buildings and everything around them would be destroyed before nature was left to regrow as it saw fit.

By the time they began pumping the neutralizer, no sane restaurant would be open. "No noo-dles with sea bugs tonight," I said to my husband, who stayed closer than anyone else liked to the contaminated building. "Is okay. We get some tomorrow."

"You're still getting your noodles with sea bugs, but the husband of one of the CDC reps will be making it for you. She lives thirty minutes from here, so he'll start making your noodles and sea bugs once we leave, we'll eat there, and then head to a hotel for the night. Then we'll continue our vacation. Again."

"We get to spot on time?"

"We will, but you'll be tired. We'll need to skip therapy tonight."

How sad. "Worth it, even if the gorgon-mice-rat doohickeys scared me at first."

"Well, to be fair, if a bunch of beady, red little eyes stared at me, I would've made it halfway home before stopping. But my beautiful cindercorn will get her noodles with sea bugs tonight. Good behavior is rewarded, and you helped the rodents."

"Gorgon-mice-rat doohickeys."

"I really hope that does not become their official species designation."

"They're the ones who must deal. Give choice of designation, make vote. Most votes win."

"For some reason, that terrifies me."

"Well, they might willfully decide to become gorgon-mice-rat doohickeys, and while awesome, also terrifying."

"All I will do is hope that they weren't being fed to gorgons."

I snorted my alarm. "No!"

"Well, they were getting rabid feeder mice from *somewhere*."

"Oh. Maybe because airborne rabies? Hope because airborne rabies? And slow onset in gorgon-mice-rat doohickeys. So it spread to gorgons through normal mice and not these mice. These mice the starter mice."

"Maybe. And even then, they've probably been here for years."

"Is okay. We let CDC figure it out, we just prepare big nice home for many gorgon-mice-rat doohickeys."

"Why do I have a feeling I'm going to regret this?"

"Because you have rabid wolf soon, rabid puppy, rabid cindercorn..." I bobbed my head. "We all rabid here."

"Heaven help me."

AT THREE IN THE MORNING, I torched the bed and breakfast. The fires burned blue and white, and I refrained from having more than a bite or two of napalm, only enough to make certain I lit the entire batch and kept the flames going until the CDC was confident in its destruction.

It took me twenty minutes to reduce everything to ash.

While satisfied the gorgon dust would never bother anyone again, I mourned for the males used in its creation.

Ten minutes after the CDC hosed down the rubble, they lowered the shield and my husband braved the destruction armed with one of the CDC's meters.

It remained silent.

"All right, my beautiful. While you were playing with your favorite treat and making fire, I had a rabies treatment, our pets were treated, the exterior of the rental was treated, and we're ready to roll. You get to be treated after you shift back to human, and Yale wants to give you enough neutralizer he'll be really annoyed if you don't switch your marker to off. He wants divine-level purging on you because you've had so much exposure to gorgons lately. Then he glared at me and told me I needed to chill out and stop giving you venom, as you're now considered to be venom addicted."

"Well, duh?" I snorted laughter. "He miss out. Poor Yale. Okay. Be sick and miserable, make grandfather flip switch. Or father? Think father flip switch?"

"I have no idea."

"We find out soon."

"That sounds remarkably like a threat, Bailey."

"Because is? Father scary. Not as scary as swarm of gorgon-mice-rat doohickeys."

"Yeah. And you invited the entire lot of them to move in with us."

"Can't help it, stupid and love animals."

"You're not stupid, but if there is someone in need of rescue, you will rescue them. That is part of what makes you beautiful. Now, prepare yourself. Yale is cranky because he's too damned old for these jobs."

EIGHTEEN

He's not the brightest crayon in
the box.

I GORGED on noodles and sea bugs, courtesy
of a man who cooked for a living. Before I
could declare my eternal love of his cook-
ing, I passed out so hard I couldn't remember anything about the trip to Long
Lake.

It took my husband convincing Sunny to
lick my face half off to wake me up.

Sunny's breath reeked of seafood and
bones and rancid dog slobber.

"You're mean, Quinn."

"We have twenty minutes before showtime, so I need you to go put on your fur coat
and enjoy the entire bucket of napalm I made
for your enjoyment. While you're doing that,
I'm checking my guns over, as I've decided
we'll compete to see who gets to kill him first.
I made the better blend Tiffany gave me the
recipe for, so try not to get too drunk on your
favorite treat."

Outside of the window, a lake surrounded

with snow-shrouded trees glimmered in the sunlight. "Oh, that's pretty."

"It's also so plagued with rabies the neighboring towns have cleared out, the residents have declared the place as condemned, and there's a disturbing number of animal bodies littering the ground. I now understand what Yale meant about the neutralizer and prayer comment. So, you're about to become a very unhappy cindercorn. I'm very unhappy, and I'm not nearly as driven by my love of animals as you are. Yes, there's a wolf. Yes, he's still alive. No, he's not in good shape. Yes, I forced a neutralizer treatment down his throat before leashing him and tying him to a nearby tree. No, I didn't get bitten. Yes, I used neutralizer where he slobbered on me."

Oh. "Poor wolf."

"Yeah. He came over to the rental shortly after I parked, and he didn't try to bite my head off, so I did what I could for him. It's my equivalent of dumpster diving for new pets."

"You want to keep the wolf?"

"I didn't know any wolves other than Sunny mastered sad wolf eyes, but he used them on me. We're going to end up with a wild animal sanctuary in our yard, and now I'm just as bad as you are. Damn it."

"It's hard being a compassionate man. I'm sure you'll survive." I fended Sunny off, kissed her nose, and herded her to the back where she belonged. I stripped out of my clothes, grabbed the blanket Quinn brought to contain any blood and preserve my dignity, wrapped in it, and popped one of the transformative pills before getting out of the vehicle.

Long Lake took the top prize for being chilly, and I huffed while waiting for the drug to kick in and punt my ass to cindercorn form.

One day, I would master transforming without the assistance of a highly restricted substance.

Ten minutes later, I stomped my hooves, bucked, and ran around until I snorted blue flame. Quinn gave me the promised bucket of napalm, which I devoured in record time.

It burned nicely on the way down, but the buzz I associated with napalm didn't come. Breathing blue flame amused me and dulled the blow of my denied bender.

Dealing with Morrison would have been so much better on a napalm bender.

My husband's wolf flopped in the snow near the tree he'd tied it to, and I regarded the scrawny animal with my ears turned back. "Give bones? We have extra bones? May need more napalm. That only burn nicely, not make good bender? Where my bender go?"

"Your bender probably is being burned off because your body temperature is so high."

"Nooooo. Not my bender! Bring it back. I get napalm and I just get big flame?" I moaned my dismay and bowed my head.

"I'm sure you'll be okay. Think about it

this way. No bender equals no hangover." Quinn went into the SUV, got out a small cooler, and retrieved some of Sunny's bones, which he brought over and put in front of the wolf's nose. To my relief, the animal gave a few sniffs before struggling to chew. While he had some difficulties, he managed.

"It's fairly advanced rabies, but it's a good sign he can still eat," my husband said. "This is going to cost me a fortune, isn't it?"

"Late rabies treatment expensive," I agreed. "Oh, well. Bye, money. We have new wolf. Maybe friend with Sunny?"

"Or our other wolf. At least he'll have a pack if he can't be rehabilitated."

"Okay. What we do now?"

Sam pointed at a small building near the lake. "Long Lake, the town, is basically nothing but a few homes scattered along the shore. They go to other neighboring towns, all of which are abandoned due to the outbreak. I drove around the entire lake checking. I couldn't figure out where Long Lake was, discovering that the narrow areas between the actual towns is what most mean by Long Lake. That used to be a tackle shop, and it was the last building in the area open before the whole thing shut down."

"Wow. You learned a lot."

"I got here an hour ago, but you were exhausted, so I wanted to let you rest. So, I figure with nothing near here, if Morrison shows up, he'll come to the only drivable vehicle in the entire area. We should be easy enough for him to find. Morrison has a high magic rating, but he's best if he's given a lot of time to prepare, and he forgets guns exist. It's his weakness."

"He forgets I blow big fire."

"Bailey, I don't even know if he actually realizes you're a cindercorn. He's not the brightest crayon in the box."

"But it in CDC file."

"That means nothing when it comes to egotistical police chiefs. I mean, I didn't think you were an actual cindercorn until I got scolded by my family for having found an actual unicorn without telling them about it. I mean, I knew you became a fire-breathing lawbreaker, but that's different from actually *being* one."

"Right. Me think vanilla human for long time. We inn-o-cent. Where you want me to be?"

Quinn pointed at a shadowy stretch of forest between the tackle shop and the water. "Hide in the shadows there. Be a stealthy cindercorn, and should Morrison show up, we will race. I'm not sure what he's going to do, so I'm going to loosen the wolf's leash in case we can't take care of him right away. I've protected the rental as much as I can, so our pets should be okay. But if you get a chance at him, snort your biggest flame."

"Okay. Will do that. Set wolf loose. Poor

thing can't do much. Leave more bones for him. Keep busy. He hungry? Maybe food?"

"Sunny won't mind sharing some of her lunch." Quinn returned to the rental, grabbed a handful of meat, and left it for the wolf before loosening where the leash connected to the tree, leaving it in place. "Hopefully, he won't notice it's not tied and stay put while he eats. I'd rather not have to chase a rabid wolf around a lake loaded with dead animals."

"Poor puppy hungry. I go hide, be good. Make big fire when needed. If needed."

I headed for the shadows and my husband went back to the SUV, leaning against it while facing the road circling the lake. As hoped, the wolf stayed put, pausing in his bone chewing long enough to eat the meat.

Hiding in the shadows didn't work while a steaming unicorn, but snowbanks from the wind off the lake gave me a few places I could burrow into my former nemesis, which did a good job of keeping me comfortable while also offering a place to stay out of sight. My husband, to all appearances, relaxed while he waited. Considering the size of the lake, I could only hope it didn't take too long for our unwanted guest to arrive.

Then again, with my luck, our unwanted guest would leave us waiting for hours. Would Quinn notice if I took a nap in the snowbank?

I could use a few extra hours of sleep and an entire tanker of napalm.

I deserved a good napalm bender, and if I needed to torch the entirety of a rabies-infested lake, I would work hard to have a record-breaking bender.

How much napalm could a determined cindercorn consume? Would the CDC bring an entire tanker just for me?

For some reason, I doubted anyone in the CDC would be kind *or* crazy enough to give me an entire tanker of my favorite treat.

Morrison didn't leave us waiting for long. He drove a rustbucket of a pickup truck, parked not far from my husband, and got out of his vehicle.

I recognized him, but beyond that, I remembered nothing of the man beyond a general awareness I had good reason to dislike him. No, not dislike. Hate.

It was easy to hate a man who'd brought so much suffering to others.

I wondered if my flames would reach him if I snorted my biggest flame, but I waited as my husband did, wondering what he would do now that he faced the man who'd caused our family so much heartache.

"Samuel," Morrison greeted.

"What do you want?" According to my husband's body language, he didn't have a care in the world, and his tone came across as more curious than anything else.

"I'd like to cut you a deal."

My mouth dropped open. It was well enough I'd burrowed into a snowbank, as I would've fallen over had I been standing. After everything he'd done, Morrison wanted to cut a deal? How could any man be so stupid and egotistical at the same time?

Apparently, my husband had expected something like that, as he asked, "What deal?"

I didn't know which shocked me more: that Quinn was even capable of playing the bad cop or that Morrison seemed to think my husband would play ball. Movement caught my attention, and the rabid wolf got to his paws, staggered a few steps, and picked up one of the larger bones before wobbling towards the men.

Morrison approached my husband, stopping in the middle of the road. After a moment of thought, my husband joined the asshole.

"I need that girl for something, and she cooperates with you sometimes. It'll take a few minutes, and she won't come to any harm, but I must finish what I set out to do."

That girl? Me? Had Morrison missed the memo 'that girl' was a unicorn who ate meat, breathed fire, and was *married* to the police chief he spoke to? The breathe fire part would play a very important role in the end of that bastard's life if I had anything to say about it.

But first, I needed to figure out what my husband was up to, because him *talking* to the bastard hadn't been part of the plan. We hadn't had much of a plan to begin with, but we definitely hadn't discussed being civil.

How rude.

"And what, precisely, did you set out to do?"

"Reestablish who is human and who is not. We have a responsibility to our people. To humans."

My husband stared at the man who'd caused us so many problems. "What do you mean by that?"

I wondered if Morrison underestimated my husband like most. Did the asshole really believe my husband would play ball rather than gather information to finish the flame game?

Knowing Quinn, he recorded every word of the discussion to make certain Morrison's plans died with him.

"Humanity has become severely polluted. Centaurs and humans make humans. Pixies and satyrs? They make humans. Angels and demons? Make humans. Even gorgons can create humans. Vanilla humans and humans with truly dominant human genes are dying. We need to identify those of us who are still human and make sure they are truly protected. These false humans are making it so the real ones can't be properly safeguarded."

How awfully twisted. If I scratched at the surface of Morrison's insanity, I could understand his motivations—and why he would do something like use gorgon dust to flush out anyone who wasn't human enough.

I bet, in his twisted little mind, he truly believed if someone was human enough, the gorgon dust wouldn't infect them. Worse, he would have tested the dust himself to make certain he counted as human enough.

How disgusting.

"I see." My husband gestured, and I realized he pointed to one of the dead animals littering the side of the road. "I stopped because of that," he lied. "I've never seen anything like it."

"Ah. Rabies. Yes. Nature's most efficient form of population control."

Morrison viewed rabies as population control? The math made sense; airborne rabies plus time equaled a heavily reduced population, although everything I'd heard about it implied it would take years before any people actually died from the outbreak.

Hitting the gorgons first made sense if he wanted to get rid of non-humans, and his project with the gorgon-mice-rat doohickeys would have made certain there were enough infected mice not showing symptoms to infect the gorgons without signs of rabies taking hold until it was far too late to save them.

The wolf, which neither man noticed, continued his slow march to the road. Once on the snow-covered asphalt, his stride smoothed out, his ears pricked forward, and he walked better, as though somehow the infection killing him eased its relentless hold on his worn body.

He dropped the bone near my husband's foot.

So focused on each other, the men still failed to notice the rabid animal.

Idiots, both of them. My idiot gorgon-incubus doohickey would pay for his idiocy through chores and intensive corrective therapy. I hoped the other idiot learned the hard way why it was a terrible idea to ignore his surroundings.

If Morrison even looked at my new wolf wrong, nothing more than a smear would remain when I finished with him.

I wiggled out of my snowbank and wormed to the shadows behind the abandoned tackle shop. I poked my head around the corner to keep an eye on my husband, the wolf, and Morrison.

"How are you hoping for rabies to control the population? I mean, it's definitely an efficient killer." Quinn once again gestured to the dead animals along the side of the road.

Now that I looked for them, there were a disturbing number of lumps under the snow that could easily be dead animals.

What an asshole.

"Oh, yes. You wouldn't know. That's simple. The filthy non-humans, with their disgusting habits, interact with even rodents. Those who act like wild animals and feed off wild animals deserve to die like wild animals."

Marriage to my gorgon-incubus doohickey had taught me when he wanted to, he could beat any mere human to the draw, and in the blink of an eye, Quinn socked the asshole in the nose and dropped him to the road with a single hit. Bright red blood splashed onto the snow.

The wolf recognized prey when he saw it, and before my husband could even kick the downed asshole, the rabid animal lunged for the fallen man, froth flying from his mouth while he bared and snapped his teeth. The first bite missed with an audible clack. The second landed in the tender flesh of Morrison's throat.

In the prime of health, wolves weighed over eighty pounds, although the rabid animal was more skin and bones than anything else. His scrawny build and poor health did little to hamper his ability to kill his prey.

Several shakes and hard bites later, and Morrison's body twitched on the ground.

Quinn reached down, picked up the wolf's bone, secured his hold on the leash, and lured the animal away from the corpse. I galloped over, skidding to a halt and snorting flames.

The wolf accepted Quinn's praise and offering of the bone, lying down and gnawing on his treat rather than on Morrison's body.

"Wolf steal kill?" I blurted. "Wolf!"

The wolf continued to chew on his bone,

and my husband bent over and scratched the animal behind his ears. "Good boy. Relax, Bailey. Wolves are smart, and he knew we were helping him. That, plus we just fed him. We're acting like a pack for him, and he's by himself and hungry."

"No save you from wolf. Wolf eat you? Give rabies."

"I can defend myself from a wolf, I'm sure."

"He could, too."

My husband regarded Morrison's body with a frown. "Huh. You're right. I'm being stupid, aren't I?"

"Wolf sad and cute, easy to fall prey to. Poor hus-band. We teach wolf no eat us. No lie to help wolf? CDC get mad about wolf killings."

"Shit. Right. I'll make sure the wolf isn't put down for killing him. I was about to, anyway."

"With what? Fist?"

"No. My gun. At point blank range. I punched him because I wanted to. He pissed me off."

"Okay." I approached and sniffed the wolf, who was in a dire need of a bath. "Call. Request tanker. Much napalm. This area? This area bad."

"I'm not sure how burning it to the ground will help."

"Much rot, no scav-en-gers. Frozen until spring. More infection."

My husband retrieved his phone and called someone, explaining how Morrison had somehow located them and had attempted to recruit him. With a smug smile in place, he reported that the local wildlife, quite rabid, had taken offense to Morrison.

"No hurt my puppy," I warned, flattening my ears.

"My wife, apparently, is very fond of the rabid wolf and wishes to rehabilitate him. I'm not brave enough to tell the cranky and pregnant cindercorn she can't turn our home into a zoo. Right now, her new pet wolf is chewing on some of Sunny's bones and behaving himself. Yes, we're feeding a wild, rabid animal. What? He's hungry, and I'd rather not get eaten by a hungry, rabid wolf. That he handled a rather bad problem with grace tells me he should be rewarded with more bones. He's pretty bad off, though. Bailey thinks this whole place needs to be napalmed. The towns are abandoned and there are dead animals everywhere."

The wolf finished with his bone and stretched out in the snow, resting his muzzle on my husband's foot.

I worried the wolf was yet another victim of transformatives, as I couldn't imagine a wild animal behaving in such a way, especially not while rabid.

Either way, we'd find out soon enough.

QUINN KEPT the sick wolf on a tight leash, and I worried the animal cooperated because my husband kept feeding him. As I expected I would need to help light a massive fire, I remained a cindercorn. Our pets slept in the SUV, which we kept running with a window slightly cracked open so they got fresh air.

"Sleepy puppers, sleepy kitten, Quinn," I said, lifting a hoof to point at the rental. "Good puppers, good kitten."

Quinn stared down at the wolf, who had polished off our entire supply of food for Sunny and was working on Blizzard's. "I know I asked for something to feed him, but I hope they're anticipating how much a starved wolf can eat. He's really well behaved, though."

"Trained or transformative?"

"I think trained." Quinn sat, clucked his tongue, and held out his hand. "Shake."

The wolf immediately lifted his paw and placed it on my husband's hand.

"Oh, knows trick!"

"He failed the sentience test."

"You tested?"

"Yes. I gave verbal instructions to do something, and he just stared at me in confusion. But he knows shake and some other commands. So, he's probably trained."

"Why nice for us, not nice for Morrison?"

"No idea. Good taste in people, better sense for assholes."

I eyed the wolf with interest. "Make police

dog! With Sunny. I have *two* police dogs. He already do good work. Kill bad guy. I hire. Pay in bones, love, meat, and more love."

My husband opened his mouth, his brows furrowed, and he closed his mouth, his teeth clacking together.

"Idea good, yes?"

"I'll pitch the commissioner if he can be cured of rabies, but I'm not promising anything more than that."

The first of the CDC's vans rolled up, and the wolf whined, grabbing the rest of his meal in his paws and pulling it closer. I took the leash in my teeth so Quinn could handle the reps.

A cranky Professor Yale emerged from the front passenger seat, and Alan came out of the back.

My husband chuckled. "No hand shaking. I'm surely rabid now. Honestly, if you're here, you're infected. There are dead animals everywhere, and the wolf's pretty sick."

Alan crouched near the animal, careful to stay out of biting range, and turned his meter on. Within a minute, it squealed an alarm. "Yep. It's the bad strain. Concentration is moderate. Is the animal already frothing?"

"There was froth, yes. He's had some trouble chewing, but he's been able to obey basic commands. He knows a few tricks. He's generally wobbly, but he *can* move like he means it." Quinn pointed at Morrison's body. In the time it'd taken the CDC to arrive, snow had dusted his corpse. "I punched him in the nose because he pissed me off, but the wolf got the kill. I'll verify with an angel, but he wanted to purge as many non-vanilla humans as possible, and he wanted Bailey for something. Unfortunately, after hearing about his desire to use rabies for population control purposes, I lost my temper and socked him. The wolf went after him then. Bailey wants him for a police dog. I believe she may think the wolf was protecting me."

"Did good job, very good wolf. Just a little rabid."

Yale lifted a hand and rubbed his forehead. "I'm too old for this, Bailey."

"Me rabid with time. Much excited, yes?"

"No. The last thing anyone needs is to deal with a rabid cindercorn. I would rather force feed you napalm and set you loose in my living room."

"Much napalm needed to burn entire lake."

"We wouldn't be burning the lake. We'd put a barrier between the shoreline and the water and protect as much of the water from the ash as possible. We don't want to completely destroy the environment. But yes, we're going to napalm the entire area."

"How much area?"

"Three miles around the shore. The CDC has already begun making certain there is no human life to evacuate. While you're burning that, we will be doing a neutralizer test using the next three miles of terrain; there are still some living animals after the three mile mark. If the test works, we'll do mass treatments of wildlife. But this section is to be razed."

"Sad," I said, turning my head to stare at some of the lumps beneath the snow. "Why they all die in big mass?"

"We're not sure. We're going to grab a few of the bodies for autopsy, and we'll do a full test on your wolf before we begin full treatments. I played ball when your husband mentioned you were wanting to adopt yet another rabid animal, so we'll test treatments for late-stage rabies patients on him. That does *not* guarantee his survival, but that's the goal. If the test treatment goes well, he'll be our first proof of concept."

I could live with that. "Okay. Accept. But CDC pay bill because not option, and CDC make care good. Like wolf. Wolf pet if no release to wild?"

Quinn once again held his hand out to the wolf. "Shake."

The wolf sighed but stopped guarding his meal to shake with my husband.

With a smug smile, my husband raised a brow at Professor Yale.

"Right. The wolf has been trained to shake. Please tell me you've done the sentience test."

"He doesn't seem to be a sentient, not like

Bailey's gorgon-mice-rat doohickeys. How are they doing?" my husband asked.

"We lost five of them so far, and it looks like we'll lose a few more. They have funeral rituals for their dead, and after much confusion, the lab attendants let them handle their burials. They use cairns. So, they're definitely sentient, they have a culture, and they're multilingual. We think they have the ability to understand any form of spoken language, although they can't communicate in anything other than their language. In good news, that means you'll have an easy time housing them. After they built their cairns, they allowed the technicians to dispose of the bodies, but we're trying to figure out how to handle communicating with them. It's a challenge. We think the first generation of them was transformative victims, and they had children—these are their children. Or their children. Or their children's children. We're not really sure."

"Poor gorgon-mice-rat doohickeys."

"Yeah. We'll probably get them separated into family units and building a community habitat for them once we figure out their family structure. They have one, so we now have a real mess on our hands, as we have laws we have to follow regarding newly discovered sentients. Since you're housing them, that'll help simplify some things down the road."

"We need very big house, Sam. Very big. Two wolf, one husky, ocelot, many gorgon-mice-rat doohickeys, three gorgons, a cinder-corn, a gorgon-incubus doohickey, gorgon fosters, two gorgon-incubus-cindercorn doohickeys. Many beings, one building. Where we find that near work?" I heaved a sigh. "Hard. Not sure CDC check big enough."

"You're still getting some compensation for this and the Vegas jobs, Bailey. You're on vacation, and you're on contract still for six months, so you get your hazard pays and so on. I just have to talk to the locals to figure out what that compensation is," Professor Yale informed me.

"Oh. Maybe enough money for big house."

"And since you're solving a major problem with the new sentients, the CDC can probably help with your housing problems. At the very least you'll get a real estate agent who will be compensated by the CDC, which will lower the final bill." Yale heaved a sigh. "And I can't authorize putting the wolf down even if I wanted to at this point. This is not an excessively aggressive animal."

"I think he reacted to the situation. Bailey's idea of making him a police wolf might be a good one. It looks like he has the right base instinct, but he'll need a lot of work."

"And since the idea of giving her a wolf is to give her extra protection *and* you protection, he did exactly right, because the last thing any of us needed was an actual fight between two chiefs."

"He wanted to talk, and that cost him."

"Insane," I added.

We regarded the corpse with disgust.

"Yes, I'll buy into that. Still. The *wolf* killed him?"

"Is what I said. Wolf steal kill!"

Professor Yale shrugged. "It's for the best. The wolf wouldn't deal with guilt. You two? You two would need therapy."

"Like hell I would. He wanted to use my wife!" Sam crossed his arms over his chest and grumbled curses. "My pregnant wife. Guilt would not have been an issue."

"Yes, but your wife would have had enough guilt for both of you." Yale pressed both of his hands to his cheeks. "Oh, no! My husband killed someone for me. He will be burdened. Everything is my fault. Woe is me."

The bastard of an old man even managed to do a damned good impression of me at my worst. I flattened my ears. "Eat you, Yale!"

He laughed in my face, and with zero fear, he rubbed my brow, careful to avoid my steaming nose. "You wouldn't. You'd miss me."

"Hate it true," I complained.

"Now, come along. We have a new blend of napalm for you to try. It's even stronger than your absolute favorite. I've been told to gas you up and let you loose. Apparently, if you're shit-faced drunk, you won't feel as bad about setting a major fire. We also want to test how badly you dehydrate. We're not going to let you suffer, though. We have hangover medication for you, and we brought enough to give it to you before you transform and after, too."

"It's your lucky day, Bailey. Looks like you get that bender you wanted. View it as celebrating your successful adoption spree. Yale, did you find any other living animals in the burn zone?"

"There's limited wildlife still alive, but they're on the verge of death. We'll set up a drop zone for her while we're setting up the first barrier. If she can herd out anything before we start pumping the napalm, we'll save what we can. Don't get your hopes up, Bailey. We scanned on our way in, and just about everything here is sick and dying. Your wolf probably came out of the zone we'll be hosing down with neutralizer."

"Okay. Will look. Help as can. Make rest burn."

Yale led me to one of the tankers, and at our approach, one of the workers, who wore a gas mask, brought a sparkling bucket over. To my delight, he pulled a bottle of hot sauce out of his utility belt, opened it, and dumped it on top before giving it a stir.

"Spicy!" I pranced in place, bobbing my head.

"The capsaicin is a legitimate ingredient, but we were told cindercorns appreciate when the capsaicin comes in hot sauce format. This blend uses capsaicin as a catalyst ingredient. We'll pump a tanker of the na-palm into the zone, and then we'll layer cap-saicin onto it. Within sixty seconds, the batch is ready, and it'll last for three hours before it begins to degrade and lose general potency. The ignition point is three thousand degrees."

"F or C?"

"F."

I turned my head and snorted blue flame. "I can do that."

"And we haven't even gassed you up yet. That's impressive, Chief Quinn."

"Mr. Chief Quinn's fault. Him and his tiny terrors. Tiny terrors make me run very hot. Very hot. So hot." To prove how hot, I rolled into the nearest snowbank I could find and burrowed into it. My coat steamed, and I surged back to my hooves and snorted more blue flame for them to admire.

"Really?" my husband asked. "It's my fault, Mrs. Chief Quinn, who conspired with my relatives to make sure we had twins? I promise you, I would not have asked for twins. I would have gone for healthy, person-ally. You're the one who wanted twins for Christmas."

I dove towards my husband, thumped onto the ground, and slid his way, wiggling across the ground before coming to a halt on my back nearby, pawing at him with a hoof, taking care to keep from hurting him. "I in-no-cent cindercorn."

"You had one little snack earlier. That is

not an excuse to be waving your hooves in the air. If you want to wave your hooves in the air, go eat your treat."

Whinnying my laughter, I got up and went to the bucket, taking a tentative bite to test it.

It burned in the best ways possible, and I abandoned my manners to get the sparkling gel into my stomach. I licked the bucket clean. Before I had a chance to whine over my treat being gone, the tech grabbed it, refilled it, and dumped another large-sized bottle of hot sauce into the mixture before stirring.

He made me wait a full minute before giving it to me, and I almost choked in my hurry to eat it before it got taken away from me.

"They're not going to take your treat away, my beautiful. It makes no sense for them to stop gassing up the only real cinder-corn present when they need you to light fires for them. Take your time," my husband chided. "While you do that, I'm going to go give our new wolf a neutralizer bath and see about feeding him some more."

Alan pointed at one of the vans parked nearby. "They can help you with that. I'll keep an eye on her and make sure she's running hot enough to light the napalm. We're on a timer with this blend, and I'd rather not lose two tankers of capsaicin along with our napalm. The snow will help, though. We're going to use it to replicate the napalm, and we'll use lake water as needed to make sure we have full coverage."

"This very big fire."

"Our active burn zone will be approximately seventy thousand acres. Some zones are wider than others. We're trying to limit it to the areas with complete loss of wildlife." The tech went to the tanker and returned with a map, which he showed me. It featured Long Lake in the middle with the burn zone colored red while the neutralizer zone was colored blue. The blue zone went beyond my expectations from Professor Yale's descriptions of what would burn and what would be salvaged.

"Bigger than thought?"

"We've had as many personnel checking around the area as we can, and we're redrawing the burn and neutralizer zones accordingly. The burn zone has grown substantially, and I expect we'll be adding another five thousand acres along the northern shore, which was hit particularly hard," the tech explained. "You're going to have your work cut out for you, and we're prepared to make a gap in the shield if you need more fuel to keep lighting the napalm. You'll need to encourage the burn spread, so you'll have to do a pattern from barrier to barrier to make sure everything gets lit. We think once you get a quarter of it lit, firestorms will begin igniting and help your efforts. We have a few practitioners on hand who will be attempting to encourage the development of fire twisters within the shield."

"Oh. That cool. Sad we must burn so much, but very cool. Hot. Very hot. Yes, much hot."

The tech chuckled. "This won't be too bad. After you're done and we've extinguished the burn zone, we have a bunch of trainee fire-fighters who'll get in some practice, and once they're done practicing, the novice practitioners will get to do cleanup. They'll start mass replanting in the spring, and within a year, nobody'll know this place was reduced to ash."

"Much cool!"

Yale checked my bucket, which I'd emptied of napalm again. "Drunk yet?"

I thought about it before shaking my head. "Hot. Run much. Make barrier, eat while pumping. Make super drunk, super hot cindercorn!"

"Oh boy," Yale muttered. "May somebody forgive me this, but give the cindercorn what she wants. Get the tone going. Maybe the sound will scare the little surviving wildlife away. Have fun, Bailey, but try not to have too much fun."

"I have all the fun. You have the magic orange medicine." I trotted to the rental to check on my pets, who played in the back seat. Somehow, the ocelot battled wolf and husky and managed to stay on top, ruling over her furry friends with an iron paw.

"Make sure rental safe. No burn· rental or puppers or kitten."

"Your pets will be safe," Yale promised.

I CONSUMED SO much napalm I wanted to die, but the blessed bender never came. I wanted to wade into the lake and mourn for my non-existent bender, but the barrier blocked me from reaching the water. Whining over my foul luck won me exactly nothing, and I plodded along the shoreline in search of anything living, but I found nothing.

I could only hope the bone-deep thrumming tone warning of mass destruction scared the living animals away.

The CDC brought in aerial tankers to help spread napalm faster, and the pink, sparkly, and spicy gel rained down, splattering onto the snow-laden trees and shimmering in the air. Had I not known its purpose, I would have thought it was beautiful.

I considered that as some napalm splattered onto my nose and I licked it off. No, the gel was beautiful, but it would destroy all it touched, which made me sad.

I preferred when such beautiful destruction was limited to the works of man rather than nature.

To test if I could light the napalm, I transitioned from a walk to a canter, weaving through the trees until my coat burst into flame. The napalm raining from the sky ignited when it came into contact with me, and pools of fire spread around me.

Perfect.

With nothing else to do, I waited.

NO NAPALM BENDER equaled no hangover, but no napalm bender also equaled general exhaustion. I made three circuits around Long Lake before I managed to get the fire lit sufficiently for the inferno to gain a life of its own. Playing in the flames amused me, but within an hour, I grew bored, wandered to the barrier closest to my husband and pets, and rolled around in the smoldering ash while complaining over the unfairness of it all.

Quinn approached the shield, chuckling his amusement at my antics. "Problem, my beautiful?"

"Tiny terrors steal my bender," I whined. "Now it just work, work, work. Work, work, work, work. More work. And more work. Run hard, fire burn. Bored. Not be bored if bendering!"

"I won't argue with that. You all right?"

"Bored."

"How terrible for you, to be bored but safe. I grieve for you."

"Sarcasm in good form today, Queeny. Do more."

"I'll think about it. Are you all right?"

"Snow gone, no bender. Hungry." I flopped and stretched out my neck until my nose touched the barrier. "Why sound pass but not fire or ash?"

"Magic."

Right. Of course. "Hungry."

My husband checked his phone. "Even after that much napalm?"

"Run a lot, napalm all gone. No bender. Life not fair."

According to the sounds coming from Quinn's phone, he was taking pictures of me. "You will be pleased to find out a standard rabies treatment eradicated the disease in our new pet wolf. However, he's very ill, so he's going to a CDC vet to see how they can aid in his recovery. I'm going to end up begging my grandfather to help heal your new pet wolf. After they bring the barrier down, which will be in about thirty minutes judging from the burn rates around the lake, we will both get treated for rabies. Our pets are not being treated, but we'll be returning the rental in a suspicious shade of pink they'll eventually get washed off. The CDC has contacted the company so we're not responsible for damage to the paint, as they'll repaint the vehicle if needed. They're saying they claimed our rental for official business. After that, we get to go on our merry way. So, my beautiful, where would you like to go for the rest of our actual vacation?"

"Home. I done with vay-cay-shun! No more vay-cay-shun. Tired."

"Sure, my beautiful. We can go home."

I got to my hooves and shook myself off. "Get map. One more task. Chalk, ink, map, paper, and marbles."

"Ah. Dowry's uncle."

"Yes. Find uncle and then go home. Or at least a general location, then go home, sleep for week, and then go to location?"

"You're so tired." My husband headed off, returning several minutes later with my box of wayfinding tricks. He sat in the snow near the barrier and put down a towel. Once he had that situated to his liking, he spread out a map of the United States, set a sheet of paper beside it, got out the ink vial and opened it, and pulled out a stick of chalk. "Okay. What do you want me to do with this stuff?"

I pointed a claw at the map. "Crush chalk, dump on map."

Quinn obeyed, and he crushed it in one hand with little effort before brushing off his hands and leaving a dusty pile all over the map.

"Sexy," I stated. "Crush with no effort. Much manly. All mine."

He laughed. "If that's all it takes to make you think I'm sexy, I'll crush chalk for you whenever you want."

I glared at the map and paper. "Where

Dowry missing uncle? Be nice, magic, much tired, no games. No games, be *nice*. Guide me to Dowry missing uncle. Or give add-dress. Add-dress good. Alive or dead also good. No more mean magic. Please."

My husband laughed so hard he doubled over. "Every time I think I can't possibly love you any more, you go and do something like that."

I glared at the pile of chalk, the paper, and ink, which did absolutely nothing.

"Now!" I barked at the uncooperative supplies.

My order only made my husband laugh harder, and he fell over into the snow.

Maybe my husband wasn't taking me seriously, but my magic decided to behave itself. A shimmering, pink blotch appeared on the map, and black text appeared on the paper, which I couldn't read between my unwillingness to lift my head from where I sulked on the ground and the shimmering barrier dividing me from my husband. "Stop laughing, start reading."

It took him several minutes, but he sat up, picked up the paper, and read it. "Well, according to this, he's alive, there's a name, there's a phone number, and an address in Delaware." Quinn referenced the map. "And the pink splotch on the map is over Delaware."

"Can I nap now?"

"Sure, Bailey. You can nap now. What do you want to do about this?"

"Del-a-ware on way home. We go in-ves-ti-gate before home. Then we go home, and no more vay-cay-shun. Only home, where sleep for month."

"It's not quite on the way home, but I guess it's close enough. Alas, we don't have a month to sleep, my beautiful."

"Well, that is sad."

"I'm sure you'll be okay."

WHILE LIFE WAS OFTEN NOT fair, it wasn't always cruel, and not all disappearances ended with grief or sorrow.

Before we headed home, we went to the address in Delaware, which proved to be a state-run mental institution, and the name was that of the doctor in charge of Commissioner Dowry's uncle, who was known as John Doe to them, for they'd never been able to find any leads on the man's family due to his Alzheimer's.

They hadn't known he hadn't been diagnosed prior—and they hadn't known he'd been a sudden onset victim listed as a missing person in a different state.

As the state couldn't pay for an angel to reverse the damage without familial request, Dowry's uncle lived a quiet life in a wing dedicated to dementia patients.

In the paperwork we were permitted to review due to our badges and that the Dowry case was our jurisdiction, we learned Dowry's uncle would need months to be able to recover—assuming he received the right care. The hospital had laid out a treatment plan, including everything they thought was needed to let him live happily outside of their walls. He had a good record, calm disposition, and was considered to be an ideal long-term patient who caused no trouble beyond needing to use a script to remind him why he was there and distract him when he wanted to remember his past.

At sixty-three and otherwise healthier than an ox, he'd be a long time dying, living in a fog without memory or identity.

It took us two hours at the hospital, a trip back to our precinct, more forms than I liked, and another few hours at the hospital to begin the mandatory treatments required to let him go home. The effort exhausted me, and I wondered how Quinn handled his day-to-day work, as it somehow seemed routine to him.

Instead of asking, I watched and tried to learn—and wondered how much would have changed if I'd known about the man.

According to the angel who came to begin the treatment, he would be ready to meet his family and resume life sometime near Easter.

The drive to our house went by in silence while I tried to make sense of my magic, how easy it had been to solve such an old case, and what would have changed if only I'd known to look for him sooner.

"Okay, Bailey. Spill. What's wrong?"

"I wouldn't call it wrong. I was just wondering what would have happened if I hadn't hid what I am."

"That you're my most beautiful cindercorn and wife?"

"Wayfinder."

"I don't know. What I do know is that when we invite Commissioner Dowry to spend Easter with us, we'll be bringing quite the surprise with us. I've decided we'll be visiting Delaware at least three times a week during his treatments, and I'll be bringing the familial records from the case. His family did a lot of work trying to find him."

"How did they miss him in Delaware?"

"He had no symptoms of the disease, Bailey. That's why. Why would we look for that? We had queried about *amnesia* patients. He's not an amnesia patient. He's an Alzheimer's patient. And so you now see one of the many failings of law enforcement." My husband sighed. "I don't know if you would have found him sooner. Was your magic strong enough then? How does your magic work? Does it need the weight of longing from others to work? When you looked for proof of Audrey's guilt, it was one of the most important things I needed in my life."

I understood what he meant. "When I

went to find you, you were the most important thing in my life."

"When you found Avalanche, you wanted her for me."

"Returning to being among the most important things in my life. And then Janet would have counted, too."

"My point is, every time you've used your magic, it has been something truly and desperately important to you. Finding him wasn't necessarily that important to *you*, but years of not knowing creates a sense of desperation. I'm willing to bet that fueled your magic more than your personal desire. Have you ever looked for anything truly trivial?"

I spent the rest of the drive thinking about that. When he pulled into our driveway, a cruiser waited for us. "No, I've never looked for anything truly trivial. Why are there cops in our driveway again? I swear, Sam, if someone tried to burn down our house again, I'm going to kick ass, take names, and need bail."

"It's a deterrent cruiser the Queens cops parked with a camera running to monitor. Don't take your clothes off until we're inside."

"Why would I take my clothes off before we're inside?"

"I'm that sexy, and I failed in my duties to provide to your every need two nights in a row. You're thirsty for me."

I was? I mean, when wasn't I? I stared at him. "Do you need something, Sam?"

"Desperately. Please."

I laughed. "The faster we get our pets and our shit inside, the sooner I take care of your special needs. Move it, Samuel Leviticus Quinn. I don't have all night."

Damn, he sure could move when motivated.

Epilogue: It was the little things in life.

Easter Morning.

I RECRUITED the Devil to help me with my dirty work, tricked my mother-in-law into recruiting Sam to help with everything, gave the kids to The Grandfather Quinns, all bazillion of them spread over a ridiculous number of generations, and took Sunny, Rabies the Wonder Wolf, Blizzard, and Avalanche to retrieve Jeffrey Dowry so he could be reunited with his family.

Rabies the Wonder Wolf, cured of the disease that had almost killed him, suffered from severe separation anxiety and couldn't handle life without Sam or I nearby. One day, he might adapt better, but of all the problems we could have with our latest rescue, we could handle separation anxiety.

Until then, we accommodated him, although I wouldn't mind when he learned he could wait *outside* of the bathroom rather than on my feet.

Nothing made going to the bathroom more interesting or complicated than dealing with a ninety-five pound wolf firmly pressed to my legs the entire damned time. As far as I could tell, he feared the toilet might rise up and get me if he didn't keep a close and careful eye on me.

In good news for my sanity, Rabies the Wonder Wolf loved car rides.

It was the little things in life.

The Devil heaved a sigh. "I can't believe you're making me do good deeds on Easter. I'm going to catch some disease if I do this. Face eternal shame. I might die."

"Look, I can't drive two vehicles at the same time, Lucy. You need to drive this so I can drive my present for Sam. You know, the one you helped me acquire?"

"Yes, I seem to recall striking a bargain with a naughty cindercorn so my wife wouldn't be stolen from me, potentially permanently, as the caretaker of your gorgons, your gorgon-mice-rat doohickeys, and the rest of your menagerie. It's bad enough you've recruited me to make sure your various doohickeys have the perfect Easter. I had to recruit the fucking assholes to make rodent-sized dishes, furniture, and everything they might need to be happy in their basement mansion. At least you were willing to accept quails as replacements for miniature turkeys."

"Okay, I can accept I may have gotten slightly overenthusiastic over my varied Easter preparations."

"We're going to end up triggering an apocalypse in the Plaza, and you invited every single member of your family to help end the world."

"Lucy, it's dinner. You won't die. Or face eternal shame. Your father might want a hug, but I'm not responsible for *that*. Just hug him and act happy."

"Do you know who you're talking to?"

"Yes. Uncle Lucy, who likes unicorns. Not just unicorns, cindercorns. And as you like cindercorns, and I'm precisely a hundred percent of the current breeding population of the entire species, you *love* me." As I was driving, I couldn't point at my stomach, which was already beginning to show evidence of the tiny terrors occupying my insides. "You particularly love the tiny terrors on the way. And naughty uncles don't get invited to hold the babies right away, where nice uncles who dance to my tune get invited to the delivery and get to hold the babies."

"You win."

"I had this figured out, but thank you for reaffirming that."

The Devil laughed, and we spent the rest of the drive to the hospital talking about how best to integrate Jeffrey with his family.

We both needed some serious tutoring on how to handle important and serious things with grace, as neither one of us came up with any good ideas on how to make sure things worked out as we wanted.

My husband's new SUV, which the Devil's wife had brought to the hospital, waited in the secure lot, and I loaded the pets into it after making sure everything was in good order. I giggled at the flame-orange bow in the back. Leaving the animals in the Devil's care, I went inside to discover Jeffrey waited in the entry fiddling with his tie and fidgeting.

"Ready?" I asked, painfully aware he had nothing to take home with him.

"As ready as I can be. Dr. Rassen says it'll be difficult to adjust, especially since I keep remembering things. But I remember my sister and brother. And their children."

"If you're not ready, we can always reschedule. They just think we invited them to dinner because I'm a new chief, and apparently, family dinners with the commissioner and his family is a thing the new chiefs do at least once. And since my family is as ridiculous as my husband's family, we had to take over an entire damned hotel to fit everybody. I brought my uncle with me, so you get a choice of vehicles. You can go on a ride with the Devil, or you can join me with two wolves, a husky, and an ocelot."

"Did you just say I could go on a ride with *the Devil*? Is he your uncle?"

"Yes, and yes."

Jeffrey blinked. "But how?"

As he handled the news my uncle was the Devil, I figured he might be able to handle the insanity waiting for us at the hotel. "I married the Devil's nephew. Well, great nephew. It's complicated. He's a pretty nice guy, he just likes to pretend he's all evil. Really, he's not all that good at being evil. Just pretend you're awed. His native language is sarcasm."

"Are you going to be offended if I go with the Devil?"

"Absolutely not, especially since the Devil is probably trying to convince Rabies the Wonder Wolf the world is not ending. I dared to leave him in the SUV."

"You have a wolf you named Rabies?"

"Well, he was rabid when we found him, and it's a miracle he's recovered so well, so he's Rabies the Wonder Wolf. That plus he immediately developed separation anxiety, so we have to take him everywhere until we can convince him he won't be abandoned."

"You have a wolf."

"Technically, we have three wolves, but Belinda is more standoffish, and she doesn't like to leave home. She loves people, but car rides scare her, and she's not good about going new places. We're working on that, but it'll take time. She just likes people too much to be released into the wild. Belinda is a very good wolf! We have a big enclosure for our pack, although Rabies the Wonder Wolf and

Sunny sleep in our room. Belinda has herself a cozy den in her enclosure, so she's happy. Apparently, Belinda needs a friend that's not Rabies the Wonder Wolf or Sunny, so we're waiting for a rescue so she can have a proper pack. That will be fun. By fun, I mean, we don't need more wolves, but we're going to end up with more wolves. We're going to need a bigger house. Again."

Jeffrey stared at me. "Are you nervous?"

Damn. Jeffrey had learned my ways. "Maybe."

"I can tell. You're positively babbling."

"I just want everything to be perfect today, and I neglected to tell my husband I was bringing you to dinner. In fact, my husband still thinks we're three weeks out from the reunion."

"I see. You are being sneaky, and you are afraid he will disapprove."

"Maybe you should become a therapist, because that is something my therapist would say."

"Why do you have a therapist?"

I laughed. "Well, apparently, all police chiefs get therapists, because we have a tough job. I had no idea Sam was seeing one, but he only gets a session once a month. I get a session once a week. Apparently, I really do have more self-esteem issues than an entire ward can readily handle, so my therapist is trying to undo the harm from my idiot parents. Rabies the Wonder Wolf comes to my sessions, and he's basically a police wolf in training *and* a therapy animal. Sunny is also a police wolf in training, but she's learning how to be a bomb wolf among other things, so she's learning different skills. My husband will mostly handle Sunny while I get Rabies the Wonder Wolf."

"I'm amazed you have time to deal with someone like me."

"Someone like you? Please. Your nephew is my boss, and nothing is more annoying that watching my damned boss get mopey because of a cold case he can't pester us about no matter how badly he wants to come into my office daily and ask me to use the damned magic I already used to close that damned case. I have plenty of time to 'deal with you' because you're nice, you deserve to have your life back, and you have a family who loves you. And for once in my life, I get to say helping people like you is my job, and I really like that." I dragged Jeffrey to the damned rental SUV we kept around because the convertible couldn't fit everybody, I didn't want to keep two cop cars in our driveway, and we needed to be able to cart our entire menagerie around. "Hey, Lucy. This is Jeffrey."

The Devil played nice, smiled, and shook hands with the commissioner's uncle. "It's a pleasure to meet you. Please forgive my niece. Pregnancy plus nerves means her mouth surely runneth over."

"She's been wonderful."

"Well, that's her default. She's just really weird about it. Get on in, and I'll fill you in on everything you need to know to get through today without taking one of those anxiety pills you have in your pocket. Bailey, I'll make sure he has a good time, so try not to worry. If there are any problems, it's not as if you don't have an entire hotel full of those who can fix it if you ask. And unfortunately for all of us, we have learned you are not afraid to ask."

I laughed at that. "Blame Sam. It's his fault. He taught me nobody is going to hate me if I can't do everything myself. It turns out life's a lot better when you aren't constantly sabotaging yourself."

"That it is," the Devil agreed.

I CONSIDERED HIDING in the lobby, but after I gathered the flock of pets and my purse, the valet made off with my keys to park my husband's new baby in the safety of the parking garage. I heaved a sigh, went inside, and waited for the Devil to escort Jeffrey inside.

Even from the lobby, I could hear evidence of a family feud in progress somewhere deeper in the hotel. I gulped, heading to the lobby desk. "Please tell me the Quinn party isn't destroying the hotel."

The woman nearest to me grinned.

"They aren't destroying the hotel, Chief Quinn. They're doing a demonstration. It seems your family has decided to test their skills against your husband's family, and they're doing spars. This has resulted in everyone having quite the good time, although it is noisy. None of the guests are complaining, as they have been invited to watch. This kind of entertainment can't be bought."

Well, that was something. At least our families were keeping themselves amused before dinner. "And lunch and dinner preparations?"

"The lunch spreads are being prepared right now, and all is going well. Dinner plans are on schedule. The caterers are checking in with us every hour as you asked. There was one issue, but it turns out there is excess food rather than insufficient food."

"What we don't eat should be delivered to the nearby soup kitchens."

"They are expecting to have so much they will overflow. It seems the estimated amount of food was accidentally tripled."

I frowned. The regular order of food had been deliberately designed to provide meals for the homeless, with various dinners prepackaged to be taken out. At triple the volume, we could feed the homeless in the entire city with extra to spare. "Let me get back to you about that problem in an hour. Just instruct them to package the excess for shelters and the homeless, and I'll worry about distribution."

The Devil had minions, and the heavens had its fair share of angels. Given twenty minutes, I bet I could set up a competition for who could get the most food passed around to those in need.

"Excellent. I'll let them know. Chief Quinn was looking for you earlier. It seems he noticed you had staged an escape."

Damn it. "I swear. He gets worse separation anxiety than Rabies the Wonder Wolf."

"Yes, I do," my husband said from behind me. "I see you've been causing mayhem again.

Busted. I turned around and wielded my best smile like a weapon. "Oh, it's the best husband in the entire world. How are you doing?"

"I'm wondering why my wife ran away."

"The Devil made me do it!"

"I really did not," my uncle complained. "Why are you blaming me? I helped you because you're holding visitation rights over my head."

"Well, you *are* the Devil, and as I like my soul where it's at, and I have what you want. I will ruthlessly use what I have to get what I want. But thank you for cooperating with minimum complaint. I had a good time."

"You're teaching her to be extra feisty, Sam," the Devil muttered.

"Honestly, I'm really pleased with the results. Ah." My husband chuckled and went to

Jeffrey, holding out his hand. "I understand now. It seems my wife has hoodwinked me again."

"She seems to be quite talented at that," the commissioner's uncle replied with a smile. "I really appreciate everything you've done."

"I'll take the Dowry family to one of the smaller meeting rooms, Bailey. Some things don't need to be public, so we'll make the delivery and go watch your father and Anubis pick fights with each other while everybody make bets and laughs. Your mother's already here, though she won't be able to manifest until later in the afternoon, so you'll get to see both of your parents at the same time. Please try not to cry."

I'd learned one thing: pregnancy hormones meant I was going to cry. Early, often, and without remorse. "That's not happening, Sam."

My husband sighed. "A man can dream."

"Yes, you can. Go get his family gathered."

"I'll go with him," Jeffrey offered. "It's not as though anyone will recognize me anyway. Time has done its work. I can't even recognize myself."

"No," my husband disagreed, giving the commissioner's uncle a pat on the shoulder. "Trust me on this one. They'll see you, and they'll know. They've been waiting for this moment for years. Stay with Bailey until I text her phone, and then we'll send you in. Your family needs this as much as you do."

I gave it ten minutes before he managed to herd everyone, as my husband had a talent for making people do what he wanted. "Excited?" I asked.

"Terrified," he admitted.

I understood that. "Well, do your best. They're good people, and they've been looking for you for a long time."

"That's why I'm terrified."

MY HUSBAND TOSSED me to the wolves, chickening out on delivering Jeffrey to his family. After shooting him a glare promising retribution in some part, I decided I'd get my revenge in one simple way.

I asked Jeffrey to wait in the hall with my husband, went into the conference room, and took a piece of paper, a map of New York, a piece of chalk, and some ink with me. I left the door open behind me, as I expected the family would be following a pink, shimmering path soon enough.

Commissioner Dowry raised a brow. "When Sam said there was something we needed to see, I wasn't expecting you with some paper. Is that chalk?"

"It's a map, a sheet of paper, some chalk, and ink. Honestly, I don't really need all of this stuff, but it works when I do it this way, and that's that. Sam gave me your case."

The entire family stilled, and I took the moment to look over the gathering, which consisted of Commissioner Dowry, his wife, six older people I could only presume were parents or grandparents, and several men and women around Dowry's age, likely siblings or cousins judging from the similarities in appearance along with their wives. All in all, twenty-three people filled the room, all waiting for what I had to show them.

"I see."

"I'm a wayfinder, Commissioner Dowry, and this is what I need to find where you need to go." I frowned, eyeing the paper and the rest of my supplies. "Honestly, I'm just being an ass and could tell you where you need to go, but it seemed like a good idea at the time."

"You know what happened to my uncle?" Dowry asked.

"Yes."

I gave the family a chance to process my single word, and a myriad of emotions played across their faces, ranging from hope to grief.

"The wayfinders we spoke to all said the same thing. It cost more than we could afford to do what we needed," he said, his brows furrowing. "Why are you different?"

"I wanted it bad enough, as do you. Sam seems to think my magic is directly tied to need. The more need I have for it to work, the more likely it is to work. That's his theory, at least. Was it *easy* finding your uncle? Not precisely. I had to throw a bit of a fit to make my magic work, but that's fine. It worked. Are you ready?"

The Dowry family exchanged glances, and after a long time, the commissioner nodded.

"Severe fast onset Alzheimer's resulted in your uncle's disappearance. One day, he was fine. The next, he couldn't remember anything, and because he's an Alzheimer's patient rather than suffering from standard amnesia, the missing person's databases didn't align when the NYPD searched."

"Alzheimer's?" the commissioner blurted.

"You would have to ask an angel what induced it. I can't tell you that."

"What happened to him?"

Poor Commissioner Dowry. His tone led me to believe he expected the disease had finished its wretched work. "I established a trail, and on our way home from our honeymoon, we visited a mental hospital in Delaware, which is a long-stay facility run by the state. We identified him, and the state began treatments. He was released this morning and is waiting with Sam to see you. Sam, however, seems to be a chickenshit today, and he's making me come in here and tell you all about this."

"I'm not a chickenshit, Bailey. I'm just not the one who found him, so I shouldn't steal your thunder. You did the hard work. I just drove the rental." My husband poked his head into the door. "Please don't stir the ire of the tiny terrors starting a path that leads right around the corner."

Damn. I threw my hands in the air, gathered up my supplies, and faked a sniff. "You're mean, Samuel Quinn."

"I'm sure I'll find some way to make it up to you later. Your father is looking sad and lonely down the hallway. Apparently, he hasn't gotten a hug yet today."

For fuck's sake. I loved my father, but sometimes, he drove me to the end of my rope and gave a few tugs to see how crazy he could make me. "I hugged him yesterday. Numerous times."

"Yes, but that was yesterday. That's not today. I'm siding with him, my beautiful. It's a sad day without a hug from our cindercorn. Now that you've done your part, I'll go do mine. Go enjoy some time with your family and try not to cause more trouble than you can handle."

"I like that you're acknowledging I'm going to cause trouble."

"I love you, but you are the Calamity Queen. Where you go, trouble surely follows."

That I was, and yes it did. "Whatever you say, Trouble."

Afterword

Dear Reader,

In 2016, Bailey tumbled to life as a NaNo-WriMo (National Novel Writing Month) project, written because a close friend (Diana Pharaoh Francis, and she writes some of my favorite books!) was having a hard time in her life and needed some laughter. So, while I wrote Playing with Fire, I shared it with her, hiccups and all.

She laughed. So did I.

The Flame Game is the last Bailey & Quinn novel, although they will show up here and there as side characters in other stories set in this world. They may also make short appearances in future Magical Romantic Comedy anthologies of short stories and novels.

All things must come to an end, and I hope you enjoyed their books. No, no matter how much you beg and plead, there won't be a fourth Bailey & Quinn novel. I'm sorry to disappoint you, but I'm not sorry for making that decision.

They have the happily ever after they deserve.

But since I'm here, I'd like to answer a question about the Magical Romantic Comedy (with a body count) series.

This 'series' won't last forever. While I enjoy writing them, I am tired of being typecast against a series that represents approximately a *quarter* of what I actually write.

I'm tired of people leaving nasty, low-star reviews because my other books "aren't Magical Romantic Comedies (with a body count.)" Or that "This isn't funny!" Or that "I was here for fluff!"

Please stop it.

If you think the Mag Rom Coms are fluff, *you haven't been paying attention to what you're reading.*

FLUFF MEANS 'LACKING IN VALUE OR SUBSTANCE.' If you are missing the substance of these books, you are not paying attention. It's there. It's dressed up in humor *to make you laugh and enjoy yourself*, but there is substance.

Something being funny does not mean it lacks substance.

Leaving unhappy reviews because the *majority* of my books aren't Mag Rom Coms accomplishes one thing and only one thing: It makes me want to cease writing Mag Rom Coms.

There comes a point where the only

person who isn't laughing is me, the author. I want to write exciting, fun, adventurous, and somewhat *dark* books. I also want to write exciting, fun, adventurous, and somewhat *hilarious* books.

It's okay to like only one series.

It's not okay to sabotage other series because you want more of something else.

So please. Stop doing that. All you're doing is sabotaging the series you like.

I want to keep writing Mag Rom Coms as cleansers between my darker and more serious fare, so please respect that I'm not a one-trick pony.

I enjoy writing (and reading) a variety of books, and the Mag Rom Com series is only one facet of what I like to write.

I'm not going to quit writing the other series because people are leaving unhappy reviews the books 'aren't Mag Rom Coms' or 'they aren't funny like the Mag Rom Coms!'

I will quit writing the Mag Rom Coms first, so please keep that in mind when you want to vent in reviews my other books aren't just like them.

Next year, there are only two Mag Rom Coms scheduled. I want to get caught up on other series, and I need a break from trying to be funny all the time. Sorry.

Writing comedy is hard. Please do me a solid and don't make it harder, as I really do want to keep writing it.

Stay safe, stay well, and happy reading.

~R.J. Blain

If you like darker books with some hints of humor, you can try Outfoxed (The Fox Witch Book 1), Booked for Murder (Vigilante Magical Librarians Book 1), or the Witch & Wolf Series. (Get the completed series set, as that will save you money.)

I also write as Susan Copperfield, and those books are darker while still having some humor.

Just don't expect them to be Mag Rom Coms, because they aren't.

About R.J. Blain

RJ BLAIN suffers from a Moleskine journal obsession, a pen fixation, and a terrible tendency to pun without warning.

When she isn't playing pretend, she likes to think she's a cartographer and a sumi-e painter.

In her spare time, she daydreams about being a spy. Should that fail, her contingency plan involves tying her best of enemies to spinning wheels and quoting James Bond villains until she is satisfied.

RJ also writes as Susan Copperfield and Bernadette Franklin. Visit RJ and her pets (the Management) at thesneakykittycrit ic.com.

FOLLOW RJ & HER ALTER EGOS ON BOOKBUB: RJ BLAIN

SUSAN COPPERFIELD
BERNADETTE FRANKLIN

CPSIA information can be obtained
at www.ICGtesting.com
Printed in the USA
BVHW081852020123
R14486300001B/R144863PG655236BVX00002B/1